Highlan

BARBARA MAGOON

CHAMPAGNE BOOK GROUP

Sam,
always follow your
dreams!
Happy Reading
~ Barbara

Highland Gold

This is a work of fiction. The characters, incidents, and dialogues in this book are of the author's imagination and are not to be construed as real. Any resemblance to actual events or persons, living or dead, is completely coincidental.

Published by Champagne Book Group
2373 NE Evergreen Avenue, Albany OR 97321 U.S.A.

~ * ~

First Edition

pISBN: 979-8-564655-88-0

Cover Art by Melody Pond

www.champagnebooks.com

Version_1

To my husband, Douglas John.

Prologue

Inverness, 1641
Just before dawn

"Something was pounding…"

Blaine Michael MacKinnon peeled one eyelid open. For a moment, he thought the pounding was in his head. He had spent the night drinking and wenching, and it couldn't possibly be time to rise. He half-smiled when he touched Lil's soft warm body, her breasts plastered against his chest. He looked down with one eye and saw her fiery hair spread out like a blanket covering them both.

"Bloody hell," he swore under his breath. There was definitely someone pounding the door to his bedchamber. He was going tell them to leave or face his wrath when he heard a familiar voice.

"Blaine, open up, 'tis important."

Blaine rolled his eyes and cursed again.

Lil stirred and gazed up at him. "I'll get it, my lord," she said with a seductive smile. Slowly she untangled her long legs which were intertwined with his and padded over to the door—completely naked.

Blaine grinned at the fetching lass, admiring her shapely form and wishing for more time to sample her loveliness.

She opened the door, and he saw Ewan, his brother's first-in-command. He didn't even raise a brow at Lil's lack of apparel.

"Ye best be get'n dressed, my lord, there be an angry mob want'n yer neck." Ewan entered the bedchamber and began to gather articles of clothing that were strewn about.

Lil padded back to the bed and crawled back in, as Blaine once again wrapped her in his arms. "What in bloody hell are ye yapping about?" He settled back. The sooner he rid himself of Ewan, the sooner he could attend to more pleasurable business.

"'Tis serious, Blaine, now please get dressed."

Serious was how annoyed he was. "Who…or what is it that I am being accused of?" Blaine snapped.

Ewan looked at Lil with a cocky grin. "Seems yer husband be up in arms that ye be here, ah…let's just say…warming the wrong bed."

"Nay," Lil said adamantly. "I 'ave no 'usband."

Blaine raised both brows then looked down the other side of the bed. Moving around the rumpled covers, he exposed a set of lovely legs, then a shapely bottom which he swatted rather firmly.

"Oomph," was heard down by his feet, as a disheveled, lass with curly-blonde hair popped her head up.

"Katie darling, what have ye done?" he admonished her. "Ye know the rules." Sensing the urgency of the situation, he jumped out of bed, snatching his breeks from Ewan. "Why didn't ye tell me ye married?"

"Forgive me, my lord, but 'tis only been a few months," Katie pleaded. "I grew tired of waitin' fer ye, but when I saw ye returned—"

"Hurry and get dressed, lass," Ewan interrupted, attempting to throw each of them the right article of clothing. "I'm afraid yer husband is not so understanding as Blaine. He's out for blood."

As Blaine pulled his boots on, he heard some loud voices coming from below. Ewan ran over to the window, throwing it open. Blaine looked down to see his horse tethered and waiting for him. He gave Ewan an approving smile.

Blaine walked up to Katie and lifted her chin with two fingers. "Ye have a place to go, lass?" he asked, in genuine concern, "till yer husband has a chance to cool his ire."

Katie nodded. "Aye, me sis."

"Good." He winked at her and then turned his attention back to Ewan. Walking over to the window, Blaine lifted one leg over the sill. "Here, lend me a hand, then take the back stairs and see that she is safe."

Ewan, being a large man, grabbed his arm and effortlessly lowered Blaine out the window. He dropped quietly to the ground, then mounted his horse and rode away.

Chapter One

Blaine rode alongside his cousin Brode as they inspected the repairs that had been completed while he was away. Stonegate was a thriving fishing community, and unlike his brothers, Caelan and Douglas John, Blaine did not farm the land. The sea sustained them, as well as the ships which docked at his port. The king himself had invested handsomely, making it possible to increase Blaine's fleet of boats by more than half. The improvements to the docks and piers allowed for larger ships to berth and trade their wares as well. To accommodate the shipping vessels, crew and passengers, he constructed a large tavern and inn right on the wharf.

The people of Stonegate were not made up entirely of MacKinnons. In fact, only a dozen clansmen lived there. As people ventured to Stonegate to peddle their wares, they found the land, and its laird, quite hospitable, so many stayed. It had become a melting pot of clansmen, merchants, sailors and travelers who swore fealty to Blaine and would not hesitate to raise a sword to protect him.

The increase in his fleet resulted in an abundance of fish and therefore, preserving them became a problem. During his travels abroad, Blaine discovered the Italians use of ice houses. Stonegate was far enough north that ice was not a problem; however, building the ice house cost more than he anticipated. The king had shown great interest in the idea of constructing an ice house, yet he had not offered to provide any funding. Blaine was not willing to compromise the structure and went as far as to have the stones directly shipped from Italy.

Blaine spent the afternoon in his study, bent over his ledgers and scrutinizing his latest entries. The cost of the ice house was mounting at an alarming rate. He still held out hope that he would attain some funding from the king. Still, with the pesky English continually plaguing them, Blaine could not get a definitive answer. The increase in productivity would recoup the cost and pay for itself in the long run. When the door opened and Brode marched in, Blaine startled.

"My lord, Laird MacKinnon is here to see—" Brode did not have a chance to finish before Caelan MacKinnon brushed past him.

"You may dispense with the formalities, Brode," he snapped.

Caelan MacKinnon was the eldest son of Robert and Anna MacKinnon. He was also laird and clan chieftain. Blaine was accustomed to his brother's somewhat austere demeanor and was rarely affected by it. Over the years, he had learned when it was best to remain silent, and this was one of them.

"What a pleasant surprise," he said, wary of the dark scowl on Caelan's face. "What brings ye to Stonegate?"

"'Tis not a social call. I would like a word with ye...in private." He turned a frosty blue gaze toward Brode who nodded then hastened from the room.

Blaine walked over to the sideboard. "Would ye care for a drink, Caelan?"

His brother did not respond; instead, he started pacing, clearly agitated. Not waiting for a response, he poured a glass of whisky, which Caelan waved away. Blaine tossed back the contents and contemplated having another one.

"I would have ye fully coherent," Caelan warned him.

Blaine reluctantly re-corked the bottle.

"I want ye to listen to what I have to say."

"Would ye prefer that I sit down?" Blaine asked a bit too sarcastically, earning him a stern look.

"Do ye think I find joy in traipsing across all of Scotland, leaving my wife's side...so close to her time?" Now Caelan was yelling. "I swear Blaine if ye make me miss the birth of my bairn, I'll tear yer head off and feed it to..." Taking a deep breath, he ran his fingers through his thick black hair.

Caelan was tall and broad-shouldered, but the similarities ended there. Blaine's siblings featured their mother's raven locks and stellar blue eyes, yet his own golden hair and leaf green eyes were like their father, Robert.

He said nothing as Caelan's scowl grew darker. "I have tolerated your garish behavior long enough. Your insatiable appetite for the fairer sex has to end."

Blaine walked back slowly and sat down as Caelan continued with his tirade. *This is going to be a long one.*

"Ye are the ever-consummate libertine, the relentless seducer—"

"Libertine?" Blaine interrupted. "I take umbrage." Now it was his turn to get angry. "I live by a strict rule Caelan, and ye are fully aware of it."

"Do I?" Caelan drawled. "Seems ye forgot yer rule about a month ago, and if it wasn't for Ewan…"

Blaine held up both hands. Caelan stopped. It was true, Ewan had saved him from an awkward entanglement. There was some fall out with the innkeeper when Katie's husband stormed into the inn with his men. They brought havoc and destruction as they searched for his wife.

Blaine thought the matter closed when he sent the innkeeper payment for the damages. "I must admit that it was in poor form, and I regret my actions, but I considered the matter—"

"Resolved? I think not." Again, Caelan ran his fingers through his thick hair, a habit of his when distraught. "It seems the young lady was married and not to just any man, but to a MacDonnell."

He paused, letting his words sink in. Blaine clenched his jaw.

"When Boyd MacDonnell was unable to find ye, he brought his grievance to me."

Blaine bristled at this. "'Tis not yer fight. He has no business involving ye. Just tell me when and where, and I will meet the cur."

"Hold on Blaine, 'tis fortunate for ye that yer reputation as a skilled swordsman surpasses the one ye have with the ladies. Boyd demands compensation."

"What are ye saying?"

"The man wants coin," Caelan gritted out. "He claims the affront was planned by Rory Macleod, and because we are allied with them, they say we put ye up to it."

"That's insane," Blaine shouted. "The man has no grounds."

It was the first time in his life he was embarrassed by his behavior. Lauded as a man with the ability to charm the snakes from Medusa's head, he never thought his actions would have consequences that would affect his clan. Well now, he too wanted retribution.

"How much is he demanding?" His gaze flew to the ledgers on his desk. This was not a good time with his coffers so depleted.

Caelan snarled, "Ye need not worry, I paid the man."

"I will repay ye, Caelan," Blaine promised, the taste of bitterness in his mouth.

"Aye, ye will and every last coin," he scoffed. "However, the man wants more."

Icy cold dread slipped down Blaine's back. "Look here. I had no idea the lass was married. She neglected to tell me."

"Aye, and the lass defended ye. She told the tribunal she duped ye."

He was shocked to learn there was a trial and wondered why he wasn't asked to attend. Then his anger turned to concern, fearing that her husband might harm her.

"Ye need not concern yerself, brother, she is fine. Ye canna expect a man to harm a lass in her condition."

Blaine blanched. "What do ye mean…condition?"

"I mean the lass is with child."

His eyes grew wide.

"Nay, 'tis not yers."

"How can ye be sure?"

"She is too far along; the babe moves in her womb," Caelan explained. "Even ye can't change nature's course, although ye act as if ye can."

Blaine breathed a sigh of relief. His mind wandered to that night at the inn. Katie looked enticing in the firelight—her skin glowed with supple youth. He remembered her heavy breasts and how she gasped at their sensitivity when he suckled and laved them.

Walking over to the sideboard, he decided he wanted that second drink. "As ye said brother, the lass concurred. I had no idea she was married. That's my rule; I never take what is not freely given."

"Reluctantly I said the same." Caelan cast his gaze down. Silence hung in the air like a dark cloud. "The MacDonnells want absolute assurance that this will never happen again. I gave them my word, but it wasn't enough. They believe that your disregard…"

Blaine once again tried to argue, but Caelan held up his hand.

"The clan wants absolute assurance," he repeated, "otherwise they will bring the fight to my shores." He scowled, a glacier glow behind his blue eyes. "I told them that there is one oath ye hold dearer than all others."

Blaine looked at him in disbelief. "What are ye saying?"

"I told them ye will marry by the end of the harvest season."

He closed his eyes. "Ye canna be serious, Caelan, the harvest is nearly over."

"Aye, I expect ye best start looking for a bride then." His brother strode over to pour himself a drink. "I gave them my word, that in a month's time ye will wed."

Blaine wanted to argue but it would be pointless. As his chieftain and laird, Blaine could not disobey him. The whisky soured his stomach.

"As laird, I could simply tell ye who ye should marry and be done with it. Rory MacLeod has been after me fer years to join our families through marriage. Cenna is a bonny lass—ye could have her."

"Are ye jesting?" Blaine threw his hands in the air. "Ewan would have my head; he claimed her years ago."

"Aye, but the dolt seems afflicted by the same sickness as ye, and she will not have any part of him until he stops his womanizing ways," he said. "Ye will marry and be thankful I give ye freedom to choose who."

"How am I supposed to choose a bride in a month?"

Caelan finished his drink. "That's not my problem." Turning to leave, he picked up his riding gloves. "Well, it matters not to me who, just as long as ye are wed."

Regardless of how upsetting their conversation, Blaine did not want his brother to leave without offering him food or drink. "Please, sit down and let me have Mrs. Anderson bring ye some refreshments."

"No need, I am leaving,"

"But ye just arrived." Blaine hoped he might persuade him to allow him more time to find a wife or perhaps agree to a handfasting.

Unfortunately, the look on Caelan's face said he was determined to get back to Calderglen and his expecting wife. "If I leave now, I can reach Dunn Leigh Keep before dark. I intend to be home as soon as possible."

"Very well, if ye insist, but allow me to pack some provisions."

Caelan agreed, and they went in search of Brode.

Within the hour Caelan was mounted and ready to depart. "Do not think to tarry in this task, Blaine. I will not tolerate it. And just to be sure, I sent a missive to the king of yer intentions to wed, so unless ye want a bride picked by our sovereign leader, ye best get to it." With that last comment, he kneed his warhorse and rode out the gate, flanked by his outriders.

~ * ~

Blaine brooded for a few days after Caelan left. His usual exuberant manner was replaced by a sulking one.

Blaine scowled as Brode hesitantly entered his study. "Ye received a missive from yer family today. It seems Fenny is finally wedding yer cousin Kaylee."

"Hmm."

"I don't suppose ye will be attending?"

"I am a bit preoccupied, or have ye forgotten, I too, am supposed to wed?" Blaine hated upsetting his cousin, but Blaine had not been the same since Caelan delivered his ultimatum.

Brode frowned. "Ye've done nothing about finding a wife. There will be a large gathering of clans; I don't suppose ye might find yerself a bride amongst the guests instead of acting so petulant."

Even though Blaine knew Brode worried, he just glared at him and turned on his heel, leaving Brode staring at his back. Blaine didn't move until he heard the door shut.

Later that day Blaine was in his study, lost in the bright dance of the fire when he heard a knock on the door.

"Enter," he barked. "I was beginning to think ye'd gotten lost, Mrs. Anderson."

"I'm not Mrs. Anderson," came the gruff voice of his cousin.

Blaine looked over his shoulder and scowled. "Good, I don't suppose ye brought a bottle with ye. This one is near empty." He clutched a missive in his hand and with the other hand, he scratched at the length of new beard.

Brode's face turned grim. He jerked his head at the letter bearing the king's seal. "Bad news?" he asked, in a hesitant tone.

Blaine thrust the letter at him as he walked past him to pour himself the last bit of whisky. His cousin scanned the page. His expression darkened as he read. When he lifted his head, Blaine let out a bark of disgust.

"Aye. I've been summoned to court."

Chapter Two

Jocelyn looked at the clouds that gathered overhead. They should have left earlier, but she was determined to sell every loaf of bread. The weight of the purse tied to her belt gave her reassurance that she had made the right decision. Although her shoulders ached from the long hours of baking and selling their goods at the market, it was worth it.

Arching her back to relieve some of the soreness, she looked up again at the dark and angry sky. Their cart was pulled by a single mare, so it would take hours to get back home. They would be soaked within the hour.

Seated next to her was her brother. "Are ye tired, Braedan? I can take over if ye like."

He gave her a smirk and tossed her the reins. Closing his eyes, he leaned back, stretching his long legs. A handsome lad, he had the same deep brown hair and blue-gray eyes as she. He had filled out since his twentieth birthday, losing that boyish look but gone too was his innocence. It had been ten years since their mother passed away.

Jocelyn, being older, immediately took over the family's bakery. It was their only source of income when their father unexpectedly died, leaving them penniless and destitute. Jocelyn and Braedan both suffered by the loss. She had dreams for her brother, and selling bread wasn't one of them. She wanted a better life for him and vowed she would do anything to see their family home and land restored.

She smiled as she mentally tallied the coins in her purse. If they were careful, they could pay the women they had hired to help them with the baking and buy enough flour for the following week's order. She could put a substantial amount away and maybe buy back some of the lands their father lost to their neighbor.

"Ugh," she said under her breath.

The very thought of that man made her stomach roil. Sir Walrick Graham was the most morally despicable man in all of Scotland. He had taken advantage of their father when he was deep in his grief. The man had no scruples and duped their father into investing in several businesses using their land as collateral. When the companies failed, they lost each parcel to him. If she had been born a man, she would run him through with her sword and rid the world of his vileness.

Guiding their cart along the dusty road, Jocelyn noticed two men blocking the road.

"Ho, there," one of them shouted while a second one strolled up, grabbing the mare's bridle.

His face bore a sinister looking scar down one side. "Ye 'ould mind share'n some of yer goods wi' a few hungry men?" He sneered.

Braedan laid his hand on the hilt of his sword as two more men approached. "Ye be too late, sir, we have nothing left. I'd be appreciating if ye let go of my horse. We want to be on our way."

"All in good time, lad," the first man said, and then nodded to the other two who began rifling through the baskets and boxes. When it was obvious, in truth, she and Braedan had nothing, they stepped away. Two more men emerged from the brush and surrounded them.

"I told ye, we have nothing," Braedan repeated. "Now, please step aside."

The man smiled lasciviously at her. "I am sure ye have some'n," he drawled, eyeing her intently. "I be think'n ye 'ave some coin or may'ap ye care to let the lads and me a sample o' what the lass ha' tae offer."

As the first man reached for Jocelyn, Braedan took his sword and slapped the mare hard on the rump. The horse reared, knocking loose the hold the scarred man had. "Go, Jocelyn, get out of here," he yelled, leaping from the cart and slashing at the assailants.

A hand grabbed Jocelyn by the back of her cloak. As the cart lunged forward, she was jerked off the cart, landing hard on the ground. Stunned, she struggled to regain her breath as the sound of swords clashing surrounded her. She scrambled to her feet and managed to run a few steps only to be tackled back to the ground by the first man.

He lay nearly on top of her. "No so fast, lass, I'm no done wi' ye yet." His rank breath assaulted her as he flipped her over. "I still be want'n some of yer sweetness."

"Get off her," she heard Braedan yell but saw that he was soon divested of his sword and held captive by two men. "I swear, ye lay a hand on her, and I'll kill ye."

At the blood seeping from a gaping wound on the side of Braedan's head, she gasped but had other fears. The man just laughed as he straddled her. He began searching through the pockets of her cloak.

When he discovered the heavy purse tied to her belt, he

laughed. "Ah, I knew ye be 'iding some'tin." Taking his dirk, he cut the leather ties and tossed it to one of his men.

Jocelyn managed to free her hand and proceeded to slap and scratch with all her might. This worked for a minute, but the man captured both her hands and held them over her head. His gaze boring into her, he bared his lips, showing his rotting teeth.

"So ye like it rough, eh?" He grabbed the hem of her gown and pulled it up. "I be more n 'appy to oblige."

At the cold air on her thighs, she prayed. *Dear Lord, save me.* She closed her eyes waiting for the assault. Surprisingly the man loosened his grip. Opening her eyes, she watched as his mouth opened and closed like a fish out of water. Then blood began to foam from his loose lips.

She tried to scoot away, but the man pitched forward, pinning her to the ground. Her eyes widened at the sight of a jeweled dirk protruding from his back.

The air was pierced by the sound of a blood-curdling warrior's cry, and all hell broke loose. From her position, she saw boots stamping about, dirt flying and the sound of swords clashing. Try as she might, she couldn't budge the dead man off her.

No sooner did the skirmish start, then it was over. The only noise was that of running feet. She arched her back to see what was going on when a pair of high booted legs walked over to her. Much to her relief, the dead man was lifted off her like some discarded refuse.

A large hand reached toward her. "Are ye all right?" the man asked in a deep, rich voice.

At that moment, the sun broke through the clouds and bathed the stranger in warm light. A halo glowed around his golden head. Although his face was shadowed, she expected him to be handsome. Nodding, he helped her onto legs that threatened to give way. Lightheaded, Jocelyn saw the ground rushing up to meet her.

Steel-banded arms grasped around her waist and crushed her against his hard body. "Whoa there, hang on to me," the angel said to her.

Yes, this golden man is like an angel. An avenging archangel like Michael or Gabriel. She attempted to stand again, but when she swayed, she was swept up into solid arms.

"Kindly take yer hands off of her," Braedan demanded.

"I mean no offense, young man." The man's voice thrummed through his massive chest. "I only mean to prevent yer wife from injuring herself."

With a stern expression, Braedan watched as the imposing

warrior carried her over to a flat rock, setting her down gently. "Forgive me, my lord," Braedan said, "and she is my sister, nay my wife,"

The man handed her his skin of water which Jocelyn accepted it with trembling hands. "Thank ye," she said, her voice quavering.

"Caleb!" the man barked. Caleb, who was tending to Braedan's head, ran over. Whispering something, the man nodded in agreement. "We best be leaving afore they return."

"But they are gone, my lord," Braedan said.

"Aye, but they will return. We used the element of surprise to best them. Once those men realize they outnumber us, they will be back to avenge the killing of their leader," he motioned to the dead man lying on the ground, "or to steal his boots."

Jocelyn heard the word steal and grasped at the severed leather ties on her belt. Her heart sank when she remembered they had taken all their money. "We must go after them," she begged. "They robbed us of everything."

The other man, who was standing next to Braedan, walked to where Jocelyn was seated. "I am afraid this was all we could recover." He pressed a few coins in the palm of her hand.

Looking down at what little she had, the sting of tears pooled behind her eyes. They had worked tirelessly through the night and traveled hours to the market and for what? Less than what they would make in a day at the bakery? Her sorrow turned to anger. She didn't know how, but she would find the men responsible and make them pay.

"My lord, we need to go," Caleb urged him.

The man nodded. "Do ye have a horse? I thought we saw a cart."

"Aye," Braedan said, "but ye will not find it. I am sure our mare is halfway home by now."

"Where do ye hale from?"

"A small town near Glen Garry,"

The man frowned. "Are ye MacDonnells then from Glen Garry?"

"Nay, my lord," Braedan said. "We are south of Glen Garry, near Loch Rannoch. A small village called Killie Kern. My name is Braedan MacAulay. This is my sister Jocelyn."

"Well then Braedan MacAulay of Killie Kern, ye best come with us." The man whistled for his horse. "Caleb, ye take Braedan as the lad is not too steady." He walked to where Jocelyn sat. "Let me help ye up. You will ride with me."

When she finally saw her champion. Her breath caught in her

throat. Jocelyn was entranced by eyes so green that they resembled the lush meadows that surrounded her home. His cheeks were planed and chiseled, with a strong, square chin. But it was his mouth that held her captive, full lips, luscious and perfectly shaped. She wanted to touch those lips with the tips of her fingers, to see if they were as soft as they looked.

Her cheeks heated when she realized how much she would like to feel them against her own lips. Even as she took his hand, never taking her eyes off his face…his perfect face, the warmth spread to her neck and chest.

"May I ask yer name, my lord?" she asked timidly.

"This is our laird, Laird MacKinnon of Stonegate," Caleb spoke up, making something of an announcement. "I am Caleb, and this here is Peter." He motioned to his companion.

"Well, I thank ye for saving us." Jocelyn smiled.

Laird MacKinnon returned her smile. Sweeping her up in his arms again, he carefully lifted her onto his horse. As soon as he was mounted behind her, he gave the signal. They took off as fast as their horses could manage with two riders. Her hair blew back in his face, and she heard him breathe in deeply as his arm brought her closer to him.

Taking the left fork away from home, Jocelyn worried what their housekeeper, Heddy, would think when their cart arrived without them. But then their horse was a stubborn mare, and it would not be the first time she took off and found her way to her feed-bag—the tenacious old mare. Resigned, Jocelyn leaned back against a solid wall of man.

At the warmth against her back, she relaxed a bit as she enjoyed his arm around her waist. *I wonder which one?*

The MacKinnons were a large and wealthy clan. She recalled their clan chieftain had recently wed. *Oh, I hope 'tis not this one*, she silently prayed. She also remembered the MacKinnons were said to be raven-haired with startlingly blue eyes. Her archangel was not dark; instead, he was light as the sun and golden. She thought back to when she caught a glimpse of him fighting. His hair hung long past his shoulders with colors that resembled a lion's mane. She wanted to run her fingers through its silky strands.

There was one MacKinnon people gossiped about, one who was considered a rogue, a man with a slippery tongue, like the devil himself—believed to charm a lass with words of sweet promises and fulfilled desires. It was said he ruined many without a care for her or her reputation. He left them unmistakably compromised as he slipped out of town to let them face humiliation alone. Jocelyn tried in vain to remember the name of that blackheart but gave up. Well, her defender was not him. He was her hero, her savior.

When they were at a safe distance, Laird MacKinnon slowed their pace. "Where are we going, my lord?" Braedan asked as he and Caleb came alongside.

"We are going to my good friend, Sir Roderick MacPherson. His home is a few miles up the road."

Braedan's brows knitted. "We are in yer debt, my lord, but if we could inconvenience ye again, mayhap ye might lend us one of your horses so we may continue on home? We have kin who will worry if we do not return. I give ye my word. We will return yer horse on the morrow." He searched the man's face.

Selfishly Jocelyn did not want to be parted from her angel, but her brother was right, people expected them.

"I am afraid Killie Kern is a good distance away. We've traveled far ourselves and ridden these poor beasts hard. I would not risk them. I will make sure to send word to your kin at the first opportunity." Laird Mackinnon looked up at the heavy-laden sky. "It will be a miracle if we arrive unscathed."

Just then the sky opened, and the rain fell like a torrent upon their heads. The wind flew around from all directions. Jocelyn could not shield one side before the rain pelted them from the other. Her cloak was inadequate for keeping her warm or dry. She smiled when Laird MacKinnon wrapped his cloak around them both. Sighing contently, she was not bothered at all by the dreadful weather.

The way was unfamiliar, and she noticed they were quickly losing light. Whipped by the wind, the tree branches reached out at them like tentacles, forcing the group to ride single file. The road twisted and turned, then they began to climb. Labored breathing came from their horse, and she worried that carrying them both was too much. She breathed a sigh of relief when they started to descend.

They rode down the winding path toward a gate that lifted at their approach. Once inside, men came running to take the reins and helping them with their baggage. Without the protection of his cloak, Jocelyn was soaked in the few minutes it took to get inside. The great door opened, and an elderly man ushered them into an adjacent room where a fire burned in the hearth.

They stood in a large receiving hall, which had a sweeping staircase that led to the upper levels. The room to the right was a large banquet room, but on the left was more of a receiving salon. Jocelyn looked about, awed by its grandeur.

"My lords, lady, welcome to Castle Ballindoch," the chatelaine said dryly, tsking at their appearance. "I will bring hot drinks immediately."

"Thank ye, Carsen," Laird MacKinnon said and led the group to stand before the hearth.

Jocelyn was half-frozen, standing next to the fire with her hands stretched out. She was hesitant to let Carsen take her cloak as the wet wool kept some of the heat in her body, but she agreed when a servant girl brought her a cup of steaming hot tea.

She and the others huddled around the fire. The door swung open, and a giant warrior with flaming red hair entered.

"You're late," he said in a booming voice.

Jocelyn swore the timbers reverberated overhead.

Not bothering to respond, Laird MacKinnon rolled his eyes. "Don't look at me that way, brother. I have been expecting ye fer days."

Brother? Jocelyn thought. Well, that was an unusual thing to say, considering they looked nothing alike.

The giant warrior smiled and then gave Laird MacKinnon a big bear hug, slapping him not too gently in the back. "Makes no difference, ye are here and..." The man's gaze fell on Jocelyn. Walking up to her, he lifted her hand to kiss the back. His soft lips lingered a touch too long. "Well, well, I must say this is a pleasant surprise."

"I am remiss in my introductions, Sir Roderick." Laird MacKinnon laughed. "May I introduce ye to, Lady—"

"Miss MacAulay." Jocelyn lifted her chin slightly. "And my brother Braedan MacAulay."

"Tis a pleasure." Sir Roderick stepped forward to take Braedan's hand. His expression changed when he noticed fresh blood seeping from his head and down his neck. "Yer brother is injured," he said, in a worried tone. "Peter, Caleb, please take him upstairs and have Mrs. Westershire tend to him. She will show ye which bedchamber. Also, ask her to prepare another bedchamber for Miss MacAulay."

Jocelyn had started to follow when her hero took a gentle hold of her arm.

"Stay here, lass, and warm yerself by the fire. Finish yer tea, and I will escort ye."

The warmth of his hand tingled through the material of her gown.

After sitting in the chair that was brought for her, she turned her attention to the red-headed warrior. "I thank ye for yer hospitality, Sir Roderick."

"Aye, my dear, any friend of Blaine MacKinnon is a friend of mine," Sir Roderick said and then winked at her. "I don't suppose ye care to tell me what befell yer brother to cause his injury?" He waited politely for Jocelyn to respond, but she said nothing. She lost all expression, blood draining from her face. "Are ye all right, my dear?" He was about to press the issue when the door flew open.

"Blaine MacKinnon, you are late."

Standing at the doorway of the salon, with her hands on her hip, was the most gorgeous creature Jocelyn ever laid eyes on. The woman had shiny blonde hair one would swear was spun out of gold. She had the flawless milky white complexion bards sang about. Her dark blue eyes sparkled like the sea. She was swathed in light blue silk that left little to the imagination. Her full breasts looked like they might tumble out of her bodice at any moment. Although she was heavily powdered, with rouge and painted lips, she looked breathtaking.

"'Tis very naughty of you to keep me waiting," she gently admonished Blaine while extending her hand so that he could kiss it.

"My sincerest apologies, Lady Charlotte." He smiled charmingly. "I was unavoidably detained."

"I see," she said with a pout. She raised a perfectly arched brow when she caught sight of Jocelyn. "I don't suppose you were the detainer?"

Jocelyn stood, her back ramrod straight.

"May I introduce to ye, Lady Charlotte Wickstrom," Blaine said.

Jocelyn politely curtseyed.

"This is…"

"Miss MacAulay," she introduced herself, "but please, call me Jocelyn."

"I see you brought a little friend with you," Lady Charlotte said, turning her back.

"We are not friends, Lady Charlotte," Jocelyn said, her tone flat. "In fact, we made our acquaintances just today."

Lady Charlotte turned slowly to look at her, an amusing smile on her red lips. "MacAulay, you say? Isn't that Irish?"

"Aye, Lady Charlotte," Jocelyn said proudly. "Wickstrom? Isn't that…English?"

The silence hung in the room like a weighted shroud as both men looked with bewilderment at her and Lady Charlotte.

Jocelyn reached for her cup and took a sip of the scalding tea, not minding that it burned the roof of her mouth. "Thank ye, Sir Roderick," she said, putting the cup down. "If ye don't mind, I would like to see my brother."

Sir Roderick stammered something and then offered her his arm. She turned to look at Blaine. "Thank ye again, Sir Blaine, for your assistance today. We are indebted to ye."

Blaine watched as she left the salon, her held her head up like a princess. From behind, he heard a hissing sound. Jocelyn had not properly excuse herself, and the affront had not gone unnoticed.

"Well, Charlotte…what brings ye to Scotland?"

~ * ~

"Blaine MacKinnon? It canna be." Jocelyn groaned as she submerged into the steaming hot water.

Although the bath was effectively warming her body, it was doing nothing to soothe her emotional state. "Of all the people to come to my rescue, why the infamous womanizer of the Highlands?" She laughed pitifully. "What was it they said about him?"

She tried to remember the words in the right order. "Ah yes, he will take ye to bed, but never will he wed, so virgins and wives, best run for yer lives."

Except, there had been many a young lass who lost her heart to that scoundrel, and he left them reciting his golden rule as the reason.

Disappointment had sliced straight through her heart when Jocelyn heard his name. She had only herself to blame. Shaken by the robbery and being spared the unthinkable, well, it was natural to be more than appreciative, and she couldn't deny she was attracted to him. But to be subjected to Lady Charlotte's venom—well that whole encounter set her teeth on edge.

"And what did the rogue do? Nothing."

She was sure he thought it entertaining. Jocelyn was determined to separate Braedan and her from his company. Taking a washcloth, she applied scented soap and scrubbed vigorously.

She was not the only one wanting to be gone. Later, before she was shown to her bedchamber, Roderick took her to check on her brother. Entering Braedan's bedchamber, they saw Mrs. Westershire tending to his head and clucking like a mother hen.

Jocelyn was relieved to see him in good spirits. Once alone, he insisted they leave at first light. She suspected he was worried about Heddy, but she wondered if there was another reason. Perhaps Braedan knew of Blaine's reputation. He was very protective of her and wouldn't want her near that blackheart.

Well, tomorrow they would leave at first light, and she would never have to lay eyes on him again.

~ * ~

Blaine stared at the clock on the mantel. Lady Charlotte was not the only guest at the castle. Roderick's friend, Jackson Ferguson, and his cousin, Terence, arrived a week before, and Lady Charlotte was accompanied by her friend John McDermott. While Blaine usually enjoyed their company, tonight he found the conversation stale and boring.

"You should have seen the chit standing there, a veritable puddle forming under her tattered gown." Lady Charlotte laughed. "I swear to you, she had six inches of mud on her hem."

"Retract the claws Charlotte," Blaine said through gritted teeth. She was in a mood tonight, and it was futile to curb her diatribe.

"Oh, dear me, have I upset you, Blaine?" she said, swaying her hips as she walked toward him. "I don't know where you find these urchins, but darling, you need not rescue every damsel in distress."

"What happened to the lad?" Rod asked. "Did ye say he fell?"

Blaine decided not to say anything about the robbery. Strangely he felt the need to protect the MacAulays' privacy. "Nay, I didn't."

Sauntering up to the sideboard, Blaine refilled his glass of wine. Lady Charlotte was beside him in seconds, holding up her empty glass. She eyed him as if he were a bowl of sweet cream and she the fat feline ready to lap him up.

"Why are you so secretive, lover?" she purred. "What tidbit are you keeping from us?"

Desperately wanting to change the subject, he told Roderick of Fenny and Kaylee's upcoming wedding and the clans that would be attending. He told them of Lady Ilyssa's cousin, Davina, and her upcoming nuptials to Sir Kieran MacNeil.

Thankfully, this prompted Charlotte to go into her account of Davina's trip to France in search of a wedding gown. She took stage describing everything from the dress to the shoes with all the trappings. She paused a few times to make sure she had his attention. He lost interest anyway, unable to keep from staring at the little crumb of cake that was stuck to her bottom lip. He wondered how long it would take before it would dislodge and fall into the crevice between her breasts.

"Blaine, don't you find that extravagant even for Davina?" Charlotte asked, finally licking her lips and dragging the crumb into her mouth.

"If ye will excuse me, I find myself somewhat fatigued this evening." He put his glass down, not bothering to finish it. "My lady…gentlemen." He bowed, taking his leave.

He completely ignored the look Charlotte shot his way. He supposed she wasn't too pleased with being dismissed twice in one evening, but he had enough. Walking up the stairs, he saw Mrs. Westershire. "My usual room?" She nodded and smiled at him with genuine affection. "Oh, and by the by, where did ye put Miss MacAulay?"

"Now lad, ye be leaving the lass alone. She is not yer kind of game," scolded Mrs. Westershire.

"I am not inquiring for myself." This was partly the truth. It would be best to keep Lady Charlotte and Jocelyn away from each other. No doubt, Lady Charlotte would have the room next to his as most of the servants were aware of their relationship.

"Then fer who?" Mrs. Westershire asked in disbelief. "Well, ye might as well know, ye have Miss MacAulay right across the hall, and I put her brother next to ye. So ye best not be making a nuisance of yerself."

He was surprised Braedan was next to him and not Charlotte.

"If ye are wondering which chamber is Lady Charlotte's…"

"That's all, Franny." As he called her by her Christian name, he winked at her.

"Aye my lord." Mrs. Westershire smiled fondly. "If ye be retiring, I will have yer bath brought up."

~ * ~

Blaine leaned back in the tub and watched the wisps of steam rising. He tried to relax, but he felt unsettled. He could not rid himself of the image of Jocelyn when she heard his name. It was like the light had gone from her face. At first, he thought it might be something else. Still, after going over every detail of when they met, he recalled being introduced only as Laird MacKinnon, never by his given name. It wasn't until she heard his given name that her attitude changed toward him.

It was fortunate that he and his men came upon them when they did. Seeing that vermin lying on top of Jocelyn with his hands on her thighs incensed Blaine. He was most impressed by Jocelyn's demeanor when faced with her assailant and he admired her for it.

Blaine thought himself as an admirer of all women. It mattered naught if they were big or small, dark-haired or blonde. He could always find something about them that was unique and beautiful. Once he chased a lass for a month solely for her laugh. She wasn't comely or wealthy, but she was intelligent and joyous in nature. They could sit and talk for hours, but when she laughed, it was like a burst of sunshine all around them. Grinning, he remembered how she laughed after she reached her release.

By the Saints' holy breath, Blaine chastised himself. Here he was lamenting over the loss of Jocelyn's favor one moment and then reliving one of his past sexual escapades. He needed to find the truth, why the lass turned frosty toward him. Could it have been because of Charlotte? Nay, Jocelyn handled herself well, not allowing Charlotte to intimidate her. The lass was bold.

After a time, the water grew cold, and he rose to dry himself. Wrapping the drying cloth around his narrow hips, he stood near the fire. He picked up the glass on the table, taking a hefty sip of the potent wine. A light rap on the door broke through his thoughts, most likely one of the servants. It would be an excellent opportunity to ask for something to eat. Opening the door, he was dismayed to find Lady Charlotte on the other side.

"I wondered where you went off to." Her gaze raked his form from top to bottom. "I can see you are dressed for company. I hope ye don't mind?"

He minded very much. "My dear Charlotte, although I would love yer company, I'm afraid I am not entertaining this evening."

"What game are you playing?" She tried to look past him. "Tell me you don't have that little bit of fluff in there." Pushing her way past him, she eyes his empty bed. She went as far as to look underneath.

"Forgive me, my darling, but I as ye can see, I am quite alone, and I would prefer to stay that way." Taking her arm firmly, Blaine led her out of the room.

She tried to wiggle free from his grasp but caught site of Mrs. Westershire approaching with a couple of servants in tow.

"What's going on here?" Mrs. Westershire asked.

Charlotte hovered, fuming, while a nearly naked Blaine was doing his best to keep his temper in check.

"Ah Mrs. Westershire, just in time." He poured on the charm as he said, "It seems Lady Charlotte has lost her way. She usually occupies the bedchamber next door. Would ye be a dear and show her to her room?"

Charlotte looked ready to scream. Her face was pinched with red splotches. "Well, I never." She turned on her heal, practically running over the housekeeper.

"Poppycock. The lady knows exactly where her room is. She's been here nigh a week." Franny said it loud enough for Lady Charlotte to hear. "Now let's get ye settled, love. Is there anything I can get ye?" She brightly smiled at him.

He gave her a lopsided grin. He suspected she enjoyed seeing Lady Charlotte at a disadvantage. "I wouldn't mind something to eat."

"Aye lad." She poked him in the stomach. "Someone's got to

feed ye. Yer looking rather scrawny these days and what are ye doing with all this hair, 'tis past time ye had it cut."

He laughed. Mrs. Westershire was never one to mince words. Donning his robe, he picked up his glass of wine. His encounter with Charlotte was most unfortunate, and he would pay for it later. But tonight, he wanted to relax. He would deal with Lady Charlotte Wickstrom in the morning.

Chapter Three

Jocelyn finally fell asleep in the wee hours of the morning. She spent the night tossing and turning, unable to calm her mind. After her bath, she realized that all her clothes had been removed, most likely to be cleaned. Not having a change of clothes, the young maid, Heather, provided Jocelyn with a night-rail that she could borrow.

Finding a book on the shelf, she curled up next to the fire to read. Realizing she had not eaten much, her stomach kept growling, which made it difficult to concentrate. She jumped and ran to the door when she heard voices outside her room. Hoping it might be Heather, she cracked the door open just a bit and peered out.

Jocelyn was shocked to see Lady Charlotte leaving Blaine's bedchamber as he stood in the doorway wearing nothing more than a drying cloth. Jocelyn shut the door quietly, not wanting to be caught snooping. Her heart sank. She had suspected Lady Charlotte might be something more to him than just a friend, but to see them carry on…well, it was too much. She could not forget what she saw. Tears fell.

"What a ninny ye are carrying on for a man who's nothing but a rake." It was good that she was aware of his true nature before she became too attached.

After a time, she gave up the notion of reading and found she had lost her appetite. Blowing out the candle, she buried herself deep under her covers and attempted to sleep. She did manage to set aside any thoughts of Blaine, but then her mind was flooded with images of the men who robbed them. Releasing a heavy breath, she worried it was going to be a long night.

When she finally awoke, she couldn't tell what time it was. The sky was so dark, and the rain had not lessened at all. She thought to rise, when she remembered she had nothing to wear. With no other option, she got back into bed.

Thankfully it wasn't long before Heather came to start a fire in the hearth. "Good morrow, my lady, I take it ye slept well?"

Jocelyn lied, nodding that she had.

Heather carried a gown in her arms. "Och, I hope ye don't mind, I thought you might wear this seeing that yer gown was badly stained and torn in a few places. My sisters and I are working on repairing it, but 'tis not finished," she held up the gown she brought, "I think this will fit ye nicely."

Jocelyn blushed; the gown was better than any she owned. The dark blue material contrasted beautifully with the ivory lace around the neck and sleeves. Underneath, the ivory counterpane narrowed to a V at the waist. "I'm not sure it will fit."

"Och, it will fit all right. My sisters took yer measurements from your gown. We had to alter verra little," Heather said as Jocelyn helped her put it on.

The dress, in fact, fit perfectly.

She could not help admiring her reflection in the mirror. Heather kindly brought her a chemise, petticoats, stockings and garters. The only thing that didn't fit was the shoes.

"Och. Well, ye can use yer boots. They should be dry." She left to retrieve them.

Jocelyn brushed her dark brown hair until it shined and then plaited it in one long braid. She wondered where the dress came from and then paled at the thought that she might be wearing one of Lady Charlotte's. There was no way the woman would be that generous, so she decided not to give it another thought. When Heather returned, she explained that the gown belonged to Sir Roderick's sister, Lady Angela.

"I will have to thank her."

"Lady Angela is at court. But I will pass along the message. She will be greatly pleased to know ye like it."

After Jocelyn ate, she went in search of Braedan, as it was time to find a way home. She knocked on the door and entered when she heard his voice. Propped up in bed, he was enjoying his own breakfast.

"How do ye fare?" she asked, kissing him on the top of his head. "Any pain?"

"Only when I move my head," he said, bobbing it from side-to-side. She giggled. His smile faded. "I figure we best see about getting home."

"Aye, I be thinking the same, but have ye noticed?" she tilted her head toward the window, "'tis raining."

"Aye, but what's a bit of rain?"

She agreed there was nothing wrong with a bit of rain. Still, it was pouring outside, and her brother had sustained a nasty head injury. Perhaps leaving was not an option…unless. "There's no reason we need to get wet, Brae. I am sure Sir Roderick has a carriage. I will seek him out and ask if we may borrow it."

He shook his head slightly. "'Tis a grand idea, but I will be doing the asking. Ye just stay in yer bedchamber until we can leave."

She started to argue, but he would not listen. Walking over, she sat on the bed next to him. "What are ye worried about?"

"What do ye mean?" His voice raised slightly. "We are facing serious financial ruin and having all our money stolen has set us back. We need to find a way to stave off Graham from gaining our home until we can find a way to recoup what we lost. The last thing I need to worry about is ye and those…men." He closed his eyes.

"I know ye are worried about Sir Walrick. I saw ye talking to him."

Braedan looked at her strangely.

"Ye can tell me. Was he pressuring ye for payment?"

"I need to tell ye something."

A cold thread of dread crept down her back.

Taking a deep breath, he continued, "Aye, Graham came to see me. He claimed to be concerned about our welfare and how we planned to repay him. He told me he too had solicitors haranguing him, and we didn't have much time." His expression darkened. "He made me an offer."

"What did Graham propose?" Jocelyn pulled her bottom lip between her teeth. The last thing they needed was another business venture.

"He suggested we could align our families through marriage, we…" Braedan shook his head.

"Marriage? To whom?"

"He offered to dissolve the debt if ye agree to marry him."

"For what purpose? Graham has a son and grandsons, so there's no need for an heir."

"Aye, I said as much. Told him that I would see ye wed to someone ye chose. Graham said that unless ye wed, he would petition to have Heatherwood deeded to him."

Jocelyn couldn't believe what she was hearing, making the loss of their money even more painful. If they hadn't been robbed, they might have had enough to reclaim one of the smaller parcels of land. The mockery of Graham's offer chafed her too. "Well, I will tell ye this, Braedan. I would never agree to marry that man. I would prefer a life in a convent."

"Don't fash yerself, Joce, I did not consent to the match. If we lose Heatherwood, we will find a new home." Braedan squeezed her hand.

"Nay, Father gave ye Heatherwood, and I will not see it taken from us." She squeezed his hand back. "I will see if Sir Roderick will lend us a carriage. Once we are home, we will find a solution." He would not release her hand when she tried to stand. "Ye have nothing to worry about. Sir Roderick has behaved like a perfect gentleman."

"I shouldn't judge men based on gossip, but both Sir Blaine and Sir Roderick have quite a reputation."

She remembered what she witnessed the night before and sensed an unfamiliar ache in her chest. "I am afraid 'tis more than just gossip…last night…"

He cocked his head. "What happened last night?"

"I am afraid I behaved badly. I heard voices and," she went to stand by the windows, not wanting Braedan to see her flushed cheeks, "Sir Roderick has other guests staying at the castle, one of them being an attractive woman by the name of Lady Charlotte. I saw her leave Sir Blaine's bedchamber."

"Ah, so that was the blonde woman. Aye, she is more than attractive, she's beautiful. But I find nothing wrong in the lady stopping by to have a word with Sir Blaine."

"Really Braedan, you are so obtuse at times. It was not a visit; it was an *assignation*." She hoped her voice sounded indifferent.

"Then it was a failed *assignation*."

Jocelyn spun around, nailing him with her gaze. "Ye saw?"

"Aye, I too am guilty of spying." He flushed slightly. "I heard voices, and for a moment I thought Sir Blaine was trying to …let's just say, I was worried that he might…Oh hell, I don't care for the way the man looks at ye, and I feared he may try to compromise ye. So, I too watched as she entered his room, but soon after, she left. There was somewhat of a commotion, and well, let's just say the lady was'na happy."

"Are ye saying Sir Blaine asked Lady Charlotte to leave?'

"Nay, more like he threw her out." Jocelyn's eyes grew wide. "Mrs. Westershire was there too, and…I canna believe ye didn't hear here all the commotion. Ye must have just missed her."

Surprisingly Jocelyn experienced immense relief. She still believed Blaine was a rogue of the worst kind, but it made her happy that he had not succumbed to Lady Charlotte's wiles. "I shouldn't care at all as 'tis naught our business."

Braedan lifted a brow at her.

"No, 'tis true. Brae, we have more important matters to contend with, and the sooner we leave, the better." Leaning over, she kissed her brother on the top of his head and told him she would go find Sir Roderick.

"Be careful, Joce," Braedan warned her.

~ * ~

Blaine awoke, exhausted. Dressing quickly, he went downstairs to break his fast. When he saw there was no one in the dining salon, he decided to find Roderick instead. He found him in his study working on his correspondence.

"What in the Saint's name has gotten into ye?" Rod said when he saw him. "'Tis not like ye, brother."

His greeting did nothing to improve Blaine's mood. "Good morrow to ye as well." He went over to the sideboard and saw a tray of warm biscuits.

Rod leaned back in his chair, his expression losing its humor. "Would you care to tell me what transpired between ye and Lady Charlotte?"

"Not really." When he took a bite of the biscuit, it tasted dry in his mouth. Blaine poured himself some ale and sat next to the fire. "At the first opportunity, I will smooth things over with Charlotte. It may take some doing, but I assure ye, she will be fine."

"Lady Charlotte left," Rod said flatly.

He was surprised by the news. "I don't suppose she gave a reason?"

"Nay, but 'tis no surprise. Every person under this roof knows how ye rejected her—erm, company."

Blaine scoffed in disbelief.

"Hell's fire, Blaine, the lass waited days for ye to arrive. Then when ye finally do, ye canna even be decent toward her. She has always been discrete when it came to the two of ye."

Rod's query embarrassed Blaine, causing him to grit his teeth.

"Does this have anything to do with the lass ye brought?"

"Nay, I told ye, we came upon them, and they needed help. We offered assistance."

"Then why be so vague? What are ye not telling me?"

"I dinna think 'tis my place to say."

Rod prodded until Blaine gave in. He briefly told him what happened, leaving out the part of Jocelyn being attacked.

"Besides, the lass disdains me, so there's nothing to speak of. She had nothing to do with Charlotte's leaving."

Rod laughed. "There is not a lass in all of Scotland who doesn't fall to yer charms. Ye will naught convince me otherwise. I believe this whole nonsense of yer brother forcing ye to wed has taken its toll. I explained this to Charlotte, and she appeared to improve some."

There was a light tap on the door. "My lord, Miss MacAulay is 'ere to see ye," Carsen announced.

Blaine did not expect to see Jocelyn dressed in such a fetching gown. The dark blue accentuated her fair complexion and lithe figure. Her hair was a glossy dark brown, utterly void of any red. Her braid hung to her waist, and he longed to thread his fingers through its silky tresses.

"Good morrow, Miss Jocelyn, I take it ye slept well?" Rod smiled, getting up to greet her.

Jocelyn smiled brightly at him and curtseyed.

"Now, we need not stand on such formalities," he said, taking her hand. "How may I be of service?"

"Good morrow, Miss Jocelyn," Blaine said.

Her smiled faded at his voice. She had not seen him sitting next to the fire, his long legs stretched out. "Good morrow, Sir Blaine." She bobbed an awkward curtsey.

"How do ye fare this morning?" he pressed on.

"I am fine. Thank ye fer asking." Jocelyn sounded uneasy and looked away.

Seemingly amused by their awkward interaction, Rod winked at Blaine. "I must say ye look splendid."

"I must thank yer sister, Sir Roderick. 'Tis one of hers. I am very grateful for lending me—"

"Nonsense." He waved his hand. "My sister's wardrobes are filled to overflowing. She could wear a different gown each day and not repeat for a year. Besides, ye look positively beautiful."

Jocelyn blushed. "I do thank ye for yer hospitality, but I am afraid 'tis most imperative that my brother and I leave immediately. We have urgent matters at home that need our attention."

Rod looked out the window. "I would be happy to assist ye, but as ye can see, the weather is not cooperating."

"I am aware of that, but I thought perhaps ye might lend us a carriage?"

"I am afraid I have none at my disposal," Rod said. "My parents took one of the carriages to visit my brother, and earlier today Lady Charlotte asked to use the other. I do have open carriages, and once the rain lifts, I can have them readied."

"I appreciate the offer, my lord. However, I will only inconvenience ye with the use of a couple of horses, so my brother and I might be on our way."

Blaine was surprised to find he was not happy at the notion of Jocelyn leaving.

"I'm afraid that it will not be possible." All heads turned to see

Mrs. Westershire standing at the doorway. "Forgive me, my lady, but Mr. MacAulay has developed a fever. It would be in his best interest if he stayed abed for a few days."

"How can this be?" Jocelyn said. "I just left him. He appeared much improved, and the wound in his head was less painful."

"Aye, the wound in his head is healing nicely, but his leg may be infected." Jocelyn's mouth fell open. "Yer brother sustained two wounds that required stitching. I think 'tis best for him to stay here."

She had to return home, with or without Brae. "I would then appreciate it if ye could lend me a horse, my lord. I will go alone."

"My dear, I don't think it would be wise for a young woman to travel alone, especially in this weather," said Rod as he tried to reason with her.

"If ye are so determined to leave, Miss Jocelyn, I will escort ye." Blaine rose to stand next to her. Much to his dismay, she stepped back. "I can assure ye, ye will arrive home safely."

Jocelyn looked at him coldly. "I appreciate yer offer, Sir Blaine, but I am afraid that is out of the question." She turned to Rod. "When do ye expect yer carriage back, my lord?"

"Taking into account the rain and the muddy roads," Rod furrowed his brow, "I say a few days. But I must insist that ye wait until yer brother is ready to travel."

"Ye forget, that we are expected at court," Blaine said, throwing a wrinkle into her plans. "We will need the use of yer carriage; I believe Lady Angela is waiting for ye to escort her home?"

"Aye, and yer already late as is," Rod concurred. "It may be best to send word to yer kin and then hope for the weather to clear."

Firming her lips, she hesitated a moment then spoke. "Sir Roderick, if ye could send word to my kin, I would be most appreciative."

Roderick placed his hand on her arm, giving it a squeeze. "I will be more than happy to dispatch one of my servants."

Mrs. Westershire stood next to her. "Let's see about getting ye something to write with as I am sure ye will want to send a letter." With that, the two women quit the room.

When the door closed, Rod looked at Blaine with humor in his eyes. "Aye, the lass hates ye."

~ * ~

Jocelyn followed Mrs. Westershire back upstairs. "Ye have foolscap in yer writing desk, but I am sure the ink well is dry," she said. "I will return in a moment."

Instead of waiting, Jocelyn decided to check on Braedan. She wanted to scold him for not telling her the extent of his injuries.

When she reached his room, she saw the door slightly ajar. Pushing it open, she saw Heather and another woman, who had to be her sister.

"Good morrow, miss." Heather smiled. "Oh, Lily, see how nicely the gown fits. Ye did right by yer measurements."

Heather quickly introduced them and went to stand next to Jocelyn as Lily walked around, appreciating their handiwork.

"Oh miss, ye look lovely," she exclaimed.

Not accustomed to so much fuss, Jocelyn thanked them. She worried when she realized Braedan was missing. "Oh, ye need not worry," Heather said. "We thought it best that the mister rests in the library, where 'tis quite warm and comfortable."

"Aye," Lily concurred. "We needed to change his linens and tidy up a bit."

Jocelyn's concerns grew more at the sight of blood on the sheets.

"I can take ye to him," Lily said.

She followed Lily to the other side of the castle. It was a short distance, but the twisting corridor made it seem endless. Lily opened the door to a small but well-stocked library where a cheery fire burned in the hearth. To one side, a set of tall windows ran the length of the room, allowing in plenty of light. Overstuffed chairs and lounges sat on top a plush Aubusson rug. Looking around, they still did not see Braedan. There was a blanket draped on one of chaise lounge with an open book lying on top.

Before Jocelyn could comment, Lily pointed to a doorway. "He must be in the gallery."

They walked into the adjoining room to find him standing before a painting of a young woman. The picture must have captivated him for he did not hear their approach.

"Beautiful," he whispered.

"Aye, Lady Angela is beautiful indeed," Lily agreed, "but she is also beautiful within, having a gentle and caring nature."

Jocelyn noticed the flush creeping up Braedan's neck.

The gallery was just that, a room full of portraits displaying different members of the MacPherson clan, but this one was enthralling. The young woman possessed the same red hair as most of her kin. She was seated, her face looking slightly off to the left, with just the barest hint of a smile on her lips. She looked as if she might turn at any moment, gifting you with an alluring smile.

The painter brilliantly painted her in a gown that looked

diaphanous and delicate as dragonfly wings. It offset her perfectly creamy shoulders. Her hair was swept up and held by a blue ribbon that showed the delicate curve of her neck. She was, in fact, stunning.

"Ye should lie down." Jocelyn broke the silence.

Braedan nodded, reluctantly tearing his gaze away from the painting.

Once settled back on the lounge, Lily tucked the blanket around him. "I will check back soon to see if ye need anything."

Finally, alone, Jocelyn scolded him for not revealing the extent of his injuries. After a time, he held up his hands. "Joce, I had a bloody headache and was chilled to the bone. In all honestly, I hurt all over."

"Ye have never been hurt before, and I feel so helpless." Images of her own assault came flooding back.

Wanting to change the subject, she told him of Sir Roderick's offer to send word. Together they composed the letter and instructed Heddy to sell one of the cows. The money would sustain the bakery until they returned. They made a point of telling her that under no circumstance was she to let Sir Walrick know of their whereabouts. The less he knew, the better.

Within the hour the messenger left with their letter and the few coins they had recovered. Jocelyn watched as he galloped through the gates. She insisted that he stay the night and not return till the following day.

Sighing deeply, she crossed her arms against the chill through the window.

Chapter Four

The messenger was not the only one who left that day. Lady Charlotte's companion, John McDermott, decided they should leave for Edinburgh. Without her to keep them entertained, Jackson and his cousin Terence agreed to accompany John.

"Are ye sure ye don't want to come along?" Terence asked Blaine. "There be plenty of room."

"I canna leave yet."

"That's unfortunate," drawled John. "I would so like to witness yer arrival. Since ye announced yer decision to marry, the vultures have been circling."

The group laughed as Rod slapped Blaine on his back. "I will be along shortly, so ye need not worry," he retorted. "I wouldn't want to keep ye from yer entertainment."

"Well, don't tarry too long," John teased and bid him goodbye as he rushed to his carriage amid the torrent of rain.

Jackson shook Blaine's hand. "Blaine, there's many a man who wouldn't mind the opportunity to choose a wife from Scotland's wealthiest families. The most beautiful and eligible women will be presented to ye. Ye will have yer pick." He winked at him and left to join the others. The carriage took off, the thunder signaling their exit.

Roderick laughed. "Jackson is right, ye will have yer pick of the finest women in Scotland."

Blaine followed him back to his study and walked straight to the sideboard for a drink. "I am afraid ye are wrong, ye are all wrong." He tossed the whisky down his dry throat. "The king has already made his choice of who I will wed. I will be shackled and led to the chapel the moment I step foot in Edinburgh."

Rod joined him in a drink. "'Tis said many petitioned their daughters' hand and held a silent auction." He grinned.

"I swear, Roddy, ye are taking great pleasure in my misfortune," Blaine growled.

"Brother, ye are not taking the situation seriously enough," Rod snapped back. "Per Caelan's command, ye should have been wed months ago."

Blaine groaned loudly. "I am living in a nightmare," he

lamented. "I hoped that somehow, someone would cross my path and present me with a solution. I swear, I wish I could just fight the man who put me in this position."

"Why marriage?" Rod asked. "Why do the MacDonnells insist on this?"

"There be one oath I hold more sacred than any other, and that is the vows of marriage. My parents had a trust between them, and from that trust grew love. They were happily married until my father died. My mother never remarried. Once I wed, I will never betray my wife, and that's why I have stayed away from marriage because I have never met a lass whom I would want to spend the rest of my life with."

"Well, ye might consider finding a lass who would agree to a betrothal, which may satisfy the king and yer brother," Rod suggested.

"Then what?"

"Then, after some time, ye could say that the lass broke off the engagement. Yer brother couldn't fault ye fer that. The MacDonnells may eventually forget this need that ye wed if ye promise not to assault another one of their women."

"I did not assault her," Blaine yelled but saw that Rod was only jesting with him. "Yer plan has merit, but who do ye think I could find to agree to such a plan?"

"If ye hadn't insulted Lady Charlotte, I am sure she would have agreed."

"Nay, the king would never believe we are engaged. Too many are aware of our liaisons, and she is English to boot."

"What of Laird McClellan's daughter?" Rod piped up. "The lass is comely, to say the least, and most agreeable. Their land connects with ours; ye can ride there in an hour."

"The lass is most agreeable, but so is her father," Blaine rolled his eyes, "meaning he would make sure we wed. There would be no chance of her begging off."

"Would that be so bad? I mean, there's nothing wrong in wedding such a fine young lass."

"If she's so grand then you marry her," Blaine snapped and got up to pour himself another drink.

He took a sip of the fiery brew, knitting his brows in contemplation. He needed to find someone who wouldn't mind becoming involved in his ruse, someone unknown to his friend. Then, like a splash of cold water, he thought of the perfect person who could play the part of the lovely lady who graciously consents to be his bride and then begs off at the last minute. He smiled at Roderick, his future brighter for the first time since Caelan's visit.

Roderick arched a brow. "I know that look," he said with a lopsided grin. "Ye have a plan."

"Aye, I have the perfect lass to be my sham of a bride, and she is a lot closer than the McClellan lass."

Rod shook his head. "The lass hates ye."

Blaine rubbed his jaw with two fingers. "The lass has good business sense, and I only need to make sure it is lucrative for all parties involved." He looked out the window at the pouring rain, grateful for the time it would give him. "I will keep as close to the truth as possible. We met when I gallantly came to her rescue..."

"Aye, but the lass abhors your very presence," Rod argued.

"...we fell in love, and I was delayed arriving to court because I was busy wooing her. Ye canna expect a lass to agree to marriage without some reservations..."

"Fell in love? The lass loathes ye," Rod reiterated.

Blaine raised his voice as he said, "Aye, she hates me. So how can I convince her otherwise?"

His friend looked doubtful. "Well ye only have two days at most," he said. "Ye best make the offer a good one."

Blaine looked at him, incredulously.

"Och. Whom do I think I am talking to? The lass will melt at yer feet just for the opportunity to toy with yer affections."

Blaine needed to tread carefully. He wondered why the thought of Jocelyn acting like his adoring fiancée appealed to him. It irked him that she disliked him so. He thought it perplexing, but also challenging. For him to win over the lass, he needed more information, and he knew exactly who to ask.

"What are ye going to do?"

"I believe it's time I have a serious conversation with Mr. MacAulay." Blaine went to find his quarry.

~ * ~

Jocelyn left Braedan sleeping in the library. Although he assured her, he was fine, his red cheeks told her otherwise. What she wanted now was a cup of hot tea, and she ventured downstairs.

Walking into the kitchen, she felt immediately at home. James, the cook, introduced his wife, Dinah. Married for eleven years, they planned their daily menu, all the while gently bickering with one another. An act of total affection.

"Are ye sure ye wouldn't want to take yer tea in the salon?" Dinah asked. "'Tis more comfortable."

Jocelyn explained how she enjoyed watching her mother cook and that she spent many hours in the kitchen learning.

"Well, then ye best pull up a chair, dearie, I 'ave som'tin tae show ye."

They used honey to sweeten their nuts for the morning buns. Seeing a small number of walnuts leftover, she showed them how to finely chop them and bake them into a dinner bread. The nuts created a delicate crunch and flavor.

"How are ye with spices?" James handed her a small package. "Sir Blaine brought these at his last visit."

At the strands of deep orange, she smiled approvingly. "This is saffron from Spain," she said. "I see that ye have some fish." The brined fish was soaking in milk to leach out the salt. "The spice would make a delicious sauce."

"What about this?" Dinah held up nutmeg. "Do ye have another use other than custard?"

"Aye, ye could shave some and grind it to a fine powder," Jocelyn explained, "then add to yer boiled carrots with butter. It adds a nice taste that reminds me of Christmastide."

As it was nearing the evening meal, Jocelyn excused herself. Just as she reached her bedchamber, she saw Heather leaving Braedan's room.

"My lady, Sir Roderick requested that ye join him and the gentlemen for dinner tonight." Jocelyn wasn't sure to whom she was referring to, so Heather clarified, "Yer brother has declined the invitation because he needs to rest. So, it will be Sir Roderick, Sir Blaine and his outriders, Caleb and Peter."

Jocelyn would have preferred eating alone but decided it would be rude to refuse. "I will be happy to join them," she said and went in to freshen up.

~ * ~

Jocelyn entered the private dining hall only to see Blaine. He was leaning against the hearth in a casual manner. A faint smile touched his lips. Pushing off, he crossed the room to greet her.

He greeted her cheerfully. "Good evening, Miss MacAulay."

Jocelyn looked around disapprovingly. "I thought we were dining at seven?"

"Ye need not worry, Miss MacAulay. Roderick will be along shortly." Blaine offered her a glass of wine.

Her first reaction was to refuse, but then she thought the drink might help steel her nerves. She nodded and took the glass he handed her. She was too hasty in taking a sip that, for a second, she thought she might choke. Swallowing hard, she cleared her throat.

"Tell me about yerself, Miss MacAulay," he asked politely.

His query annoyed her. "There's not much to tell, Laird MacKinnon." Taking another sip, she put her glass down. It would not serve her to get intoxicated before the others arrived. And speaking of others, where the hell were they? "I come from a small village called Killie Kern, where I run my family's small bakery." She looked away, brushing off an imaginary piece of lint from her sleeve.

This was not going well at all, so Blaine tried a different approach. "Come now, my dear, this is not an interview. I would like to know ye, what yer life is like. I would like to learn more about the lass I rescued."

"So ye can decide if I was worth the effort?" she said teasingly. He stood there saying nothing. He gave her a sly grin while waiting patiently. "Since I am not accustomed to talking about myself, why don't ye tell me about *you*."

He arched a well-shaped brow. "Not much to say either." He sipped of his wine. "At home, north from here, I am a simple fisherman."

"A simple fisherman?" she slightly mocked him. "I believe yer men referred to ye as laird. This would make ye a landowner and titled."

"Aye, I served the king for six years and was knighted. I inherited Stonegate from my mother; 'tis a modest tower house." He looked at her intensely.

"Heatherwood is my home. My grandfather built it years before my father was born. 'Tis a good size manor, and the surrounding lands are fertile. My hopes are to restore the house one day so my brother may raise his family with pride. We have sustained ourselves through the bakery, but because Killie Kern is such a small village, I thought to increase our profits by selling at the larger markets. I hope to gain customers from local shops and taverns."

"I thought most shops and pubs made their own breads?" Blaine raised his brows

"Aye, my lord, but we make specialty breads and cakes. I am also looking to expand to other goods such as cheese and butter."

"I wonder why those thieves attacked ye," Blaine said, changing the subject. "It seems odd that they would have gained much in stealing from someone coming from the market."

Jocelyn didn't mind his observations, for those very thoughts bothered her too. "We don't appear to be people of substantial wealth."

"Perhaps they saw yer heavy purse worth their trouble?"

"What they took was far less than the cost of a nobleman's ring or a lady's bauble."

"Yer beauty alone would have been enough."

Jocelyn's spine jerked stiff at the compliment, although he didn't seem to notice. There was nothing behind the praise, and for that reason alone, some of her resolve thawed. He was about to say something when the door opened, and Roderick came in with Peter and Caleb behind him.

"My apologies, my lady, Blaine, but I had some issues with the tenants. Seems two of them had roof leaks, and Peter and Caleb kindly assisted in the repairs."

Jocelyn thought the excuse flimsy until she noticed both men had wet hair.

"If ye will follow me, I believe supper is served." Rod led them to the family salon where they sat around a table laden with platters of meats and roasted vegetables. The dinner was exceptional, and everyone complimented Jocelyn for her contributions.

Peter commented on her roasted carrots with butter and seasonings. "The nutmeg is like Christmas—'tis the smell of the evergreens."

They sampled each dish while Roderick entertained them with the latest gossip from court, excluding any mention of Blaine's predicament. He went on to relay stories of what it was like growing up with the three MacKinnon brothers and the mischief they got into. They had played a prank on their tutor, putting a mouse in her boot. Unfortunately, the mouse had escaped and went into Caelan's room. During the night, the mouse gnawed a hole in his favorite slipper. Blaine and Rod hid from Caelan in a nearby dry well.

Caelan saw where the two were hiding, cut the rope and refused to aid them until they promised to buy him a new pair. They agreed, but much to their dismay, both sets of parents decided that their punishment was not enough and made them spend the night in the well.

Jocelyn laughed at the thought of Rod and Blaine clinging to each other for comfort. She noticed that Blaine took the teasing in stride, smiling and laughing along. He had a natural ease about him. Seated across from him, she observed him as he ate.

Blaine savored each dish rather than shovel the food in as Peter and Caleb were doing. It wasn't that he ate sparingly, as there was a good amount of food on his plate. Instead he chewed each bite methodically and slowly. His full lips pursed seductively, and occasionally he licked his lips with his tongue then dabbed with his napkin.

She could watch him eat for hours, wishing she was a morsel he was about to consume. It was ridiculous to observe how a person ate, but no matter, she couldn't help it.

The evening continued long after the platters were removed. She stifled a yawn; it was time she sought her bed. She thanked Rod for the lovely evening and excused herself. Roderick offered to escort her to her room, but she declined.

"Nay, my lord," she assured him, "I can find my way."

Walking down the long hall toward her bedchamber, her emotions tumbled about tipping her heart this way and that. She had watched Blaine, like a young lass with her first crush. She needed to stop fantasizing about the man and remember who he really was.

She ran down the hall and into her bedchamber, throwing herself on her bed, feeling completely and utterly confused.

~ * ~

Blaine decided to retire early and left Rod and his companions to their drink. The evening turned out well regardless of Rod's interruption. Blaine had specifically asked him to delay their appearance so he could have a chance to speak to Jocelyn privately. Perhaps get to know her better and find out why she disliked him. However, seeing Jocelyn relaxed and enjoying herself pleased him. Just as he reached the landing, he heard his name. Right then, soft, warm arms wrapped around his waist from behind. He thought for a moment, it might be Jocelyn when he heard her voice.

"Ar' ye up for a wee bit 'av sport, milord?" Cottie, the upstairs chambermaid pressed her body tightly against his.

She was a pretty lass, and he had contemplated taking her to bed in the past, but, for some reason, he was not interested now.

After he turned around to face her, she gave him a provocative smile. "'Av what ye need tae relax ye."

Grateful they were alone, he pulled away from her embrace. He would not want anyone seeing them together. "Cottie my dear, ye are a tempting little flower, but tonight I need my rest." He took her face in his hands. "I will seek ye out another time."

He brushed a quick kiss on her lips and couldn't help but notice that her breath was far from fresh, and her clothes smelled a bit musty. He gave her his most charming smile before turning to leave.

Relieved to be finally alone, he quickly undressed and dove under the covers even though the room was far from cold. It surprised him that he thought Cottie less than adequate. He had never noticed her breath or her appearance before. He saw all women beautiful, each in her own way. Not wanting to dwell on the matter, he pushed away those thoughts and concentrated on the evening.

He thought about Jocelyn's smile and how it lit up her entire face. Her laughter was light and tinkled like bells. He was also quite aware that she spent most of the evening discreetly observing him. Why the fascination when she went out of her way to dislike him?

Before Rod interrupted them, she opened up and shared something of her life. When the subject turned to the robbery, they were of the same belief that it was not some random attack. She too thought they might have been targeted.

Blaine wished they had more time since his conversation with her brother earlier proved futile. There was something more to what was going on in their life than just being bakers in a small village. He would find out and when he did, he would earn her trust and eventually her loyalty.

If he could win her affection in the course, he would consider it a boon. Bottom line, he wanted Jocelyn—he desired her, and he admired her at the same time. Together they would get him out of his predicament, and once it was all over, perhaps he would keep her as his mistress. The prospect was appealing.

Chapter Five

Jocelyn awoke having slept better than the night before, but images of Blaine kept creeping into her thoughts. The man was simply gorgeous and popular with the ladies. Therefore, it was possible he was subjected to all sorts of gossip that could be exaggerated and perhaps even untrue. She decided to judge him by his merit and experience.

He was strong and brave, and he saved her from a potentially dangerous situation. He brought them to his friend, who provided them with food and shelter. Since coming to Castle Ballindalloch, Blaine had treated her and Braedan with kindness, and in her presence, acted like a perfect gentleman. Soon they would return home, never to see him again, and so it would be best to remember only the good.

Satisfied, she proceeded to detail a plan on how they could best utilize the money from the sale of the cow. She needed to recuperate what they lost, and if careful, they could possibly produce enough baked goods for two markets. Then this terrible misfortune would be only a setback to attaining their goal.

The goal to no longer to be indebted to Walrick Graham.

Hungry, she decided not to wait for a tray. She went downstairs and straight to the kitchen to break her fast. Mrs. Westershire directing servants and upon seeing her, was told to go to the family dining salon. "'Tis not necessary," she assured her and went to where the other servants were seated, enjoying their repast.

Jocelyn spied Heather sitting next to Lily and two others. They waved her over to join them. Seeing their resemblance, she was introduced to sisters Rose and Violet. All in all, there were five girls in the family, and all were named after a flower.

Violet, who was the oldest, was the talent behind the alterations and why the borrowed dress fit Jocelyn perfectly. Violet usually accompanied Lady Angela abroad and to court. On those occasions, she saw firsthand the fashion trends, then duplicated them for family and friends. The rest of the sisters were expert seamstresses, and it was their goal to one day own their own dress shop.

Jocelyn was enjoying herself of their company when there was a sudden change in the hall, specifically from the females. She did not need to turn around to know who had made his appearance. There were gasps and whispering. Some giggled while others were patting down their hair or adjusting their gowns. Jocelyn groaned out loud when she sensed *him* standing behind her.

"Good morrow, Miss MacAulay. Are you well?"

Heather and her sisters immediately moved over to make room for Blaine.

"Good morrow, Sir Blaine," Jocelyn said politely. "Please take my seat as I have finished." She jumped up, taking her trencher.

But before she took two steps, he grasped her arm.

"There's no need to leave on my account," he said apologetically.

"Whatever do ye mean, my lord?" she said, looking up into those amazing green eyes. "I have finished."

He looked hurt by her response. "I don't suppose ye would stay and keep me company?"

She hesitated for a moment. "Perhaps another time."

Pulling her arm free, she retreated as swiftly as possible. Her heart pounded in her chest. There was no doubt he had an effect on her. Dressed in all dark brown, with tall brown boots, his tunic hugged his muscular chest and narrow waist. His long hair was still wet, and he smelled like heaven. Every fiber of her being was drawn to him, and yet she wanted to keep to her plans, to leave on good terms and never see him again.

It was too early to seek out her brother, she went in search of a good book from the library. Taking a few books on herbs and plants, she went back to her bedchamber to read. The books themselves were fascinating and contained a wealth of information on plants and their medicinal properties. Each of them had been inscribed in the front by Anna MacKinnon. No one needed to tell her who Lady Anna MacKinnon was. Her reputation as a talented healer was known throughout the Highlands. She was also Blaine's mother.

Finding it difficult to concentrate, Jocelyn went to see if Braedan might be awake. When she entered his room, he was no better than before. His leg was infected, the area around the incision red and swollen. Mrs. Westershire came in to change his bandages and assured her that he would be fine. She slathered some ointment and bound his leg with clean wrappings.

Jocelyn spent the rest of the morning with Braedan. Together they planned on what they needed to do when they got home. After enjoying a mid-day meal together, they decided he needed to rest, she left. She went back to her room to read some more. After an hour or so, she heard a knock. It was Mrs. Westershire to say that the messenger had finally returned carrying with him a letter.

Taking the letter, Jocelyn broke the seal and started to read. Her eyes widened. "Good heavens…this can't be." She gasped. She needed to talk to Braedan. Not bothering to knock, she burst in to see him sitting up and drinking a cup of tea.

"What is it, Joce, what's happened?"

She thrust the letter at him. "Graham."

Braedan scanned the letter in dismay. "The bastard."

"Aye," she said, pacing. "Not only did Graham take the cow, but Heddy also says that if we do not pay him by the end of the week, he will take the other cow."

Lord Graham came to Heatherwood and turned irate when told they were not at home. He accused Heddy of lying when he saw their cart. Having been instructed not to say anything about their whereabouts, she said they were visiting friends. They had been provided transportation because of the rain.

Heddy wrote that he said, "Well, if MacAulay has time for a holiday, then he won't mind if I take matters into hand."

"We need at least one of the cows just for the bakery," Jocelyn lamented. "He has no right."

Braedan chewed his bottom lip, his face flushed with anger.

"Perhaps I should just wed the man."

"I will not consent, Jocelyn. I will never hand over my sister to that wastrel. He took advantage of father at his most vulnerable, and now he takes our cow? I will not abide by this farce."

Jocelyn sat next to him and took his hand. It felt hot in hers. "Heddy says the coins we sent will keep the bakery going, and they have had two days of profit. As soon as ye are well, we will go and take back our cow." She could see his anger was not good for him. "Get some rest, Brae, I will return. I need some fresh air."

Leaving his room, she passed by one of the tall windows. It was raining harder than before, pelting the glass by gusting winds. Deciding to return to the cold dark library, the solitude did nothing to quell her emotions. She looked at all the tomes lining the walls. If only one of them might hold the answer to her problems.

Jocelyn had reached her breaking point. For ten years she had labored to make ends meet, taking on the arduous task of keeping them fed and a roof over their heads. It was disheartening that someone like Graham could take away the results of their hard work and leave them at his mercy.

In that dim and silent room, she let go, allowing tears to flow down her cheeks.

~ * ~

Blaine received a message to meet Rod in his study. "What news have ye?" he asked, taking his usual seat next to the fire.

"I thought ye might be interested in learning a bit about our guests," Rod said, offering him a glass of whisky. "It might help ye in yer quest to inspire a more affable relationship with the fair Miss MacAulay."

"What have ye gleaned?"

"Maury just returned from Heatherwood—that's the name of their estate." Rod looked rather smug with that bit of information. "Says the housekeeper, Heddy, was mighty pleased to learn that the lass and her brother were safe. Did as he was told and stayed the night." He took a sip of his drink. "Says the gal can cook." Rod went on to describe what he ate and the soft bed he was given. Blaine perceived Rod's inane rambling was on purpose, so he bit his tongue.

"The following morning, Maury said they had a visit from a neighbor. The man is unscrupulous and not looked upon favorably by my family."

Blaine raised both brows.

"Are ye acquainted with Walrick Graham?"

He shook his head.

"'Tis not a loss—the man has a reputation to be shady when it comes to business. Unfortunately, my kin learned the hard way."

"What did this Graham want?"

"Maury wasn't sure. Said the man caused quite a commotion. Apparently, he was taking one of their cows. Heard them arguing about being late on payment."

"Hmmm, seems our friends here might be in some sort of trouble." Blaine got up to pour himself another drink. "Did Maury say anything else?"

"Just that the manor is of good size but in need of repairs. He also said the bakery was well managed, and business was good."

Blaine pondered for a moment. This explained why Jocelyn became so distraught when their money was stolen. No doubt it was money they needed and could ill afford to lose. "Do ye know where Miss MacAulay is?"

Rod shook his head. "I haven't seen her today."

Blaine slammed back his drink and walked out the door.

~ * ~

Blaine ran upstairs, taking the steps two at a time. He was through biding his time. He wanted the truth. What was the MacAulay's association with Graham? They were in trouble, and he wanted to help.

He saw Heather walking toward him. "Is Miss MacAulay in her—"

"Nay, my lord," she answered before he could finish. "I believe ye can find her in the library and…"

"And what?" he said, not meaning to yell.

"I believe Miss MacAulay is distraught."

Thanking her, Blaine headed to the other side of the castle when he saw Braedan who said, "Excuse me, my lord," as he rushed past him.

Something was terribly wrong. Blaine needed to find Jocelyn. The library was dark, and there was no fire in the hearth. He wondered if she had left then he saw a faint light coming from the gallery.

She was standing next to the window watching the drops of rain streaking down the pane.

"Jocelyn?" he said, barely above a whisper.

She turned around. The faint light from the lone candle illuminated the tears that coursed down her cheeks.

"Oh sweeting," he said, holding open his arms. To his amazement, she flew into his embrace. He held her tightly against him, murmuring endearments. "Ye are safe, no harm will come to ye."

After a time, Blaine saw that she had stopped trembling. He heard some muffled sniffles along with a hiccup or two. Stepping back a bit, he lifted her face with his two fingers. He wiped away a tear with his thumb. Her eyes were closed, her long lashes wet and spikey along her cheekbones. Her lips were red and slightly parted. She was a vision.

When she opened her eyes, he fell into their dusky blue-gray pools. Without thought, he gradually bent his head and barely brushed her lips with his. He pulled back, relieved to see she was not at all offended. In fact, she snaked her arms up around his neck, threading her fingers through his long hair and drew him closer.

~ * ~

Lost in his soft lips, she never imagined the mere touch of them could evoke such sensations. She realized she wanted more. Looking into eyes that looked like emeralds, she held her breath as he slowly bent down. She gasped as his mouth took complete possession of hers. He kissed her gently, caressing her lips with his own. It was like no other kiss before, not that she had many to compare with. She was fascinated by his mouth. She could have written an ode just to the way he ate, but his kisses deserved a ballad.

Blaine responded when she pressed her body against his, by cradling the nape of her neck. He kept up his onslaught and she decided she never wanted him to stop.

Then something happened, something so small and so insignificant that it was her total undoing—he groaned. It wasn't loud or done in a particular way, it was just pure and exemplified her pleasure. He wanted her.

His kiss deepened and became ardent. Jocelyn opened her mouth to say something when he plunged his tongue into the warmth of her mouth, assailing her senses. It was sensuous and intoxicating at the same time. He tasted of whisky, and the bristles on his chin rasped her cheek. The act itself was thrilling, and she felt utterly drugged, losing all control of thoughts or notions. Their tongues dueled and danced. *Oh, Blaine, don't ever stop.*

Unfortunately for Jocelyn things were happening too fast. When he should have stopped, he didn't. Without thought or care for her innocence, he brought his hand down low, grabbing her buttocks and pressing her hard against his groin.

Bells sounded off in her head, and her eyes flew open. He paused for a moment when she stiffened in his arms. He looked at her, and there within the depths of his eyes glowed pure sexual need. She immediately pushed him away, but he would not release his hold on her.

"What are ye doing?" she cried out.

"What do ye mean, what am I doing?" He laughed. "I am kissing ye, and I must say, ye were enjoying it."

"Take yer hands off me." She whirled away. "How dare ye...how!" But she couldn't finish. She was just as much to blame as he. She had gone eagerly into his arms, and somehow everything changed. The kissing went from sweet to seductive in a matter of minutes.

"Jocelyn, please..." Blaine held up hands in surrender. "I apologize, Miss MacAulay; my intentions were to merely comfort ye. I saw that ye were distraught. I was caught up in the moment and lost my good sense."

His admissions let the wind out of her anger. She could not fault him entirely, and her cheeks heated. "I-I accept yer apology, but I must take partial blame," she stammered. "I was distraught as ye say and I ..." She looked down at her feet, unable to meet his eyes. Her humiliation bared before him, and she didn't want to see his amusement.

She was about to say that she was as much to blame when she heard someone clearing their throat. Mrs. Westershire was standing in the doorway. She worried about what she might have seen or overheard.

"I apologize for interrupting," her words were clipped, "but Sir Roderick requests an audience with ye. The both of ye."

Blaine and Jocelyn followed Mrs. Westershire down the hall. She suggested that Jocelyn freshen up. She had no doubt that the perceptive housekeeper was well aware of what she had walked in on.

"Ye go on ahead. I will be down in just a moment," she suggested, but Mrs. Westershire insisted they wait. Something was amiss.

Jocelyn's reflection in the mirror confirmed what she feared. She looked every bit like a person who had been thoroughly kissed. Her lips were red and swollen, and her cheeks were flushed pink. After splashing water on her face, she patted it dry, hoping some of the red would fade. She undid her braid and started brushing her hair, braiding it back as quickly as possible. She wound it in a coil at the base of her neck and prayed her red nose and swollen eyes would go unnoticed. In a matter of minutes, she was ready and joined them in the hallway.

Blaine held out his arm to escort her, which she kindly refused but then received a disapproving look from Mrs. Westershire. Admonished, she took his arm. *There's definitely something wrong.*

When they entered the study, Jocelyn was stunned to see Braedan seated next to Rod.

"What's going on, Roddy?" Blaine asked.

Rod smiled and motioned for them to sit. He also requested that Mrs. Westershire stay.

"Are ye well, Brae?" Jocelyn asked. He was still dressed in his bedclothes and was rather pale.

"Aye, Joce," he said flatly.

"Please, Miss MacAulay, if ye will sit down, I will explain," Rod said. "Mrs. Westershire, would ye kindly pour everyone some wine?"

Mrs. Westershire did as she was bid, the silence grating Jocelyn's nerves. When they all had a glass, including Mrs. Westershire, Rod stood to address them. "It has come to my attention that I have two acquaintances who are in dire straits and in need of help. From what I have gathered, I believe if we work together, we may find a solution that will help both parties."

Jocelyn leveled her gaze at her brother.

"Please, Joce, don't look at me that way," Braedan whispered. "Hear what Sir Roderick has to say."

"Aye, we are getting ahead of ourselves," Rod said. "Let me start from the beginning." He paused a bit, his expression turning serious. "I understand yer desire for privacy, my lady, but I believe yer brother was right to come to me for help." He looked at Blaine. "It appears as if some unexpected issues have arisen, and he finds that he and his family are facing some financial problems."

"I said we are facing financial ruin," Braedan added, avoiding his sister's glare.

"Please tell me ye didn't ask for a loan," Jocelyn said.

"Nay, my lady, yer brother came to me looking for work. I told him I would consider it, but first I demand absolute honesty of anyone I employ. He agreed and told me about the business dealings your father had with a certain man whom I consider of questionable character. Without having to go into details, I agreed to help him. I already have a man of affairs—"

"I can help ye," Blaine interrupted. "Braedan, ye are a man of intelligence and well educated. I could use someone to manage my business."

She was touched by Blaine and Rod's offer. "I thank ye, but I need Braedan to help me run the estate and the bakery."

"Ye don't need me, Joce, ye have been running everything since mother died. 'Tis time I do my part."

"I believe I have a solution that may benefit us all," Rod said. "I thought that perhaps Miss MacAulay could perform a service for me."

"You want me to bake for ye?" Jocelyn said not quite understanding what Roderick was referring to.

"Nay, my dear, I am asking ye to help my friend, Blaine, as a personal favor to me. He too has found himself in a predicament. In exchange, I am willing to pay the debt ye owe to Sir Walrick Graham."

Blaine finished his wine in one gulp. "I don't think this is how we should go about explaining things, Rod, I believe I just need more time—"

"Time is not what ye have, Blaine," Rod said, looking serious. "I received word from my sister today, and she says the king is incensed that ye have yet to arrive to court. Ye canna delay any longer. I have already explained the situation to Braedan, and he is in accord. We simply need Miss Jocelyn to agree, that's all."

"Agree to what?" Jocelyn felt the room grow too warm.

"Why don't ye explain, Blaine?" Mrs. Westershire suggested.

"Dear heavens, what kind of trouble are ye in?" Jocelyn said, looking at him.

"Two months ago, I was commanded by my brother to wed. He is my laird, and I have sworn fealty so I canna refuse."

"Two months is not nearly enough time for such an important decision," Rod added.

"My plans to wed reached our king's ears, and he has amassed every eligible lass from all of Scotland. Basically, I will be told to wed whom the king chooses."

"Unless he was already married or at least is engaged," Braedan said.

Jocelyn looked at her brother as if he lost his mind. "Are ye saying that I am to wed Sir Blaine?"

"Nay lass, not wed, just betrothed." Rod smiled. "All we are asking is for you to accompany him to court, convince the king that ye are betrothed, and once ye leave then ye can break off the engagement and go on with your life. Of course, there will be compensation for your time and trouble."

She could not believe what she was hearing. She jumped to her feet. "So ye wouldn't sell me to Graham, but ye sold me to this man."

"I can assure ye, lass, that I have no intentions of buying anyone, least of all you," Blaine bit out.

"Then why don't ye find someone else to portray your loving fiancée? Surely women are falling at yer feet for the opportunity."

"Jocelyn," Braedan's voice catching attention. "I have already agreed, speaking as yer brother and the head of this family, we will aid Sir Blaine in his predicament."

She opened her mouth to argue, but her own words echoed in her head. The very idea of being forced to wed Graham was revolting, so why wouldn't she be sympathetic to Blaine's plight? Still, the thought of being part of this ruse did not sit well.

Mrs. Westershire came over to where she stood. "My lady, ye have been given an opportunity to aid a great man. Ye are not being asked to wed him but to help him attain more time. Once the king and Sir Caelan are convinced that Sir Blaine is betrothed, then ye can cry off and part ways. He still has to marry."

"Ye make it sound so simple, but what about me? If my name is associated with his, my reputation will be ruined."

"Nay, yer reputation will not be sullied," Mrs. Westershire assured her. "We only need a convincing reason why ye begged off and ended yer betrothal. People often become engaged and then find they are not suited."

"Exactly, thank ye, Mrs. Westershire," Rod said.

"I believe it should be a more convincing reason than just being ill-suited," Jocelyn said, her eyes narrowing at them. "The king would never believe it. However, I could say that I refused to wed because I discovered Sir Blaine not to be the man he claims to be, but rather a rake of the first degree. His reputation would certainly support this."

Blaine locked gazes with her. "My reputation is untarnished, my lady. Surely ye are not saying otherwise."

"Oh, please, my lord, ye canna deny you have a reputation with the ladies. That ye have left a trail of broken hearts from here to the English border."

Anger darkened his eyes. "If the idea of being my betrothed repulses ye so, then I will understand if ye decline. At this point, I would rather find myself engaged to Mrs. Westershire."

Jocelyn closed her eyes, shaking her head slightly. Accepting such a proposition was ludicrous. However, to be finally free of Walrick Graham would be a dream come true. "I need time to think."

"Of course, my lady, but please do not tarry in making yer decision," Rod warned her. "Time is of the essence."

"My lords, if ye will excuse me. I sense a headache coming on."

Blaine rose to his feet and took her arm. "I will escort ye, my lady."

"'Tis not necessary, Sir Blaine." Jocelyn tried to free herself.

"Ye will escort the lady," Mrs. Westershire said firmly. "'Tis important that ye are seen together as much as possible. From now on when ye are in public, ye will act affectionately toward each other. Ye will not be without the other. Ye must be able to convince everyone."

"Miss MacAulay has not yet accepted," Blaine said in her defense, and together they left the study.

When they reached her bedchamber, she turned to look at Blaine. "If ye will give me an hour to…" She took a deep breath. "I will meet ye in the library."

Blaine nodded and left.

Once inside her bedchamber, she collapsed into the chair by the fire. Staring into the flames, she gave in to her fears. Her mind raced, and thoughts clashed, but after a while, the internal war settled.

She made her decision and realized her life would be changed forever.

Chapter Six

Jocelyn was surprised to find the library comfortably warm. Blaine sat next to the window, apparently lost in thought, an open book on his lap. It seemed to take only a moment for him to alert to her presence. He quickly rose to his feet.

"I have decided to help ye," she said.

He did not react.

"In exchange for portraying yer betrothed—"

"Convincingly."

"In exchange for portraying yer betrothed convincingly, Sir Roderick will pay—"

"I will pay."

Blaine was not making this easy for her. "Ye will pay our debt to Walrick Graham," she finished.

"Aye, then we are in accord," he stated.

"Not exactly." He looked at her skeptically. "I want my brother to accompany us to court."

"I can understand yer wanting a proper escort, so I will arrange for Violet to assist ye as yer personal maid."

"Thank ye; however, I still want my brother to come, but for another reason." She paused for a moment, biting her bottom lip. "Even if we settle our debt to Graham, he holds the deed to our lands. We do not have the money to repurchase them."

"What are ye proposing?"

"I would like ye to sponsor my brother, provide him with the proper introductions and make sure he meets the right people."

"Go on."

Her cheeks heated. "If all these eligible young ladies have gathered in anticipation of your arrival, perhaps my brother will find a suitable wife."

"Ye mean a wealthy wife," Blaine said without a hint of sarcasm.

"Aye, 'tis not unusual for men to seek wives with substantial dowries. If Braedan can marry well, then he can restore Heatherwood and hopefully gain back our lands."

"I agree to yer terms." He reached into his pocket and pressed a gold sovereign into the palm of her hand.

"What is this?" It was more than they needed to satisfy the loan.

"Ye will meet with Rod's solicitor tomorrow morning. Give this to him. Instruct him to pay the loan in full and see that the deeds to the land are returned. Tell him ye want any promissory notes and all contracts. If Rod is right, Graham most likely obtained yer land illegally, but it will be our burden to prove."

"I know not what to say." She gazed up at him. "I am not sure of all my father's obligations."

"It matters naught," Blaine said, his tone reassuring. "If I am going to present yer brother as Laird of Heatherwood, he should have land."

Jocelyn nodded and another chip fell from around her heart. She squeezed the coin painfully in her palm reveling in the strength that gave credence to its existence. She opened her mouth to say something when her stomach let out a most unladylike growl. Her eyes widened then she giggled. He joined her with a chuckle.

"I believe they are serving the evening meal." He smiled. "May I escort ye, Miss MacAulay?"

She returned his smile. "I believe ye should call me Jocelyn."

~ * ~

The next day Jocelyn and Braedan met with Ascar MacPherson, Rod's man-of-affairs. He was a large and imposing man whose muscular arms were meant for wielding a sword rather than the pen. Perched on a nose that had been broken many times was a delicate pair of spectacles. At first, he appeared intimidating, but his intelligence and soft-spoken nature seemed to put them at ease. Not that they would likely dare test him.

Ascar instructed Braedan to write a letter to Heddy, introducing him and the purpose for his visit. For them to settle their debt to Graham, they would need Heddy's assistance in locating all their father's paperwork. In the same letter, they would announce Jocelyn's betrothal to Blaine.

Jocelyn would have preferred waiting to make the announcement in person, Rod insisted that everyone be told as soon as possible. Jocelyn's attitude was entirely different when they penned the letter of introduction to Walrick Graham. In fact, she felt quite empowered. She delighted in the statement that Ascar was acting on behalf of her fiancé. She secretly wished she could see his reaction.

Blaine too sent letters, one to the king and one to Caelan, announcing his betrothal to Jocelyn. In his letters, he explained how they met, keeping the details as close to the truth. Blaine begged the king's forgiveness for his absence and explained he had been busy courting Jocelyn. He was happy to say his persistence was rewarded when the lady accepted.

He smiled as he handed his letters to a servant to post. With these matters out of the way, the next was preparing for the trip to Edinburgh.

~ * ~

"Is it necessary? All of...this?" Braedan complained as he stood with his arms up while Violet pinned and fitted the heavy decorative coat. "I do possess clothes."

"Aye, but ye canna be presented to the king in just any clothes. Ye need to be properly attired when at court," Mrs. Westershire said.

In truth, neither Braedan nor Jocelyn owned court clothes. Fortunately, they were able to find some of Rod's old coats, vests and trousers from when he was Braedan's age. They were severely outdated, but the cloth was of excellent quality, and Violet was working her magic. Keeping in mind that the MacAulays came from a small village, they would not be expected to own the same opulent garments worn by lairds and ladies.

Jocelyn was thrilled to be wearing anything other than wool dresses. Violet turned her old dress into an overcoat for traveling. The stained front panel was removed, the sleeves cut away and the back sewn closed, so the front closed with two shiny silver buttons. The sisters altered a gown of dark burgundy that went well with the dark gray. With full sleeves and a V-drop waste, it looked elegant.

With the help of her sisters, Violet finished two other gowns, but she would be hard-pressed to complete the ballgown in time. Blaine suggested they buy a ballgown, but Violet wouldn't have it. Instead, she took one of Angela's old ballgown and added a few panels and trim. In the end, she created a simple light blue dress that beautifully accentuated Jocelyn's creamy complexion and rich chestnut brown hair. She just needed to add a few embellishments.

Braedan and Jocelyn were uncomfortable with the gift of expensive clothes and shoes. Still, they understood it was necessary if Braedan wanted to find a wife. He needed to look like a gentleman of means.

~ * ~

At last, the rain stopped, and Braedan's fever broke. Rod announced they would leave the following day. Tonight, everyone would be dining in the great hall, and James and Dinah were preparing a special meal.

Jocelyn decided to wear the dark burgundy gown. Heather put her hair up, intertwining a matching ribbon with jet black beads. Jocelyn liked how the beads glittered in the light. As she looked in the mirror, admiring Heather's handiwork, she heard a knock.

Braedan entered, smiling warmly. "Ye look beautiful, Joce."

She brushed a kiss on his smooth cheek. "Ye look quite handsome yerself. Ye will have all the lasses in court clamoring to be introduced." She worried when she saw him lose his smile. "Are ye well? Has the fever returned?"

Assuring her he felt fine, he presented his arm. Jocelyn sensed something wasn't right as they walked down to the great hall.

There was an air of excitement as they entered the hall. The clansmen were all gathered drinking while a bard sat in the corner, singing softly. Children ran about chasing each other, as women gathered in small groups exchanging the latest gossip.

"I wonder what 'tis going on?" Jocelyn said, but Braedan didn't answer; instead, he escorted her to the head table where she saw Roderick and Blaine.

Next to Rod sat a man Jocelyn had not seen before and, judging by his expensive clothes, he appeared a person of importance. She assumed he was the reason for the festivity.

Blaine introduced her to Laird Reginald MacAlister. He said the laird's daughter, Lady Cecelia MacAlister, was engaged to a MacKinnon. She would have the chance to meet Colin, and his sister Arabella, once they reached Edinburgh.

"Ye must meet my daughter," the older gentlemen remarked, "since ye two have much in common."

Jocelyn wasn't sure what he was referring to, unless, she too, liked to bake. Jocelyn was about to inquire when the dinner was announced. Servants entered the hall; their arms were laden with platters of roasted meats and vegetables. There was an assortment of cheeses, pies and bread. She beamed to see some of her favorites, an Abroath Smokie which was a delicately smoked haddock and a Scotch pie filled with tender lamb.

As she took her first bite of the savory pie, Rod rose from his chair. "Welcome everyone. We have a special guest this evening." He turned to Laird MacAlister. "Please welcome Sir Reginald of Rosewood and his clansmen who accompanied him." He raised his glass. "I must say we are especially pleased with the news that the Inverness tournament will be held next spring at Rosewood, and all are invited to participate."

The hall burst into cheers with a couple hoots and hollers.

Once they settled, Rod continued, "I have asked ye all here today for another reason." He paused to allow goblets to be filled. "It is my honor to announce the betrothal of my dear friend, Sir Blaine MacKinnon, to the lovely Lady Jocelyn MacAulay." A hush descended in the great hall. "Please join me in congratulating the couple and wishing them a long life of happiness and prosperity."

Blaine raised his goblet to her. She brought her own to her lips with a hand that trembled.

Rod positively beamed at the couple. Braedan, on the other hand, was not smiling. He tried to catch his sister's eyes, but Jocelyn looked away.

"Are ye all right, my dear?" Blaine whispered, reaching over to cover her hand with his.

Jocelyn tried to pull her hand free then she caught sight of Mrs. Westershire's approving nod. "Aye, 'tis only… I-I was surprised." She tried to appear calm. She picked up her glass again and this time drained half the contents, making her eyes water.

"I don't suppose 'tis too late to apologize for not speaking to ye before tonight's gathering." He looked genuinely remorseful. "It was in poor form and doesn't speak well of my character." She gave him a weak smile and murmured something to the effect that she would be fine.

He took the hand he held, raised it to his lips. His action was witnessed by a group of men who encouraged Blaine to give his betrothed a proper kiss. She feared that he may take their when he gave her hand a gentle squeeze instead and released it.

The interminable evening wore on and offered no end in sight. The well-prepared food turned to sand in her mouth, and the wine soured in her stomach. A group of musicians began playing, and everyone was up and dancing. She was barraged with well-wishers as well as flagrant stares from some of the women. Not everyone took well to the news either. In fact, several women gasped in dismay while another burst into tears.

Blaine asked if she would care to dance, but she declined, graciously promising to dance another time. She directed her conversation to Sir Reginald and saw him to be a genuinely kind man. He spoke adoringly of his daughter and his desire the two of them meet. They were both engaged and would have a lot to talk about.

After a time, Sir Reginald decided he would like to retire, giving the excuse Jocelyn needed to retire herself. She agreed when Braedan offered to escort her upstairs.

Blaine rose as she stood to leave. He gently kissed her on the lips as he bid her goodnight. She ignored the encouragement of those who witnessed the exchange. She plastered a smile on her face as she said goodnight to Rod and Sir Reginald.

It took every ounce of willpower not to hike up her skirts and run to her bedchamber, locking herself in and the world out. When they finally reached her room, she said something incoherent and turned to go.

Braedan took hold of her arm. "Forgive me, Joce, I should have told ye of Roderick's plan to announce yer betrothal."

Jocelyn was surprised by his admission. "I don't understand. If ye knew, then…"

He cast down his gaze. "Sir Blaine wanted to tell ye, but I thought it better that it came from me, so he charged me with the task."

"But ye didn't, ye didn't say anything. Why?"

"I-I," he stammered. "Oh Joce, ye are just so obstinate and…and…"

"Are ye accusing me of being rash? Is that the reason ye didn't tell yer own sister?"

"I wouldn't put it past ye to run away or bar the door. Or worse, threaten not to go to dinner until I yielded."

"Braedan Michael MacAulay, ye think me a harpy," Jocelyn bit out angrily, but then flushed profusely. He knew her well. She would have found a way of avoiding the evening. It embarrassed her, and she allowed her anger to ebb. Jocelyn said she forgave him. "Go and enjoy the rest of the evening."

He declined, saying he too was tired.

As she readied for bed, she couldn't stop the nagging question that bounced in her head. Why did Blaine take the blame for not telling her about the announcement? Clearly, the fault lay with Braedan. He had entrusted him to warn her. Each time she thought she understood him, he did something that surprised her. It confused her.

"Who is this man?"

~ * ~

Blaine awoke the next morning filled with inspiration. Although the challenge was yet before them, he thought they were on the right path to resolving his predicament. The king may have already received his missive, and he may not need to be at court, but then he remembered his promise to promote Braedan. Well, there may be a way around that too. Blaine bound out of bed and hastily performed his morning ablutions before going downstairs to break his fast.

Entering the hall, he decided not to linger, grabbing a tart apple and biscuit instead. Anything would be better than having to endure the forlorn faces of some of the women. He stepped outside to a sunny day. There wasn't a cloud in the sky, but this was Scotland, and the weather could change in an hour.

He decided to check on his horse, thinking that a ride would do them good. "Aye, 'tis the truth, I swear to ye." He heard a voice say.

"Nay, I heard it sae he kill 'em wi 'is dagger," the other voice replied.

He entered the stables where he spied two stable lads busy at their task. Their faces lit up when they spotted him.

"Milord," a freckled face lad piped up. "I 'ere ye killed the mon wi yer sword, and Tate sae it were yer dagger."

"Aye and that's 'ow ye won the Lady Jocelyn's hand," Tate said not giving Blaine a chance to respond.

"Nay, I told ye, Tate, it was Lord Braedan that rewarded Sir Blaine wi 'is sister's hand."

The two lads started to argue who was right.

"Lads," he shouted, barely able to keep his smile restrained. "Please saddle my horse." He turned. "And it was with my dagger, and the lady rewarded me by consenting to be my wife," he said over his shoulder.

~ * ~

Jocelyn stared at a cloudless sky that did little to improve her mood. She was committed to playing the adoring fiancée, but she feared being close to Blaine would compromise her. She admitted that her initial treatment of him was her way of protecting herself, but after the kiss they shared, he stirred some tenderness.

"Just be strong," she whispered, her breath vaporizing against the cold pane.

"Did ye say something, milady?"

She spun around to see Heather standing near the hearth. She was about to respond when the chambermaid came to start the fire and tidy the room.

"Ye are late, Cottie," Heather scolded her. "Ye should have had the fire started hours ago."

In fact, the room was quite chilly, but Jocelyn was so miserable she hadn't noticed. The lass muttered something and quickly went about her duties. Jocelyn heard her sniffle and saw her eyes were red as if she had been crying.

"It's perfectly all right, Heather. I plan to go for a walk, so there's no need for a fire." Jocelyn picked up two small apples and wrapped up a hunk of cheese. Donning her cloak, she put the bundle in her pocket.

She had reached the door to the garden when she heard her name.

"Lady Jocelyn, where are ye going?"

She turned to see Mrs. Westershire. "I thought I would take advantage of the mild weather and go for a walk," she explained giving her a wide grin. "And please, it's miss, not lady."

Mrs. Westershire gave her a stern look. "Now that ye are betrothed to Sir Blaine, ye shall be addressed as 'lady' and as a lady, ye are not to go walking about without an escort." She guided her back inside.

"Mrs. Westershire, I assure ye, I will only go as far as the gardens. I just want to get some fresh air," Jocelyn said, attempting to sway her.

"Aye, and ye may, and ye will, but ye will take an escort with ye," Mrs. Westershire insisted.

"I will be more than happy to escort Lady Jocelyn." The ladies turned around to see Sir Reginald standing behind them. He smiled, offering Jocelyn his arm.

Sir Reginald was a kind man, a fatherly figure, and she quickly became fond of him. They walked while Sir Reginald told her about his daughter and his soon to be son-in-law. She laughed at his daughter's antics and sympathized with his struggles as a doting father. Few men would take the full responsibility of rearing a daughter, albeit Sir Reginald confessed of being too indulgent. She liked the man and kept her opinions to herself. Finding a bench, she shared her small bounty with the aging knight.

"I have been going on long enough about myself." He took a bite of the tart apple. "Tell me about you and where ye hale from."

She gave him a brief recount of her life at Heatherwood, her mother's bakery and how they hoped to someday restore the family estate. She did not need to relay the details of her father's failed business ventures.

"I can understand how aligning with the MacKinnon family will make this possible," he concurred. "Ye are a fortunate young woman. The MacKinnons are a wealthy and powerful clan."

Staring off into the distance, Jocelyn caught sight of a rider. She watched as he easily cleared the stone wall. Giving his horse the lead, he tore down the road at a breakneck speed.

Sir Reginald followed her gaze and smiled broadly. "Here comes yer betrothed now."

Her breath caught in her throat as she watched Blaine ride toward them. His long hair blew in the wind; the golden hues glistened in the light. His gaze bored into hers, the same hue as the green hills behind him. He looked powerful astride his horse, once again the personification of the avenging angel bearing down upon his enemies. And then when she thought he couldn't look more magnificent, he smiled at her. A smile that said more than words could convey.

~ * ~

Blaine spotted Jocelyn from a distance. It alarmed him to see her sitting with a man who wasn't her brother. He was protective of her, if not possessive. As he neared, he was relieved to see Laird MacAlister.

Blaine smiled when their eyes met. When she returned his smile, warmth ran straight through him. After slowing his horse to a stop, he dismounted and walked toward the pair, never losing eye contact.

"Good morrow, my lord." Sir Reginald said with a smile on his face. "I see ye have a proper escort, my lady. Although I appreciate your generosity in sharing yer breakfast, I feel the need for something a bit more robust. Now if ye will excuse me." He nodded at Blaine.

Jocelyn uttered something under her breath to Sir Reginald, then looked at Blaine. "Good morrow my lord," Her face was unusually flushed. Sensing she was awkward being alone with him, he gave her his best smile.

"Going for a walk, my lady?" he asked.

She nodded and stood up to feed his horse the rest of her apple.

"Would ye mind if I join ye?" He held out his arm. They led his horse down the path toward the stables.

He handed the reins to the stable boy who had run out to greet him. "Rub him down good," he instructed the lad. He threw him a shilling for his troubles.

Her hand slightly trembled, evident of how he affected her.

"Are ye cold, my dear?"

"Just a bit. 'Tis sunny, still very chilly."

"Would ye like to go back?" He fingered the material of the cloak she wore and saw it offered little protection. She assured him she was fine. "I was thinking Jocelyn," oh, how he loved the sound of her name as it rolled off his tongue, "we should get to know each other better."

"But ye know where I come from, about the bakery," Jocelyn said.

"I am no' talking about that." Blaine looked into her eyes. "We are supposed to be betrothed. What flower is yer favorite, what colors ye favor."

"Is this necessary, my lord? Even couples who were genuinely engaged dinna think it necessary to share much of themselves. Frankly, few men cared."

He assured her and insisted.

"I suppose my favorite flower would be heather. I love to look out over the meadows blanketed with them, the air sweet with their fragrance.

"I remembered when we met, ye smelled like heather…and something else." Blaine looked off into the distance as the memory played in his mind. Her hair blowing back by the wind as he held her close.

Jocelyn arched her brow. "When I make soap, I like to add crushed heather with a wee bit of violet."

"Ah, that is what I remembered," he said, nodding in approval. "'Tis a bonny scent, and it suits ye." He wondered if he could find a perfume with the same combination. "Is there a particular fruit?"

They continued walking and talking about her likes and dislikes. Eased by their conversation, he saw her relax and even laughed a time or two. When they reached the edge of the pond, Blaine picked up a flat stone and skipped it across the smooth surface. The wind had just started to pick up, so he moved them over to where some trees might offer a bit of protection.

She looked up at him as he scanned the distance. "Blaine?" she asked timidly, "what do ye like?"

He didn't respond immediately, instead he wrapped his arms around her when she shivered. "I like it when ye say my name." He smiled down at her. "I love the sound of yer laugh."

"I wonder," she stammered. "What ye like to eat?"

Blaine wished he could say he wanted to devour her. He wanted to strip her of her clothes and lay her on a blanket of heather and violets, while his lips tasted every inch of her body. Thinking back to the library, he wanted to avoid making the same mistake by being too hasty.

"I like the taste of yer lips." He gave her a crooked smile. "Especially when they taste of apples." He leaned down and gently brushed her lips with his own. "I love the feel of ye in my arms and the sound of yer heart so close to mine."

Jocelyn instinctively placed her arms around his neck, encouraging him to kiss her again. Blaine needed little encouragement. Inch by inch, he neared, his lips, hovering over her own. He closed his eyes to truly experience the tough of her lips, to taste the sweetness of her mouth. His kiss was gentle at first, and then he pressed a bit harder when she kissed him back.

Blaine became aroused and worried she would notice him starting to thicken. So, he deepened his kiss and sucked and nibbled her lips while holding the nape of her neck with one hand and her lower back with the other. She leaned hard against his arousal.

Blaine tried to pull away, but she held onto him, so it was very difficult to disengage without making it awkward. So instead, he gave her the lead and happily followed, tumbling into an erotic abyss. Her lips were soft like rose petals, plump and divine. It was impossible to describe how she felt in his arms, kissing him with such fervor. To have her responding to him was an aphrodisiac which intoxicated him.

She protested when he left her lips until he began to kiss along her jawline and down the long column of her neck. Soon she was gasping and calling out his name. He kissed up the other side of her neck to nibble on her earlobe and then once again captured her lips in a most searing and sensuous kiss that left them both panting.

Blaine stopped. His body stiffened as he looked around. "Someone's coming."

Walking around the screen of trees, he saw Caleb riding toward them, leading his horse. "Come, my lord, we must get ye back to the castle immediately."

"What is it?" Blaine asked, irritated.

"'Tis the king."

Chapter Seven

It wasn't the king himself, as Blaine feared. The king was incensed when McDermott and his friends arrived without Blaine and thus sent his men to retrieve him.

The message was clear.

"Blaine, ye must leave immediately. I would not tarry for another minute," Roderick pressed. "This is not a command ye can refuse."

Blaine shook his head. "The king has not received my missive. He is not aware of my betrothal. If we but wait a couple of days—"

"Are ye mad? I was able to buy ye enough time to pack what ye will need, but the coachman will not wait. He has been instructed to bring ye immediately, ready or not. At least I had the foresight to plead to his good senses and allow the horses to rest. Ye have but a few hours."

Blaine knew it was futile to argue. He still held out hope that the king would receive his missive by the time they arrived. "I best see about packing."

~ * ~

"Braedan, I have been looking for ye," Jocelyn said, finding him in the gallery.

In truth, Braedan spent most of his time in the gallery. He told her he enjoyed the peace and quiet among the portraits of the MacPhersons. She suspected it was Lady Angela's image that drew him. She wondered if it was possible to fall in love with a painting.

"The king has sent for Sir Blaine. We are leaving soon."

"Ye seem worried." He saw the handkerchief she held was nearly in tatters. "Haven't ye noticed that everyone here believes ye betrothed? The tale of how ye met and fell in love is on everyone's lips. 'Tis said Sir Blaine truly esteems ye."

She rolled her eyes. "Oh, Braedan, do ye take me for a fool? The man is a rogue, a scoundrel. He is merely playing his part of the devoted fiancé. He has no real interest in me, save to help him escape the matrimonial noose."

"Believe what ye want, but I have seen with my own eyes how he looks at ye."

"Like he wants to consume me, bonnet and all."

"Nay, but since ye dinna care to listen," Braedan argued.

She was about to ask what he meant by this when they were interrupted by Mrs. Westershire. "Braedan, the cobbler is waiting for ye in yer room. He has the boots that ye ordered." She looked at Jocelyn. "Violet needs ye for the final fitting. She will be the one accompanying ye to Edinburgh. She is the best choice since she has experienced court life and what is expected. Now go." She scooted them out.

Jocelyn headed down the hall but stopped when she heard voices coming from one of the bedchambers. Her curiosity was piqued at the sound of a woman crying.

"He sae he wan'ed me," the woman sniffled.

"Och, Cottie, why ye do this to yerself? Ye ken ye canna 'ave the mon."

Jocelyn recognized Lily's voice.

"He is betrothed, and soon he will wed. He will no' change 'is mind."

"Mayhap no, but if he wants, I am will'in to be 'is mistress."

"Ye are a young gel, Cottie. Go find a nice lad. Get married and 'ave lots of wee ones and stop with this impossible dream."

"'Tis no' a dream, Lily. He sae to me the first nigh' he wan' me and that I was 'is forbidden flower."

Jocelyn feared the two women could walk out any minute and see her standing there.

"Blaine wants me and 'e will send for me when all 'tis over. Ye wi' see. I wi' be 'is leman."

Jocelyn picked up her skirts and ran, all her doubts ringing in her head. "What in heavens am I doing?"

~ * ~

It was past midday when they finally left for Edinburgh. The king's spacious carriage could easily carry six of them comfortably. However, Roderick insisted on taking his horse. Braedan offered to ride to keep him company.

Jocelyn and Violet rode in the carriage along with Sir Reginald, who decided to join them. Since there would not be privacy for him to get to know his fiancée, Blaine decided to join the ride as well. The rain held off even though the clouds overhead looked ominous.

They stayed the first night at a local inn. It was crowded, and rooms were limited, but Blaine insisted on having his own. He soon regretted his decision. Apparently, one of the tavern wenches remembered him all too clearly and spent entirely too much time trying to meet his needs, all his needs.

"I dinna suppose ye be wantin' some company…luv," she whispered loud enough for all to hear.

He cringed when he saw Jocelyn look away in disgust. Even when he referred to her as his betrothed, did not the dimwitted lass curb her behavior. He attempted to elicit polite conversation with Jocelyn in the hope to smooth things over.

"I believe I will retire. I am exhausted," she said flatly.

"I will escort ye," he offered, only to be turned down with firmness.

"I am sure ye have more stimulating plans for the evening. I wouldn't want to detain ye," she bit out motioning to Braedan.

She practically stormed out of the dining hall, no doubt thinking the worse. She wasn't far off her mark. When he finally retired, it was to find the tavern wench waiting for him in his bed dressed in nothing but one of his shirts.

It took more than an hour to remove her. She went from pleading to crying and then to disbelief. When he finally persuaded her to leave, he made sure to bolt the door. Never had he ever regretted his popularity with the ladies. He wished he had led the life of a monk—well almost. It certainly convinced him to be more discriminate in the future.

The following morning did nothing to improve Jocelyn's demeanor. When the time came to rest and water the horses, he did not hesitate to take her by the arm and lead her to a spot where they could have a private conversation.

"I believe we have an agreement, my lady," he bit out. "I don't see ye meeting the terms."

She looked at him with feigned innocence. "Whatever do ye mean, my lord? I have been most attentive."

He gritted his teeth. "Ye are supposed to be my betrothed. Ye are supposed to be convincing and thrilled at the prospect of becoming my wife."

"I believe ye too are to be convincing, but who would believe we are engaged when ye flaunt women in my very presence?"

"I dinna flaunt anyone," he yelled. Never had a woman ever made him raise his voice or any man for that fact. "I canna help it if the lass wouldna take no for an answer."

"Oh please, ye did not dissuade, nor discourage her. As a matter of fact, ye looked quite pleased when she fawned all over ye. 'My lord would care for more ale; my lord do ye need more bread?' I am surprised she didn't wipe yer lips with her sleeve."

She had a point. At first, he didn't mind the attention,

preferring to be served immediately and keeping his tankard filled. Still, it soon wore thin when she kept bending over to display her ample breasts for all to see.

"I have no interest in the lass, which I made very clear," he defended himself. "I did little to encourage her..." He stopped when Jocelyn walked away from him.

"Tell that to someone who believes ye," she threw over her shoulder.

He ran after her, taking hold of her arm.

"Please let me go," she pleaded, "allow me some dignity."

His heart ached when he saw her tears. He dragged her into his arms. "Oh sweeting, I never meant to..." His words sounded shallow. "Please love, don't cry, I canna bear to see ye hurt."

"Mmrph niff nerf," she mumbled against his chest.

He lifted her face. "What did ye say?"

She refused to meet his gaze. "I am not hurt," she said as more tears fell.

He took out his handkerchief and wiped away her tears. Then without thinking, he leaned down and kissed her lightly at first and then more passionately. She tried to pull away, but he deepened his kiss, plunging his tongue into her sweet mouth. She responded by wrapping her arms around his neck and returning his kiss with unbridled ardor.

It was time they returned. The others would wonder of their absence.

"I apologize to ye, Jocelyn, for my behavior and for any pain I have caused ye."

Jocelyn nodded.

"From this point on, I swear I will conduct myself with utmost decorum befitting as yer betrothed."

Relieved that she forgave him, he escorted her to the waiting carriages.

Jocelyn climbed in and looked out the window. He met her gaze and gave her a half-smile that made her blush. Guiding his horse, he joined the others.

~ * ~

It had been years since Jocelyn and Braedan had been to Edinburgh. She recalled that their mother was still alive then. When they reached the castle, it began to drizzle, the damp permeating even the king's carriage. She wished she had a warmer cloak. No sooner did they enter the palace courtyard, when the door swung open, and Roderick was escorting her inside.

Looking around, she noticed Blaine was nowhere to be seen.

Guests crowded the corridors as servants dashed in and around them. They walked together up a staircase to find a rather purse-lipped gray-haired woman waiting for them at the top.

"Aggie, my dear, so kind of ye to meet us," Roderick introduced them to the MacKinnon's long-time servant.

"Lady Anna commanded me to be here, so here I am," she retorted much to Jocelyn's surprise.

She had never known a servant to be quite so caustic toward a man of nobility.

"Please follow me." Aggie turned, not bothering with introductions and led them down another series of stairways and corridors.

Braedan pulled Jocelyn back and whispered so only she could hear, "They took Sir Blaine."

Jocelyn gasped, her hand covering her heart.

"No sooner had he dismounted then the king's guards surrounded him and escorted him into the palace."

She wanted to ask him more, but they arrived in her room.

"Violet, make sure ye have Lady Jocelyn's best dress pressed." Aggie looked Jocelyn up and down disapprovingly. "I expect ye will be dining with the king this evening," she said, pursing her lips. "Oh, and she will need a proper gown for the ball tomorrow night as there's a celebration for the newly knighted."

Jocelyn wanted to inquire as to the location of Braedan's room, but she received such a dismissal that she dared not. Entering the bedchamber, Jocelyn whirled around, her eyes grew wide with amazement. The walls were ivory paneled and gilded in gold. The sconces were also gold, and the trio of crystal drops that hung at the base sparkled in the light.

Her feet sank into the thick plush carpet. The bed and canopy covers were of matching material beautifully embroidered. She stood in awe of her surroundings; still, all this opulence did little to ease her mind. What could have happened to Blaine? Surely the king wouldn't just have him arrested.

She chewed her bottom lip and decided to change the subject. "Is Aggie always so surly?" she asked Violet.

"Och, dinna pay no mind to Aggie. She's been in the family since Sir Blaine was a wee one," Violet said cheerfully. "And dinna worry about Sir Blaine, he be fine."

Clearly Violet must have overheard Braedan's comments and wanted to assure her. Still, it did not settle her nerves. Was she beginning to care for him?

Blaine was not surprised when the king's guards were waiting for him when he arrived. He thought he would be taken to the king. Instead, he was locked in a large room with a chair and a clock. At least a fire burned in the hearth, keeping the room comfortably warm. The sound of the ticking irritated him as the hours dragged on. No one came to check on him or to see to his needs. He was growing impatient, he was hungry and worst of all, he needed to find a chamber pot.

Checking the door for the fifth time, he considered relieving himself in the wood box. Just then he heard a key turning the lock. He waited, apprehensively, as the door swung open.

"Ah, there ye are. I wondered where they be keeping ye." In walked his younger brother, the last person he expected.

Without bothering to greet him, he dashed past his Douglas John in search of the nearest retiring room. Upon returning, Blaine was annoyed by the humorous look in his brother's face. There was nothing funny about the situation.

"What are ye doing here?" Blaine questioned.

Douglas John was the youngest of the brothers. He had their mother's raven black hair and cerulean blue eyes. He was slightly taller, and some would say more handsome, in a pretty sort of way. In personality, he was a combination. Serious like Caelan and then easygoing like Blaine. Since wedding the beautiful Lady Arrabella, his temperament leaned toward agreeable.

"Caelan bade me come and see that ye are not treated too unkindly. Sought to make sure the family was available to represent should things become serious," Douglas John said. "Seems the king is verra annoyed by ye, and so is our brother. Did ye forget? Ye was to be married months ago."

"It seems ye have not been informed, little brother, for I am betrothed," Blaine said sardonically. "I have been busy wooing said lass, and I am happy to say she has agreed to be my wife."

Douglas John stared at Blaine for a moment before he burst out laughing.

"I do not see the humor in this, and it shows a lack of respect for me and my intended."

"Save yer indignation, Blaine." He laughed again. "If ye believe ye have hoodwinked anyone with this supposed betrothal than ye are a fool. Caelan said ye would try something like this. He even wagered that ye would come to court dragging some poor lass ye either duped into believing ye will wed or paid her to pose as yer devoted bride. We all expected it." His expression then turned more serious.

"And I am afraid so has the king."

This did not sit well with Blaine, for now he feared he may have endangered Jocelyn. If the king thought they were trying to deceive him, they could be arrested for treason. The situation had changed drastically.

Schooling his features, he put on a look of exasperation. "Believe what you want, Douglas John, but I have all intentions of marrying Lady Jocelyn MacAulay."

"Are ye sure ye want to carry on with this ruse, brother?" he asked, his brows lifted.

Not bothering to answer, he motioned with his head. "Come along. Let us see the king."

~ * ~

After another excruciating long wait, they were finally ushered into the king's study. King Charles II sat behind an enormous desk piled high with papers. Two advisors hovered as they reviewed the documents he was signing. The king looked up when Blaine and Douglas John were announced.

"Leave us," he barked at his men who scurried out. "Take a seat, Douglas John." He motioned with his head to a chair next to one of the tall windows. He went back to his papers as Blaine stood directly before him.

It had been several hours since he had eaten, and his stomach growled in protest. If the king heard it, he took no notice. He stood at full attention and did not waiver. The king expected this. At last, the king set aside the document he was perusing and started rummaging through a stack to his left. He withdrew a piece of parchment Blaine immediately recognized as his letter announcing his betrothal to Jocelyn.

"What nonsense is this?" He held the letter in the air. "Ye expect me to believe are betrothed?"

"Aye, my liege, I am indeed betrothed to be married," Blaine said, hoping to sound confident and convincing.

"To whom?" the king asked. "To some country lass, ye coerced by promising her what? Money?"

"My liege, it is as I said in my letter. We met, and I fell in…"

"Cease!" The king slammed his fist down on his desk. "I will not listen to this absurdness." His face turned red. "And from you…of all my subjects I never would have thought ye would try to cuckold me. Ye served me for six years, Blaine. I favored ye. When I heard ye were looking to wed, I took great care in finding ye a proper wife. Someone whose family would be an asset to yer clan, strengthening yer alliance against the MacDonnells. And knowing yer penchant for a comelier lass, I even went as far as to make sure she was beautiful and intelligent." He threw the missive down in disgust. "Yet ye dare send me this…this rubbish? Ye canna expect me to believe it. You are in love? Then why are ye not wed?"

Douglas John rose to say something, but the king gave him a look, so he sat back down.

"I did not wed her because I came here to ask if ye would grant us yer permission," Blaine said firmly.

"And if I say nay? What then?"

"Ye are my sovereign. I will do as ye command."

The king thought for a moment, his fingers gently stroking his bare chin, "Tonight ye will dine with the queen and me. Bring this…proposed bride before me. You too, Douglas John, I will expect ye and yer wife to attend." He rose to leave. "I will see ye in an hour. Don't be late."

~ * ~

Jocelyn paced the floor of her bedchamber. Blaine had finally sent word that all was well, and they would be meeting the king and queen in little less than an hour. Fortunately, Violet heeded Addie's warning and began preparing her hours in advance.

"Please, my lady, sit down," Violet said. "Everything will be fine."

But Jocelyn was ready to jump out of her skin. She was about to say something when they heard a knock on the door.

Violet stopped her when she tried to open it. "My lady, we are at court. I will get the door." She positioned her and adjusted the train of her gown.

Jocelyn relaxed when she saw Blaine standing on the other side, a look of approval on his handsome face.

He looked incredible dressed in a dark blue jacket and waistcoat that accentuated his broad shoulders, trim waist and narrow hips. His cravat was tied intricately, and there was a small ruffle around the cuffs of his shirt. The britches hugged his muscular thighs, and instead of wearing stockings, he wore tall black boots that were polished to a high sheen. His long hair was tied in a queue. Just when she thought he couldn't look more handsome; he gave her his unique smile leaving her breathless.

"Ye look beautiful, my dear," he said as he walked over to where she stood. He lifted her hand and placed a gentle kiss on the back. "I am a most fortunate man to have the privilege of escorting ye before the king. I believe he will agree with me that ye are the most beautiful woman in Scotland."

Jocelyn's cheeks heated at the compliment. The dark brown gown she wore complimented her figure. The neckline was off her shoulders and highlighted her creamy complexion. The waist fell to a deep V, and the sleeves were full and edged in gold lace. The full skirt split in the front, revealing an underskirt made of a light brown satin. Pinned to the center of the bodice sparkled a large topaz broach.

Violet had swept up her hair leaving small curls framing each side of her face. Looking deep into his eyes, she relished in his approval.

"Please, Violet, can you give us a moment? I would like a word with Lady Jocelyn."

Violet smiled and left the bedchamber.

No sooner did the door close than Jocelyn grabbed Blaine around his waist, pulling him into a tight hug. "Oh, Blaine, I was so worried. I heard ye were taken away by the king."

Blaine quieted her by placing his fingers to her lips and then he followed that with a soft kiss. "'Tis all right sweeting, I am fine."

"I waited for hours, not knowing what had become of ye. Did ye speak with the king? Was he angered?"

"Aye, I was detained, but I explained everything to the king. Ye will be presented to him this evening. I believe he will be as charmed by you as I am." He kissed her again. "Shall we go?"

Comforted by his words, she smiled when he offered his arm. She did remind herself that they were only playing the part of a happy couple, and soon all this would end.

Don't fall for his pretty words.

Chapter Eight

The dinner was held in the royal family's private quarters. Jocelyn asked if her brother or Roderick would be in attendance but was told they were not invited. However, Roderick met up with McDermott, and he and the Fergusons had quite an evening planned for Braedan. She wasn't sure if this was a good thing or not.

The footman opened the door to a spacious salon filled with people. She half expected it would be more intimate, but there had to be at least thirty or more. The room grew quiet when they entered, all heads turning in their direction.

Blaine scanned the crowd and broke into a smile. "Come, my dear, I have someone I want ye to meet."

They walked over to where a tall and very handsome man was conversing with an older gentleman. The tall man had raven black hair and the most incredible blue eyes. She smiled demurely. He must be kin to Blaine as there was a family resemblance. Next to him sat a beautiful woman with dark auburn hair and eyes the color of liquid amber. They glowed in a face that too had a golden complexion. She stood when they approached.

"My dear, may I introduce to ye my brother, Douglas John MacKinnon, and his lovely wife, Lady Arrabella."

Jocelyn curtseyed and took the hand he offered.

"'Tis a pleasure, Lady Jocelyn." Douglas John was said to be the handsome brother, but she thought him to be a bit too attractive.

She much preferred Blaine's look and coloring.

"I have heard so much about ye." He kissed the back of her hand.

"I am somewhat at a disadvantage since yer brother neglected to tell me ye were at court," she replied. "I am, however, glad to meet someone who might have the grace to teach him better manners."

Douglas John laughed easily, making him appear even more handsome. "I am afraid nothing we say or do will make a difference where my brother is concerned. I fear it takes the skill of my own wife to keep me in line." He looked adoringly at his wife.

"I see my keeping ye from my betrothed's company was a wise idea. I should have known she would join forces and see that my self-esteem is shredded." Blaine laughed, taking two glasses from a passing servant.

The four of them fell into a natural conversation, keeping the subject light. Jocelyn started to relax and talked about herself without giving too much information. She told them about the bakery and the small village where she lived. Lady Arrabella asked questions, showing genuine interest. She told Jocelyn that for years she helped run the farmlands around their estate and had an interest in experimenting with crops too see what grew best.

Even as she had a good time, Jocelyn noticed that Lady Arrabella was looking pale. She had not drunk any of the wine and had lost some of her spunk. "Are ye well, Lady Arrabella?"

Douglas John stopped talking the minute he heard Jocelyn's query. He took the glass his wife held, putting it on the table next to her. "Are ye feeling ill my love?" he asked, with a concerned look.

"I am fine," she assured him. "I think I will find a retiring room and freshen up a bit."

"I will go with ye," Jocelyn volunteered.

"Oh no, 'tis not necessary," she said. "I wouldn't want ye to miss any of the festivities."

Jocelyn insisted, "We will be back momentarily." Taking Arrabella's arm, she led her out of the salon.

~ * ~

It was some time before Jocelyn and Arrabella were able to join the men. When they returned to the salon, Blaine was in the midst of telling a tale.

"He leapt onto the table, sending dishes and glassware crashing to the floor, withdrew his saber from its scabbard and declared, 'I shall have another butt of malmsey, by God.'"

The group burst into laughter some holding their bellies, others wiping away tears. Through all the noise and commotion, Blaine immediately made his way, weaving through the throng, and was at her side in seconds. He didn't hesitate to lift her hand to his lips. Douglas John was close behind.

"I am sorry we tarried so long; apparently we missed a good tale." Jocelyn smiled at him. "I don't suppose ye care to repeat it?"

Blaine returned her smile as the door opened, announcing the arrival of the king and queen. Immediately everyone lined up on either side of the room as the king and queen greeted their guests. The men all bowed, and the women curtseyed as they passed.

Jocelyn dipped down low as the king approached. With her head bowed, she noticed a pair of bejeweled slippers before her. Lifting her eyes, she saw the king, his stare boring straight through her.

"Sire, may I introduce ye to Miss Jocelyn MacAulay," Blaine said, holding out his hand as he assisted her up.

The king said nothing, barely nodding in acknowledgment.

The guests were ushered to an adjoining room where sat a long table that could accommodate the people who were invited to dine. As they were shown to their seats, the king motioned to Blaine. "I would like it if you would sit here." He indicated an empty chair to his left.

Jocelyn was thankful to be seated next to Douglas John and Arrabella.

The meal turned out to be delicious yet surprisingly simple. It started with a rich, clear broth followed by a fragrant soft cheese, roasted nuts and fruits. She was delighted to taste for the first time a roasted chestnut dipped in fig jam. The combination with the warm bread was heaven. Even though Blaine was seated a bit too far for conversation, Douglas John and Arrabella kept her happily entertained.

During most of the meal, Blaine was in deep conversation with the king. Douglas John explained how the king had invested in Blaine's fishing business. "Has he told ye about the ice house he is constructing?"

Jocelyn found it interesting, but Douglas John could only provide a vague description. "Ye will have to ask Blaine to explain."

She glanced over to where Blaine sat, and their eyes met. He lifted his glass in a silent toast and took a sip. She did the same, smiling at him with genuine happiness.

The main course consisted of a variety of roasted meats and vegetables. They were excellently seasoned and prepared. The meal was just about concluded when Jocelyn noticed a beautiful young woman seated on the other side of Blaine. To say she was beautiful was an understatement. The lass was stunning. Finding it difficult not to stare, Jocelyn saw Blaine whisper something to her that made her laugh. She lifted long tapered fingers up to her lips. Her face blushed charmingly.

"Isn't she lovely?" Lady Arrabella whispered. "She is Sir George Buchanan's youngest daughter, Lady Clara. She has just been appointed lady-in-waiting to the queen. 'Tis quite an honor."

Jocelyn nodded but said nothing. She could only stare.

The dinner concluded, and as the guests were leaving the king motioned for Blaine and Douglas John to remain, along with a couple more men. Seeing that their escorts would be detained, the queen invited Jocelyn and Arabella to join her for a cup of tea. Jocelyn followed Lady Arrabella to the adjoining salon and worried she looked a bit weary.

"I am well, ye need not worry," Arabella assured her. "This will be a good opportunity for you to be presented to the queen."

She had just sat down when the queen approached them. Rising to her feet, Lady Arrabella introduced Jocelyn. The queen smiled warmly and politely asked a few questions. She tilted her head toward the pianoforte that stood in the corner. "Do you play, Miss MacAulay?"

Jocelyn dipped her head briefly. "Nay, Your Majesty, I am afraid I do not."

Queen Catherine smiled again. "No matter," she said kindly. Turning to Lady Clara, she motioned for her to play.

Soon, it was apparent to Jocelyn that Lady Clara was an accomplished musician, and Jocelyn listened to her in awe.

Arrabella leaned in and whispered, "I confess, I too canna play the pianoforte, but with young ladies like Clara, I suppose I don't need to."

As Lady Clara continued to entertain them, Lady Arrabella covered her mouth to keep from yawning. Seeing this the queen approached them. "Arrabella dear, ye should get some rest. After all, tomorrow is the ball."

Lady Arrabella thanked her majesty, and this time didn't argue about Jocelyn's offer to accompany her. "Are ye sure ye don't want to stay?"

"I too am tired, and frankly my nerves have been stretched to their limits. I did not expect to meet the king and queen so soon."

Lady Arrabella patted her arm. "It may appear overwhelming, but ye must keep in mind that although our king is a great leader, he is still just a man. He breathes the same air as we."

~ * ~

Violet was waiting for Jocelyn when she finally reached her bedchamber. She was eager to hear all about the evening. "Did ye meet the queen too? Isn't she lovely?" Violet helped her undress. "I understand her gowns are designed by the best modiste in all of France."

"I didn't have much of a conversation with the queen," Jocelyn admitted, "but with so many people in attendance, their attention was much in demand." When Violet questioned her about Blaine, and if he too enjoyed the evening, Jocelyn thought of how the king monopolized him the entire time. "Aye, he seemed to."

She went on to describe what they ate and what the ladies wore. She made sure to give Violet as many details of the queen's gown, seeing it was what interested Violet the most.

She excused herself once she had Jocelyn tucked into bed. Lying in the dark, she couldn't help thinking how drastically her life had changed in a little less than two weeks. Here she was at court, meeting the king and queen, pretending to be engaged to one of the most handsome men in Scotland.

She was disappointed when the king showed little interest in her; however, it might not be a bad sign. With his numerous responsibilities and the pressure of running a country, the last thing on his mind would be her marriage to Blaine. She did notice that twice during dinner, she caught the king looking at her. When she met his gaze, he quickly looked away. Oh well, there was no reason to make much of the situation.

Tomorrow, at the ball, she would be presented to the king again. She would do her best to conduct herself favorably in hopes that he would be satisfied with their betrothal. Then she and Braedan could return home, to the simple life they led. It was a life she had grown accustomed to and one she preferred, rather than all this pomp and circumstance. No, this wasn't the life she wanted for herself, and she knew it deep in her heart.

~ * ~

When Blaine joined the ladies, he was disappointed to learn that Arrabella and Jocelyn had retired for the evening. He remained for as long as he thought necessary before he too sought his own bed. The stress from the day had drained him of his energy and made him short-tempered. He could not deny that the king's disinterest in Jocelyn had him irked. Even though he was grateful the king didn't make any references to their earlier conversation, he made little effort to get to know Jocelyn. He was proud of the way she conducted herself. She looked refined and acted like a well-bred lady. Thankfully, his brother and Arrabella seemed to be taken by her.

"Blaine, although I have spent little time with Miss MacAulay, I can see she is a remarkable young woman. I hope ye are truthful in your plans to wed her," Douglas John said.

Blaine reassured him although he had no intentions of wedding Jocelyn. He sincerely hoped that in the end, they could come to some sort of agreement. He toyed with the idea of keeping her as his mistress and thought the prospect most enticing. He only needed to convince Jocelyn, which could prove a challenge, but it was a challenge he thoroughly planned to enjoy.

He decided to get some rest. Before he excused himself for the evening, the king requested his company for a morning ride. He had thought to show Jocelyn the city. Thinking how lovely she looked this evening, he wanted to find something special for her wear to the ball. Smiling to himself, he thought that this was the beginning of the seduction of his future leman. The prospect of having all of her was more than tempting; it was turning into an obsession. He wanted Jocelyn MacAulay. He wanted her naked and writhing beneath him as he brought her to her release. He wanted Jocelyn.

~ * ~

In the main dining hall, Jocelyn sat next to her brother, who was looking a bit piqued. He was holding his head, moaning that it was too early. "Bloody hell, Joce, ye could 'ave went to breakfast without me."

"Sit up," she hissed under her breath when she saw Douglas John and Arrabella approach. She introduced them to Braedan, silently wishing she had left him upstairs.

"Ah, I see all the earmarks of a night spent with Roderick MacPherson." Douglas John grinned.

"Ye need not be embarrassed, Lady Jocelyn," Arrabella added, seeing the look on her face. "I have seen my share of sick men in the morning after a night with that scoundrel."

"Scoundrel?" They spun around to see a quite fresh-looking Roderick standing directly behind. "Why ye cut me to the quick Lady Arrabella. I was only making sure the lad was well entertained."

"Exactly what did ye do to our young friend here?" Douglas John said. "Seems a good tot should help when the cups have been hard on ye."

"Dear heavens, Douglas John, yer not suggesting the lad drink more?" Arrabella scolded him. "I believe food and rest are all that is needed."

"I think ye are right," Braedan said, excusing himself.

Jocelyn watched as he quickly bolted up the stairs thinking he might get sick.

"Ye should be ashamed of yourself." Arrabella shook her finger at Rod. "He is not one of yer cronies."

"What is that supposed to mean? One of my cronies?" Rod feigned innocence. "The lads and I showed him a good time." He winked at Douglas John.

"Ye didn't take him down to Sal's, did ye?" Arrabella asked, her brows knitting together.

"Aye, and she was in the most charitable mood." Rod laughed when she slapped him on the arm.

"What is Sal's?" Jocelyn asked, but Arrabella shook her head and explained it was not a 'what' but a 'who'. At this point, Jocelyn decided she didn't care to know.

"I was thinking of taking a walk through the gardens. Would ye like to join me?" Arrabella asked.

Jocelyn smiled and accepted the invitation. As soon as they finished eating, they left to fetch their cloaks.

~ * ~

When Blaine saw that the queen and her entourage had joined them for the morning ride, he hoped Jocelyn might have been invited. Disappointed, he held back, choosing to ride with Warren, the king's personal guard. He was an old friend and came from a good family. They talked about the latest news from home. Blaine was thankful that Warren did not ask him any questions regarding his current dilemma.

The ride was more like a walk, and Loki became fidgety, dancing beneath him. "I think I will give him the lead," he said to Warren and turned him toward the open pasture.

With a squeeze of his thighs, Loki broke into a run. Blaine leaned forward, moving along with Loki's stride. The wind was cold against his face, and he thought the speed exhilarating. He was letting Loki set the pace when he heard the approach of a horse behind him. Glancing over his shoulder, he was stunned to see Lady Clara riding a massive warhorse, and she was gaining on him. By the look of determination on her face, the race was on.

"Ha!" he yelled. There was no horse faster than Loki, and he dug in his heels, urging him, but even as they drew away, Lady Clara was right on his tail. "Ha!" he yelled again.

As they started to climb the knoll, she was right next to him. She, too, was bent low over her horse, digging in her heels and expertly using her crop. They were neck and neck as they crested the knoll, but she took the lead at the last minute, making her the clear winner.

They burst out laughing as they reined in their horses. "Bravo, Lady Clara, I declare ye the winner."

Lady Clara's cheeks were flushed bright pink. "I had the advantage, my lord." She laughed when he raised one brow. "I am much smaller, and I was able to gain on the rise. Otherwise, I believe ye would have kept yer lead and won."

Blaine appreciated her modesty. "I had a bit of a head start my lady, and therefore it was a fair race."

"Well if ye want, I would be more than happy to challenge ye again," she said. "We can determine then who is the real winner."

"I fear Laird Buchannan would not approve of his daughter riding at such a speed."

Lady Clara tilted her head back and laughed, "Aye, yer fear

would be substantiated; however, I don't see my father here, so 'tis always good to capitalize when the opportunity presents itself."

Blaine shook his head in amusement and said, "Lady Clara, ye are full of surprises."

They walked their horses back to the group. Lady Clara was intelligent and undoubtedly an impressive horsewoman. She came from a good family and didn't appear conceited. The latter was not something commonly seen amongst the peerage. He smiled broadly as a brilliant idea snuck into his head. He needed to find Jocelyn.

~ * ~

The clouds covered the sky, but there was no wind, making the walk through the garden tolerable. Jocelyn and Arrabella came upon a stone wall and gazed out at the loch in the distance. Directly below, Jocelyn saw a group of riders. One rider had separated from the group and was racing across the field at a good pace. A second rider was in pursuit.

From a distance, it was difficult to identify them when suddenly Jocelyn caught site of long golden hair. "Blaine," she said under her breath.

Arrabella looked to where Jocelyn was pointing. The riders raced across the field and both cleared a low rock wall at the same time, but one eked out ahead when they reached the rise.

"Blaine won."

Arrabella gave her a curious look. "Well, if that 'tis Blaine, it looks to me they were tied."

"Oh, it was Blaine," Jocelyn said with confidence.

Jocelyn and Arrabella made their way down to the hothouse, excited to see what was growing. Arrabella introduced her to Alain who had been the castle groundskeeper for the past ten years. The ladies sat down on a bench among the various blooms and delightful fragrances.

"I understand that ye met Sir Blaine when he came to yer aide," Arrabella said. "What happened?"

Jocelyn's smile faded, and she looked away.

"I beg yer forgiveness; I did not mean to pry."

"Nay, Lady Arrabella, 'tis just that so much has happened; I suppose I have put that horrible experience in the back of my mind." Jocelyn smiled at her and then told her all that happened…everything.

Lady Arrabella listened quietly and gasped when Joselyn described the attack in detail.

"Sir Blaine risked his life to save us. We were outnumbered, and if he hadn't been there…"

Arrabella reached over to give her hand a squeeze. "Nonsense, 'tis perfectly understandable that ye are upset." She smiled warmly. "'Tis good for ye to talk."

Jocelyn wiped her cheek with her gloved hands. "Sir Blaine was like an archangel coming to my rescue. Ye can understand why I would be grateful to him, why I—"

"Have fallen in love?" Arrabella finished for her.

Jocelyn's face blushed hot.

"Ye need not worry my dear—'tis natural to feel more than appreciation for one's hero." She patted her arm. "Ye two are well suited, and I am sure ye will have a lovely life together."

Jocelyn started to panic. She didn't want a life with Blaine. She didn't want to have feelings for him either. She needed to rein in her emotions if she were going to survive this intolerable plan. Wanting to change the subject, she suggested they continue with their walk.

The ladies arrived at the stables just as a group of riders could be seen approaching. Blaine was in the lead and dismounted when he saw them. Jocelyn met his smile and walked over to where he was helping Lady Clara off her horse. Jocelyn then realized it was Lady Buchanan who had raced him, and she had to admit the lass was genuinely remarkable.

Lady Arrabella shook her head and gently admonished Lady Clara. If her father were present, he would consider her reckless. Lady Clara laughed and thanked Arabella for her concern and promised to be mindful in the future.

As they walked up the path toward the castle, Blaine held Jocelyn back from the other two. "I believe I have a rather grand idea, Lady Jocelyn." He beamed.

"I, too, have one," Jocelyn said not letting him finish. "I believe I have found our heiress for my brother."

"Lady Clara," they said together and then laughed.

Chapter Nine

When they returned to the castle, Blaine asked Jocelyn if she would be interested in taking a tour of the city. Jocelyn had accepted when they saw the queen.

"I expect to see ye at tea, Lady Arrabella," she said, walking past them. "Please bring Miss MacAulay."

Jocelyn turned to Blaine with regret on her face. "Mayhap after tea we might take that tour?"

It was vital that she attend and agreed to go later. When he reached up to kiss the back of her hand, he noticed that she shivered a bit. The cloak she was wearing did nothing to keep her warm. He kissed her again, but this time on the cheek. He laughed when she blushed bright red.

Blaine watched as Arrabella and Jocelyn ran to catch up with the queen and her entourage. He was about to see if he could find Roderick when he came up with an idea.

Turning around, he walked back to the stables. He was glad to see that Loki had yet to be unsaddled.

"Hold on there," he said to the stable lad. "I need to run an errand."

Blaine mounted and took the road that led to the city.

~ * ~

The time spent with the queen was far from entertaining. In fact, Jocelyn found it nerve-wracking. She sensed her every movements were being scrutinized. Most of the time was spent listening to Lady Clara playing the pianoforte as others worked on their embroidery.

Neither Jocelyn nor Arrabella had brought theirs, so there was nothing to keep their hands busy. Lady Clara offered to bring them a hoop, but they politely declined. Looking at the needlework Lady Clara was working on, Jocelyn couldn't help admiring it.

"Is there nothing this lass can't do?" she whispered to Arrabella.

After a few hours of polite conversation and enough tea to float them all to China, the queen finally retired but not before suggesting that Arrabella rest before the ball. "We can't have ye tired tonight."

Finally excused, Jocelyn and Arrabella left to find their

bedchambers. Jocelyn was so excited it took everything she had not to pick up her skirts and run. When she finally did arrive, she slammed the door, calling for Violet.

"Has Sir Blaine left word where I am to meet him?" She worried she might have missed him.

"Nay, my lady," Violet said, walking out of their adjoining room, "but a parcel did arrive for ye."

She pointed to a rather large package on the bed. Jocelyn went over and unwrap it. Inside she withdrew a thick winter cloak. It was made of fine black wool lined in dark gray satin. It was the most beautiful cloak she had ever seen. She lifted it up to admire it when a note floated to the floor. Picking it up, she saw that it was from Blaine.

J

Please consider this gift a small token of my esteem. I await ye in the Great Hall.

B

Jocelyn freshened up and changed into her traveling gown. When she donned the new cloak, she noted it would keep her very warm. Violet offered to escort her to the Great Hall. Still, Jocelyn declined not wanting to keep Blaine waiting a minute longer.

It took a considerable effort to walk down the stairs and through the open courtyard. Hearing loud voices, she followed them to the double doors. Peering inside she worried she might not be able to find Blaine with so many people gathered.

As she stepped in, she noticed everyone stopping their conversation to stare at her. The crowd parted the way as she walked in and within seconds, she spotted Blaine surrounded by a group of women.

Seeing her, he stopped in midsentence and politely excused himself. A broad smile graced his face, and his eyes sparkled with acknowledgment. When he reached her, he lifted her gloved hand to his lips. "Ye look beautiful, my dear," he whispered, "and definitely warmer."

"I can't thank ye enough for yer thoughtfulness," she said. "'Tis exquisite. I have never owned such a beautiful cloak."

"Nay, 'tis only a garment. Ye are exquisite." He looked deep into her eyes.

For a moment they were the only two in the hall. The spell was broken when she heard her name.

Jocelyn turned to see her brother, who looked remarkably

better.

"Are ye going somewhere?" he asked, looking at her cloak approvingly.

"Aye, and ye are not invited." She smiled, giving him a buss on the cheek. "But I must say ye are looking much improved."

Braedan grinned, rolling his eyes. "I must admit I was somewhat reckless last night, but I am fully recovered and looking forward to the ball."

Jocelyn told him briefly of Lady Clara. She was surprised when he didn't seem too interested.

"She is lovely, and if ye met her, ye too would agree. Blaine thinks 'tis a good match and is willing to promote ye."

"Jocelyn, I appreciate all that ye are doing, but she is a Buchanan and the queen's lady-in-waiting. I don't believe her family would be too pleased if she wed a poor..."

"Dinna say it, Braedan. Ye are a gentleman, and any young lady would be proud to be yer wife."

"I am just saying..." but he didn't finish when he saw Blaine. "I believe yer betrothed is ready to leave." He kissed her on the cheek. "Have a good time." Turning on his heel, he returned to where Rod and his friends were entertaining a group of ladies.

"Aye, 'tis time we leave." Blaine smiled, ushering her out the door and down to the lower courtyard. Waiting for them was a black lacquer phaeton. It was sleek and harnessed to a matching pair of black horses.

"Oh, Blaine, 'tis glorious." She gasped in disbelief and took his hand as he helped her up.

Taking the reins from the footman, he jumped in after her. He drove down the long road toward the heart of the city. They passed by St. Giles Cathedral, more appropriately termed the High Kirk of Scotland. It was the principal place of worship in the Church of Scotland. The tall impressive crown steeple could be seen from miles around.

They passed down Royal Mile till they reached Holyrood Palace. The palace was the residential home of the king and queen; however, when there was a special occasion like celebrating the newly appointed knights, the dragoons held the celebration at Edinburgh castle. They proceeded to the park, stopping to walk around a bit and admire the view of the palace.

"'Tis grand Blaine. I can just imagine how beautiful it must be inside," she said as he helped her down.

Holding his arm, they walked around the grounds. Around the

back stood the old abbey. It was constructed in 1128 and then later expanded to become the royal residence.

"My parents were married in the abbey. I presume the king will see many of his subjects married here."

"Perhaps we shall marry here." She clamped her mouth shut, shocked at what she had said aloud. "That's if the king had his way." She recovered.

Blaine shook his head. "Nay we would not marry here. My mother would never allow it without her being present. As a matter of fact, each one of my siblings would have to be present. She is most adamant about this. We would most likely be married at Calderglen, the home of my brother Caelan."

"Well, I am sure when ye do decide to wed, it will be a grand occasion," Jocelyn said, hoping to sound nonchalant. He gave her a serious look. "I gest with ye, Blaine. We have an agreement to see ye out of this predicament and nothing more. I long to return to my home and my simple life. Please understand I am agreeable to saying goodbye to ye when this is over." She turned and walked back to the phaeton.

~ * ~

Blaine eyed her with her back straight, and her head held high. What was it about this woman that attracted him so? The thought of having to say goodbye to her was not agreeable at all. Was it because she wasn't throwing herself at his feet, waiting at his beck and call?

No, many women played the game of showing little to no interest in him, and it never worked in the past. She had stopped her cold disregard of him, but he still sought her company and reveled when he made her smile. The cloak was nothing more than something that he thought she needed, yet it meant everything to him that she was pleased with his gift.

It then struck him like a bolt of lightning with a new acuity he had never considered. It mattered to him that he pleased Jocelyn. His past relationships were based on women he found attractive, and they pleased him in one way or another. This brought about his own wants and desire to please them in return, usually in the bed. But she was a young woman whom he honestly admired, and her heart mattered. He realized he wanted to make her happy and to see to her needs no matter how small or insignificant.

Blaine drove them back through the winding roads, pointing out places of interest. He stopped the phaeton in front of the "Locked Booths" a series of seven buildings exclusive to fine jewelers and goldsmiths. He loved watching her eyes light up as she perused through the shops, gazing at the assortments of broaches and necklaces. One vendor had a collection of beautifully hand-painted fans. There was one who caught her interest. It was gold with small blue flowers painted on the outer slats.

He insisted on buying it for her although she protested. "Trust me, my dear; you will be grateful to have something to cool ye. The hall will get very hot."

She reluctantly agreed. A few shops down, sitting on a white satin pillow, was a gold necklace with brilliantly cut sapphires. There were three stones on each side, graduating in size toward the middle and in the center was a sizeable tear-drop sapphire the size of a grape. The superb workmanship was akin no other and the gems of the highest quality.

"Oh my," she said, her eyes growing round. "Have ye ever seen anything more splendid? I have always favored this stone. 'Tis said the blue sapphire is the stone of wisdom." She told him of stories her mother would tell her about gems and their meaning.

Pressing the package that held her fan, he ushered her outside. "The ball starts at eight. 'Tis time to get ye back so ye can ready yourself."

Tucked into their phaeton and huddled close, they made their way up the long and narrow road.

~ * ~

By the time Jocelyn returned, Violet was in a tiff. Immediately stripped of her clothes, Jocelyn was dunked into a waiting bath.

"Well, the water was warm," she scolded when Jocelyn complained it was cold.

She thought they had plenty of time, but she soon realized why Violet's temper. It took more than an hour to style her hair, sweeping it up on the top of her head as she curled the ends that cascaded between her shoulder blades. Violet had managed to create something Jocelyn never thought possible.

Next came the torturous corset that squeezed her waist to a tiny size so she could fit into the ballgown. Light blue satin hung off her shoulders, the neckline, bodice, sleeves and hem edged in gold lace. Jocelyn showed Violet the fan Blaine had purchased which complimented the gown perfectly. Small sparkling gold beads lined the hem and embellished the tops of her shoes. Violet used the same sparkling beads sewn onto a gold ribbon and wove it in and around her hair. Looking at her reflection, Jocelyn felt like a princess.

Violet stepped back to admire her work. "Ye look beautiful, my lady. Sir Blaine will be so proud."

Just then Jocelyn heard a knock on the door. Looking at the clock, she thought they still had some time before he was expected.

Violet opened the door to see it was indeed Blaine. "Please forgive me for intruding but I was hoping to have a word with my fiancée."

Jocelyn loved to hear him refer to her as his fiancée. She chided herself for her foolishness but decided that just for tonight, she wouldn't put any restrictions on the evening and planned to enjoy herself. Making sure her dress was perfectly arranged, Violet opened the door.

"My lady, I am speechless by your beauty." He smiled. Taking her hand, he pressed it up to his lips.

Jocelyn's uneasiness almost made her giggle but managed to stifle it, so as not to offend. Looking at him, she saw that he was once again in his navy-blue court clothes. Instead of wearing the heavy overcoat, he had replaced it with a lightweight navy jacket that accentuated his shoulders and chest. His plaid was across his chest like a sash and draped over one broad shoulder. The MacKinnon badge secured it into place. He looked magnificent.

They stood gazing into each other's eyes until they were interrupted by another knock at the door. Violet opened it to two servants carrying trays of food and drink.

"I hope ye don't mind, but I took liberties in having refreshments brought up. I thought ye might want to eat a little something before we go. The ball starts at eight, but the evening meal will not be served till midnight." The servants set up the small table next to the fireplace, placing two chairs on either side. "Please bring another chair." Blaine turned to wink at Violet, "I thought ye might want to join us."

"Och, nay, my lord." She blushed. She went on to explain that she had plans to meet with friends when he insisted. She left them for the adjoining bedroom to ready herself.

He took Jocelyn into his arms as if to kiss her then he stepped back. A slight furrow formed between his brows. "I admit that I find yer appearance flawless, but I canna help think that perhaps something is missing."

Jocelyn giggled when he walked around her, perusing her from top to bottom. He stopped to stand before her with a rakish grin on his handsome face. He withdrew a small leather pouch. Placing it in her hand, he closed her fingers around it and placed a small kiss.

Cocking her head to one side, she eyed him suspiciously. "What is this?" Giving her a lopsided grin, he told her to open it.

Jocelyn gasped aloud when she saw the sapphire necklace. Her mouth agape, she looked at Blaine and then at the necklace. "I don't know what to say, I canna, I canna…"

"Of course, ye can," he finished for her. He took the necklace from her, the deep blue gems sparkling in the candlelight. Walking around, he moved aside her hair and fastened it around her neck, placing a light kiss on her shoulder. "Now ye look perfect."

Jocelyn's hand reached up to touch the stones that were instantly warmed by her body. At a loss for words, she was spared when Violet came rushing out of her bedchamber.

"Oh my, 'tis positively beautiful, and it goes so well with the gown. Oh, my lady, I have never seen it's equal. I canna wait to tell Addie. She has such opinions. She will be as flabbergasted when she finds out what Sir Blaine gifted ye, and she said ye would never wed, ha!"

Jocelyn took a breath at the last comment. But what did she expect? People would question the legitimacy of their betrothal. Violet bid the couple goodnight and rushed out the door.

As soon as Violet left, Blaine motioned for her to sit. Still shocked by the gift, Jocelyn couldn't help touching the necklace, enjoying the weight around her neck. "Ye shouldn't have, Blaine. I canna accept such an extravagant gift."

He poured them some wine. "Dinna be silly, of course, ye can. Ye are my betrothed."

"In name only," she smiled, taking the glass, "and ye ken this."

"I can't imagine a more perfect gift." He took a sip, his full lips caressing the lip of the goblet.

Her breath caught in her throat. "Ye ken what I am saying, Blaine. In a few weeks, we will part ways. I will go back to Heatherwood and return to my life as a baker. I see no occasions where I will be able to wear such an exquisite piece of jewelry. It would be a shame for it to sit in my jewel box."

"At this moment, ye are my betrothed, my dear, and, as I see it, I am allowed to give ye what I want." He uncovered one of the trays.

Jocelyn lost all desires to argue when she saw the bowl of roasted chestnuts in fig jam and warm slices of bread.

"How did ye know?" she asked in astonishment.

Taking a piece of bread, he smeared some of the nut-jam on it and handed it to her. "I might not have been sitting next to ye last night at dinner; however, I am not blind. I saw how much ye liked it, so I arranged to have some brought up."

He watched her like on the night before, closing her eyes as she relished the taste. He looked as if he might want to devour her. Jocelyn couldn't help but be flattered.

The gift of the necklace was by far too generous, but his awareness of what food she favored pleased her even more. His observance touched her heart. If she didn't guard herself, she would find herself heartbroken.

"I am touched by yer thoughtfulness."

"All I want is your happiness."

~ * ~

The ballroom was a crush of people. Jocelyn noticed many men dressed in military uniforms and all the ladies were in their finest. They found Douglas John and Arrabella immediately, talking to a young man in uniform who looked very much like Arrabella.

"May I introduce to ye my brother, Colin Murray." She smiled. "'Tis the real reason why we came to court."

Colin smiled as he took her hand. "I just completed my first year of training at Douglas Castle and have been assigned to Fort Williams. I leave at the end of the week." Colin had the same dark auburn hair as his sister, but his eyes were a silver-gray.

Jocelyn thought the contrast quite striking.

Blaine slapped him on the back. "Looks like ye are ready. What happened to the gangling lad I once knew?" Colin flushed. "I don't believe ye will like Fort William as much as Douglas Castle as it tends to be a might colder up north."

"Of course, he won't like it. He will be away from me." A young blonde lass escorted by Sir Reginald MacAlister pouted.

Colin smiled ear to ear and placed a kiss on the young woman's cheek. "I understand ye have met Sir Reginald," he said, puffing out his chest. "May I introduce to ye his daughter, Lady Cecelia MacAlister." Jocelyn curtseyed. "My soon-to-be betrothed."

Looking a bit put off, Lady Cecelia went into a long explanation about their status. "I do declare, ye can dispense with the soon-to-be part, just because Papa wants us to wait until after yer time in the king's service…"

Jocelyn never knew anyone who could talk without needing a breath. Lady Cecelia launched into a diatribe of complaints at having to suffer Colin's absence. She continued for so long Jocelyn lost interest in what she was saying. She found herself distracted by the curls on top of Cecelia's head that appeared to spring out from the center like a fountain. She just smiled and watched her curls bob up and down as she carried on.

"Do ye agree, Miss Jocelyn?"

Jocelyn was mortified to have been caught not paying attention. Lady Cecelia stared at her waiting for her to respond. Looking around, she saw that no one else had been paying attention.

"Of course, she doesn't agree," Sir Reginald answered. "I believe ye are too young, and there's plenty of time before we announce yer betrothal." He winked at Jocelyn.

"Well, I wondered if she was of the same opinion," Lady Cecelia argued, undoubtedly looking for an ally.

"Even if she did, she is a lady and would never contradict," Laird MacAlister said.

Jocelyn was relieved to see the crowd had moved to either side of the room, signaling that the king and queen were soon to make their entrance.

The guards sounded their horns. King Charles and Queen Catherine made their way into the ballroom followed by a dozen knights. The king addressed the crowd, announcing the titles of the newly appointed. Jocelyn could see the pride in their faces. After a rather lengthy speech, the musicians began to play, and the dancing commenced.

The king and queen began the first dance then nodded to the other distinguished guest to join them. Jocelyn was shocked when the king nodded to Blaine, and she herself was being pulled to the center of the room. They were dancing the quadrille, and the king and queen were part of their foursome. Jocelyn prayed she wouldn't stumble, or worse, step on the king's foot.

Much to her amazement, she did well, taking the king's arms as he swung her around, then back to his side. She smiled and much to her surprise, the king smiled back.

The dance ended, and Jocelyn curtseyed to the king. "Thank ye for the dance, Sire," she said sincerely.

"It was my pleasure, Miss MacAulay," the king replied before taking his wife's arm and escorting her from the dance floor.

Jocelyn was elated. She never would have dreamed that one day she would meet the king, let alone dance with him. When they rejoined their group, they saw Braedan had joined them. Unfortunately, Lady Cecelia was next to him explaining something, and he looked miserable.

"Braedan, I see ye have met Lady Cecelia," Blaine came to his aide. "Perhaps ye would like to take yer sister out on the dance floor."

Braedan agreed and offered Jocelyn his arm. They joined the other couples in a quick-step Bourrée. Jocelyn couldn't help admiring how her brother looked in his new clothes. He looked every bit the gentleman. She was so proud.

Laughing, they walked off the dance floor. "Please spare me the company of Lady Cecelia. I canna bear another explanation of her betrothal status."

Jocelyn looked through the crowd and saw that Lady MacAlister had moved on. "Brae?" She tried to get his attention, but he was completely mesmerized. "Braedan MacAulay."

Looking in the direction to where he was staring, she spied Roderick MacPherson walking toward them, and he wasn't alone.

"It's her," Braedan whispered.

For a second she didn't know whom he was referring to. Still, when she looked again, she saw that it was none other than Lady Angela MacPherson, the lass whose portrait captured Braedan's interest.

Roderick smiled at them broadly as he introduced his sister.

"'Tis a pleasure to meet ye, Lady Angela. I must tell ye I am most appreciative of your generosity. I am not sure if Violet told ye, but I am wearing many of yer gowns," Jocelyn said.

Lady Angela smiled brightly. "It pleases me that I can share my good fortune with ye. Ye have met Violet and her sisters, and therefore ye must have been told that I have been given more gowns than I can possibly wear in a year's time."

Jocelyn was charmed by the lass, and apparently, she was not the only one.

Lady Angela turned her attention to Braedan. "How do ye like Edinburgh, Mr. MacAulay? Is this yer first visit?"

He didn't answer her immediate, and Jocelyn had to discretely prod him. "Nay, I have been to the city before but not for many years."

She noticed her brother was having a difficult time forming his words, and she couldn't help finding humor in the situation.

"Braedan, why don't ye take my wee sister out on the dance floor?" Rod asked. "I am sure she would rather have ye then her old brother as a dance partner."

Braedan agreed and offered her his arm. They were lost in the crowd in a matter of seconds. "I believe ye made my brother very happy," Jocelyn said as she accepted Rod's arm.

"Well, he's a good bloke, and I canna see him being a nuisance," Rod said, and together they went to join the others.

~ * ~

Jocelyn enjoyed the ball immensely. She danced several times with Blaine, once with Douglas John and twice with Rod. She never caught sight of her brother except to see him and Lady Angela on the dance floor.

The room was becoming stifling hot, and she was grateful for her fan. However, it was getting to the point where it offered little relief.

"Would ye care to go outside?" Blaine suggested. No sooner did they walk out into the freezing cold, that the wind forced them back. "Perhaps we can go to the dining hall and get something to drink."

Jocelyn agreed, and together they walked arm in arm toward the adjoining room. Much to her relief, this room was much cooler. As he handed her a glass of champagne, she heard a shrilling laugh. Standing among a group of young women was Lady Cecelia.

Whatever she was saying, it must have been juicy gossip as the group all gasped collectively. Unfortunately, all eyes turned to Jocelyn and then followed by a gaggle of giggles. She decided not to pay any mind to a bunch of ninnies.

"Sir Blaine?"

Blaine was greeted by Warren, the king's personal guard.

"The king would like a word with ye."

"Aye, I will be there, momentarily." Blaine smiled regretfully at Jocelyn. "I shouldn't be too long. Would ye care to stay here and wait?"

She turned again to see Lady Cecelia and her companions staring at them. "If it's all right with you, I believe I will freshen up. If ye could point me in the direction of the nearest retiring room?"

He nodded, and they left together. They decided they would meet where Douglas John and Arrabella were sitting. She assured him she would be fine, and he left, but not before kissing her on the hand.

"When I return, I'll be wanting to kiss more than just yer hand." He smiled roguishly.

Jocelyn's stomach fluttered like a dozen butterflies. She enjoyed his attentions. If only they could go on like this forever.

Jocelyn was behind one of the screens adjusting her gown when she heard a familiar voice. "I swear to ye, Margaret, she is no more betrothed than I am."

"Honestly, Cecelia, I don't know where ye get yer information. Ye have not been kind at all," a woman said. "What has she done to earn yer scorn?"

"I have no idea what ye are talking about. I am simply stating a fact. Sir Blaine is quite single. The king has not granted him permission to wed that woman. So, if ye still have yer cap set for the man, then I say ye should go after him."

Jocelyn closed her eyes and gritted her teeth. Although Cecelia was annoying, the woman was right. She wasn't engaged to Blaine, and in a few weeks, he would be available. Tears welled up in her eyes. She wished she could escape the retiring room, but she was stuck. At least until they left.

"Don't encourage Margaret," another voice said. "If the king does not give his permission, then he will have to wed who the king chooses."

"Ugh," said the one Jocelyn assumed was Margaret. "Not Lady Pure and Perfect?"

"Aye," said the first woman. "If Blaine MacKinnon does not wed Miss MacAulay, then he will have to marry Lady Clara."

"That's enough," Cecelia growled. "I tire of the subject."

"Ye brought it up," Margaret chastised her.

"I don't have to listen to any of this," said the first lass. "Come along, Miss Soon-to-Be, I believe yer betroth is waiting."

The three women finally left the retiring room, leaving Jocelyn with her fingers at her temple. Of course, it would be Lady Clara, she would be perfect for Blaine. There went any hopes of matching her up with Braedan.

Disappointment left her wishing she didn't have to return to the ball. In fact, Jocelyn wished she had never entered into such a foolish agreement in the first place.

Taking a deep breath, she wiped away the tears that were threatening. Checking her image in the mirror, at the splendid gown, with her hair swept up like a princess, the glitter from the sapphire necklace caught her attention. Reaching up, she stroked the beautiful piece, admiring its quality and elegance. It looked stunning against her pale skin.

Determined not to let a group of ill-mannered women ruin her evening, Jocelyn straightened her gown and squared her shoulders. Yes, she would hold her head up, and yes, she would keep the necklace as a reminder of the wonderful time she spent with a wonderful man.

Entering the ballroom, it took little time to find Douglas John and Arrabella. They were surrounded by Roderick and his friends, the Ferguson cousins and John McDermott. Their conversation was lively, and they soon had her laughing.

She looked around to see if she could find Blaine, but he wasn't with the king, and as far as she could tell, he wasn't with Warren either.

Looking out on the dance floor she saw Braedan still dancing with Lady Angela. That's when she saw him, or rather…them.

Blaine was dancing with none other than Lady Clara, and they looked perfectly suited to each other. Both golden-haired, both strikingly beautiful, both from powerful clans. Why did she ever think she could have him?

Jocelyn's self-confidence drained out of her like sand in a sieve.

Chapter Ten

Blaine followed Warren to where the king was seated at a private table. He hoped the reason for the meeting might have to do with his request to wed Jocelyn. He appeared quite taken by her when they danced earlier. The king waved away his other guests and motioned for Blaine to sit in their place.

The conversation did not go quite as he hoped. The king was only interested in hearing how he was progressing with the construction of the ice house. Pleased that he wanted to invest in the project, Blaine promised to bring the construction plans the following day. The king excused him but not before suggesting he take Lady Clara out on the dance floor. Unable to refuse, Blaine walked over to where she stood next to the queen and offered his arm.

Lady Clara Buchanan looked stunning in a silk pink gown, her long blonde hair twisted intricately on top of her head. Her cheeks flushed brightly as she accepted his offer. Leading her to the dance floor, he couldn't help noticing that all eyes followed them. He overheard someone say they made a striking pair, another referred to them as the golden couple. He prayed Jocelyn was still in the retiring room and would be spared their comments.

The musicians began playing a Scottish reel, an energetic dance. Lady Clara was an excellent partner. He admired her grace and skill and thought her to be utterly charming. She would make any man a wonderful wife, especially for Braedan. When the dance ended, Blaine decided it would be a good time to introduce the two. He only needed to find the prospective groom.

Guiding Lady Clara through the crowd, he couldn't believe his good fortune when they bumped right into Braedan and Lady Angela. The ladies, being well acquainted, chatted away. Blaine's ability to read people served him well throughout his life. Within minutes after their initial introduction, he concluded that Braedan was not interested in Lady Clara. Braedan MacAulay was positively and unequivocally smitten by Angela MacPherson.

Blaine watched as the lad's eyes followed Angela's every move, he hung on each word and his smile held a surprising tenderness. He was happy for Braedan, but worried if a future together was at all possible. Leaving the trio to their conversation, Blaine excused himself and went in search of Jocelyn.

~ * ~

The ball was nearing the end, and Jocelyn decided that overall she had a wonderful time. She danced so much her feet ached. When Blaine found her, she chose not to mention what she overheard in the retiring room. There was no need to upset him, nor ruin the evening. Clearly, Lady Cecelia was just a spoilt child who enjoyed spreading gossip. Since Jocelyn saw little of them during the remainder of the night, she put little thought to what was said.

"Are ye ready to retire, my lady?" Blaine smiled suggestively. "Or ye care to join me for a drink?"

She arched one brow. "And where do ye suggest we have this drink?"

"My quarters, naturally." He tucked her hand in his arm.

"Surely ye jest, my lord." She giggled as they made their way through the crowded corridors.

"I would never joke about entertaining a lady in my bedchamber."

She should refuse, but quite frankly she wanted to accept. She hoped everyone saw them leave together. If they assumed, they were having an assignation, so be it.

She gasped when they walked into his quarters. Awestruck by the sheer size of the suite, she thought it was evident that he was considered a man of importance. The suite consisted of a sitting room, a bedroom, a bathing chamber and an adjoining room for the valet. She wondered if he had a valet when an older gentleman emerged. He didn't look at all surprised to see her.

Respectful of her reputation, Blaine introduced her as his fiancée.

"I was made aware of yer engagement, my lord, may I extend my congratulations?"

Blaine thanked him and dismissed him for the evening. Guiding Jocelyn to a settee next to the fire, he brought her a glass of whisky. She lifted a brow.

"What? Do ye not like whisky? I promise ye, 'tis the king's best."

"I am not accustomed to drinking strong spirits," she said, taking a sip.

Her eyes grew wide, and she coughed a little. He laughed and offered her a glass of wine instead. With watering eyes, she accepted.

He sat next to her and took a sip of his drink. Jocelyn watched him in the firelight as he licked his lips, her body reacting to being so close to him. She realized that she shouldn't be alone in his bedchamber, but perhaps because of the drink or the excitement of the ball, she didn't care.

"Give me yer wine," he said, reaching for her glass.

She hesitated and held back her drink.

"Trust me and do as I bid."

He grinned, taking the glass from her hand. He had her scoot back against the side and through the layers of petticoats then he lifted her feet onto his lap. Taking off her satin slippers, he started massaging her tired and aching feet.

"Oh," Jocelyn exclaimed, relishing in his administrations. "I canna believe how good that feels." She sighed contently.

A hunger reflected in his eyes. A longing that made her wonder what other things he wanted to do with her. She imagined his strong hands caressing her skin, touching her most tender regions.

"Did ye enjoy the evening?" he asked.

"Hmmm, it was grand, my lord," she said, closing her eyes. "The dancing, the music, and everyone in their finest. I could never have imagined."

"I don't suppose ye noticed that Braedan spent most of the evening with Lady Angela."

Her eyes flew open. "Ye would have to be blind not to have noticed," she said with humor. "I dinna believe he will consider Lady Clara as his wife."

She and Blaine laughed at their failed attempt at putting the two together. She told him about Braedan's interest in Angela's portrait.

"I was not aware of that," he admitted.

"I didn't mention it," she confessed. "I thought it only a passing interest, but now I see the error of my thinking." She grew slightly pensive. "I don't suppose Sir Roderick will object should he offer for her?"

Blaine shrugged. "'Tis out of our hands, my love, we can only hope for the best."

Jocelyn thought differently. Sir Roderick was his closest friend, and if anyone could convince him to consider her brother as a suitor, it was Blaine. Not wanting to ruin the moment she closed her eyes again to enjoy her massage.

They talked about the ball and the people she met. He told her about his conversation with the king and his interest in his ice house. He promised to show her the plans, so she could better understand what he was undertaking. He went on to tell her how the king asked him to take Lady Clara dancing, and that he thought it an excellent opportunity to introduce her to Braedan.

Jocelyn tamped the urge to smile when she heard this. She secretly was pleased that it wasn't his idea to dance with Lady Clara. They spoke a little more about Braedan's interest in Lady Angela, but she noticed that Blaine remained non-committal. Jocelyn stifled a yawn, smiling sheepishly at him.

"Come, my dear, the hour is late. I best get ye back to your bedchamber." He slipped on her shoes and helped her up. "I am sure Violet is wondering where ye are."

Jocelyn smiled at him as she wrapped her arms around his neck, pulling him closer to her. "I am sure she is asleep." She stood on her tiptoes, just inches from his face. "Now why don't ye kiss me?"

His lips came crashing down with a searing kiss leaving her breathless. She parted her lips so his tongue could explore her mouth, sending a wave of heat that coursed through her body. She loved the way he consumed her as if she were some forbidden fruit. He planted little kisses down the long column of her neck, then nuzzled between the soft mounds of her breasts. His tongue dipped, and his teeth nibbled her soft flesh.

She arched her back to give him better access. She wanted more and encouraged him with her gasps of delight. Before she realized it, his hands deftly unbuttoned the back of her gown, allowing it to slide down her arms to her waist.

Blaine reached into her corset, freeing her breast then he sensuously licked and suckled her nipple, intensifying the sensation.

"I must have ye," he said, his voice hoarse with passion. "Please do not deny me, my love. I dinna think I can bear it." He then released the other breast from its confines and continued with the same administrations making her body ache with need.

She should stop him, but something inside her wanted him as much as he wanted her. She threw caution to the wind and allowed her need for him to be her directive. "Aye, Blaine, I want ye too."

Blaine lifted his head and looked directly into her eyes, perhaps to assure himself that he heard correctly.

"I want this, and I am ready to give myself to ye."

Within seconds her dress and petticoats billowed to the floor. He lifted her over the pile of material. She giggled when he picked up her gown to lay it over the back of the settee; he really was thoughtful.

She glanced up to say something when she saw a look in his eyes that somewhat frightened and excited her at the same time. "Wait a moment, please."

She reached down and pick up the glass of whisky. She drank the whole contents in one gulp and immediately began to cough, her blue-gray eyes tearing up.

"Oh," she said. "Verra verra warm."

Shaking his head, he went over to the sideboard to pour her a glass of water. "Here, this will help."

With tears streaking down her face, she choked out her thanks. No sooner did she recover when she was back in his arms. He kissed her lips, her eyes, even the tip of her nose. She wondered at her willingness to trust him.

He carefully removed her necklace. "I believe ye like yer gift?"

Jocelyn nodded, watching him place it on the table. "Aye, I received many compliments." She eyed him. "Curious how so many knew the necklace came from ye." She shot him an accusatory look. "I wondered at yer invitation that Violet dine with us—now I think I understand."

"Ye are a clever lass," he admitted. "If ye want people to know anything, just tell a servant, and the information is sure to spread."

She laughed but stopped suddenly when he unlaced her corset and removed it.

"Better?"

She nodded, and he resumed kissing her, his hands running down her back and then up her sides to cup her breasts again. Her breasts were perfect, full and enticing.

He bent, taking one into his mouth when she stopped him. "Here, let me help ye with yer waistcoat."

Jocelyn surprised herself. Was she attempting to take control of the seduction? Her delicate fingers slowly unbuttoned the vest, sliding it off his wide shoulders. She unlaced the top of his shirt, kissing the exposed smooth patch of skin. Blaine was too impatient and pulled his shirt over his head, throwing the garment onto the floor.

Jocelyn gasped when she saw his bare chest, gloriously tan and rippling with muscles. Her hands explored every indentation and ridge, down to his flat stomach. She became mesmerized by his beauty and perfection. Her hands reached up to his large pectoral muscles, her fingers circling his flat copper nipples. She smiled when he inhaled sharply between his teeth.

Her exploration of him was driving him senseless, his arousal pressing hard against the fabric of his breeches. Her hands caressed his shoulders and then trailed down his arms, she heard him sigh with approval as they glided over his biceps and down to his forearms.

"Do ye like what ye see love?" he whispered.

"Aye, I like what I feel." She smiled, gazing up at him from beneath her lashes.

Her look completely undid him; it was beyond what any normal man could endure. He picked her up in his arms and carried her to his bed. By the light of a single taper.

He laid her down on his bed and then divested himself of his boots and breeches. Dressed still in his breeks, he lay down next to her and resumed his assault on her lips, neck, shoulders and breasts. Engulfed in a warm cloud of pervasive sensations she shuddered as it radiated through her body that left her core pooling with bold desires.

He caressed her silk-clad leg, reaching up to touch the soft, warm flesh above her stocking. When he reached the apex between her legs, she let out a soft yelp.

Regretfully he saw fear cloud her eyes. "Shhh love, we can take this slow."

Her body relaxed. He wanted Jocelyn to enjoy the experience. Holding her close to him, she trembled slightly in his arms. Rolling onto his back, he pulled her on top of him. Carefully, he unpinned her hair and reveled in its silky softness as he ran his fingers through its length. She lifted her face to look at him and gave him a reassuring smile. He continued to massage her head, neck and back, causing Joselyn to literally purr. He laughed softly and closed his eyes as his hands explored her body.

Pulling down her chemise to her waist, he massaged the length of her back. It amazed him by how well-toned she was—no doubt years of kneading dough had a beautiful effect on her body. He ran his hands down to cup her pert little derrière and wanted nothing more than to press her skin against his.

That was when he heard her purring sounding somewhat rhythmic. "Jocelyn?"

He repeated her name, and much to his dismay, she was fast asleep. Careful not to wake her, he pulled up her chemise and then rolled her on her side. She stirred a bit, pressing her adorable bottom up against his arousal. It leaped inside of its restraints, and it took a herculean effort for him not to release his manhood and bury it inside her sweet supple body.

He continued to stroke her, his fingers trailing along her side and over the curve of her hip. Her body was flawless and entirely feminine. As he held her, something happened deep inside his soul. He felt a burdening pain. Was it guilt for having put her in this absurd position? The fact that once they were free of the king's scrutiny, he would part ways with her? Or his desires to make her his leman?

Blaine closed his eyes, the heavy yoke of guilt becoming a burden. If it hadn't been for that throbbing member in his pants, he too would have drifted to sleep. After a while, the angry beast subsided, and he nuzzled closer to her, smelling the scent of heather in her hair. He fell into a peaceful sleep and dreamt of blue-gray eyes and honeyed lips.

~ * ~

Blaine awoke at the first sign of light. He nudged Jocelyn until she finally opened her eyes. She gave him the most delightful smile, wrapping her arms around his neck and kissing him full on the mouth. He kissed her soundly back. He needed to get her back to her room before she was missed.

Half asleep, she managed to dress and get her shoes back on but forego any attempts of putting on her corset. She giggled when she tried to button her gown.

"Here, let's leave it unbuttoned. This way ye will not need Violet's help."

She agreed as he handed her the necklace and fan. Jocelyn thought she should be worried that someone might see her leaving his room, but for some reason, she didn't care. Blaine opened his door to find the corridor empty. Seeming to forget something, he rushed back into his bedchamber and then was back at her side. Since he didn't say anything, she didn't remark, and they hurried to her bedchamber.

It was still early, and they reach her room without being seen. Jocelyn opened the door and slipped inside. Turning around, she leaned against the door frame gazing wistfully at him. Blaine bent down and kissed her softly on the lips.

"Sleep well, my love," he said and then kissed her again.

She was about to close the door when he motioned for her to wait. Reaching inside his pocket, he withdrew a small mound of hairpins. She smiled at his thoughtfulness. She whispered her thanks as she closed the door.

Back in his room, Blaine rid himself of all his clothes and dove under the still-warm covers. Lying on his back, he folded his arms behind his head. He had never cared for any lass as much as he did for Jocelyn. Nor did it bother him that he had not taken advantage of her.

Jocelyn was different. He only needed to resolve a few issues, and then he could settle back with her and work on building his icehouse. He just needed to find a way not to get married.

~ * ~

It had been five days since arriving at Edinburgh, and Blaine tired of court life. His spirits lifted when his usual ride with the king had been canceled because of rain. Finding himself free of any obligations, he went in search of Jocelyn. After not finding her in her room, Violet told him that she and Arrabella had decided to go to the library.

He was on his way when he saw Douglas John walking toward him. "Good morrow, brother, I am on my way to find Jocelyn and yer wife. Would ye care to join me?"

"We canna right now. Roderick asked me to fetch ye—says 'tis important."

Together they went to Roderick's quarters and found the red-headed knight furiously pacing.

He looked relieved when he saw them. "Thank ye for coming so quickly Blaine. I am afraid I have some bad news." He handed Blaine a letter. "I think 'tis best we find Braedan since this also concerns him. I was told he is with Angela at Holyrood Palace."

Blaine read the letter in disbelief. "We must leave immediately."

"I agree. I sent a messenger asking Angela to pack her things."

Blaine gave the letter to Douglas John.

"We must speak with the king. I have requested an audience," Roderick said. "I pray we will not wait long."

"I will accompany ye when ye speak with the king," Douglas John offered.

Blaine told him it wasn't necessary, but Rod countered, "We need the king's permission if ye want to leave court. The king will listen to yer brother."

Blaine tried to argue but if the king refused to let him leave, Douglas John would be his only hope.

~ * ~

Much to everyone's relief, Rod received a summons from the king. They watched in silence as he read the letter then threw it down in disgust.

"Walrick Graham has been a thorn in my side for far too long. 'Tis not the first grievance against him." He narrowed his eyes at Blaine and the others. "How can ye be certain that it is he who attacked yer solicitor?"

"I am not certain, but as ye know…" Roderick stopped when the king held his hand up.

"Blaine, ye say you sent Ascar MacKinnon to settle a debt for the MacAulays. You did not accompany him to make sure the deed was carried out?"

Blaine started to explain when he realized it was a rhetorical question.

"And now ye are telling me that once your solicitor settled the debt, the papers were stolen."

"Sire, he was ambushed by thieves not far from where Miss Jocelyn and her brother were attacked," he explained.

"And yet all they took were the documents?" Turning to Roderick, King Charles gave him a reproving look. "Clearly ye have an issue with thieves, Roderick, ye may want to send your guards out to better patrol your land." He did not sound pleased at all. "I understand yer concerns, Roderick, and ye have my permission to go. I assume ye will be taking Lady Angela with ye?"

Roderick nodded.

"'Tis a shame, I will be sorry to see her leave. She has been a delight."

The king swung around in Blaine's direction. "Why is it important for you to go? Surely Roderick and Mr. MacAulay can handle the matter."

"Sire, I have pledged to help the MacAulays. When I offered for Miss Jocelyn's hand, I agreed to pay the debt owed to Walrick Graham. I believe Ascar has something to incriminate Graham and prove that he is doing something nefarious…"

"Nefarious? Good God, must ye be so dramatic?" The king laughed.

Blaine gritted his teeth, trying his best to remain calm.

The king leveled his gaze. "See here, the man is a cad, and I would give anything to strip him of his title and holdings. I have had my fill of complaints. If ye need to go with Roderick, so be it, but I want ye back as soon as possible so we may have this wedding business concluded."

"Have ye made yer decision about my betrothal?" Blaine asked, hoping he didn't sound desperate.

"Let me ask you this," he leaned forward on his desk, "do you still plan to wed Miss MacAulay?"

Blaine looked straight into the king's eyes. "Aye yer grace, I do."

"Fine, then you will not oppose if I arrange for you to wed the lady before you leave." The king said matter of fact. "The ceremony can take place today."

Jocelyn would never agree. "Your grace, my brother would insist on being present at my wedding. He is my laird and clan chieftain. I doubt he would be willing to leave his wife's side."

"'Tis true, Sire," Douglas John said as the king continued to look skeptical. "Lady Ilyssa just gave birth to their first child."

Much to their surprise, he laughed. "I don't suppose your mother would agree, considering her proclivity for wanting all her family gathered for weddings."

His comment was directed to Douglas John, whose own wedding had been delayed because of missing family members.

"Aye and our sister, Miranda, is traveling abroad, so it will take time for a message to reach her," Douglas John said.

Blaine relaxed a bit, thankful they had averted this hasty wedding idea.

The king laughed again and sat back eyeing Blaine sarcastically. "You are clever, Blaine, 'tis one of the reasons I like you so much. Fine, we will wait, and when spring comes, ye will gather your kin and bring them here. But…you will wed Lady Clara."

At first, Blaine was not sure he heard correctly. "I canna marry Lady Clara; she is only a child."

He regretted his words when the king glowered at him.

"Be assured that Lady Clara *is* of age, and she offers your clan an alliance to one of the wealthiest and powerful clans. With their support, Caelan will no longer be bothered by the MacDonnells or even the MacLeods and their incessant feuding. Ye should consider yourself fortunate."

"And what about Miss Jocelyn?" Blaine asked, keeping his features stoic.

"I will let you continue with this farce. Go and be with the lady, and when she calls off your betrothal, you will return and marry Lady Clara," the king said. "But do compensate her well. I was impressed by her." He then added, "So, rid us of Graham, and then Miss MacAulay can find some country lad to settle down with."

Bowing to the king, Blaine left with Rod and Douglas John in tow. He was about to say something acerbic when a thought crossed his mind, and he smiled.

"For someone who has just been told he must wed someone not of his choosing, ye look pleased," Rod said.

"I have no intentions of wedding Lady Clara."

"The king did not grant ye permission to wed Lady Jocelyn," Rod quipped.

"Aye, but he didn't say I could *not* marry her."

Douglas John shook his head. "Are ye saying ye want to wed the lass?"

"Nay, I do not want to wed her, but I…" Blaine wasn't sure

how well his brother would receive the idea of Jocelyn becoming his mistress. "Let's just say I am relieved that I have till spring to find a solution to my predicament. In the meantime, I mean to see Walrick Graham removed from Jocelyn's life."

Chapter Eleven

Jocelyn positioned herself closer to the hearth. The library wasn't cold, but all morning she was chilled to the bone. Picking up her book, Jocelyn tried again to read. After adjusting her shawl for the second time, she realized she had read the same paragraph twice.

"Is there something troubling ye?" Arrabella peered over her book, giving her a friendly smile.

Jocelyn smiled back, shaking her head.

"Would ye prefer to converse?"

"Nay, I am all right, truly, I just will miss..." Jocelyn couldn't finish.

Aggie told her earlier that she and Blaine would be attending a small soiree for the newly trained soldiers. The following day Douglas John and Arrabella planned to leave for home.

"I will miss ye too," Lady Arrabella said perceptively. "Dinna be sad. Soon ye will wed Blaine, and then we will see much of each other. Are ye aware that Stonegate is only a few hours from Dunn Leigh Keep?"

Jocelyn's eyes brimmed with tears.

"We will see each other often, I promise. Our children will grow up together," Arrabella assured again.

She felt horrible. Arrabella was a kind and honest woman. What would her opinion be if she knew the truth? A single tear slipped down her cheek.

"Oh, Jocelyn." Arrabella got up to wrap her arms around her shoulders. She reached inside the pocket of her gown and handed her a handkerchief. "Now, now, there's no need for tears."

"Tears? Who's in tears?" Startled by a booming voice, Jocelyn looked up to see Blaine and Douglas John standing behind them.

Blaine walked around to kneel before her. Taking her hand in his, he kissed the back of it. "I will not see ye upset, my lady. Pray tell, what has happened to distress ye so?"

Jocelyn shook her head and smiled at him. "Nay, 'tis nothing. I was just saying to Lady Arrabella that I will miss her when they leave tomorrow."

"Well, ye will not have time to miss her since we are leaving too," Blain announced. "We received word from Ascar, and we must return home as soon as possible."

"Was he successful? Did he manage to get my land back?" Jocelyn said, not caring who might be listening.

"We can discuss this later, my dear. In the meantime, I am starving. The midday meal is being served—care to join me?" He offered his arm, which she gladly accepted. "Are ye coming?" he asked Douglas John over his shoulder.

~ * ~

Jocelyn sat before the mirror while Violet put the finishing touches on her hair. Lost in thought, Jocelyn tried to make sense of what Blaine told her earlier. Ascar had been successful in settling their debt with Graham.

However, he became wary when Graham couldn't provide the documents ascertaining the legitimacy of the investments, he claimed to have purchased on behalf of their father.

Ascar was satisfied that the initial debt had been signed and settled. Soon after leaving Castle Mugdock, Ascar was accosted, and the documents taken. Jocelyn knitted her brows. Something didn't make sense. Why would thieves be after the contents inside of a satchel, unless…

"Did ye say ye be wearing the dark blue gown, miss?"

It took Jocelyn a moment to answer. Nodding, she sent Violet to fetch the navy-blue gown she was first given. Jocelyn thought it would go nicely with her sapphire necklace.

She was just slipping on her shoes when she heard a knock. It was Blaine right on time to escort her to the evening soiree. Striding into her quarters, he looked handsome in dark gray breeches, with a silver waistcoat and a matching gray quilted jacket.

His long hair hung loose, sans the queue he usually wore to formal occasions. This suggested the evening would be a casual affair.

Jocelyn thought about what had happened the night of the ball and wondered if tonight would end the same way. If so, she was determined not to fall asleep.

"Ye look beautiful, my dear." Blaine's eyes narrowed seductively. "Are ye ready for tonight?"

She smiled, perceptive of what his words suggested. "Aye, I am most eager.

~ * ~

The crowd was much smaller, but it took no time for the room to turn stiflingly hot. Jocelyn and Blaine joined Arrabella who was standing next to her brother, Colin. Jocelyn noticed again how handsome he was, with his light silver-gray eyes. They were most unusual and attractive.

Once the dancing commenced, he was claimed by Sir Reginald's daughter, Lady Cecilia, and not seen for the rest of the evening.

After dancing the waltz with Blaine and a reel with Douglas John, Jocelyn suggested to Arrabella they find the retiring room, so they could freshen up.

"I must say 'tis a wonderful party, but I for one am looking forward to going home," Arrabella said.

Jocelyn agreed. "I am not accustomed to court life, although I have enjoyed myself."

Enjoyed was an understatement, more like relished it. Blaine was especially attentive to her and sought her for every dance. He also introduced her to his friends who had just arrived at court. Jocelyn was spoiled by his attention. She planned to enjoy every minute.

"I don't suppose ye noticed that yer brother is quite taken by Lady Angela," Arrabella said out of the blue. "They are always in each other's company."

Jocelyn raised her brows. "Aye, I noticed."

"I don't suppose he plans to offer for her?"

"He would be a fortunate man if she accepted," Jocelyn said. When they returned to the ball, neither of them was able to find Blaine or Douglas John.

"I see Sir Roderick and the Fergusons."

Jocelyn looked to where Arrabella was pointing. Spotting Roderick's fiery red hair they made their way through the crowd. As they approached the group, Jocelyn noticed a woman standing in the middle.

She recognized her immediately. Dressed in a lavender silk gown and dripping in diamonds was none other than Lady Charlotte Wickstrom.

Lady Charlotte turned, sensing their approach. "My word, if my eyes don't deceive me." She gasped in mock surprise. "I heard you were at court, and quite frankly I couldn't begin to imagine why—but there you are, Miss MacAulay." The woman perused her from top to bottom, pausing to gaze at the sapphire necklace around her neck.

Jocelyn straightened her back and looked directly into the woman's eyes. "Good evening Mrs. Wickstrom, what a pleasant surprise," she said politely.

"I must say the pleasure is all yours," Charlotte responded sweetly, but the insult was not lost. "What brings you to court, Lady

Arrabella?" She turned toward Arrabella so her back was to Jocelyn.

"I came to see my brother before he leaves for Fort Williams." Arrabella adjusted her position forcing Lady Charlotte to face them both. "And, of course, to celebrate Blaine's betrothal to Lady Jocelyn."

Lady Charlotte's expression turned sour at the mention of Blaine's betrothal. "What nonsense; the man will never wed. He is just buying time till all this nasty business with the MacDonnells is put to rest. Soon he will be charming the drawers off every lass in Scotland."

"Really Lady Charlotte, I don't think ye need to be so prickly." Arrabella lowered her voice to say, "Ye can set aside yer displeasure for once and wish the happy couple the best."

"Well, I don't wish them the best," Lady Charlotte snapped.

"That's in poor taste, Charlotte." Arrabella's voice was laced with anger. She started to further reprimand the woman when Jocelyn stopped her.

"No need to intercede for me, Lady Arrabella." Jocelyn smiled. "Not everyone has received the news of our betrothal well. 'Tis no surprise either."

Lady Charlotte's face grew pinched and red with anger. "What is that supposed to mean?" she snarled.

"All I am saying, Mrs. Wickstrom, is that ye are of the same opinion of most of Blaine's castoffs." With that Jocelyn curtseyed and left.

Lady Charlotte was not about to let the matter go and ran after her, grabbing her arm and pulling her so close Jocelyn choked from her cloying perfume.

"Perhaps you should be told the real reason Blaine is marrying you." Lady Charlotte was seething. "Seems he tupped some laird's wife and even after paying the man restitution, he still has to marry or the MacDonnells will bring a feud to the MacKinnon shores. So, you see, little miss, your purpose is solely for convenience."

Jocelyn tore her arm from Charlotte's grasp and calmly adjusted the sleeve of her gown. "Nay, Mrs. Wickstrom. If Blaine were marrying someone out of convenience, he would have proposed to you."

Lady Charlotte's eyes glittered with hatred. She lifted her hand as if to strike. "Why you little…"

A hand reached out to grasp hers. "I suggest ye gain control of yerself, Charlotte."

She and Lady Charlotte startled at the sound of Blaine's voice.

"That is my fiancée ye are attempting to strike, and, if you think I will tolerate your rudeness, then ye are mistaken."

Lady Charlotte looked as if she were about to burst into tears. Wrenching her hand out of his, she spun on her heel and stormed out of the ballroom. Unfortunately, the exchange between the women was witnessed by many. Blaine took Jocelyn's arm and guided her toward the dance floor.

Arrabella ran up to the couple. "What happened? I didn't realize that Charlotte went after ye until it was too late."

"Don't worry, Arrabella, our Jocelyn here handled herself quite well." Blaine smiled at her. "Ye are a little tigress when someone ruffles yer feathers,"

Jocelyn assured Arrabella that she was fine but declined Blaine's invitation to dance. The altercation had left her unsettled. As a matter of fact, learning that Blaine's need to marry involved another man's wife was more than she could tolerate.

Wanting to get away and think, she made an excuse of needing some air. But once she left the ballroom, she ran straight to her bedchamber.

When Jocelyn entered her room, she was relieved to see that Violet was still out. She paced for a while before throwing herself into the chaise lounge near the dying fire. Her mind whirled with the words that spewed from Lady Charlotte lips, like venom from an asp. She knew that the woman spoke the truth.

Closing her eyes, she wracked her memory, trying to remember the conversation with Rod and the reason for Blaine's plight. Why was she under the impression that it was his brother, Caelan, who was pushing the issue of marriage? Wasn't there something about having to meet his obligations and providing an heir?

Trying to suppress a headache that was starting behind her eyes, she pinched the bridge of her nose. The more she thought about it, the more she realized the futility of hoping that somehow, someway, she could have a future with Blaine.

Staring into the dying embers, she took deep breaths forcing herself to relax. Just as she closed her eyes, she heard a knock at the door. *Oh, good heavens.* Knowing full well who it was, she thought to keep silent in hopes he might go away. Then he knocked again.

"Jocelyn, please let me in."

~ * ~

Blaine was doing his best to sound calm even though he was brimming with anger. He believed Jocelyn handled the encounter with Lady Charlotte very well. That was until she left to 'get a breath of air' and didn't return. When he went in search for her, he found Charlotte instead.

"You have made a fool of yourself, Blaine, and shamed your clan," Charlotte spewed at him. "I have heard you are to wed Lady Clara, and yet you dangle that urchin on your arm expecting us all to play along. Well, I don't believe you have any intention of actually marrying her."

"Whether ye do matters naught, Charlotte," he said. His tone void of any emotion. "I do not seek yer opinion nor yer approval. The fact is, I have every intention of wedding Jocelyn."

"Don't play me for a fool," Lady Charlotte shouted at him. "I know you. I know who you are, and no one will convince me otherwise. You will never wed that country mouse. Why are you lying to yourself and to me?"

He was entirely unprepared for what happened next. Before he could move away, she was in his arms, her arms wrapped around his neck like a vise. She pressed herself up against him and kissed him hard on the mouth.

It took more effort than he expected to extricate himself from her clutch. Pulling away, he unconsciously wiped her kiss with the back of his hand.

That small gesture tore at her, and she burst into tears. "I can't believe you would treat me so callously after all we have meant to each other. I knew one day you would wed, but once you met your obligations, we would still have each other," she sobbed.

He looked at the woman, her face contorted in resentment and could not find an ounce of sympathy. Charlotte Wickstrom was and has always been a selfish, power-hungry woman who used people. He had turned a blind eye to her treatment of those less fortunate, stepping on them when they got in her way. No, she had climbed every social ladder on the backs of those she used and abused, relying on her beauty and family name, to achieve status.

"I have no desires to continue a relationship with ye, Charlotte, now or ever," he said and turned to go back to the ball. "And one more thing," he narrowed his eyes, "if ye ever speak to my betrothed in the same manner as ye did tonight, I will personally drag ye by yer hair and throw ye back to England."

Now, standing on the other side of the door, Blaine wanted nothing more than to take Jocelyn into his arms and kiss her senseless until she forgot about Charlotte. He was about to knock again when the door opened.

Without hesitation, he slipped inside and closed the door quickly. When he reached for her, she spun away and casually walked to the other side of the room. He half expected Jocelyn to be tearful, but he did not imagine she would respond in anger. Staring into her blue-gray eyes, his heart ached when he saw that distrust had returned.

"Why didn't ye tell anyone ye were retiring for the evening. I would have been happy to escort ye," Blaine said, immediately regretting the irritation in his voice.

"I said I needed a breath of..." She stopped as he clenched his jaw.

"Whatever Lady Charlotte said to upset ye, she will make amends. If it's an apology ye want, then—"

"I want nothing from that woman. I have endured enough of her virulence to warrant never having to see her again."

"What did she say to ye then? Why are ye so distraught? I can assure ye she spoke falsely just to hurt you...to hurt us."

Jocelyn shook her head. "Don't blame her for what is wrong with us." She turned her back to stare at the embers, blinking rapidly to keep from crying.

"What did she say?"

"Nothing of importance, just a minor detail ye neglected to tell me."

"About what?"

"The true reason why ye must wed." She spun around to look him square in the eyes.

"Enlighten me."

"Seems ye offended an entire clan by yer dalliance with a man's wife." She sounded smug. "So, to keep them from warring on your kin, ye must wed."

"It was a misunderstanding," he gritted out.

She stared at him for a moment before laughing ironically. "Of course, it was. The virtuous Blaine MacKinnon to commit an offense a purpose?" She moved up to stand before him. "What is it said about ye? He doth not take what is not freely given? I suppose the lady in question omitted the fact that she was married?"

"Aye, 'tis exactly what happened."

"Who takes a woman to bed without knowing about her? How is it that something so important was kept from ye?" Her eyes were cold as slate. "Did ye think to ask?"

He was about to answer when the door opened and in walked Violet.

"Oh," was all she said as she eyed the two. "Forgive me, my lord, I dinna realized ye were back."

"'Tis fine Violet." Blaine forced a smile. "My fiancée is tired, and since we depart early tomorrow, I thought it best she gets some rest. I was just keeping her company until ye returned." With that, he leaned over to brush a small kiss on Jocelyn's forehead. "Sleep well, my dear."

He left, not bothering to look back. He walked down the corridor toward his room but stopped short. What he really wanted was a drink, so he went in search of his brother.

Chapter Twelve

Lady Arrabella and Jocelyn hugged each other goodbye. Jocelyn felt terrible when Arrabella insisted she stay in touch and keep her abreast of her wedding plans. Jocelyn promised and climbed into the waiting carriage with a heavy heart.

Her sadness waned some when she realized Braedan, Violet and now Lady Angela would be her traveling companions. She was thrilled for her brother to have the opportunity to spend the next three days in Lady Angela's company. Within the first hour, it was apparent how well the young couple got along. Their conversations flowed, and at times the light bantering between them kept them entertained.

Blaine did his best to be pleasant. Whenever they stopped to rest the horses, Jocelyn could feel his eyes upon her. In the evenings he played the attentive fiancé so effortlessly, it was easy to forget her anger. Soon she was enjoying his attention. Yes, he had deceived her, but slowly her anger dissipated.

Try as she might, she tried to focus on the real reason for their return to Castle Ballindalloch. The attack on Ascar had complicated matters and left the poor man injured. However, when they finally reached their destination, she could not deny her disappointment that her time with Blaine was nearly over.

"How is Ascar?" Roderick asked Mrs. Westershire when she greeted them.

"Recovering well, and he is most anxious to speak with ye..." Mrs. Westershire stopped when Lady Angela climbed out of the carriage. "Oh, praise the Saints, my wee bairn is home." She ran and threw her arms around the lass.

Angela laughed, assuring her that it hadn't been that long.

"Ye were with yer brother for a month, then to court. I swear ye have grown taller in yer absence."

Lady Angela hugged the older woman. "I haven't grown in two years."

Laughing, Mrs. Westershire ushered the group to the main salon where servants were ready to take their cloaks and provide them with refreshments. Although the rain had held off, it was still frigid.

Violet's sisters were very excited to see her return. Mrs.

Westershire gave her the evening off. "I will personally see to Lady Angela and Lady Jocelyn. I am sure ye have much to share."

Jocelyn was not given much of an opportunity to rest before Braedan was knocking at her door. Apparently, Ascar wanted to speak to them immediately. When they arrived at Ascar's bedchamber, Rod and Blaine were already there. Aside from the bandage around his head, the other man appeared fine.

Propped up on his bed with a score of pillows, he bade them enter. Jocelyn forgot what a large man he was. It wasn't until she drew closer, did she notice his pallor and the dark circles under his eyes.

"Oh, dear me," she exclaimed. "I am so sorry ye were injured, Ascar."

Ascar smiled and motioned for her to sit. "Nay, Miss Jocelyn, 'tis nothing…only a wee scratch."

She was not convinced when she saw that both his arms were bandaged.

"I am most anxious to speak with ye," he blurted out. "Asides from Northern Star Shipping company, what other ventures did Graham invest in with your father?"

She looked at Braedan then both shook their heads.

"Graham claims there were five ventures in all."

Rod and Blaine, who were standing on the other side of the bed, looked concerned.

"Ascar, ye are getting ahead of yerself. Why don't ye start from the beginning," Rod suggested.

Ascar nodded. "As ye directed, I went to Heatherwood. Yer housekeeper, Miss Heddy, aided me in locating your father's paperwork and schedule of payments. I was able to ascertain the outstanding balance owed to Graham." He paused, taking a breath then said, "I decided it would be best to send for my secretary, Malcolm, so he could record and witness any transactions. We've had the misfortune of doing business with the man in the past and he canna be trusted. No sooner did Malcolm arrive, we left for Castle Mugdock. At first, Graham refused to see us but changed his mind when I said I was there on behalf of Lady Jocelyn." Ascar winced. "He was not pleased that I came to settle yer family's debt and demanded information on how ye came by so much money. His lack of hospitality goes without saying. Still, when I told him of your betrothal to Sir Blaine, Graham became enraged. He claimed to be betrothed to ye and that Braedan agreed to the marriage."

"That's a lie," Braedan snapped. "I told that swine I would never accept his offer."

"Please Braedan, don't fash yerself." Roderick put his hand on the younger man's shoulder. "We all agree he is a two-headed asp."

Ascar smiled sympathetically. "I told him he only needed to provide me with the betrothal contract, and I would be on my way. Naturally, he couldn't. I presented him with a written contract settling the outstanding accounts. I also proposed that he sell back two of the four parcels your father used as collateral." He paused to take a sip of water. "I am afraid that the news of your pending marriage had an adverse effect on the man. He delighted in showing me four more business contracts your father invested in and the outstanding loans associated with them. I questioned their validity, considering there were no such documents amongst your father's things. Graham assured me they were valid and that your father signed them."

"Do you believe he might have forged my father's signature?" Jocelyn asked.

"I am not certain. Once we agreed upon the amount owed, I insisted on keeping the contracts. Graham offered to give me a receipt, but I refused." He considered Braedan. "'Tis usual business practice that all investors receive copies of the contract once they are signed. For those copies to be missing concerned me."

"So ye believe Graham swindled Jocelyn's father," Blaine surmised. "I assume those were the documents that were stolen?"

Ascar nodded. "I don't understand,"

Jocelyn looked at Blaine then at Ascar. "Sir Blaine gave me a sovereign, and surely the debt was substantially less."

"Aye, and he offered to pay ye the difference, but I insisted on a bank draft," Ascar said. "I was not about to traipse through the countryside with that much coin and not be heavily guarded."

"'Twas good thinking," Braedan said.

"I want to take another look at your ledgers and the original Northern Star contract."

"Wait, I thought ye said the documents were taken?" Blaine commented.

"I assumed there was only the one venture, Northern Star, and Graham would have his copy. I did not take the original document."

"So ye are saying we are still in possession of the original contract?" Jocelyn smiled for the first time.

"Aye, 'tis my belief the contract holds the answers we seek." Ascar closed his eyes for a moment. "I also wrote down the names of the other four businesses your father supposedly invested in. Fortunately, I was able to study the documents carefully before they were taken.

"That will be enough for today." Everyone turned to see Mrs. Westershire standing at the door. "'Tis time for Ascar to rest."

Everyone stood to leave.

"As soon as I am fit, I would like to return to Heatherwood," Ascar said.

"When ye are healed, ye can go, but not until I say so," Mrs. Westershire said as she shooed them out the door.

Roderick suggested they meet in his study once everyone had a chance to rest. An hour later, Jocelyn received a message to meet. Happy to see everyone gathered she graciously accepted the glass of wine Blaine offered her.

"Good, now that ye are here, I have some information I think ye will find interesting," Roderick said as each took a seat. "Ascar was on his way back to Heatherwood when he and Malcolm were attacked."

"Aye, and when I asked him what happened, he said five men encircled them and without provocation drew their swords. Once they had the satchel they left," Blaine said.

"Lady Jocelyn, ye were attacked by six men," Roderick continued, "in which Blaine dispatched one of them."

"Ye think they are the same men who attacked us?" Braedan asked.

"Well it may be a coincidence, but I suspect they are. There's another detail I find interesting. Graham did not possess a copy of the Northern Star contract. Why is that?"

Blaine raised a brow. "I must say, the name of the shipping company sounds familiar to me. I would need to look at my ledgers. A ship from Northern Star may have berthed at Stonegate."

"Or perhaps ye did business with them?" Braedan asked.

"But it could have been years ago," Jocelyn added.

"Aye, but I keep a record of every ship that comes into my harbor. Also, my brother Caelan has ships that transport his goods from the Isle of Skye to the mainland. He may have information."

"It might be a good idea for ye to return to Stonegate," Roderick suggested. "I would be more than happy to accompany ye."

Jocelyn was struck by a sense of sadness at the thought of being parted from Blaine. Even if it was for her benefit.

"There's much to be planned in the next few days," Rod said. "In the meantime, I suggest we all retire to the dining room. It's my understanding that Dinah has prepared a lovely meal to welcome my sister home."

Jocelyn accepted Blaine's arm as he escorted her to dinner. At least it would be a few days before Ascar would be able to travel. She intended to enjoy the time she had left with Blaine.

~ * ~

Jocelyn awoke as the first faint rays of light illuminated her bedchamber. Dressing quickly, she headed downstairs and straight into the kitchen. She couldn't help giggling at the look on Dinah and James's faces at her sudden appearance.

"My lady, I am afraid we do not have anything prepared yet," James stammered, looking around to see what he could offer her.

Jocelyn smiled brightly at Dinah as she took the mixing bowls from her arms.

"If ye care to return to yer bedchamber, I be 'appy to 'ave a tray brought up," Dinah offered.

"No need Dinah, I am here to help ye this morn." Jocelyn placed the bowls on the long table and helped herself to one of the aprons hanging on a peg. "Oh, I hope ye don't mind," she said as she perused the shelf of spices.

James broke into a huge grin and left to retrieve the bag of flour from the larder. Within minutes she and the others were happily chatting and swapping stories. James and Dinah marveled at Jocelyn's epicurean talents. This was precisely what she needed, to lose herself in her baking, to feel the fine grit of the flour and the earthy scent of rising yeast. When she immersed herself in her baking, life stopped for a spell, worries were set aside, and she felt happy and alive.

Jocelyn was seated amongst the servants when she spied Blaine standing at the opening to the kitchen, his mouth opened in disbelief. Trying to appear as if she hadn't seen him, she self-consciously used her apron to wipe her hands, face and even the tail end of her braid. Jocelyn chewed on a warm piece of bread as she regarded the pastries, pies, bread and assorted buns, cooling on every surface.

"'Tis like 'eaven in mi mouth," exclaimed one lass as she devoured a morning bun.

"I ne'er tasted better," said a second.

"Och, nay let yer mum 'ear ye sae that." Dinah laughed. After she removed a tray of assorted cross buns out of the oven, the group collectively took in a deep breath.

"Ye need to teach me," James exclaimed. "I fear I may lose my position if I canna replicate it."

"Ye best wed Sir Roderick, dearie," Dinah said to Jocelyn, "for ye can never leave."

Jocelyn tilted her head back and laughed heartily. It was good to be amongst those who appreciated her and the simple ways of life. She suddenly became filled with a deep longing for home.

Blaine's deep voice caught their attention. "If ye think I will allow ye to keep my betrothed ye are sadly mistaken." He winked at them.

Jocelyn's cheeks heated at being caught looking so disheveled. Blaine walked over and lifted her dusty hand to his lips. His eyes smoldered, turning the green into dark emeralds. All gazes were upon her as they smiled.

"Now if ye would please excuse us, I would like to spend some time with my betrothed. Ye have had her long enough, 'tis my turn." He helped her to his feet and spun her around to untie her apron.

Jocelyn's heart sputtered.

"I was thinking of going for a ride," he said as they walked out.

"I am not much of a rider," she answered truthfully.

"I will find ye a gentle mount."

"'Tis supposed to rain."

"We will return before it does."

"I am a mess," she said teasingly.

"Then I will wait for ye." The words came out like a caress.

There was no point in arguing. "I will return momentarily."

As promised, she was back in less than a quarter-hour. Blaine asked why she did not carry the cloak he had given her. Seeing his disapproval, she explained, "'Tis too grand to take riding. I borrowed this one from Violet."

"Very well, but I believe the cloak I gave ye will be warmer."

"Aye, 'tis true." She looked up at him through her lashes. "Ye will just need to keep me warm." There was nothing lost by her meaning, and he smiled roguishly.

As soon as they stepped foot outside, the first drops of rain hit her head. By the time they reached the stables, they had to run to avoid getting drenched. Looking around, they saw that the stable boys had left. "They must have left to break their fast," she surmised.

"I will return momentarily." Blaine disappeared into the tack room and returned with two large blankets. "This way, my lady."

Taking hold of her hand, he led them up a ramp to the loft above. At the top, he took one of the blankets and laid it over a pile of hay. Motioning for her to sit, he plopped down next to her and covered their legs with the second blanket. The blankets were clean and provided substantial warmth. To her delight, Blaine produced a small bundle from inside his cloak. Wrapped in cloth were the biscuits, bread and sweet rolls she had baked earlier.

Although she wasn't hungry, she accepted the half he offered.

"Ye have quite the talent, my dear." He took a bite and closed his eyes.

"'Tis something I enjoy."

"Ye forget, I am but a simple fisherman." He laughed when she scrunched up her face. "'Tis true, my life at home is much the same as yers. We rise up early with the sun and return once our nets are filled."

She shook her head. "Ye are a laird and knighted. Ye are well known in court and favored by the king. Ye are anything but simple."

He shrugged. "Stonegate is a modest tower house, and I have only a few servants. Those who live in the village hail from various clans. They have sworn fealty under the MacKinnon banner and made the port their home. The king invested in my fleet a year ago, and since then, we have more than doubled our productivity. 'Tis gotten to the point we need to find a way to preserve our fish, so they don't spoil before we can get them to market."

"Do ye not salt the fish to preserve them?" she asked.

"Aye, but I would like to extend my distribution and be able to sell them fresh. Therefore, I am building an ice house."

Jocelyn smiled. Blaine went on to explain how he saw ice houses when abroad in Italy and how the Italians could preserve fish for days.

"To assure my ice house works just as well, I used the same material. The type of stone is hard, yet easy to cut." He described how ice houses varied in design depending on the builder. Most were conical and rounded at the bottom to hold the ice. He paused, "I apologize, my lady, I don't mean to bore ye."

"Nay Blaine, I find it fascinating," she said. "I would very much like to see this ice house."

Blaine looked deep into her eyes. After a few moments when neither said a word, he gave her a seductive smile that drove straight into her heart. "There is no pretense, Jocelyn. I am very attracted to ye, and I desire ye above all else."

Even as she desperately wanted to believe him, her common sense warned her. Blaine was nothing more than a smooth-talking rake. She started to say something when he lifted her chin.

"Hold," he whispered and then leaned over to lick a drop of currant from her bottom lip. He left her breathless. He then kissed one corner of her mouth and then on the other side. "I canna express to ye how much I adore doing that."

She could only nod. She was captivated by the moment.

"I want to show ye how much."

Before she could reply, he leaned in slowly, inch by inch, keeping his eyes open until just before their lips touched. He caressed her lips with his own, and he released a sensuous groan deep in this throat. He continued kissing her, leaning her backward until she lay beneath him.

Soon he was kissing her with such urgency she couldn't help but gasp. This gave him access to her open mouth which he took advantage of, licking and stroking her tongue with his. He tasted sweet as honey.

He then positioned himself until he lay between her legs, he ground his groin against her, showing how much he desired her. She did not retreat, as a matter of fact, her hands grasp his shapely buttocks and pull him harder against her. If her gown had allowed, she would have wrapped her legs around him.

Jocelyn gave him all her passion, an unspoken language that he knew well. Her body betrayed her rational thinking and responded with total carnal lust. She wanted this man, mind, body and soul.

He left her lips to trail little nibbles down her neck. His hand cupped her breast over her gown, and her nipple hardened beneath his hand. "I must have ye, Jocelyn…tonight please." She groaned something into his mouth when his lips took possession of hers. "Let me love ye, give me the gift of being mine." Throwing all cares to the wind she nodded. "I will cherish ye with my body; I will awaken the light in your soul. Ye will know the song of my staff…" Blaine paused when she trembled beneath him. He looked down and saw that she was biting her lips…biting to keep from laughing. Arching his body up, he raised a brow. "Do ye finding something amusing, my dear?"

Jocelyn could hear the hurt in his voice. "Nay, please, my lord. I just, I…" She couldn't continue, sealing her lips together.

"Jocelyn, I am trying to express my feelings for ye."

"Nay Blaine, ye are trying too hard," she said when she gained some control. "I will know the song of yer staff?"

She giggled again even though he looked a bit peeved, but then he too smiled. Within seconds they were both laughing. Voices could be heard beneath them; Jocelyn realized the stable lads were back from their morning meal.

She liked laying in the sweet-smelling hay while a storm blew outside. The heat of Blaine's body still clung to her as he helped her up.

Before releasing her, he pulled her to him for another searing kiss. "Until tonight, *mo cheach*."

~ * ~

Blaine and Jocelyn ran to the castle, arriving with their cloaks dripping wet. She was thankful the rain offered a good excuse for her ruffled appearance. He started to say something when they saw

Braedan storming out of Roderick's study.

"Good, ye are dressed," Braedan said when he saw her. "Go upstairs and gather your things. We are leaving." He nodded curtly at Blaine and headed out into the storm.

Jocelyn looked at Blaine curiously. What could have happened to upset Braedan? She had never seen her amiable brother so angry. His gray eyes were like steel when he looked at her.

"Go on upstairs, love," Blaine said. "I will find out what has happened."

She thanked him and hurried along. No sooner did she open the door to her bedchamber when she saw Lady Angela.

"Oh, Lady Jocelyn, ye must help us." The young woman ran and threw herself into her arms. She was distraught.

Jocelyn couldn't understand what she was saying. "Please, Lady Angela, everything will be all right," she tried to soothe the poor girl. Reaching into her pocket, she pressed a clean handkerchief into her hand. Angela hiccupped, then managed to calm down a bit. "Please tell me what has ye so upset?"

Angela took a deep breath, wiping the tears that ran down her smooth cheeks. "We must find Blaine. He...he must speak to my brother. Roddy was so angry."

"'Tis all right. Blaine is with him now. Tell me what happened?"

"'Tis yer brother, my lady, 'tis Braedan." She looked at Jocelyn, worry etched on her face. She wiped her eyes again and blew her red nose. "I have enjoyed your brother's company these past few days, and I find that I have grown quite fond of him. Imagine my surprise when Braedan told me last night that he returned my affection."

Jocelyn would have been thrilled but something did not bode well. "I am pleased to hear. I do believe ye are well suited."

"Aye, I believed so too, but I knew for certain when he kissed me last night. I have never known anything like it before." She blushed as Jocelyn took her hand. "Rod received a message from my parents. They will arrive any day, and they plan to stay a week before continuing to court. They want me to join them for the new year." Tears welled in her eyes. "I can't bear the thought of spending another month at court. I thought if I were already engaged, I would not have to return."

"Did my brother offer for ye?" She was surprised things had progressed so swiftly.

"Aye, and I accepted. Braedan is most considerate. He said he would insist on a long engagement, to give us a chance to become better acquainted with one another. He also wants to make sure he regains his lands and restores Heatherwood. 'Tis not necessary to wait. With my dowry alone, we can buy back his land. If not, we could simply buy another home. I receive a sizable monthly stipend from my grandmother. Braedan is determined to support us when we wed. He cares nothing for my money. But that's not what my brother believes. He said terrible things."

"Wait, why would ye speak to Sir Roderick?"

"Braedan must ask my father for my hand, but I fear he will refuse him. They have rather high expectations for me. They might not give Braedan a chance to prove himself. So together we went to speak to Roddy. We asked if he would talk to his father…to convince him of Braedan's worth. He…he…yelled and…"

"It's all right Angela, Blaine is with yer brother now. He will put things to right." Jocelyn put her arms around her and prayed she spoke the truth.

~ * ~

Blaine walked into Rod's study to find the man standing next to the hearth, a glass of whisky in his hand.

"'Tis a bit early to be drinking. Dinna ye think?" Blaine said but went to the sideboard to pour his own.

"I am in no mind to talk, Blaine." Rod ran his fingers through his fiery hair. Before Blaine could respond, he started to vent. "Can't believe the imp would offer for her? My sister? She is meant for a laird. A wife to a powerful chieftain, someone like yer brother or…even you." He pointed his finger at him. "Not some country whelp with no land nor coin."

It didn't take long for Blaine to figure out what happened. "Ye liked him well enough when ye brought him to court and threw him in with yer cronies," he retorted.

"Aye, I did, and I took him under my wing and showed him the…erm, the finer things court had to offer. I am willing to help him with Graham but this…this?" he sputtered. "How does he repay me? By trying to seduce my sister. The interloper."

"Rod, I wish ye would consider Angela's happiness." Seeing the murderous look on Rod's face, there was no use in continuing the conversation. Instead, Blaine left the study as swiftly as possible but not before he heard the distinct sound of breaking glass.

He needed to speak to Jocelyn and to find a way of postponing her departure. Knocking on her bedchamber door, he entered to see Angela in Jocelyn's arms.

"Oh, Blaine. Oh, praise the Saints, ye have come," she cried when she saw him. "Please tell me ye have set things right with my brother and I can wed the man I love."

He was at a loss for words for a moment then he said, "Come along, lass, let us go to yer bedchamber. I will have Mrs. Westershire attend ye."

Angela wrapped her arms around his waist, hugging him firmly and then stood up on her tiptoes to brush a kiss on his cheek.

Sniffling, she thanked Jocelyn, then handed her back her handkerchief and left with Blaine.

He was glad to see Mrs. Westershire waiting for Angela when he escorted her to her bedchamber. Apparently, the staff was aware of what transpired between Rod and Braedan. Blaine went back to Jocelyn's room to find her pacing. She ran right into his arms.

He stroked her back and whispered soothing words until she relaxed. "Ye need not be so upset, matters will work themselves right. Roderick is still determined to help ye with Graham—that has not changed."

"But what about Braedan and Angela? Did ye to speak to Sir Roderick? Is he willing to support them?"

Blaine took a deep breath. "I know Rod well, and he is most protective of his sister. I think 'tis best we set aside this matter between yer brother and Angela and focus on what's more important—finding proof that Graham swindled yer father." She stiffened in his arms. That wasn't a good sign.

She pushed him away, walking to the other side of the room. "Ye did not convince Sir Roderick to support my brother? Ye will not help them?" Her eyes filled with disappointment.

Walking toward her again, he hoped to make her understand. "Rod was incensed. He refused to listen to anything I had to say." He stopped to take both her hands in his. "I canna interfere right now."

"Cannot…or will not." She tore her hands free. "We had an agreement, Blaine. Ye promised to help Braedan find a suitable heiress. Ye have done that, and what 'tis more remarkable she esteems my brother. She fancies herself in love."

Her accusation did not sit well with him, and unfortunately, he let his anger guide his words. "I have done all that ye asked of me, Jocelyn. I took yer brother to court, introduced him to society and championed him. However, this is different. Rod is family, and I have respect for his opinions and his wishes. I did not guarantee a match or marriage."

"Nor would I ask it of ye." Blaine was stunned to see Braedan standing in the doorway. "The carriage is waiting, Jocelyn."

Blaine felt sorry for him. "There's no need to rush off, Braedan. 'Tis raining hard, and ye can wait till it lets up a wee bit. Let's sit down and talk."

"Thank ye, my lord, but 'tis time my sister and I left. Laird MacPherson has extended his hospitality long enough." Braedan went over to where Jocelyn's trunk lay open and muttered something about helping her pack. "If ye will excuse us, my lord, we are somewhat in a hurry."

Blaine stared at her, hoping she would agree to delay their departure.

Instead she said, "I thank ye, my lord, for all your help. Now, if ye will excuse me."

A half-hour later, he watched her climb into the waiting carriage as she politely bid him goodbye and, just like that, Jocelyn was gone.

Chapter Thirteen

It had been four days since Jocelyn left. The rain never let up, and the cold turned bitter. Blaine suspected the roads would be laden with snow, making it difficult to return to his home. With Rod confined to his study, refusing to see anyone, he spent his time with Ascar. Together they reviewed past contracts between the MacPhersons and Graham, hoping for any similarities.

Waiting for the man to recover tried Blaine's patience. To bide time, they made plans for when Ascar could leave. First, they would go to the registrar's office in Glen Garry. There they might find information on Northern Star Shipping Company. Next, they would go to Ascar's office and see if Malcolm was able to discover anything about the other investments Graham claimed to have.

It gnawed at him that he couldn't remember where he had heard the name 'Northern Star'. He also hated the emptiness that echoed within. He caught himself daydreaming of chestnut hair and blue-gray eyes. He heard her laugh and swore he could smell the scent of heather and violets. He never knew anyone to leave such an indelible impression upon him. Jocelyn somehow managed to imprint herself onto his thoughts and, at night, his dreams.

In his dreams, he could taste her lips, the feel of her heavy breasts in his hands. He woke up every morning raging with need. If he didn't find some sort of release, he feared he would go mad. A few lasses offered to comfort him, but he wasn't interested.

He was not the only one miserable. Once Angela discovered Braedan gone, she locked herself in her room, refusing to speak to anyone. To make matters worse, the foul weather forced their parents to travel directly to Edinburgh. Rod told him that he tried to convince Angela to join their parents at court, but Angela flatly refused, sending shoes and her hairbrush sailing over his head.

Blaine was going over some correspondence when he saw Violet standing in the doorway.

"A moment, my lord?"

"Is there something amiss, Violet?"

"When Lady Jocelyn left, she took none of her gowns." Violet looked uncomfortable. "I dinna mention this, assuming she may return soon."

"I am leaving shortly and plan to stop by Heatherwood. If you would kindly pack all of Lady Jocelyn's belongings, I will be more than happy to deliver them." He turned away, displeased by the news.

"I also found this." She reached into her pocket and withdrew a small leather pouch then handed it to him. "There's a note inside... I-I dinna read it." She curtseyed and left.

Blaine immediately recognized the pouch that held the sapphire necklace. He reached in and extracted the note. His jaw clenched as he read the few words.

Blaine,
I am sure ye will find someone who will appreciate such a gracious gift.
J

He crumpled up the note in his fist. "Violet," he yelled, storming out of the library. When he caught up to her, he handed back the pouch. "Make sure to include this in Lady Jocelyn's things. I am certain my fiancée will be relieved to see it returned."

The day was getting worse.

~ * ~

Heddy was beside herself when Jocelyn and Braedan finally arrived home. She barraged them with questions. Who was this Blaine MacKinnon? Is he the handsome brother from Clan MacKinnon? What was court like? Did they meet the king and the queen?

Jocelyn politely answered them, not wanting to go into too much detail. Braedan, on the other hand, was only focused on seeing to their most immediate needs. They needed supplies for the bakery so they could meet the demands of the customers they had met at the market.

Anxious to cash the banknote from Graham, Braedan told her he decided to leave for Glen Garry the following day. Concerned for his safety, she insisted he take Martin, their groundskeeper and Heddy's brother Sam.

With Heddy at the bakery, Jocelyn decided to see about recreating some of the delicacies she had tasted at court. One confectionery consisted of vanilla custard. She wondered if it could be replaced with a lemon curd since vanilla beans could be challenging to locate. Looking through the larder, she came across a vial of saffron.

Holding it in her palm, she thought about the fish she had made for Blaine. Her mind flooded with visions of him smiling at her approvingly, his beautiful green eyes glowing with appreciation. It seemed a lifetime ago now and her heart ached at the loss.

Gathering the items that she needed, Jocelyn went back into the kitchen. When she looked down at the list of ingredients, the words started to blur, and tears fell onto the parchment, smearing the ink. Oh, who was she fooling?

She was miserable. She needed to face the truth, something she had denied herself since arriving home: she was positively and unmistakably in love with Blaine Michael MacKinnon. Still, it was futile to refute what was in her heart and hope for a future together.

Her time with him had come to an end.

Looking for a clean cloth to wipe her eyes, she used the end of her apron. Lost in her misery, she did not notice that someone had entered the kitchen until a shadow fell on the flour she was measuring. Dropping the cup, she gasped out loud, clutching her hands to her heart.

~ * ~

Blaine received the news he had been waiting for: Ascar was healthy enough to travel. With the weather cooperating, they would be able to leave within the hour. Ascar's secretary, Malcolm, had advised them that at least one of the businesses that Graham had purportedly invested in was defunct and therefore could not be legitimate. Blaine was anxious to leave.

Heading to the stables, he stopped when he heard his name. Rod stood at the doorway to his study. "A moment before ye leave?"

Blaine regretted his behavior the past week. He should have tried to talk to his friend or at least lend some support. He knew Rod was upset over the rift between he and his sister. Rod gave him a weak smile, handing him a missive. "What is this?"

"'Tis from Caelan," he said and went back to his desk. "Ye need not fret, Blaine, 'tis only an invitation to the christening of his son."

Blaine didn't understand why but hearing Caelan had a son oddly affected him. "How do ye know he had a son?"

Rod tilted his head. "I asked Douglas John. He told me Ilyssa gave birth to a boy and that Caelan was beside himself. He says the lad is fair-haired like ye."

Blaine opened the missive. It wasn't implausible that the babe was fair-haired considering Caelan's wife possessed glorious blond hair. He quickly scanned the letter and tossed it onto a nearby table. It was more of a command than an invitation. Caelan expected him at Calderglen in a fortnight to attend the christening. "I see no reason why I must be present. I still have business with the MacAulays, and I haven't been home in a month."

"I assume it's because ye are to be the lad's godfather," Rod said. "I am only assuming."

"Why would ye assume this?"

"Why not, the lad is named after ye." He smiled.

Blaine picked up the letter again and this time read it thoroughly. There it was—the birth announcement of Michael Blaine MacKinnon, son to Caelan and Ilyssa MacKinnon. There was a handwritten invitation from Ilyssa explaining how crucial it was that he be present. Caelan added that he was expected, and no excuses.

"Michael Blaine MacKinnon," he said barely above a whisper.

The babe didn't have his exact name, but he still felt a wave of warmth run through him. He wondered what it would be like to have a son, his son. An ache grew in his chest. There was only one woman he would want to bear his son. He saw Jocelyn ripe with child, smiling serenely. He saw their home filled with children, each of them with glorious chestnut hair and blue-gray eyes. The ache intensified. He walked straight to the sideboard to pour himself a drink.

"Will ye pour me one too?" Rod asked. "Do ye remember when Angela was born?" Blaine shook his head. "I remember it all too well." Taking the drink from him, Rod tilted his head back, swallowing the whisky in one gulp. "There's quite an age difference between us. I was almost twelve summers when Angela was born. My mother lost two bairns before she carried Angela. I feared the wee lass might not survive. I remember the very moment they put her in my arms. So small, so frail. I remember thinking that I would always protect her. That's how it's always been between us. She has grown to be a beautiful and intelligent woman, although she is light in frame and delicate in nature, she has an inner strength that is bewildering." He looked out the window, seeing days gone by. "I only want the best for my sister, and 'tis not with the MacAulay lad." Blaine opened his mouth to argue, but Rod stopped him. "I could not bear to think of her struggling to make ends meet. She belongs in a home filled with servants and all the comforts that wealth can provide."

"The MacAulays are not destitute by any means," Blaine argued.

"Nay, but it matters naught. My parents' sole purpose for wanting Angela at court is to arrange a marriage with Clan Chieftain Thomas Mackenzie. They are hopeful he will agree to the union."

"Thomas MacKenzie? But the man's thrice her age."

"Nay, he is no older than your Uncle Angus when he wed Lady Katherine," Rod corrected him. "Besides, he is wealthy and a good man. His clan respects him, and he is said to be fair."

"What about love?"

Rod gave him an odd look, and quite frankly Blaine too was surprised by his words.

"Angela will want for nothing, and Thomas will keep her belly full of bairns. She will have all the love she needs."

Rod's last comment did not sit well with Blaine. It was so archaic to force a young woman into a marriage solely for the sake of the clan, yet, wasn't that what the king wanted from him? He also thought of his sister Miranda, barely a year younger than Angela. He couldn't imagine having her marry someone like Laird MacKenzie, no matter how good a man he might be.

"Is she aware of yer parent's intentions?"

Rod looked pained. "Nay, but I will prepare her before we leave for court." He doubted Rod's chances of getting Angela to court. "When my mother finds out she is here, she will not hesitate to send a carriage to bring her post-haste, and Angela will not be able to refuse."

"Are ye in accord with this arrangement?"

He leveled his gaze. "I know not what is right or whether 'tis good. What I do know is my opinion matters naught, and therefore, there is no use to lament over what I canna change."

Blaine suspected he wasn't being truthful. If Rod did not approve the marriage, he would move heaven and earth to stop it. "I will send word as soon as I learn of anything regarding Graham. Give my best to your parents when you see them."

"Are ye not going to Calderglen?"

Blaine looked stone-faced at his friend. "Ascar and I are going to meet with Malcolm and see what he has uncovered, and then I am going home."

"Ye are taking Peter and Caleb?"

"Aye."

"Good."

~ * ~

Blaine and his companions made good time reaching the registrar's office in Glen Garry. When they met with Ascar's secretary, he was shocked to learn that two of Graham's investments could not be legitimate

"What is our next move?" Malcolm asked.

"I believe we should contact the magistrate at Castletown as he has authority over this region," Ascar suggested.

"Nay, I believe we need to gather as much information about all the investments, especially Northern Star, and bring it before the king," Blaine reasoned. "I do not want to give Graham the chance of slipping away before he is brought to justice. If he catches wind, we are onto him, he may leave the country."

Ascar nodded. "Agreed, but I must go back to Castletown to retrieve the Northern Star document. I left it in my safe."

There was a cold draft in the registrar's office. Blaine felt a twinge between his shoulders and adjusted his heavy cloak. "I plan to send Caleb and Peter back to Stonegate. I need them to see how things are faring. I will have Brode review my shipping logs."

Caleb and Peter both perked up at the prospect of going home.

"Aye, and when I get back from Castletown, I need to go to Heatherwood. I want to review the MacAulays' ledgers again."

"What are ye looking for, Ascar?" Blaine felt another twinge, followed by a sense of uneasiness.

"I am not certain."

"Then, I will accompany ye." It pleased him that he would see for himself, how Jocelyn was doing.

He did not care for the way things ended between them. He hoped with his help, they would gain back their lands and she would throw herself in his arms and agree to be his mistress." He smiled at the thought and left with Caleb and Peter.

Blaine was giving them instructions when his chest tightened, and he thought he might be sick. "Are ye well, my lord?" Caleb asked.

Blaine nodded and continued, but words seem to get tangled in his thoughts. "Brode will be able to assist ye. Now ye best be off while there's light." Turning around, a wave of dread went through him that could not be ignored. "Caleb," he called out. "Before ye go, tell Ascar that I am on my way to Heatherwood now. Ask him to meet me there."

Ignoring their questions, he went in search of the stable boy.

~ * ~

The sight of Walrick Graham standing in her kitchen caused Jocelyn's legs to tremble. "I heard ye were back," he said mockingly. "Did yer betrothed abandon ye so soon?"

Straightening her shoulders, she stared at him with contempt. Standing before her was the man who stole their lands and had the unmitigated gall to walk uninvited into her home. Tamping down the words she wanted to say, she did her best to look at him with a bored expression. Walrick Graham was not a small man by any means. He was tall but lacked Blaine's broad shoulders. He was thin except for the belly, which reflected his penchant for overindulgence. Dressed in expensive clothes, she could help notice the food stains on the front of his satin vest. His hair was greasy and matted down. Pulling it back in a queue did nothing except accentuate the sag along his jawline.

"Not that 'tis any of your concern, but my fiancé," she stressed the last word, "is a very busy man. He is away attending to business and will return soon. Now if you don't mind, I too have responsibilities that have been neglected too long, so I bid ye good day."

At first, Jocelyn thought Graham might leave, but instead, he gave her a cynical smile that made him look more like a serpent than a man. "My dear, what have I ever done to deserve such discourtesy? I am here out of concern that ye are all alone and that the man ye claim to be yer betrothed is reputed to be a bounder. I certainly do not deserve yer scorn…after all I have meant to yer family.

He was so smug, she could only stare in disbelief. "Lord Graham, I would appreciate it if ye would please leave. I have too much to do, and I am not entertaining today.

He ignored her, sauntering toward her as his eyes raked her body. "I will not be dismissed like some servant," he scoffed. She retreated as he neared. "I have sacrificed everything for your family, and I am deserving of your time."

Her back hit the wall. He had backed her into a corner and the long kitchen table prevented her from escaping. Graham continued toward her until he was nearly pressed up against her. Then by some miracle or perhaps powered by anger, Jocelyn pushed against his chest with all her might. She caught him off guard, and he stumbled backward giving her enough room to slip by.

"How dare ye," she shouted at him. "Ye have sacrificed nothing. Ye have kept yer rapacious hold on my family for years, and now that we have finally settled our debt, ye refuse to sell back our lands."

"I am more than happy to give ye yer lands," he said unexpectedly. "Ye only need to consent to be my wife."

She laughed at him, "I am already betrothed, my lord, and even if it were not so, I would never agree to such a ludicrous proposition."

By the look on his face, she realized she had gone too far. There was a vicious glint in his eye. "The only one who will find themselves in a ludicrous position will be ye. MacKinnon will never wed, 'tis for appearance only. When he finally rids himself of ye, and he will, ye will be ruined. There will not be a man in Scotland that will not think that ye have spread yer legs for that rogue."

Jocelyn gasped in disgust. "Get out," she yelled. "Get out before…"

She did not finish, as he was upon her in seconds. Holding her tightly against him, he tugged viciously on her long braid, tilting her head back. His rank breath bathed her face as he panted in anger. "I will never leave. I will never give up. I care naught if ye are unchaste. I will have ye as my wife and show ye what 'tis like to be made love to by a real man."

Bile rose into her throat.

"Ye can't even take care of yerself. How will ye survive when ye are truly abandoned? Yer brother? Braedan couldn't even protect ye from the very men who robbed ye. He is useless."

She must have relaxed a bit, for he loosened his grip. "What did ye say?" A cold realization creep down her back. "Who told ye we were robbed?"

She saw the guilty look on his face and realized that he had been caught. Thinking better not to say more, she started pushing as hard as she could to get out of his grasp.

"'Tis...I heard from, there was talk..." Graham stammered, clearly trying to cover for his mistake. "There have been robberies in the area, and yer solicitor was ambushed by a band of thieves." He still held her firmly in his arms.

"Take yer hands off me, ye snake." She struggled in earnest. "Ye are the bounder. I will not tolerate another moment of yer presence."

"Ye will do more than tolerate me, my dear." He leaned down to kiss her, but she thrashed her head from side to side, and he missed.

He grabbed her braid again and pulled her head back painfully. She let out a scream and closed her eyes, not wanting to see his mouth coming down on hers. *Dear Lord, help me.*

"Take yer hands off my fiancée."

He immediately released her when the tip of a sword pierced his back then spun around to face the intruder. He was struck dumb by the man's murderous glare. Jocelyn ran into Blaine's arms, so relieved she nearly collapsed.

"MacKinnon, I presume?" Graham said when he found his voice.

"Ye make a habit of presuming, Graham. Now leave as the lady requested," Blaine growled at him.

"Ye do not know who I am? I—"

"Ye are nothing and no one."

"Miss Jocelyn and I have business—"

Blaine's brow lifted, and he thrust his sword into his face. "Any future business ye have with my betrothed will be conducted through my solicitor. I suggest ye leave while ye still can."

Graham narrowed his eyes but said nothing. He turned to face

Jocelyn and bowed, then he squared his shoulders and walked toward the door.

"Graham," Blaine called out. Graham turned around with his lips pursed which gave him a sour look. "If ye ever lay hands on my fiancée again, I will personally cut out your black heart."

With those parting words, Graham slammed the door behind him.

Her legs finally gave out. Blaine had to grab her to keep her from falling. "Oh, Blaine, ye came, ye are here," she cried out, sobbing in his arms. He clutched her to him, whispering nonsensical words to calm her. "I prayed for a miracle and there...there...."

She looked up at him, tears streaking down her cheeks. He did his best to kiss them away. "My love, ye are safe. I will not let that man near ye again. I swear."

He stared into her eyes, illuminated by tears. After giving her a reassuring smile, he then crushed her mouth with his, sealing his promise with a searing kiss. "I am here, and I never intend to let ye leave me again."

She smiled, nodding. "Oh, Blaine, Graham...he is behind the robberies," she stammered. "We were arguing, he-he said he would give the land back if..." She swallowed hard. Blaine kissed her again, hard this time, as if the very act might fortify her. "He said he would give back our land if I agreed to marry him."

"That will never happen."

"I told him the same. He grew angry, and that's when he let it slip that he heard that Braedan and I were robbed on our way home from the market." Her eyes grew wide. "Ye explicitly told me not to say to anyone what happened."

"'Tis possible that someone else might have said something. 'Tis how we claim we met."

"Nay, when I asked how he knew, he panicked. He realized he had made a mistake. I believe he is also responsible for the attack on Ascar. Why else would the robbers leave once they had Malcolm's satchel? They were not looking for money. I believe they were looking for the documents."

~ * ~

Blaine thought about what she said for a moment and had to admit the story had merit. The men could be working for Graham. Who else would benefit if the contracts went missing? "Ascar will be arriving soon, and when he does, we will ask him to describe his assailants. We may find they are one and the same. Do ye remember the men who attacked ye?"

"Aye, I will never forget the man who tried to defile me, nor the man who grabbed my mare. He had a scar that ran from the corner of his eye to his jaw."

"Any others?"

Jocelyn closed her eyes. "Aye, I will be able to describe them."

"Good." He hugged her tightly, not wanting to let go, and resumed kissing her. The warmth of her pressed against him turned his blood hot. His hunger for her became insatiable. "I want ye, my love. I need ye in my life forever."

"I too need ye, Blaine, without ye, my life holds no purpose. Ye are the air that I breathe…I love ye," she whispered.

He pulled back from her, doubting that he heard her correctly. The warmth in her eyes reflected the truth of her words and gave them credence. Instead of feeling panic or unease, he was jubilated. To have the heart of this perfect woman was an honor.

"I am so unworthy of your love, lass, but I rejoice in having it none-the-less." He kissed her again, this time with all the passion he possessed. His kisses became more urgent. And he was swept away in a wave of heated emotions and need.

Lost in the moment, he was caught unaware when a woman burst into the kitchen. She was rather robust in an attractive way, having all the right curves in the right places.

"Jocelyn, are ye all right?" The woman stopped, and her mouth fell open upon seeing her mistress in his arms.

"Heddy," Jocelyn exclaimed, stepping away from his embrace. Taking the edge of her apron, she wiped away any lingering tears. "Aye, I am fine. What are ye doing here? I thought…"

"Forgive me, I was on my way to my sister's when I saw Sir Graham riding away, and I feared he might have," she looked at Blaine wide-eyed, "tried to harm ye."

He smiled easily. "Forgive me, but I haven't had the pleasure." He walked up to Heddy and bowed slightly. "I am Sir Blaine MacKinnon, Jocelyn's betrothed."

Heddy blushed profusely as she bobbed a quick curtsey. She wasn't a young lass, but she was attractive in a youthful way, her dark brown eyes sparkled, and her smile was infectious. "'Tis an honor to finally meet ye, my lord."

"The honor is certainly mine. Ascar speaks quite fondly of ye, and I can see why."

Heddy giggled and smiled most attractively.

"Where is Braedan?" he asked of them, changing the subject. "I was hoping to speak with him."

"He has gone to town, with Martin and my brother," Heddy said. "I don't expect them till the morrow."

"Well, ye best go to yer sister's while there's still light," Blaine suggested. "I am here and will protect yer mistress until her brother returns."

Heddy agreed that she best leave and bid them both a good day.

Blaine followed Heddy out. "I will return shortly," he told Jocelyn. "I want to make sure that Graham is indeed gone. I also need to see to my horse."

Chapter Fourteen

Blaine searched the grounds, and even though his inspection confirmed there was no one hiding in the shrubbery, he sensed the house was being watched. How was it that Graham just happened to visit when Jocelyn was alone? Riding back, he dismounted and strolled to where he spied a small herb garden. Smoke billowed from the chimney, and a delicious smell wafted from the kitchen. The manor was of a decent size, with two floors, but Blaine noticed areas in desperate need of repair, especially the roof. His search of the grounds confirmed the fact that most of the land lay unused and he understood Braedan's frustration at not being able to farm them. It was wasteful, and Graham had no right to them.

When Blaine entered the stable, he saw clean stalls and the smell of sweet hay hung in the air. He groomed his horse and gave him a good portion of oats. His stomach growled in anticipation of what Jocelyn might be preparing, but there was a deeper hunger within that could not be satiated by food.

Entering the kitchen, the smell of lamb permeated the air making his mouth water. Jocelyn stood next to the pot, stirring the bubbling stew. He put his arms around her, finding he liked seeing her doing simple chores. He imagined coming home to Stonegate after a long day at sea, to the smell of baking bread and of her warm embrace.

"I hope ye are hungry? I believe I made too much," she said, leaning back. After a time, she moved out of his arms. "'Tis almost ready." She smiled. "I will be back in a moment as I need to prepare a room for ye."

Blaine reached for her. "'Tis not necessary, Jocelyn, I plan to stay in yer bedchamber." He pulled her closer. "And preferably in yer bed." Her smile faded. "Please do not deny me, lass. I don't think I could bear it if ye say nay. The days have been dark and the nights cold. I have had only a few memories of ye to keep me warm."

Seemingly touched by his words, she smiled. "Sit down, I will get some wine."

~ * ~

Comfortable in each other's company Blaine and Jocelyn sat down to eat. Their terrible argument just days before was forgotten, and neither held ill will. After they finished, they went to her father's study. Reviewing the ledgers, she pointed out some entries she thought rather interesting.

"I hope Ascar will be able to decipher these and shed some light," he said. "Are ye sure ye looked everywhere for the other contracts?"

"Aye, Braedan and I spent a good day searching. All we discovered was a letter from Graham where he mentioned the Northern Star. He wrote to say the company suffered a terrible setback and that they needed to meet to decide what to do."

The study was cold for they had not taken the time to light the fire and it was getting late. "I believe we should look again, tomorrow when there's light."

Jocelyn agreed and picked up the candle. "If ye would like, I will gladly have a bath brought..."

He laughed as he gathered her into his arms. "And who will be joining me in my bath?" She ducked her head, embarrassed by his implication. "No need, I noticed ye have a bathing chamber behind the kitchen. I can take care of myself."

She followed him out of her father's study. Her feet felt like lead and refused to move. She just stood there, foolishly at a loss of what to do.

Seeing his saddlebags in the foyer, she ran to grabbed them and followed him but then dropped them in the foyer next to where his cloak hung on a hook.

She rolled her eyes at her tepidness. The days that followed her departure from Castle Ballindoch left her with immense regret that she might never see Blaine again. And here he was, in her home and she wanted nothing more than to fulfil her desire to be truly part of him.

Sitting down on a long bench, he pulled off his boots. She walked over to the stove to make sure the pot was full of water and starting to boil. There was plenty for two.

"I don't suppose I could convince ye join me?" he said as if reading her thoughts.

She smiled as she handed him a small washing cloth, a cake of soap and drying cloth. "I will wait for ye upstairs."

"And which bedchamber is yers?"

Jocelyn bit her bottom lip trying to appear calm. "At the top of the stairs, turn left. It will be the first door on yer right." She smiled and slipped out.

Her heart beat wildly as she made her way upstairs. Thinking of all that transpired, she was still shocked by her admission that she loved him, but she had no regrets. Nor did she expect him to reciprocate by declaring his love in return. Admitting how she felt was liberating, as well as assuring that she was making the right decision in giving her virtue to Blaine. She could never love another, and it made sense to give herself to the man she loved with all her heart.

Upon entering her bedchamber, she shivered, it was freezing cold. Laying the taper on the table, she began building a fire. Her hands trembled, and it took her three times to light the kindling. Once she had a good flame going, she too wanted to bathe. It had been an easy day at the bakery, but she foolishly hoped the water might soothe her nerves. Her teeth chattered as she took off her gown and chemise.

Going behind the screen, she poured water into the basin. The water was so cold that she was instantly covered in goosebumps from head to toe. Thinking about his invitation to join him now appealed to her.

"Coward," she said aloud.

By the time she finished, she could barely move her fingers. Pulling her night-rail over her head, she managed to brush her hair until it shined. She had a hard time braiding the long tresses and was about to give up when she heard the door to her bedchamber open. Holding her breath, she quickly finished.

"Jocelyn," he called out.

She closed her eyes willing herself to be brave.

"Jocelyn?" he called again.

"Here," she squeaked from behind the screen. Mortified by the sound she made, she repeated in a lower voice. "Here."

She came out from behind the screen. Her legs trembled so she nearly stumbled. She almost did when she saw him naked except for the drying cloth wrapped around his narrow hips. He had brought up the wine and was in the middle of pouring her a glass.

She attempted to smile. "Ye need not fear me. I would never force ye to do anything."

Jocelyn shook her head, unable to form words. Clenching her teeth to keep them from chattering, she did her best to smile again. "I am cold."

"Come," he said. "Let me warm ye."

Walking toward him, she accepted the wine he offered. Blaine arched his brown when she drained the contents, handing him back an empty glass. Taking a sip of his own, he put both goblets down on the small table.

"Turn around," he said.

She didn't think she heard him right. Placing his hands gently on her shoulders, he spun her around so that she faced the growing fire. His hands kneaded the area between her neck and shoulders. He smiled when she relaxed.

Jocelyn was astonished by the heat that emanated from his body that she found herself leaning against him. "Mmm," she sighed contently as his hands continued to caress her, moving down the length of her arms.

"'Tis twice now that I have seen fear in yer eyes. The day we met," he said as he wrapped his arms around her, "and today when I saw ye in Graham's clutches." He placed a soft kiss on the side of her neck. "It would cleave my heart in two if I saw that fear return now."

She turned back around and wrapped her arms around his waist. Looking up into his eyes, her fear diminished in their emerald depth. "Nay, Blaine, 'tis only nerves." She tiptoed up to graze a light kiss on his lips. "I come willingly."

He looked deeply and longingly before caressing the side of her face with his hand, tracing his thumb along her jawline. "I am relieved." Leaning down, he kissed her lightly at first and thoroughly the next.

His tongue entered her mouth, and she opened greedily meeting his thrusts with her own. The kiss seared itself into her memory as the kiss that sealed her love.

They kissed for a long time until the drying cloth slip from his hips to land at her feet. His arousal pressed hard against her belly, making her a bit apprehensive again, but she refused to succumb. Before she could react, his fingers untied the top of her night-rail. His lips followed his fingers as he pushed the garment down her arms, exposing her breasts to the cold air. Her nipples hardened when he took each one into his mouth, suckling gently and swirling his tongue around in lazy circles.

She ran her fingers through his long blond hair, reveling in the silky strands. He continued caressing her breasts with his mouth when her night-rail slipped over her hips to pool around her feet. His lips were once again on her mouth, his hands roving down to cup her backside. He pulled her hard against his arousal.

Picking her up in his arms, he carried her over to the bed to lay her down gently. He looked at the fire that needed attention. "Get ye under the covers, lass."

She scrambled, immediately pulling the covers up to her chin. He softly laughed, shaking his head.

Confidently, he strode back to stoke the fire, utterly comfortable in his lack of clothing. Gracing her with a view of his perfect backside, he looked like a golden Greek statue. Turning, he paused to take a sip of wine, and she felt her mouth go dry at the sight of his engorged member, jutting straight out from burnished curls. Her bravery slipped away.

Before she realized it, he climbed into bed to gather her in his arms, warming her with the heat from his body. Hoping to restore her confidence, she kissed him hard. He must have sensed her unease because he rolled her gently onto her back and covered her with his body. His kiss was heated and urgent. Blaine's hand trailed down her flat stomach where he placed it between her legs, gently traipsing his fingers over her mound. He then kissed from her neck to the valley between her breasts. Just as his mouth took possession of her right nipple, his fingers dipped between the folds to stroke the sensitive flesh hidden beneath.

Jocelyn responded to him, her breath catching in her throat as he continued his torturous caresses. She experienced something deep inside when he latched onto her left nipple. As his tongue flicked, his fingers followed suit, and when he sucked in deeply, his fingers delved into her passage, coaxing the sensation to where it slowly took a life of its own. Warmth radiated out in a pulsating energy until her body started to buck in an urgent rhythm. Just as she reached the pinnacle of her release, he dipped his finger deep inside and pushed her over the precipice.

Her body convulsed around his finger causing him to exhale in a sound that culminated into a growl when he heard her gasp out his name. Just as the last wave of pleasure left her body, Blaine drove deeply into her, allowing her passage to fully envelop his length. It was so sudden and unexpected that she hardly felt him break through her maidenhead.

"Oomph," she exclaimed, her eyes flying open.

"Are ye all right, love?" he asked, a pained look on his face, his body shaking as he hovered over her.

When she nodded, he started to move in earnest, pulling out slowly and then back in again. She watched him, his eyes closed, his face reflected in carnal ecstasy.

As his rhythm grew, his expression was replaced by one of concentration and just when she thought to say something, he threw his head back and yelled, "Dear God."

~ * ~

Jocelyn pried one eye open to see her bedchamber still shrouded in darkness. It was still early, but it was time to rise if she was going to the bakery. The room was frigid cold, as the fire had burned out hours ago. Wrapped in Blaine's warm embrace, she was reluctant to leave her bed.

"Sleep, lass," he said.

"I need to go to the bakery…"

"Nay, sleep." He held her closer, his left hand reaching around to gently cup her right breast. "Ye need rest."

He was right as he had kept her up most of the night with his kisses and caresses. They had made love again, although she had been too tender to reach her own release. However, she was elated when he plunged deeply into her, arching his back and screaming her name into the dark. Snuggling closer to him, she couldn't help smiling, feeling his arousal against her backside.

"Easy, lass," he groaned. "Keep rubbing yer pert little bottom, and I may need to make love to ye again."

Jocelyn closed her eyes and allowed herself to relax, drifting back into a sound sleep.

And sleep she did, better than she had since returning home. When she surfaced from a dreamless slumber, she was surprised to find her bedchamber was still dark. She also noted that it was incredibly warm in her bedchamber. At some point, he must have risen to build a fire. Still wrapped in his arms, she decided she could afford a few more hours when her brain registered a noise that needed consideration. Straining to listen, she heard nothing and slipped back into the restful abyss.

There it was…the noise again. Except it wasn't a noise, it was a voice. "Braedan!" Bolting from the bed, she ran around her room, not quite sure what she was looking for. "Blaine, wake up."

Blaine gave her a lopsided grin folding his hands behind his head. He leaned back onto his pillow. He looked glorious. His long hair ruffled about his massive shoulders, the covers down by his waist to expose his golden physique.

"Please, get up. We must hide afore Braedan sees ye," she pleaded. Not finding his clothes, she gave up.

"Lass, Braedan knows I am here. He has seen my horse by now."

She quickly donned her chemise and gown, dragging her stockings over her legs before shoving her feet into her shoes. "We must get ye dressed…now, where are yer clothes?" She searched frantically again.

"Well, that poses a problem, ye see…"

"Don't tell me ye left them in the bathing chamber?" He raised his brows and smirked. "Go to the bedchamber across the hall. Pull the dust sheets and make the bed appear like ye slept there. I will fetch yer things." She didn't bother to brush her hair. Instead, she threaded her fingers through the heavy tresses and tied it back with a ribbon.

Jocelyn slipped downstairs as quietly as possible. She heard Martin's voice out in the courtyard. Relieved to find there was no one about, she rushed into the kitchen in search of Blaine's clothes. Thankfully she found them folded on the small stool next to his boots.

Grabbing the bundle, she ran out of the kitchen and right smack into Braedan. "Oooff," she grunted, dropping one of the boots with a loud *thunk*.

"Jocelyn, I have been calling for ye—didn't ye hear me?" He stopped, giving her an odd look.

Her cheeks grew hot. "Braedan, ye have returned so early."

"Early? 'Tis past midday," he said, turning a quizzing eye. "What is going on? I stopped by the bakery, and they said ye had not been in."

"Oh, I wanted to try my hand at recreating some of the baked goods we had at court. I still need some ingredients. Have ye brought all that I asked for?"

"Where is Laird MacKinnon?" he asked, looking around. She followed his gaze to where Blaine's cloak hung on hook and his saddlebags resting on the floor. "Where is he, Joce?"

She continued to stare at him, her mouth opening as if to say something then snapping shut.

"Where is MacKinnon?"

"Here I am, Braedan." Both of their heads snapped in the direction of Blaine's deep voice.

Then both of their jaws dropped when they saw him standing at the top of the stairs dressed in only her robe. Silence reigned as he walked down. The robe was much too small, exposing his broad chest, but thankfully it wrapped sufficiently around his narrow hips. She dropped the second boot with a *thunk*.

It must have taken Braedan's brain a moment to register but when he did, he withdrew his dirk. "What is the meaning of this?" he yelled, looking accusingly first at Blaine and then at Jocelyn.

Blaine held up his hands. "Ye can put down the dirk, Braedan, I can explain." He took a step closer, but Braedan would not lower his blade. "Yesterday Ascar and I left for Glen Garry. We went to meet his secretary at the registrar's office to see if we could find—"

"Stop," Braedan roared. "What has this to do with ye standing in my home wearing my sister's robe?"

"Let me continue…please."

Braedan dragged in an angry breath but gave a stiff nod.

"As I was saying, we discovered some useful information about your father's business, and we needed to examine the ledgers again. I sent my men to retrieve my shipping logs and then came straight here."

Her brother raised his brows mockingly at him.

"When I arrived, I was surprised to see there was no one about. I walked around the back, and that's when I heard raised voices and then Jocelyn screaming."

At this point, Braedan lowered his dirk.

"When I ran inside, I saw Graham attempting to assault your sister." Blaine looked at Jocelyn, who nodded, sure her expression was a reflection of the horrible incident. "I was able to intercede in time. Yer sister was not harmed. I also threatened to kill him if he ever touched her again."

"I see. I am once again in yer debt, Sir Blaine."

"Since Jocelyn was completely alone, I thought it best that I stay to keep her safe."

"Where is Heddy?"

"I gave her the day off, Brae. 'Tis been a long time since she has visited her kin."

"It dinna explain why ye are in such a state of…undress."

"After a day of traveling, I wanted to bathe." Blaine smiled. "Ye canna expect yer sister to be hauling buckets of water upstairs. I used the convenience of yer bathing chamber and inadvertently left my clothes behind. Miss Jocelyn was kind to retrieve them."

"Am I to assume ye slept in the guest bedchamber?" Braedan furrowed his brow at him. "If I were to go upstairs now, what would I find?" There was an awkward moment of silence. "My lord, did ye sleep in the guest bedchamber?"

Blaine hesitated. "Nay."

"What?" she screamed.

Braedan raised his dirk again. "This is not to be born," he yelled. "Ye are no gentleman."

"I beg to differ."

"Ye save my sister, and when she is emotionally vulnerable, ye seduce her to yer bed?"

"It was actually her bed, but 'tis not as you say."

"How dare ye make light of this matter," he roared, anger suffusing his face. "Ye will make this right, Blaine. Ye *will* marry my sister."

"I accept," he said simply.

"I do not," she yelled in return.

Braedan turned to look at her sternly. "Jocelyn, don't be foolish. Yer reputation has been compromised."

"I am a grown woman, Braedan, no one will decide my future. I will decide who I marry."

"I am yer brother and the head of this family. Ye will do as I say." Ignoring her protest, Braedan grabbed the clothes she held in her arms and shoved them at Blaine. "I must help Martin unload the cart before the weather worsens. If you will, please meet me in my father's study…in about an hour, we can go over the terms of the betrothal contract."

Blaine nodded. "I will." He picked up his boots and retreated upstairs.

She ran after Braedan taking hold of his arm. "Please, Braedan…I canna marry Blaine."

Braedan's face was void of any emotion, which unsettled her. "Aye Jocelyn, ye can and ye will." Donning his cloak, he walked out, slamming the door behind him.

"Well, I never," she said and went in search of Blaine.

He was pulling on his breeches when she stormed into her bedchamber. "Have ye gone mad?"

"Nay, my mind is not addled," he said as he turned to her. The sight of his bare chest defused her anger some as she could not deny he was a glorious sight to behold.

"Then what possessed ye to expose yerself wearing this?" She motioned to the robe draped over the back of the chair.

"I heard Braedan questioning ye. He was demanding to know my whereabouts. I came to yer aid."

She gritted her teeth, mindless of his good intentions. "Admitting ye shared my bed is not coming to my aid."

He dragged his shirt over his head, tucking his shirttails before lacing up his breeches. "I did what ye asked of me. I made sure the guest bedchamber appeared as if I slept there, but then I realized he would inspect yer bedchamber. Look around, lass. Braedan would have realized instantly I was lying."

She glanced about and realized he spoke the truth. Besides the two wine glasses on the small table, the condition of her bed made it evident of what they had done. The washing cloth he had used to clean them up still had traces of her virginal blood.

There was no doubt Braedan would deduce what had happened. "I still canna marry ye."

Blaine's look was between bewilderment and hurt. "I am sorry ye find the prospect of becoming my wife so revolting."

Jocelyn immediately regretted her words. "Blaine, I gave ye my heart and my..." She couldn't bring herself to say it aloud. "I am not some fickle woman. I love ye, but I canna marry a man who is not free to wed." She held up her hand when he tried to protest. "I know the truth. I know the king expects ye to wed Lady Clara."

"Ye should not pay heed to Lady Charlotte. She is vicious as well as vindictive."

"It was not just Lady Charlotte. It was on everyone's lips." Jocelyn walked over to stand before him. "When we arrived at court, I wondered why our betrothal was received with so little interest. 'Tis because the king commands ye wed—"

"Enough." Blaine gritted out. "I will never wed Lady Clara."

"Blaine, if ye refuse the king, he will see ye hanged." Tears stung behind her eyes. "I could never be the cause of yer death. I love ye too much."

Pulling her close, he wrapped his arms around her. "I will not be hanged. I will find a way to make the king understand."

"Tell me the truth." She looked up at him, her eyes brimming with unshed tears. "Did the king ever consent to our betrothal?"

"Nay." He wiped away the tear that coursed down her cheek. "The king questioned the validity of our betrothal. He said if my intentions were true, then he would see us wed before we left for home."

"What did ye say?"

"I refused, of course. I explained my clan would insist that family be present."

"It was a test, Blaine, and one that ye failed. When ye refused the king, he knew our betrothal was a ruse. Soon ye will have to return to court, and once ye do, ye will have to wed Lady Clara."

Blaine shook his head, pressing his full lips into a straight line. "I will find a way to make the king understand. In time, a solution will present itself. Now, if ye will excuse me," he gazed out the window, "I believe I will go help Braedan. Foul weather is upon us."

Chapter Fifteen

Blaine watched the ink dry on his signature. He expected to feel a wave of trepidation, but instead, there was a sense of relief. This simple piece of parchment represented something right, turning his lies into truth.

Braedan reviewed the document again before putting down his own signature. The only stipulation Blaine had was to date the contract back to when he and Jocelyn first met. This way, the king would be more inclined to believe their marriage was planned.

Satisfied, Braedan put the parchment inside the family's Bible. "I will see that ye get a copy once 'tis recorded by the Kirk."

Blaine waved his hand that it wasn't necessary.

Walking over to the sideboard Braedan picked up a bottle of whisky. "Would ye care to join me in a drink?"

He grinned and accepted the glass. Taking a sip, he was mildly surprised by how good it was. The MacAulays may not possess much, but they did serve a fine whisky.

Braedan smiled at his approval, but then his expression turned serious. "Ye will take great care of my sister? Ye will not stray—"

"I can assure ye I take marriage vows quite seriously," he said rather firmly before finishing the rest of the fiery brew.

There was an awkward moment of silence as both men stared at their empty glass. Braedan then lifted his head and breathed in deeply. "Mmm…smells like Jocelyn is preparing something special."

Blaine's stomach protested rather noisily. He had not eaten since the night before. Sitting in silence, he glanced over at the young man that would be his future brother in-law. He admired Braedan's wish to protect his sister, to make sure her future was secure. It was akin to Rod's wants and desires for Angela. Braedan would make a fine husband for Angela; he only needed to convince Rod.

~ * ~

Thankful that Heddy had returned an hour earlier, Jocelyn was rushing around the kitchen trying to finish the meal. At first, Heddy inundated her with questions about Blaine. When she found her mistress less than forthcoming, she happily chatted about Ascar's pending visit. "I recall Ascar was quite fond of my butter biscuits. I will have to make sure to bake some."

Jocelyn raised her brow, wondering what might have happened between them.

Taking the savory buns out of the oven, she heard strange voices coming from the other room. Wiping her hands on her apron, they both went to investigate. In the foyer, Martin stood next to a cloaked figure. She couldn't imagine who would be out in such foul weather?

"If ye will stay here, I will fetch the master," Martin was saying.

Jocelyn saw small delicate hands reach up to pull back the hood of her cloak to reveal bright red hair. "Lady Angela?" She gasped.

When Angela saw Jocelyn, she burst into tears and ran into her arms. "Oh, Jocelyn."

"What are ye doing here?" She took her icy hands into hers.

"I am in terrible trouble," she cried, her slender form shuddering.

"Please, Martin, find Sir Blaine and my brother." Martin did not have a chance. Both Blaine and Braedan came running in.

"Angela?" Braedan said in disbelief.

"Oh darling, I thought I would never find you." Lady Angela managed to take two steps when she swayed on her feet.

Seeing her begin to fall, he caught her before she hit the floor.

"Oh, the poor lass," Heddy cried out. "She be soaked to the bone."

Jocelyn became alarmed by Angela's pallor. "We need to get her out of these wet clothes." With Blaine's help, she managed to free Angela of her sodden cloak. "Braedan, take her upstairs."

He carried her limp form.

"Heddy bring me some drying cloths and one of my clean night-rails," she said over her shoulder.

Walking into the guest bedchamber, Braedan carefully laid her down on the bed while Blaine set to starting a fire in the hearth. They managed to strip her of her wet gown and petticoats. Braedan began rubbing her limbs vigorously with the drying cloths. When she wore only her chemise, he turned to preserve her modesty. The women finished undressing her and putting on the long nightgown.

They all breathed a sigh of relief when they saw Angela's eyes flutter open. Braedan rushed back to her side, lifting her up so they could put her under the covers. Heddy brought a large hot stone wrapped in a cloth and placed it at the foot of her bed.

"B-Braedan…I am so…so sorry…I…"

"Shhh, my sweeting, ye need to conserve yer energy." He continued to rub her hands, warming them in his large ones. The poor lass shivered violently, her teeth chattering loudly. "Perhaps she could use something warm to drink?"

"I believe Angela needs something stronger," Blaine suggested.

"P-p-pplease no, I just n-n-nneeed…"

"Ye need something warm to drink. I will return in a moment." Jocelyn smiled. Deciding to give the couple some privacy, she motioned for Blaine and Heddy to follow her.

Upon returning, Lady Angela was much improved.

"Can ye tell me why you dared to venture this way, unescorted and in such weather?" Blaine asked. "I have always taken pride in yer ability to use common sense. Ye could have been injured, or worse."

"Ye said ye were in trouble?" Braedan handed her the mug of hot tea. "What did ye mean by that."

It took a moment for Lady Angela to reply. She wiped away a tear, looking more like a child than a grown woman. "Yesterday I received a missive from my parents insisting that I return to court. Since Rod refused to speak to father and mother about Braedan's offer, I thought I would go and try to convince them to give him a chance. I hoped once they met ye," she gazed lovingly at Braedan, "they would love ye…as much as I do." She wiped away another tear. "I was busy packing when Roddy requested a word. He looked terrible, his hair standing on end. I must admit I have treated him most unkindly since ye left. He said he wanted to talk to me, to tell me something in hopes that I would be prepared for what awaited me at court. It seems my parents arranged for me to wed Sir Thomas Mackenzie." Lady Angela could no longer keep the tears from flowing. "I canna marry a man I have never met."

"Ye have met him lass, at least a time or two," Blaine said.

"Aye, when I was a wee child," she cried out. "I have no recollection, nor do I care."

Braedan touched her hand in effort to calm her.

"I was so upset. I went to the stables and had my horse saddled. I thought the fresh air might help. The wind in my face made me feel free. Free to make my own decisions. Free to live my life. I just kept riding, and it wasn't until I was a good distance away that I saw I was halfway to Killie Kern."

"Ye left without telling anyone?" Jocelyn fretted.

"As far as anyone is concerned, I am once again locked in my room and refusing to see anyone. The last thing Roddy said to me is to be ready. We would be leaving for court in the morning."

"How is it that ye found us?" Braedan asked.

"I was unsure if I would find Heatherwood. The weather was getting worse, and I was losing light. A kind man I met told me which road to take, but there came a time when I thought I might have taken the wrong path. I was terrified. But then I remembered you telling me of the Scottish pines that line the drive and the bridge where you liked to fish. I must say I knew I reached Heatherwood when I saw her ivy-covered walls."

"My darling, ye should not have risked yer life. Ye could have written me, and I would have come at once."

"There was no time, Braedan. Rod was insistent that we leave, and I could not refuse."

Tears flowed again. Not wanting to distress her further, Jocelyn took over. "Well ye are safe now, and we will help ye." She smiled.

"Aye, I am certain if Blaine speaks to Father he will listen. My parents hold ye in high regard. They will see I am meant to be with Braedan and not with Laird Mackenzie."

Seeing her yawn, Jocelyn took the opportunity to excuse them. "Ye need to rest. Why don't ye close yer eyes for a spell and in a while, I will have Heddy bring ye something to eat." She leaned over to brush a light kiss on her forehead. "Sleep."

~ * ~

The three of them sat in the salon, silently eating the delicious dinner of roasted chicken with taters and nips. Jocelyn nodded when Blaine offered to refill her glass of ale.

"I will take Lady Angela home tomorrow," Braedan said unemotionally. "Her family will be worried."

"Ye canna travel by horse in this weather, and Lady Angela has been through too much," she reasoned.

"I will hire a carriage then," he snapped. "I will escort Angela home myself to make sure she arrives safely. 'Tis the right thing to do." He grabbed his tankard, downing its contents. "I know of Laird Mackenzie. He is a good man and will take good care of Angela. She deserves to be the wife of..." He did not go on instead, he poured himself more ale.

"But she's in love with ye," Jocelyn said. "She does not want to wed another."

"Lady Angela is young. In time, she will forget about me."

Jocelyn was about to argue when she heard a loud boom and the sound of angry voices. "Now what?" All three ran into the foyer.

Standing in the middle of the room and dripping wet, stood Roderick MacPherson. He was yelling while Martin was doing his best to keep him from going upstairs. "Out of my way before I remove ye with my fist. Angela," he bellowed.

"Sir Roderick, please keep yer voice down," Jocelyn pleaded with him as he glared at her and Blaine.

When he caught sight of Braedan, he became incensed. "You!" he roared. "'Tis all yer fault. Ye filled her head with nonsense." Balling up his fist, he slammed it into Braedan's face, sending him sprawling to the floor.

"Stop," Blaine shouted. He grabbed Rod by the arm to keep him from pummeling the lad.

"Keep out of this, Blaine. 'Tis not yer concern."

"'Tis my concern when ye assault my future brother-in-law." He stood in his way, refusing to move.

Rod started to laugh. "Ye need not keep up the pretense, Blaine. I know the truth."

"I am afraid ye have not been apprised of the latest news. I am officially betrothed to Lady Jocelyn, and therefore I will not allow ye to hurt Braedan."

Jocelyn stood next to Blaine. "Please, Sir Roderick, Lady Angela is here and resting. Ye see she was…"

Roderick would not hear her out. Consumed with anger, he continued insisting on seeing his sister. "Well get her up and tell her we are leaving."

Heddy, having walked in just as Rod punched Braedan, had seen enough. Storming up to the man, she pointed her finger at him. "Ye will keep yer voice down, or I will personally see ye thrown out of this house." Rod raised a brow. "Yer sister is sleeping right now. She will see ye as soon as ye have had a chance to calm yerself."

Jocelyn held her breath fearing how Roderick would react. Surprisingly he took off his cloak and handed it to her.

"That's better. Now I will see about finding ye something to drink." Pushing him in the direction of the salon, Heddy told him to stand next to the fire and warm up. Jocelyn followed them.

"I would rather have something strong to drink," Rod growled at her.

Rubbing his chin, Braedan entered the salon and went over to the sideboard. He poured a glass of whisk, handing it to Rod who snarled at him but still took the glass. He slammed the liquid down his throat; he looked surprised.

He thrust the glass back at Braedan. "If ye don't mind, I will have another."

Braedan nodded and refilled it.

This time, he took a sip of the amber liquid, taking time to taste it.

"If ye will excuse me, I will get ye some dry clothes." Jocelyn excused herself. As she passed Blaine, she gave him a worried look.

~ * ~

Rod sat down on the hearth nursing his drink. "I thought I had lost her. I have never sensed such fear." He looked at Blaine, his eyes clouded with sadness.

"If ye recall I too have a sister. There is nothing I wouldna' do for her," Blaine commiserated.

"Do ye think I can talk to her?" Rod asked, looking positively miserable. "If she will see me?"

"Angela is safe and resting, but she went through quite an ordeal. Give yerself a moment, Rod, and when she awakens, I will tell her ye are here."

He nodded, taking another sip of his drink.

"Ye should be aware that she told us of yer parent's plans to wed her to Mackenzie."

"I thought it best to prepare her. I wanted to give her time to accept our parents' decision. Make her see what a future she would have with Mackenzie, something better than what MacAulay could ever offer." Rod looked about the room with a less than appreciative look.

"Ye should know that Braedan concurs with yer decision that Angela wed Mackenzie. He offered to escort her home."

"Should I be impressed? He is the reason she fled in the first place," Rod said. "It matters naught. My carriage should arrive by morning. When it does, we will be on our way."

Just then, Heddy came into the salon. "Lady Angela is awake and asking to see ye. If ye will follow me, I will show ye to her bedchamber." He followed her.

Shortly after, Blaine could hear raised voices, and within minutes, Rod was seen walking down the stairs with a deep scowl on his face.

With so many guests, Blaine wondered how they would accommodate everyone once Ascar and his secretary arrived. Blaine went to the kitchen in search of Jocelyn. She just finished with the dishes when he came up from behind to wrap his arm around her waist. He planted a soft kiss on the side of her neck.

"'Tis too crowded here. I preferred yesterday when I had ye all to myself." Spinning around, she wrapped her arms around his waist. He leaned down, kissing her passionately with an unspoken need. His embrace deepened, his tongue plunging into her sweet depth, leaving her breathless. "I would give anything to have ye lying next to me again, to taste your lips and enjoy the touch of yer satin skin." He kissed her again.

She kissed him back making him forget their current situation.

"We best stop afore I find myself stripping ye of yer clothes and making passionate love to ye again. I fear yer brother would not hesitate to use his dirk."

She agreed and together they finished cleaning the kitchen. "I have meant to ask ye about that letter ye have."

"Ye mean the letter from Graham?"

"Aye, did he give much detail?"

"Aye, in fact, he was explicit. It seems the company suffered a severe setback when they lost two of their ships in a storm and soon after their warehouse caught on fire."

Blaine was in the middle of putting away a stack of dishes when he froze. "What did ye say?"

"I said—"

But he didn't let her finish. "Love, can ye show me the letter?"

"Of course—'tis in my father's study."

Without another word, he dragged her down the hall. She opened the top drawer to retrieve a leather-bound folder. Handing him the letter, he held it next to the candle so he could read it. He couldn't believe it. Is it possible that this was the same company? It would be too much of a coincidence.

"What is it?"

He was positively ecstatic. "I am not sure, and I would rather not say until I am certain." He laughed at her look of disappointment. "But I do promise ye, lass, that if I am right, ye will be rewarded for yer patience." He took her back into his arms and kissed her soundly. Blaine now realized where he needed to go to find the answers. He just hoped he wasn't wrong.

Chapter Sixteen

The following day did not improve Roderick's mood in the least. No sooner did they finish their morning meal, when he announced they were leaving.

"Rod be reasonable. Ye canna expect Angela to ride so soon. Give the lass time to recover," Blaine said.

"My carriage will arrive soon. I want her readied, so we can leave immediately," he growled back.

"Why are ye so in a hurry to get to court?"

Rod shook his head, dragging his fingers through his thick red hair. "I am not taking her to court. I am unsure of what I am doing. I just know we canna stay here."

"If ye think her being here will make her less enamored with Braedan, then I'm afraid ye are too late."

"Nay, the longer I stay, the more I find myself liking the whelp."

Blaine laughed and slapped him heartily on the back. This was the good-natured Rod he knew, not the brooding overbearing bear of a brother. "Come, I want to show ye something."

The two of them went to the study. Blaine showed him the letter hoping he might remember anything that could aid them in finding out what happened to Northern Star.

Heddy entered the study and announced that Sir Roderick's carriage had arrived. "Do not think ye are taking Lady Angela anywhere," she snapped. "I am afraid the lass has developed a fever."

Blaine could tell that Rod suspected she was lying, but when they went to see her, she was indeed feverish.

Jocelyn was applying a cold compress to her forehead when they walked in. "I gave her some tea with willow bark. It will help with the fever," she reassured them. "She just needs some rest."

Wanting to let Rod and Angela have a chance to talk, Jocelyn motioned for Blaine to follow her. As they descended the stairs, a footman and coachman were carrying in several trunks. "What is all this?" She opened one to see it filled with her gowns, the other contained shoes, a pelisse, and other accessories.

"I asked that yer things be sent. I didn't expect Rod would

bring them," Blaine admitted.

Reaching in, he opened a small compartment that held her more intimate apparel and withdrew the black pouch that contained the sapphire necklace. Pressing it in her hand, he folded her fingers around it and then raised them to his lips. "I would ask that ye wear the necklace when we wed."

Jocelyn smiled and nodded, holding the pouch against her breast, tears glistening in her eyes.

~ * ~

No sooner was Rod's carriage unloaded when Ascar and his secretary, Malcolm, arrived. Heddy was beside herself, jumping up and down as she gazed out the window from Jocelyn's bedchamber. They had been busy going through her trunks.

"Isn't he magnificent?" she squealed as he dismounted from his horse. The clouds had finally cleared, and it was turning into a lovely day. The air was still cold and crisp, but the sun was shining, giving the roads a chance to dry.

Jocelyn laughed. "Well, let's not tarry. We must receive Mr. Magnificent."

Ascar greeted Braedan and Blaine with great enthusiasm but was surprised to see Rod. "My lord, 'tis a pleasure to find ye here at Heatherwood. What brings ye this way?"

Rod flushed red, mumbling something about checking in on the MacAulays as he shook the man's hand. Ascar questioned him again when he caught sight of Jocelyn coming down the stairs.

"Ascar, 'tis such a relief to see ye have recovered from yer injuries." There was only a small red mark on his forehead, but she did note that he walked with a slight limp. Bowing, he took her hand.

"Injury? Why was I not told?" Heddy walked down the stairs to stand next to Jocelyn.

Ascar's eyes lit up when he saw her. "Miss Heddy, 'tis good to see ye again." He lifted her hand to his lips, his kiss lingering a bit too long.

Looking concerned and a bit put out, Heddy snatched her hand back. "Ye didn't answer my question, Ascar. What happened?"

"'Tis nothing lass, nothing that yer butter biscuits canna cure." Heddy's ire evaporated, unable to resist his charms. Taking his arm, she led him where a fresh batch was cooling in the kitchen.

~ * ~

When Ascar had his fill of butter biscuits, he joined his secretary to begin the arduous task of trying to decipher Gordon MacAulay's ledgers. Everyone gathered in the study to see if they could aid in any way. Blaine relayed what happened between Jocelyn and Graham, and his idiotic offer to give the land back if she agreed to marry him.

"The man has no morals," Blaine grunted. "Ye yerself notified him of our pending nuptials."

Ascar adjusted his spectacles. "'Tis his nature, regardless of the situation. He will not cease until ye are, in fact, wed."

Blaine looked at Jocelyn. "I plan to rectify matters soon enough. Once I help Braedan with some repairs here at Heatherwood, we will leave for my family's home." He saw her eyes widen. "We are leaving for Calderglen."

"There's no need for ye to delay yer departure—I am more than willing to see to the repairs," Ascar offered. "I might be an accountant, but I come from a family of masons."

Jocelyn bit her bottom lip to keep it from quivering. Her life seemed to be spinning out of control. How could they leave when they just arrived? What about the bakery? What about the king?

"I believe our next step is to address Graham's generous offer to return the parcels of land." Ascar smirked. "Since Lady Jocelyn's hand in marriage is not an option, we will offer to buy back the land. Naturally, I will make him a low offer."

"Do ye believe 'tis wise to let him know when my sister is marrying? He may try to stop it." Braedan was right. The man had no scruples.

Ascar thought about it for a moment. "Aye, I will send him a proposed contract once ye are gone. It may be best to say ye are, in fact wed, unless ye think there may be some delay?"

"Nay!" both Blaine and Braedan answered in unison.

"Nay, we will leave as soon as Lady Angela is better." Braedan turned to Rod. "Naturally we would first escort ye home, my lord…just to assure ye both arrive safely."

Roderick shook his head. "We will leave as soon as my sister is healthy enough to travel; however, we will be accompanying ye to Calderglen." This revelation was indeed a surprise. "I mean, I canna refuse Caelan's invitation to his son's christening, nor miss Blaine's wedding, so we will attend. May I offer ye the use of my carriage?"

Jocelyn could see the intense look on Braedan's face and the hope in his eyes. "I welcome the company, Sir Roderick, I…" Braedan stammered.

Rod put his hand on his shoulder. "'Tis Rod, no need to stand on ceremony."

Jocelyn smiled at them. "Did ye bring the Northern Star

contract?"

"Nay, I had second thoughts about taking the risk that something might happen to it, so I had it copied, and yer father's signature traced over with this fine vellum." He withdrew the copy and handed it to her. "Can ye tell me if this is yer father's?"

Jocelyn took a close look at the signature and then gave it to Braedan. They both agreed that it was.

"Why is there only my father's signature and not Graham's?"

"'Tis exactly what has bothered me since I saw it," Ascar admitted.

"Do ye think Graham was not an investor?" Rod asked.

"Then why was my father paying him. What exactly was he in debt for and to whom?" Braedan's voice was on edge.

"We need to find out about the other investments and go from there. In the meantime, I will start with these ledgers and advise ye if I have any questions." Ascar signaled to Malcolm, and they sat down at the large oak desk.

Jocelyn decided she should go by the bakery and see about organizing the supplies. Braedan agreed to go with her.

"Take my coachmen with ye. I would prefer ye had a proper escort," Rod said, and then excused himself saying he wanted to see how Angela was faring.

Blaine watched as Jocelyn went upstairs to fetch her cloak. He went to see if Braedan needed help when he heard his name.

Ascar approached him with a concerned look on his face. "I did not mention this earlier because in truth I was unsure, but after what ye said about Graham coming here when Lady Jocelyn was alone…"

Blaine led him away from the stairs to the salon, so they could speak in private.

"I believe Graham has men watching the home. When I was riding down the drive, I spied a man on horseback just standing there. He was distracted by what was going on at Heatherwood, he didn't hear my approach. Thinking it might be some farmer, I called out a greeting."

"What did he do?"

"The man just rode away." Ascar furrowed his brow. "I didn't get a good look at him. He raised his hood and then just disappeared into the brush."

Made sense that Graham would be watching the manor; therefore, he needed to get to Calderglen as soon as possible. It had been a long time coming but at last Blaine thought he had a clear sense of what he needed to do.

"Thank ye, I will share this with Braedon. He should be made aware so that he can take necessary precautions." With that, he went in search of Rod.

~ * ~

Blaine caught up to Rod as he was quietly closing the door to Angela's bedchamber. "How is she doing?"

"Improving, I believe she will be fine to travel in a day or two."

"Good, go grab yer cloak, we're going for a ride."

The two set off on their horses across the barren fields. When they finally came to a stop, Blaine told him about Graham attacking Jocelyn and what Ascar had seen.

"If we are on Graham's land, what's not preventing him from shooting ye? Clearly yer trespassing."

Blaine gave him a skeptical look. "Aye, give me a reason to lop off his head and throw it in the jakes. 'Twould be said it was in self-defense."

"Seriously, Blaine, he might have patrols about, and we be sitting pretty fer an attack."

"Nay, he will not try anything. 'Tis also best we make our presence known so he stays away." The pair continued their inspection, sensing they were being watched. It rankled Blaine, although he did not let it show.

As they headed back to the Manor, Rod slowed his horse to a lazy walk. "So ye are serious about wedding the lass?" He chuckled a bit when Blaine glared at him. "I have no qualms about the young lady. I am rather fond of her. I am just surprised that ye changed yer mind about going through with the betrothal. Ye must be aware the king will be displeased." Rod waited, but Blaine didn't respond. Then he laughed, slapping Blaine on the arm. "I knew it. Ye took her to yer bed."

This time his comment did angered Blaine. "I would refrain from making such comments about my intended, or I will knock ye off yer horse."

"Hold on, I mean no disrespect." Rod laughed heartedly. "I just know ye and yer bloody rules, and I am curious as to why ye changed yer mind. Ye are too clever to be forced into a marriage, and ye do not do anything without a purpose."

"Just suffice to say that after long consideration, I believe 'tis best to wed Jocelyn. We are well suited, and besides, my brother will be pleased." Blaine continued to scowl.

Rod was right—he was cautious, yet what had made him linger in Jocelyn's bed when Braedan was expected in the morning. Why did he confront Braedan wearing only her robe?

"Don't fash yerself, I will be by yer side when ye wed. I would not miss the occasion. I do find myself in somewhat of a predicament. I dinna know how I will make my parents understand why we are not at court as they commanded."

"'Tis simple Rod, did ye send Caelan's invitation to the christening?"

"Nay, I brought it with me. I thought to give it to them."

"'Tis better. Send the invitation, along with a letter stating that ye and Angela are attending. They would have no idea if their letter asking ye to come to court arrived before or after ye left. Make sure to say that in addition to the christening, I plan to wed Lady Jocelyn and wish they be present."

Rod's parents would expect him to attend his wedding. He had offered a perfect solution.

Smiling broadly Rod winked at him. "Brother, I need a good stiff drink. Race ye to the stables."

Without waiting for an answer, Rod dug his heels into his horse's flank and tore across the empty field. At least for Rod, his burden was delayed. Blaine wished he felt the same. He desired Jocelyn above all else and taking her innocence left him fiercely possessive of her. The thought of any man touching her drove him mad. His conviction rooted deep within his soul.

Firmly convinced that once they arrived at Calderglen, the answers would be found there. He urged his horse back to Heatherwood.

~ * ~

Angela's health improved rather swiftly, especially after learning they would not be traveling to Edinburgh. Blaine told Jocelyn they would leave for Calderglen the following morning. Ascar would oversee the running of the manor, as well as the bakery. Heddy confided in her that she was overjoyed at the prospect of spending perhaps a month or two with Ascar.

With their packing complete, Jocelyn was in the kitchen making a list of supplies they would need for their journey. Blaine's family home was on the Isle of Sky, and it would take at least a week to reach their destination. Of course, they would stay at various inns along the way, but she wanted to be prepared.

"It will be a long time afore I will hold ye in my arms. I may perish from the wait," Blaine said, entering the kitchen. Jocelyn laughed and went back to her list. "How cruel of ye to laugh at my discomfort. Have ye no compassion for my suffering?"

She smiled. "Ye are a strong warrior. I believe ye can withstand a little suffering."

"Aye, ye are right, but if I may have just a taste of yer sweet lips, it may sustain me…at least an hour."

She laughed as he wrapped his arms around her slender waist. Tipping her head up, she lost herself in his beautiful green eyes. He bent his head and captured her lips. A slight groan rumbled deep in his throat. The sound made desire pool deep from within. She kissed him back, fervently, not being able to get enough.

He broke the kiss, trailed his lips up and down the side of her neck, stopping to gently nibble her sensitive earlobe. The sound of his breath was laced with lust. He managed to untie her apron at the same time as she managed to unbutton his vest. Their garments fell to the floor. Next, she unlaced the top of his shirt and pressed small kisses on the smooth patch of skin. Dissatisfied by not being able to touch more of him, she tugged at his shirt

"Jocelyn, my love, wait, wait…" but she wouldn't listen. "Braedan…" he warned.

She laughed, her voice sounding unusually sultry, even to her. "I canna wait. I must feed ye so that ye wilna perish." One of the buttons on his cuff popped off in her haste and clattered to the floor.

"Wait, we canna do this here…"

"Come with me," she said mischievously.

Blaine picked up his vest from the floor as she pulled him out of the kitchen to a part of the house that was rarely used. Going down a short hallway, she opened the door to reveal a small chamber on the other side of the kitchen. The room was dark, and it took her a moment to find the flint to light the taper. The storage room is where she stored some of her more precious herbs and spices. There was a small chaise lounge in the far corner.

"I used to sit here and read when I wanted to be alone," she explained.

The room smelled heavenly of cinnamon, nutmeg, and some other exotic spices. Jocelyn locked the door and walked back into his arms and began kissing him again.

"Wait…wait," he stuttered as she explored his back and sides. She reached around to pull up his shirt. When she had it all out, she stepped back and rather haughtily motioned with her index finger,

"Take it off." She smiled. "Slowly."

"As ye wish." Blaine lifted his shirt up and then over his head. He shook loose his hair from its queue, the glorious tresses settling around his broad shoulders and down his back. Jocelyn nodded approval.

She stepped closer, looking at the wonder before her. His body was perfection. Her hands touched his large pectoral muscles, while her fingertips gently circling his flat copper nipples, down the center ridge to his flat stomach. She heard the sharp intake of breath between his teeth. Her exploration of him was driving him insane, and she reveled in the power of it.

"Now 'tis yer turn." He unbuttoned the top of her gown as he pressed light kisses on the nape of her neck. "Mmmm," he groaned. "I can smell just the hint of heather and violets. 'Tis most pleasurable."

He pushed the dress down over her arms and then untied her chemise, so she stood only in her petticoats and stockings. Jocelyn arched her back so his mouth could latch onto her full breast. He sucked greedily as her fingers entwined in his silky locks.

"Dear heavens," she gasped. The sensation of his mouth sent electrical pulses between her legs.

Blaine stiffened when she reached down to caress his arousal, stroking its length that pressed tautly against the fabric of his breeches.

"I have had enough," he said, withdrawing. "I want ye naked, and I want ye now." He gave her a wicked smile as shoved aside her petticoats and lay her on top of the chaise. Kneeling, he flipped her legs over his shoulder and bent to kiss her in her most intimate area.

Jocelyn cried out as his tongue stroked and flickered over the sensitive point of flesh. She was startled by his invasion but was powerless to stop him. In fact, she wanted more. When he sucked, she gasped in pure ecstasy as he brought her higher and higher to the point of wondrous arousal, making her body tremble from the intensity. And just when she thought she could endure no more, his mouth consumed her bringing forth an intensified release.

Her body stiffened as wave after wave coursed through her body like a current from the center of her pleasure to the ends of her fingertips.

Breathing hard, she brought her hands up to cover her face, warmed by the experience. She lay there, at a loss for words. She had never experienced such pleasure, and it left her limp and satiated.

He was not finished. Still, on his knees, he unlaced his breeches, releasing his arousal. She must have gazed at him with such satisfaction, he beamed from within. With her bottom hung off the edge, he wrapped her legs around his waist. He carefully parted her lips below with the tip of his staff.

She was ultra-sensitive and bucked a bit from the intrusion. With careful movements, he penetrated her, closing his eyes. A gasp escaped his lips as he pushed forward until he was buried to the hilt, which she thought indescribably gratifying. He began to move gently at first, and then each thrust increased in its intensity and speed. With the pad of his thumb, he stroked her sensitive flesh. She brought her hand up to her mouth, biting down on her fist to keep from screaming.

He gritted out a feral growl before throwing his head back. "By the all the Saints," he yelled as his body trembled from the power of his orgasm. "I love ye," he said breathlessly as he collapsed beside her.

Wrapping his arms around her, she could feel his heart beating against hers. She was too spent to say or do anything except lie there but she was fully aware of what had escaped his lips.

~ * ~

Jocelyn looked out the window as Rod's men carried her trunk out to the waiting carriage. She realized she was leaving her home, perhaps forever. She spun around to see the door wide open and on the other side was her future as Blaine's wife. She had tried to speak to her brother that there was no need to force a marriage, but he would not listen.

"I canna see why ye object so," he said, "'tis obvious ye love the man."

She feigned a look of shock, but he only laughed at her. Her brother knew her too well. It was true, she loved Blaine with all her heart, and she would love him for all her life, but...

He was a man who craved variety. Sure, he expressed his love for her when they last made love, his words not escaping her hearing, but how long would it last? How long before he sought the arms of another woman? How would she survive? Tears pricked behind her eyes, causing her to close them. Taking a deep breath, she did her best to still the waves of doubt. She would not succumb to fear or uncertainty, she had to be strong and...and...

"Are ye ready?" His deep tenor voice reverberated through her like a warm wave.

Slowly she opened her eyes to see him standing before her. He was dressed all in black, making the contrast of his golden mane even more amazing. Praise the Saints, could the man look more beautiful? There was an intense look in his eyes while his brows angled up in concern. With a smile, she nodded. He gifted her with a boyish grin and extended his hand. Taking it, the warmth ran up her arm to curl around her heart.

"Are ye all right?"

"Aye, 'tis only nerves," she said, her voice sounding weak.

"As long as ye are with me, there is nothing to fear."

"I trust ye, I just…"

"What is in your thoughts?"

Jocelyn decided she needed to be honest. "Our future? 'Tis so unclear."

He smiled and squeezed the hand he held. "That is naught something I can control. So, let's face this together."

So, together, hand in hand, they walked out of her bedchamber to their uncertain future.

Chapter Seventeen

The first few days of their journey passed by without incident. Leading the way, Blaine and Rod road their mounts while Braedan took up the rear on Angela's mare. Well protected in Rod's cozy carriage. Angela's happiness was infectious. Jocelyn understood why her brother was so enamored by her.

Having visited Calderglen on many occasions, Angela described those whom she would soon meet. Blaine's mother, Lady Anna, was known throughout the Highlands as a great healer. Then there was the youngest MacKinnon, Miranda, Angela's dearest friend. She told her of the mischief they would get into. For the most part, this kept Jocelyn distracted from her fear in meeting the eldest brother, Caelan, who was Clan Chieftain. He was reputed to be severe and unyielding.

Jocelyn worried how he would react to the news of their pending marriage. Angela assured her she had nothing to worry about, but doubts gnawed at her nerves as they neared the Isle of Skye.

By the fourth day, Jocelyn grew reticent. When Blaine asked, she blamed it on the weather. The temperature had dropped, and the snow was imminent. He told her not to fret, in fact he thought the weather rather mild with the winter solstice just a fortnight away. When they stopped to rest the horses, Blaine suggested they stretch their legs.

Lady Angela jumped out of the carriage ahead of them and ran to where Braedan stood, apparently to fawn over her mare. Finding a distant patch of grass for her horse to graze, the pair reached for each other's hand. Jocelyn found joy in watching the couple.

Picking out the path, he took her to a clearing overlooking a large meadow. He came up behind to wrap his arms around her.

"Are ye all right, love?" he asked, leaning around to kiss her on the side of her face.

"Aye."

"What is going on in that lovely head of yers?" He hugged her closer.

Jocelyn closed her eyes, and her worries faded. "Ye will think me silly."

"Try me."

"I just hope yer family is accepting of our union. I am aware that I do not offer much."

Blaine turned her around. "My dear, my family will be thrilled to finally see me wed." She cast her face down, refusing to look at him. "Oh, lass, dinna take this wrong." He lifted her face. "My family will find ye most charming and welcome ye to their bosoms. And if they dinna, just bake them one of yer sweet rolls, and they will follow ye around like a devoted pup." He crushed her lips possessively, making her sigh aloud with his boldness. "They will find ye beautiful and intelligent—"

"And an amazing baker." She smiled.

He kissed her again hard and then softer, stroking her lips with his own full ones. "Ye have nothing to fear. Ye are mine, and I will never let anyone hurt ye."

"What about Lord Caelan? He may object."

"Caelan is the most exuberant of all. Ye met Douglas John. The two are just the same, both with hearts of gold. Ye will no find a more caring man. We MacKinnons are fiercely protective of our kin." Jocelyn sighed. "Let's be off love. We have a long way to go."

Feeling light-hearted, she walked arm in arm to the waiting carriage.

~ * ~

The group reached Port of Glenelg to find a MacKinnon ship docked at the pier. Jocelyn saw a large, well-muscled man leave the Harbormaster's office. There was a menacing look on his face when he saw them approach. She feared he may not let them stop when she heard him shout something at Blaine.

Blaine glared at the man as he jumped off his horse. He reached him in three strides and yelled back a retort. "Why in bloody hell do ye say I am late?" Then before Blaine could retreat the giant warrior had him in a big bear hug. They burst out laughing. "Let go of me, ye big lout."

"'Tis good to see ye and in such good health," the man said releasing him. "Ye must be keeping yerself far from trouble."

"Oh, shove off ye goon. I am naught the only one who dances with trouble," Blaine said, walking back to the carriage.

Braedan smiled at the two enjoying the ribald. When he opened the carriage door, Angela jumped out unassisted. She ran toward the giant and threw herself into his arms.

"Greetings, Ewan." She laughed as he picked her up, swinging her around.

Setting her down, he cocked his head to one side. "What have ye done to my freckled-faced lass? Ye canna possibly be my angel—ye are too bonny."

Angela blushed at the compliment. "Dinna be daft." She beamed at him. "I never had freckles."

"Well, freckles or no, ye are still bonny."

The three of them continued chatting when Jocelyn alighted from the carriage. Blaine smiled broadly, walking over to take her arm. Ewan arched his brow, a look of surprise on his handsome face.

"Ewan MacKinnon, may I present to ye my betrothed, Lady Jocelyn MacAulay."

Jocelyn's stomach fluttered.

The enormous man took her hand and bowed respectfully. "'Tis an honor to make yer acquaintance my lady," Ewan flashed a winning smile, "and welcome to the family." He then leaned down and planted a gentle kiss on the back of her hand.

Her cheeks heated when the kiss lasted a bit longer than was considered polite. He released her hand but not before winking at her.

"Don't mind this ogre. He has no manners." Blaine laughed, clearly unaffected by Ewan's boldness. "This here is Braedan MacAulay."

Ewan took his hand, shaking it a bit too hard. "Welcome to ye all. Please follow me." He escorted them out of the cold and into the harbormaster's quarters to warm themselves by the brazier. "It will take a while to load up the ship, so please make yerself comfortable."

He left with Blaine, leaving Braedan to keep them company. Lady Angela was full of stories about Ewan and the troubles he and Blaine would get into, especially with the ladies. Ewan himself was supposedly betrothed to Lady Cenna MacLeod, but it was said that she refused to set the date until he settled down. She launched into another story when Ewan returned to say it was time to board the waiting ship.

Jocelyn watched as they pulled away from the shore to cross the short distance to the Isle of Skye, the ancestral home of the MacKinnon's.

The morning mist lifted momentarily so they could catch sight of the coastline which consisted of a series of bays and peninsulas. The southern end, referred to as 'the Garden of Skye', rose lush and green before them. Blaine relayed the history of how the MacKinnons came to the Isle of Skye. It was Laird Lachlan MacKinnon who first took up residence in Castle Moil in the 12th century. Originally the clan had settled in Mull, sometime between the 10th and 12th century. After the Bannockburn, The Bruce rewarded the chief of the MacKinnons with lands in Skye, and it became the principal residence of the clan.

Although the MacLeods occupied most of the island, the MacKinnons ruled the southern end, which was mostly flat and ideal for farming. Castle Moil was the seat of the MacKinnon clan. The drafty castle fell into disrepair around the 16th century. The family built a large manor in the heart of Calderglen, where the clan prospered from the land as well as the sea. The MacKinnons owned ports on both sides of the straight and right next to them was Loch of Kyle, where they could export to the mainland markets.

"The isle itself is thought to have gained its name from the wing-like shape of the shore," Blaine exclaimed. "However, I have seen it when the sea is so blue and the sky so clear that one canna see where the sky ends, and the water begins, so the isle looks to be floating." His eyes reflected the love he had for his home.

The wet mist settled over the loch, and so the ladies went to the galley below where it was warm. Blaine gazed out at the blanketed loch, wiping the water droplets that formed on his face and eyelashes. He was lost in thought when Ewan's voice startled him, "'Tis been a long time since ye 'ave been back. I am sure yer ma will be happy to see ye." He leaned against the bulwarks.

"I don't suppose Caelan will be too pleased to see me." Blaine pressed his lips. "I hope the surprise will lessen his ire."

"Oh, he will no be surprised," he smirked at Blaine's expression. "There was a skiff heading back to the isle. I made sure to send word that ye arrived."

"And why would ye be so accommodating?" Blaine retorted.

"Dinna be a glaring. I thought it best that yer laird is made aware that ye be escorting yer betrothed. Give him time to get a hold of his anger and mayhap not come out a yell'n."

Blaine gave it some thought and realized it didn't matter what Ewan did. Caelan would no doubt be displeased. "Come," he said to his good friend, "let's get a drink." They went below to join the women.

~ * ~

It took little time to cross the loch and soon they were tying up against the dock. An open carriage sat waiting for them. Laying heavy fur pelts over their laps, they headed up through the bustling docks and the village. Everyone yelled out a greeting as they passed by. Jocelyn felt their eyes staring at her, and she did her best to appear calm and unaffected although her stomach was doing flips. She didn't mind in the least when some of the women called out to Blaine, asking him to visit or stop by for a chat. He was their kin and, soon enough, they would learn of their engagement. She just wished she could stop being so anxious. Sitting back against the squabs, she looked out at the countryside as they made their way up the long road toward the large manor.

Calderglen came into view. It wasn't a large manor, but it was impressive, nonetheless. The three-story structure was in the shape of a U. The front was longer, with a beautiful circular driveway lined with Silver Birch trees. As they drew closer, Jocelyn saw a man and a woman standing at the top of the stairs. Both had raven black hair, but that's where their similarities ended. The woman's smile could be seen from a distance. The closer they came, the broader the smile.

Jocelyn looked at the tall warrior standing next to her and a smile spread across her face. She immediately recognized Blaine's brother Douglas John. But then there was something odd about him. He wasn't smiling at all—as a matter of fact, the energy emanating from his anger darkened his handsome features. That was when Jocelyn felt the ice from his cerulean eyes pierce right through her. The man standing next to the woman was not Douglas John, which could only mean it was …*Caelan*.

When the carriage came to a stop. Blaine and Rod jumped down to help the ladies down. Angela was up the stairs and in the woman's arms in a flash. "Oh, Lady Anna, 'tis so good to see ye."

Lady Anna hugged the young girl fiercely and then released her, so she could take a better look. "Child, ye are positively lovely. 'Tis been far too long. Ye best go in and see Miranda. She's been wearing out the carpet in her room waiting for ye."

No sooner did she say this when the door flung open, and a younger version of the woman came running out. Both girls started screaming and hugging and talking at once. The young woman, whom Jocelyn assumed was Miranda, looked exactly like her mother, although not as beautiful.

Jocelyn stole a look toward Caelan who wore an annoyed expression on his face. It was at that moment that their eyes locked, and Jocelyn was rapt by his cold hard stare. This was the exuberant Caelan? A heart of gold like Douglas John? She stood there like a ninny, rooted to the spot. Only when he tore his eyes away from her, did she hear her name.

"Mother, Caelan, I would like to present to ye my betrothed, Lady Jocelyn MacAulay, and her brother Braedan MacAulay." Blaine dragged her up the steps where she curtseyed on unsteady legs.

Caelan's expression did not change. He was polite, as expected of Highland hospitality. "Welcome to Calderglen," he said. "This is our mother, Lady Anna. She will show ye to yer bedchambers so ye can freshen up. We will meet later before the evening meal, and we can get better acquainted."

Lady Anna took Jocelyn by the arm and escorted her inside. "My dear, I am so pleased Blaine brought ye so ye can meet yer future family."

Lady Anna had a soothing voice. Jocelyn understood why some said Lady Anna had the touch to bring comfort to those who suffered. She was still beautiful at her age with only a few gray hairs and hardly a wrinkle on her face.

Caelan greeted Rod, who brought up the rear. "Rod, I expect ye would like a drink."

He smiled and nodded. "Come, Braedan, let's find ourselves a drink." The two went toward the family salon.

Blaine thought to go with them when he heard his brother say, "My study, Blaine." Caelan turned on his heel.

Blaine followed Caelan into his study and went straight to the sideboard to pour himself a drink. Slamming it down, he poured himself a second before turning to face him.

"I should knock yer head right off yer shoulders," Caelan yelled. "What in Saint's name do ye think by coming here with...with...," he dragged his fingers through his thick hair, "...her."

"Her name is Jocelyn, and I would appreciate it if ye would remember that she is my—"

"Cease!" Caelan shouted back. "Do ye think for a moment that I believe this betrothal to be true? I heard all about yer escapades with the king. Ye didn't fool him. Why would ye think that I would believe ye plan to wed this...this—"

"I said, her name is Jocelyn," Blaine gritted out between clenched teeth. "And yes, I plan to wed her. That is why we are here."

Caelan gave him an incredulous look. "Ye are planning to wed?" Blaine nodded. "Here?" He nodded again. Caelan narrowed his eyes, clearly disgusted.

"I assume Father Maris is here for the christening?" Caelan bobbed his head. "I assume, since ye wanted me here, I would bring Jocelyn, and we would wed while the clan is gathered."

Caelan went over to the sideboard and poured himself a drink. He too slammed the contents down in one gulp. The silence was making Blaine uncomfortable. He was used to Caelan yelling and carrying on, but this silent and brooding brother made him uneasy.

"Where did ye meet the lass?" he finally said. "What did ye do to get her to agree to this charade." He turned toward the window to gaze out at the mist. Blaine believed Caelan couldn't bear to look at him and decided that it would be best, to tell the truth.

"On my way to court, I came upon Jocelyn and her brother being attacked by thieves. I came to their aid, and Braedan was injured in the fracas. I took them to Rod's. It was there that we came up with the idea of portraying Jocelyn as my intended, in hopes to give me time to find a suitable wife."

"So, ye coerced the poor lass to be part of yer ploy to deceive the king. How clever ye must have thought, knowing that she couldn't refuse since she was indebted to ye for her rescue."

Blaine would generally have considered Caelan's interpretation an affront, except he spoke the truth. "As ye say, brother, Jocelyn was in no position to refuse."

Caelan looked at him, shaking his head in disapproval.

"I did not expect the king to object to my choice of bride."

"The king chose for ye Lady Clara Buchanan. She is not only beautiful and intelligent, but she is wealthy and Laird Buchanan's only daughter. Any man would have dropped to his knees in gratitude for such an honor."

"Lady Clara is merely a child," Blaine bellowed. "I will never marry her."

"Well, brother, ye have no choice," Caelan simply stated.

"I do have a choice, Caelan, and I will wed Jocelyn."

"Ye canna deny yer king's command, Blaine."

"Why not?" he argued. "I served the king for six years. I have been a loyal subject, and his investments in my fishing fleet have brought him plenty of coin. Ye canna expect me to believe he would see me hanged for wedding the woman I desire."

"Nay, he is not so severe a ruler, but he may choose to punish ye in other ways." Caelan ran his fingers through his hair again, a sign that he was still angry. "Ye have not finished the construction of yer ice house. 'Tis winter and yer fishing is minimal at most. Yer ports are slow of passing ships, and I suspect yer coffers are depleted."

Embarrassed by his comments, Blaine clenched his jaw, aware his brother spoke the truth. "So, if the king doesn't invest in my ice house, 'tis not the end."

"Nay, but he could verra well give the idea to another. Ye did share yer plans with him?" Caelan took a deep breath. "Blaine, ye have to wed Lady Clara. I have received a missive from the king commanding I bring ye myself. And, whether ye want to or not, ye will wed this spring."

As a sign that he was dismissed, Caelan walked over to his desk and sat down. Before Blaine could say another word, Caelan lifted his hand, dismissing him. "I have nothing more to say in the matter."

Blaine stood there for only a moment before he bowed slightly and left the study. It took every ounce of control not to slam the door off its hinges.

~ * ~

Jocelyn sat in her bedchamber waiting for someone to take her to the family salon where they would spend a moment '*getting better acquainted.*' She felt as if she were heading for the noose instead of a family gathering.

She chose to wear the dark navy-blue gown that she favored but doubted anything she wore would make much of an impression with her future in-laws. Aggie, who had been assigned to help her made similar comments going as far as to complain that her hair was too thick to do anything decent with it. She hemmed and hawed, all the while tugging and pulling the tresses painfully, but in the end, she created the most becoming hairstyle.

Aggie let out a ruffle of air between her thin lips, throwing up her hands in defeat and declaring she was a hopeless cause. Jocelyn suspected the curmudgeon was most pleased with the results.

She jumped slightly at the knock at her door. Blaine entered looking magnificent in a dark blue tunic and breeches, with a black shirt underneath. He wore a green plaid over his shoulder that was belted at the waist. His hair was loose about his shoulders, and his eyes looked evergreen in contrast. Perusing her appearance, he smiled approvingly.

"Ye look beautiful, Jocelyn." He lifted her hand to his lips. "I see mother gave ye the corner bedchamber. It has quite an impressive view." He walked to the tall windows, peering out at the mist, "When 'tis not raining. This was once Caelan's bedchamber? I hope ye are comfortable."

The fact she was given Caelan's old bedchamber did surprise her. "Oh, I am most appreciative of yer family's hospitality," she said honestly.

The room was a spacious room with a desk and bookcase near the window, a beautiful canopied bed and two overstuffed chairs in front of a large fireplace. The furnishings did not appear overly masculine or feminine, more designed for comfort and warmth.

"Shall we meet the family?" Blaine offered his arm.

"Did all go well with your brother?" she asked timidly.

"Of course," he smiled assuring her. "Caelan is quite delighted by our visit.

~ * ~

Blaine and Jocelyn arrived first. He immediately poured them each a glass of wine. After ten minutes, he rose to look to see if anyone was coming. When Blaine opened the door, she heard voices coming down the hall.

"As long as I am alive, ye will bend to my will, Caelan MacKinnon, so I suggest ye set aside yer opinions and adopt a more amiable disposition." Lady Anna smiled brightly as she entered the salon. "Oh good, I am glad to see ye are here." She approached Jocelyn who had risen to her feet. "My dear, ye are so beautiful. My son is most fortunate to have such a lovely bride."

Caelan paused before Jocelyn and nodded. "Mother, may I serve ye some wine?"

"Thank ye, Caelan." She took Jocelyn's arm and guided her to a chair near the fire. "Now, tell me all about yerself, how ye came to meet my son."

"Mother, should we not wait for the rest of the family to join us?" Blaine asked.

"It will be just us for now," Caelan informed them. "My wife is momentarily detained with the babe." He handed his mother her glass and offered to refill Jocelyn's, who politely refused. "I thought we could discuss the terms of yer betrothal or would ye prefer yer brother be present, Lady Jocelyn?"

The blood drained from her face, and the ground swam before her. Clearly, Caelan was questioning the validity of their engagement. It was worse than being presented before the king, even though they were truly *affianced*.

"Oh, nonsense," Lady Anna said, getting up to stand between her sons. "This is not what I intended when I suggested we become better acquainted. Tonight, we will present her before the clan." Jocelyn gasped. Seeing her pallor, Lady Anna became concerned. "Blaine, yer betrothed appears a wee bit upset. Why don't ye sit next to her and perhaps refill her wine."

Jocelyn thanked him when he refilled her glass and then drank a reasonable amount.

"Now, that's better," Lady Anna said.

"Caelan tells me ye went to court to be introduced to the king and yet," Lady Anna looked at her, "the king is still insisting my son wed someone of his choosing." Her eyes did not waver. "Are ye aware of this?" Jocelyn nodded. "Good, now I understand the both of ye wish to wed regardless of the king's wishes and, Blaine, ye have come to yer family for support?"

"Aye, mother, but I am only asking that ye stand by our decision. I take full responsibility for what may befall when the king hears the news of our marriage."

Jocelyn stole a glance at Caelan whose expression was so stern he could have been carved from stone.

"And are ye in accord with my son?"

All gazes fell upon her. "Aye, my lady, however, I would only do so by his laird's blessing." She looked Caelan squarely in the eyes and did not falter when he locked onto hers.

"Do ye know what consequences may befall ye for yer actions?" Caelan glared her. "Ye may bring trouble to my shores."

Blaine looked like he wanted to strangle him for what he was trying to do. He thought to pressure her to the point that she might call off their engagement and end what he considered a ruse.

Blaine interceded on her behalf. "I have asked for Jocelyn's hand in marriage. I have signed a betrothal contract, and I have brought her to my family, so ye can witness our union."

There was so much conviction in his voice that Jocelyn also stood, taking his hand. "I, too, wish to wed Blaine. I love him, and I want to be his wife."

Caelan stared at them in disbelief. He turned to fill his glass of wine; Jocelyn swore she heard him say "fools" under his breath.

"Well then, that is all I needed to hear." Lady Anna clasped her hands together. "We can make the announcement tonight before the family."

Jocelyn stiffened when she saw Caelan turn to them, anger suffusing his face. He was about to say something when he stopped and smiled. When he smiled, she noticed he possessed the most delightful dimple on one cheek.

Curious as to the reason for this transformation, Jocelyn followed his gaze to see a woman standing at the doorway. She was holding a tiny babe in her arms. Caelan was at her side in seconds, his face beaming with love and affection. The woman had golden hair that was pulled back in an intricate braid. Dressed in an emerald green gown, it accentuated a figure that one could only be described as spectacular. Jocelyn was aware that women's breasts grew when nursing, but it was hard not to stare at the bounty that threatened to spill over her bodice.

Caelan guided the woman to the chair next to Lady Anna, "May I introduce to ye my wife, Lady Ilyssa." Jocelyn curtseyed. "And this young lad is my son Michael."

It was apparent that Caelan loved his wife and adored his son. She had to admire a woman who could brave his icy demeanor and still hold his heart as Caelan certainly wasn't someone, one might consider…approachable.

"Ilyssa, ye are a vision of loveliness," Blaine declared and leaned over to kiss her on each cheek. "May I say that motherhood becomes ye." He smiled and turned to take Jocelyn's hand. "This is Lady Jocelyn, my fiancée."

Jocelyn smiled and curtseyed again. "'Tis an honor to make yer acquaintance, Lady Ilyssa."

"Please call me Ilyssa. We are to be family soon," she insisted. "I am eager to learn all about ye."

"Aye, do tell us."

Lady Anna motioned for her to sit down again.

"There's nothing much to tell," Jocelyn replied honestly. "I grew up in a small village north of Glen Garry. I run a small bakery." She thought she sounded foolish.

"A bakery, how wonderful," Lady Ilyssa exclaimed. "I have always admired women who have their own professions. Lady Anna is an acclaimed healer, and I hope one to earn the same accolades. I came here to study under her tutelage, which is how I met my husband." She turned to look at Caelan, who returned her smile. "I understand ye have met Arrabella?"

Jocelyn nodded.

"Well, there's no one in the family who has more knowledge about farming than our Arrabella. She's quite the agrarian expert."

"We too have a farm," Jocelyn started to say when Braedan, Rod and Lady Angela walked into the salon. Jocelyn was grateful for the interruption.

"Are ye all done with yer family business?" Rod's booming voice reverberated through the room, "I for one am ready to partake in some company and MacKinnon hospitality."

The group laughed. All except Jocelyn. She tried to enjoy the interactions, but as far as she was concerned, the family business had just begun.

Chapter Eighteen

Jocelyn stared up at the canopy over her bed and let out a whoosh of air from between her lips. It had been a long and eventful day. Soon as Braedan, Rod, and Angela joined them in the salon, they left for the great hall where a massive crowd of people awaited their company. Caelan introduced them to family and friends, too many to remember their names. Some of the women looked at her curiously.

Seated next to Blaine on her right and Father Maris on her left, she was well protected from prying eyes. The priest turned out to be a lively dinner companion, keeping her well entertained with stories of the MacKinnon brothers. Blaine laughed at the same time defending himself. Jocelyn did enjoy herself, and the food was delicious, but the evening lasted forever, and she felt exhausted.

Just as the meal concluded, Caelan stood up to address his clan. "I would like to thank my guests, who traveled far to attend my son's christening. It is especially important to me to have my brother, Blaine, present since he will be Michael's godfather." There was a round of applause.

One man rose. "Best not be teaching him about chase'n the lassies, but how to run from 'em."

The men laughed loudly. Caelan brought his hands up. "Family is important, and it is a joy to welcome a new member to our clan."

Jocelyn's stomach dropped to the floor

"We celebrate new life," he lifted his goblet to his wife, "and celebrate new unions."

She swallowed hard.

"It is my honor to announce the betrothal of my brother Blaine to Lady Jocelyn. Please lift yer drinks and join me in welcoming Lady Jocelyn MacAulay."

Much to her surprise the news was well received. Shouts of well wishes and congratulations could be heard over the din.

Blaine got to his feet, holding his glass and waited for them to settle. "'Tis been a long time that I have avoided the snare of matrimony." They cheered at this. "At times, I thought I would live my life as a bachelor."

"Ye still can change yer mind," a man shouted.

"I have no intentions of changing my mind, Tom."

"I was no talk'n to ye Blaine, I was suggesting it to the lady." The crowd laughed.

"As I was saying, I did not think there would be a time when I would stand before my clan and say these words." Blaine put down his glass and got down on one knee. He picked up her hand in both of his, and she lost herself in his eyes, "Jocelyn, ye have made me the happiest man by agreeing to be my wife."

Her eyes brimmed with tears. He kissed her hand and then stood up, practically lifting her up in his arms and then kissing her hard on the mouth. They cheered loudly.

From the corner of her eye, Jocelyn noted that Caelan looked at them and slightly shook his head. His expression was one of happiness, albeit a bit unsure, but happy, nevertheless. When the room quieted down, he addressed them once more. "I am also pleased to announce that Blaine and Jocelyn have consented to exchange their vows here at Calderglen, and ye are all invited."

People approached her and Blaine with their good wishes. An hour passed before they could leave the hall and seek the peace and quiet of their bedchambers.

Happy that the evening was finally at an end, she saw Aggie waiting to assist her. Her temperament had changed considerably from earlier. "'Tis a shame ye had to wear that dreadful gown at the announcement of yer betrothal." She rolled her eyes at the offending garment. "I am sure we can find something better fer yer wedding day. I did notice there was a nice gown amongst yer things. I hope ye intend to wear the silver. I am sure I can find some ribbon to match…"

The more Aggie prattled, the more relaxed Jocelyn became. She was officially betrothed to Blaine. Father Maris would read the banns the following Sunday, and they would marry soon after Michael's christening.

"Lady Anna will be expecting to host a few luncheons so ye are properly introduced. Oh, dinna forget the MacLeods as they will be want'n an introduction."

Finally tucked in bed, Jocelyn found it hard to fall asleep. Turning on her side, she clutched a small pillow to her chest. She let out her breath slowly, willing herself to relax. Her eyes flew open when she the bed moved and a warm body slip behind her. She smiled in the dark as strong arms wrapped around her waist, pulling her close to his heated body.

"I thought ye might be scared, sleeping all alone in this empty, cold and dreary bedchamber." Blaine nuzzled Jocelyn's neck. "I am here to protect ye and keep ye warm." He kissed her nape.

"I didn't realize I needed protection."

"Aye, and heat…'tis too cold, ye might sicken." Jocelyn giggled. "'Tis no laughing matter when ye awaken with red eyes and a runny nose."

"The only heat will be the look of disapproval if we are caught."

"Nonsense," Blaine said, sounding like his mother. "We are practically wed now. In a few days, the banns will be read. All that is left is to say our vows." She let out a slight gasp. "Ye need not worry, lass, I promise, I will always protect ye, and as long as ye are by my side, no harm will come to ye."

She didn't want to ruin the moment, but her silly doubts began their usual bombardments. She spun around to face him. "Make love to me, Blaine." She started kissing him, his eyes, his lips, the sharp edge of his jawline.

"Hold on, lass." He laughed. "I have tasted yer loveliness when I had no right. There is nothing more in the world that I want than to take ye in my arms and make ye mine. But there's a part of me that wants the next time to be when we are wed." He laughed again when she gave him a look of disbelief. "In a few days, ye will be mine, my wife, and that 'tis when I will make love to ye and not before."

"But why are ye here? In my bed?"

"I told ye, 'tis too cold to sleep alone." With that, he settled, wrapping his arms around her again. Jocelyn thought it best not to argue. This was important to him. She just hoped she would be able to fall asleep.

And sleep she did…deep and restful sleep in Blaine's arms, dreaming of nights they would share together.

~ * ~

Trying his best not to awaken her, Blaine got up as quietly as possible. He tucked the covers around her to keep her warm. In the faint morning light, he could see her face, relaxed in slumber. Her lashes created dark crescents against her pale cheeks, and her lips were red and slightly parted. Her glorious hair fanned out behind her in thick waves. She looked so fragile lying there that Blaine's chest ached.

This differed from what he had previously experienced. This time the fierce need to protect and—something more—the need to possess her completely, mind, body, and soul. The need filled him and completed him.

"Mine!"

Closing the door to her bedchamber, he crossed the hall to his own. Silently he slipped into his room and dove under his covers, pulling them high under his chin. The fire had died down long ago, and he doubted he would sleep. After a time, he got up and dressed. Deciding he needed to find Caelan, he nearly ran down the chambermaid who was sent to light his fire. By the look in her eyes, she was interested in lighting more than just a flame.

Blaine laughed, winking at the lass. "'Tis no need, I will no be requiring yer service." He could tell by the look of disappointment that his words hit their mark.

There was no regret on his part, and he embraced this newfound desire to make only one woman swoon at his approach. Jocelyn was the only woman who now possessed his heart.

Caelan had left early that morning to attend a meeting with the MacLeods. He would have to wait to speak to him. Walking into the great hall, Blaine saw the place abuzz with activity, preparing for the christening and now his wedding. Decorated for the Yuletide, the manor looked ready for the many guests that would soon arrive. Father Maris spotted him from the hall and motioned for him to join him at the head table. Seated next to him was Lady Angela and Braedan. They looked miserable.

"Good morrow, Blaine," Father Maris said. "Come and bring these young people some good cheer."

He could not imagine what would bring them so low. Lady Angela barely acknowledged him, and Braedan looked miserable. They did their best at some polite conversation, but within minutes they excused themselves and left the hall.

Blaine guessed they might have sought Father Maris's counsel regarding their present predicament. The clergy would never divulge what they discussed, so instead, they talked about the latest news.

~ * ~

Jocelyn was busy preparing for the day. Aggie had brusquely advised her that she would be joining Lady Anna and the ladies for breakfast. Dressing in a dark gray gown, she suffered in silence as Aggie pulled and tugged her hair. Most of her hair was pulled back in a large bun, then Aggie braided several strands around her head that crisscrossed and intertwined. She left some loose strands and those she curled to frame her face. It was neat and yet elegant at the same time.

"Ye be a laird's wife soon. 'Tis best ye start looking like one," Aggie bit out. Taking a critical look, she threw up her hands. "'Tis all I can do, for now."

Aggie led her down the long hall to Lady Anna's private quarters. She entered a beautiful salon that faced the west, with a view of the garden below. She saw Lady Anna and Lady Ilyssa enjoying a cup of tea.

"Good morrow, my dear, I hope ye slept well?" Lady Anna smiled, motioning for Jocelyn to sit.

"Ye are looking quite lovely," Lady Ilyssa added.

"I hope ye don't mind breaking yer fast with us." Lady Anna pointed to the table laden with all sorts of bread, cheeses, and dried fruit. "I thought we could have a nice morning together."

Lady Ilyssa laughed, pouring her a cup of tea, "'Twould be nice to talk about yer wedding and what plans ye might have." Her faced beamed with excitement. "The last wedding, we had was a few months ago. Simply the perfect time of year. I believe yers will need to be indoors. Not much chance of holding it at the castle."

Jocelyn accepted the hot mug. "The castle?"

"Aye, Castle Moil," Lady Anna explained. "'Tis where we held the wedding for my niece, Kaylee. It was such a beautiful wedding."

"Every laird and lady have spent their wedding night at the castle." Lady Ilyssa smiled. "I hope ye will spend your wedding night there."

Jocelyn's face warmed by the query. "I thank ye, I will tell Blaine—"

"Blaine knows, but he thinks the castle is a drafty pile of stone," Lady Anna interrupted. "He will prefer to take ye to Stonegate as soon as possible. He is very proud of his home." She gestured to Ilyssa to pour some more tea.

At that moment, Miranda rushed into the room, she focused on the platter of food. "Oh, good. I am positively famished." She grabbed a small plate and started piling food while shoving a piece of bread into her mouth.

"Good heavens, child. Where are yer manners?" Lady Anna shook her head. "Ye act as if we don't feed ye."

"I am sorry, Mama." Turning to Ilyssa, she walked over and brushed her cheek with a quick kiss, "Good morrow, Lyss." She smiled at Jocelyn. "Good morrow, Lady Jocelyn."

Jocelyn watched as the lass turned her attention back to the food. She realized she had been wrong in her initial assessment. Miranda was very pretty, albeit a bit too thin. She wasn't like Lady Angela, whose reed-like figure swayed delicately as she walked. Miranda was lanky, like a young boy, but in time she would fill out and gain some womanly curves.

The lass possessed the same cerulean blue eyes that most of her siblings had, and she was blessed with glorious curly black hair. Curls puffed out from the confines of her long braid. She looked as if she had just returned from a ride.

"Child, canna ye not wait? Angela has yet to join us," Lady Anne scolded her. "Do sit down."

"Nnumph, miff herm." Miranda's hand flew to her mouth to stifle the giggle that slipped out when her mother shot her a stern look. Swallowing quickly, she smiled shyly. "Apologies, Mother," she said sincerely. "I saw Angela as I was coming here. She asked that I convey her regrets that she will not be joining us this morn."

"Is she not feeling well?"

Miranda shrugged and popped another bite of bread into her mouth. She continued eating, making all sorts of approving sounds. "This bread 'tis the best I have ever tasted," she exclaimed, taking another one from the tray. "I do not believe cook has never made these before."

"I made them." All three women stared at Jocelyn with their mouths agape.

"Truth?" Miranda blurted out. Jocelyn's face heated as she nodded. "'Tis most delicious, not salty, not sweet but—"

"Savory," Jocelyn interjected. "I discovered quite a treasure of spices, my lady," she said, turning to Lady Anna. "I combined poppy seeds and almond extract, as well as honey into the bread. 'Tis a recipe my mother made during Christmastide and 'tis one of my favorites."

"Ah, yes poppy seeds have medicinal value as well," Lady Ilyssa piped in. "Prepared in a draught, they help with coughs, and in syrup, it has a calming effect which can aid in sleep."

Miranda shook her head. "It matters naught, 'tis delicious." The ladies agreed.

It was true that Jocelyn had made the bread. She had awoken shortly after Blaine left their bed. Accustomed to rising early, she headed to the kitchen. In the past, she had known cooks to be territorial when it came to their kitchens and most did not welcome strangers, no matter their intentions.

However, with all the added guests, the cook at Calderglen was more than happy for her help. Once again, she sensed a feeling of home. She did her best thinking when kneading dough. The grit of the flour, so familiar to her hands helped clear her mind

"'Tis a shame Angela will not join us," Miranda stated absentmindedly.

"Ye did not answer me, daughter, is Angela ill?" The lass shrugged and popped another piece of bread in her mouth. Lady Anna smiled and turned to Jocelyn. "I noticed that yer brother is quite fond of our Angela. I must say they make quite an attractive pair."

Jocelyn wasn't uncomfortable discussing her brother and Angela.

Lady Anna placed her hand on her arm. "I apologize, Lady Jocelyn. I did not mean to be intrusive. I was only making an observation. They appeared attached to one another."

"Oh, 'tis not that...I..." Jocelyn stammered.

"They are in love, Mother," Miranda interrupted, clearly not being able to keep silent. "And they canna be together." The lass looked utterly despondent.

Jocelyn decided to be forthcoming—after all these ladies would soon be family. "Miranda is right, my brother is most enamored with Lady Angela, and he did offer for her. Unfortunately," she paused to compose herself, "Laird and Lady MacPherson are presently at court and in the midst of negotiating a betrothal between Lady Angela and Laird Thomas Mackenzie.

Lady Anna looked surprised. She sat quietly mulling the information for what seemed a while. Jocelyn realized she was holding her breath as if the next words from Lady Anna would resolve everything.

"Mother, isn't there something ye can do to help Angela? She loves Braedan, and they wish to wed."

"If I had been told that Laird MacKenzie was looking for a wife, I would consider wedding him myself." Lady Anna laughed warmly. "I am much closer in age."

Jocelyn felt foolish. How in heavens could Lady Anna persuade the MacPhersons to consider Jocelyn's brother, a penniless farmer, over someone as rich and powerful as Laird Thomas MacKenzie?

"Ye say the MacPhersons are at court?" Jocelyn nodded. "So, they have met yer brother and rejected his offer?"

"Nay, they have yet to meet. My brother asked Sir Roderick for Lady Angela's hand. I mean, he asked for his support."

"So, it was Roddy who rejected his offer."

"Aye."

Lady Ilyssa smiled broadly. "Mother MacKinnon, what are ye thinking?"

"I do so love a challenge," she said as she took a bite of the savory bread.

"Mother, have you given Lady Jocelyn our gift?" Miranda asked, changing the subject.

Lady Anna lifted her chin motioning to a parcel that lay on a bench near the window.

Miranda jumped up to retrieve it. She ran back and thrust the package at Jocelyn. "I think you'll be needing this, now that yer marrying my brother."

Jocelyn awkwardly opened the parcel. Her eyes grew wide when she lifted out the MacKinnon plaid. "Oh my, 'tis so beautiful."

The ladies started talking at once, each telling her how and when they received their tartans.

Jocelyn stood up, unfolding the yards of material. "Can ye help me?"

Within minutes the plaid was pleated over her gray gown and belted tightly at the waist. The remainder was thrown over one shoulder and hung down her back.

"I am so honored." She hugged Lady Anna. "I canna thank ye enough."

Seeing the approval on her future mother in-law's face, she was close to tears. She couldn't wait to show Blaine. Jocelyn quickly wiped the tear on her cheek.

"What's the matter, child?" Lady Anna inquired sincerely.

"Naught is wrong, my lady, nothing at all." Jocelyn smiled brightly.

~ * ~

Thinking the fresh air would lift his mood, Blaine left for the stables. He saddled his horse and headed north toward the ruins of Castle Moil. The wind was cold against his face. He bent down close his horse, Loki, and raced across the green meadows of Calderglen.

When he and Loki reached the rise overlooking the loch, the castle in the distance was shrouded in mist, giving it an eerie appearance. He never understood his family's fascination with the old ruin. The tradition of spending one's wedding night at the castle did not appeal to him. He had entirely different plans for Jocelyn.

Blaine wasn't sure how long he sat gazing over the water when he heard a horse approaching. Turning in his saddle, he looked behind to see a rider nearing. From that distance, it could have been either of his brothers, but he recognized the horse and realized it was Caelan.

Caelan slowed his horse when he reached him. He didn't say anything at first, taking a moment to enjoy the view.

"How was your meeting?" Blaine broke the silence.

"Tedious," he answered honestly. "Same issues as always." Caelan stared at his brother. "I thought it best we discuss yer wedding to Lady Jocelyn." Blaine did not look at him. "Keeping in mind that yer union will not sit well with our sovereign leader—"

"I love her," Blaine blurted out. His newly discovered feelings for Jocelyn filled him pervasively, and he wanted to exult in them, just not so vocally. "Forgive me, brother, I did not mean to interrupt." He waited stoically for Caelan to make some snide remark.

"I have always wished that for ye," Caelan continued unemotionally. "'Tis a gift from the Saints to hold such emotions for one's wife."

Blaine stared at his brother.

"I suppose there is no need for me to tell ye the king will not be pleased. Ye know there'll be consequences for not abiding by his commands."

He nodded.

"Fine." Caelan stared at Blaine for a moment and took a deep breath. "I assume ye plan to live at Stonegate. I can't see ye taking over the family bakery."

"Braedan will continue to run the bakery; however, some issues need to be addressed, and I need yer help."

Caelan's brows lifted.

"'Tis a complicated story."

"Then let's be off."

They headed back over the glade with the wind behind their backs. The ride gave Blaine time to formulate his thoughts. He didn't want to paint the MacAulays in a negative light, especially considering how complicated the situation.

When they arrived back at the manor, they went straight to the study. The contrast of the cold outside and the warmth in the room was stifling. Blaine immediately shed his heavy cloak, throwing it onto a chair.

"Drink?" Caelan asked and poured them a glass of whisky. He sat down on the settee. "I am listening."

Blaine took a sip of the fiery brew and decided to state the facts. "The MacAulays invested in some businesses, and as a result, they were swindled, losing their land in the process. Before the bakery, they possessed four parcels of land. Heatherwood used to be a prosperous estate until Jocelyn's father became involved with Warrick Graham." Caelan looked interested, "I have questions regarding some of the businesses that their father invested in, and I am hoping ye may shed some light."

"What kind of businesses are we speaking of?"

"Shipping." Blaine launched into a brief summary of the MacAulays investment with the shipping company and some of the details when he noticed a rather peculiar look on Caelan's face.

"Caelan, are ye ill?" Blaine asked, concerned.

Caelan got up and paced around for a moment. He stopped in front of Blaine; his mouth opened as if he was going to say something, then started walking around mumbling, "This canna be." After a moment, he dragged his fingers through his hair and looked at him. "Are ye saying that Braedan MacAulay and Lady Jocelyn are the children of Gordon MacAulay?"

"Aye, how did ye…"

"The same Gordon MacAulay who invested in Northern Star Shipping Company?"

"Aye. Have ye heard of Northern Star?"

"I believe it would be best if we bring your intended and her brother here, so we can speak to them as well." Blaine downed his drink. Caelan perused the bookshelf behind him, taking out a rather thick leather book. After a moment he looked back at Blaine with a slightly annoyed look. "Well, what are ye waiting for? I asked ye to fetch the MacAulays."

"Are ye going to tell me why? Do you know something about Northern Star?"

"Aye," he replied matter-of-factly. "I own Northern Star."

Chapter Nineteen

Jocelyn stared at her reflection in the mirror, admiring the beautiful plaid. It was a pleasant shade of green with white, yellow and burgundy lines running through it. She couldn't wait to see Blaine's reaction when he saw her. Her heart skipped a beat when someone knocked.

Smoothing down her hair, she took one last glance in the mirror before opening the door. She felt a small thread of disappointment to see Braedan on the other side. "Good evening Brea." She smiled at him.

Braedan gave her an approving smile when he saw the plaid. "Ye look especially bonny this evening Joce. 'Tis a new gown?" he teased her. His expression then turned serious. "If ye are ready, Blaine and Caelan have requested we join them in the study. Caelan would like a word."

Jocelyn nodded, and the two went downstairs.

Entering the study, Blaine greeted her with an approving smile. "Ye look beautiful," he commented, taking her hand to kiss it.

Caelan was seated at his desk, which was covered with ledgers and papers in neat piles. He stood up and walked over to the pair, holding a parchment in his hand. He handed it to Jocelyn. At first glance, Jocelyn wasn't sure what she was looking at. It appeared to be the Northern Star Shipping contract. But how could that be?

"Do ye recognize this document?" Caelan asked. "Is this your father's signature?"

"Aye." She handed it to Braedan. "How is it that ye have the contract? I thought Ascar kept our copy in his safe."

"Aye, yer copy is with Ascar, but this contract is Caelan's." Jocelyn and Braedan looked disbelievingly at Blaine and then at Caelan.

"Please sit down, and I will explain." Caelan motioned to Blaine to serve them a glass of wine. "Years ago, I heard about a shipping company that had lost two ships in a storm and a warehouse in a fire. Ye can imagine the loss was great, leaving the investors nearly bankrupt. Seeing that I wanted to expand my area of distribution, I bought the Northern Star Shipping Company for a fair price. All agreed to sell their shares except for one man, Gordon MacAulay."

Jocelyn's hand shook a bit when she took a sip of the wine.

"What about Walrick Graham, was he not an investor?" Braedan asked.

"Aye, at the start of our venture but then he too sold his share." Caelan walked over to his desk and handed them several parchments, letters from their father to Caelan's solicitor and some from Walrick Graham. "Northern Star did not do well. There's a lot of superstition amongst sailors, and as a result, they believed the ships were cursed. I thought if we changed the name, it might keep the company from failing. Five years ago, Northern Star became The White Star." Caelan pointed to the contract Blaine still held in his hand. "If ye look, there's an amendment with my signature transferring the contract to the newly named company. It was slow at first, but in time The White Star started to profit. Graham tried to sell yer father's share, saying he was acting on his behalf. I refused and instructed my solicitor to conduct business directly with Gordon MacAulay. Graham would not let the matter drop and tried to buy your father's shares stating that yer father was indebted to him. Again, I refused. A few years later, I received a letter informing me that Gordon was ill, and, upon his demise, his share of The White Star was to be transferred to his two children."

"Ye say the company was starting to make a profit. I don't recall father receiving any payments. Can ye tell me who collected them?" Braedan appeared calm but Jocelyn could see her brother was trying to keep his temper in check.

"Yer solicitor, Nigel Slagg. Do ye not know him?"

Jocelyn admitted she did not recognize the name when Braedan spoke. "Aye, Slagg works for Graham, and he brokered most of the deals for our father." He looked at Jocelyn rather sullenly. "He came to see me when Graham offered for yer hand and brought with him a betrothal contract which I tore up in his presence."

"I can't imagine why father never questioned Graham about his investment unless…"

"The White Star started doing so well we split the company into two divisions: one in the shipping of goods and the other in the building of ships. We replaced those lost at sea, with a better design. We successfully sold several to The Company of Scotland, who trade in Africa and the West Indies."

"Can ye tell me how much our father's share was?" Braedan looked uncomfortable. "I mean to say since we have no idea of the contract agreement."

"As I mentioned, we have not shown a profit until recently, I believe it was close to thirty crowns."

"Thirty crowns 'tis not a fortune but would have easily aided us in settling our debt with Graham."

"Ye are confused, Braedan. The dividends paid to yer father were quarterly," Caelan explained. Turning back to his desk, he took one of the ledgers to show him when they heard breaking glass.

Jocelyn gasped when she saw the glass her brother held in his hand shatter and blood begin to drip between his fingers. "Oh, good heavens." She ran over to him as he tried to wrap his hand with a handkerchief. "Braedan, ye are injured."

"'Tis nothing, Joce, please," he snapped at her. Embarrassed, she knelt to pick up the broken glass.

Caelan took hold of Braedan's hand to examine it. "The cut is deep and requires stitching." His voice was lacking in reproach. "Come with me. My wife is in the salon next door and can attend ye." Braedan looked as if he wanted to argue. "Plus, ye be bleeding all over my new carpet."

Blaine took the pieces of glass from Jocelyn and threw them into the fire. She picked up her glass of wine and took a sip. It didn't help, and soon tears brimmed her eyes, one slowly coursing down her smooth cheek.

"Now lass, dinna be distressed," he whispered, placing his arms around her shoulders and kissing the top of her head.

"All these years…struggling to keep food on the table, watching our home fall into shambles." A tear coursed down her other cheek. "Graham drove us into despair, all the while stealing from my father." Jocelyn covered her face with her hands, unable to stop the tears. Blaine held her in his arms.

They both jumped when Roderick came barging into the study. "I just spoke to Caelan, and he told me about Northern Star." Red-faced and charged up, he was explosive. "Finally, after all these years, ye have proof the man is nothing but a scoundrel, a criminal of the first degree."

"He must be brought to trial," Blaine said.

"We must leave at once and bring him before the king. Justice must be meted out."

"Aye, we will, but ye forget we are to wed soon."

"Blaine, we canna wait. If Graham gets wind of what we have discovered, he may flee."

"There is time and believe me when I say, there will be no place in all of Scotland he can hide. Graham will pay for what he has done."

~ * ~

The next few days were a blur for Jocelyn. With the christening and their upcoming wedding, neither Blaine nor Jocelyn had much time to think about exacting vengeance on Walrick Graham.

Douglas John and Arrabella arrived with their son the following day. Grateful to see a familiar face she flew into her welcoming embrace. "I have missed ye."

"I am so happy be part of yer wedding day." Arrabella laughed. Together they went to get her settled.

Sunday the banns were read and then the family and guests gathered in the great hall to witness the christening. Jocelyn's heart swelled as she watched Blaine hold the infant tenderly in his arms while Father Maris anointed his bald little head. She imagined the day when he would hold their son.

Blaine caught Jocelyn's gaze from across the aisle. His smile only meant for her, melted her heart. His gaze moved down to her flat stomach. Their eyes met again, and she knew without a doubt he loved her. Jocelyn smiled, joyfully at him.

~ * ~

The feast prepared after the christening was beyond compare— not just the quality of the food, but the quantity, for there were at least two hundred people in attendance. There was singing and dancing and drinking aplenty. Exhausted by the day's event, both Lady Ilyssa and Arrabella excused themselves from the festivities to see to their children. Forgetting her troubles, Angela dragged Braedan, along with Miranda and Rod, onto the dance floor.

Jocelyn smiled as she watched her brother. The way they gazed into each other's eyes; she could see they were in love. Ewan and his partner joined in the dancing. Jocelyn surmised she must be the lovely Cenna MacLeod. The clan predicted that they too would soon announce their betrothal.

Everyone was enjoying the merriment when a group of men of imposing stature walked into the hall. Their wraps concealing their faces, they strode straight to the high table to where Caelan was seated.

Caelan stood, seemingly unfazed by their intrusion. "Welcome, Magnus, I am afraid ye are a bit late for my son's christening, but there be plenty of food and drink."

The man unwrapped his cloak revealing a shock of red hair. He looked around at the group until his eyes fixed on Blaine sitting next to Father Maris.

Caelan motioned to one of the servants. "Please bring Laird MacDonnell and his men a drink."

"I thought the MacDonalds were allies of the MacKinnons," Jocelyn whispered to Lady Anna. "Why does this man appear so angry?"

Lady Anna gave her a sidelong glance. "He is not a MacDonald, my dear. He is Magnus MacDonnell of Glen Garry," she clarified. "He is not angry, 'tis his usual dispassion."

Jocelyn didn't agree for the man was far from dispassionate; in fact, he looked quite the opposite.

"Tell me, has that rogue brother of yers wed yet?" Magnus demanded in a loud voice.

Caelan did not answer; instead, he calmly walked around the table to stand before him. His glare was like brittle ice. "Magnus, ye are welcome in my hall, but yer ill manners are not."

Magnus flustered for a moment, then looked around embarrassed.

Standing next to him was a younger man with the same red hair. He was slightly larger in build, but the resemblance revealed his identity. "Father, if Blaine is not wed, then demand payment. 'Tis what was agreed upon."

"We have concluded our business as far as I am concerned," Caelan stated. "I gave ye generous restitution and my brother being married was only an added assurance there would be no…erm, further entanglements."

The hall was unusually quiet as everyone strained to hear what was being said. Blaine bolted from the table to stand next to Caelan. "If this fool is dissatisfied, we can settle this outside," he said glaring at the younger man. "What would ye prefer, Boyd, fists or swords?"

With those words, the younger man blanched.

Lady Anna suddenly appeared, standing between her sons and the MacDonnells. "Magnus, I am sure ye do not wish to disrupt my grandson's celebration. Why don't ye take off yer cloak and join us?" She motioned to the head table. "We have ample food and drink for all."

At her invitation, the rest of the MacDonnell moved toward some empty seats at one of the long tables. Magnus, in the meantime, looked as if he was raging some internal war. Magnus's son, on the other hand, looked relieved.

Jocelyn's eyes grew large when the group dispersed leaving a diminutive person in the center where they stood. Walking toward Blaine, she drew back the hood of her cloak, revealing an array of bouncy golden curls; her eyes sparkled when she looked up at him, a happy smile on her lips. Jocelyn gasped to see that she was heavy with child.

"Hello, Blaine, 'tis been a while." Her voice was light like the ringing of tiny chimes.

"Katie," Blaine greeted her. "Ye are glowing." He gazed down at her protruding belly. His comment was a succinct description because she positively beamed.

She giggled, blushing at the compliment. "Ye are too kind."

Boyd gave Blaine a murderous look, but his expression softened as he took her arm and gently led her to the table.

Magnus's expression displayed his disapproval as he watched Blaine and his daughter in-law. "I suppose we'll stay for a moment and rest, but then we will be departing," he ground out.

Caelan tried to engage the man in conversation, but he could not hold his attention. At every opportunity, Katie would glance up at Blaine.

"Magnus, I can assure ye there's no need for doubt," Caelan said. "Father Maris can attest."

"Aye," chimed in Father Maris. "The betrothal contract has been signed, and the banns have been read. They need only exchange vows."

Caelan motioned for more food to be brought. There didn't seem much that would appease Magnus, so he grabbed his goblet, draining the contents in one gulp.

No sooner did he finish than he announced they were leaving. "I thank ye for the drink. We will take our leave now." He started to rise.

"I would prefer ye stay for a while," Lady Anna said kindly. "The lass needs some respite." She tilted her head in Katie's direction.

"Thank ye for yer hospitality." He signaled to his party.

"If ye insist on leaving, I canna prevent ye, but the lass will stay." Magnus raised both brows at Lady Anna. "'Tis best for her and the bairn."

"She is sturdy, and we will not travel far." He waved her away, taking his cloak from his son. "I thank ye for yer concern."

"I am not asking ye, I am telling ye. The lass will remain."

"'Tis not her time; the babe's not due for a couple months," Boyd said.

Lady Anna arched a delicate brow and turned to Katie. "The babe has dropped low in yer belly and not much movement...aye?"

"Aye." Katie nodded. "He had been verra active, squirming all the time, but now he likes to stretch." She let out an "oomph" putting her hand on her side. "I best find a retiring room afore we depart."

Lady Anna laughed, placing her hand on Katie's swollen belly. "I will ask my daughter to show ye the way." She motioned to Miranda. She then turned her attention back to the two MacDonnells. "Listen to me. I care not what ye do, leave if ye must, but the lass stays."

Boyd started in, "Lady Anna, we have yet to be wed seven months…"

"And she was chaste on your wedding day?"

His face flushed bright red.

"We will stay," Magnus declared.

~ * ~

Jocelyn sat down in the overstuffed chair. Pulling the pins from her hair, she started brushing the long tresses. Aggie was not waiting to assist her, which was fine. She was not in the mood to listen to her complaints. That was until she realized that without her help, she would not be able to unfasten her gown.

Shaking her head, Jocelyn went back to brushing her hair. Lost in thought, she didn't hear the light tapping on her door.

"Lady Jocelyn?" a voice said. "'Tis Arrabella."

Morosely, Jocelyn rose and opened the door.

"I heard the MacDonnells arrived unexpectedly and caused quite a commotion." A commotion was an understatement, it was more like a scene, but Jocelyn didn't like arguing. "Ye seem upset. Do ye wish to talk?"

"No, 'tis nothing," she lied. "I'm just tired." Then she remembered her predicament. "Could ye please help me with my gown?"

Arrabella smiled. "Laird MacDonnell's presence requires some sort of explanation. I thought ye might want to know the situation."

"It isn't necessary," Jocelyn said. "I am aware of Blaine's involvement with Katie MacDonnell." Arrabella looked skeptical. "Lady Charlotte made sure to tell me the entire sordid tale and the true reason why Blaine had to wed."

"Ye canna believe anything Charlotte told ye. Consider the source."

"Ye don't understand—for whatever the reason, Blaine is marrying me, I am pleased, and I will keep my promise." Freed from the constraints of her gown, Jocelyn donned her wrap and tied the sash tightly. "'Tis difficult each time I meet one of Blaine's former lovers. First, there was Lady Charlotte, then the women at Castle Ballindalloch, the maids in the taverns, and now Katie MacDonnell." She plopped down in the chair and placed her face in her hands.

"Blaine was not at fault with what happened. He was duped by the woman, and he paid for his transgressions. If none of this had happened, then ye would never have met, and ye must know how much the man loves ye."

"How many of Blaine's transgressions will I have to understand? How many times will I have to endure the looks from every woman?" Jocelyn was miserable. "Ye are so fortunate yer husband was more selective before ye married him."

Arrabella laughed, her head shaking as she sat down next to her. "Ye are mistaken. I have had to learn to live with my husband's former leman." Jocelyn was flabbergasted, causing Arrabella to laugh louder. "'Tis a long story and of little significance, but aye, my husband's leman lives under our roof, and I can tell ye honestly that I have grown very close to her."

"Does it not bother ye?"

"Nay, it was long before Douglas John and I met. She was there for him during a terrible time in his life, but now she has her own family." She patted Jocelyn's shoulder. "I am not trying to dismiss your concerns."

Jocelyn gave her future sister-in-law a hug. Seeing that Arrabella was looking tired, she insisted she go and rest.

"Please remember how much Blaine adores ye and look forward to yer lives together," Arrabella reminded her as she left.

The fire was dying, and the room was growing cold. Throwing a block of peat to the flame, Jocelyn considered locking the door, assuming that Blaine would most likely sneak in during the night. She reconsidered and got into her bedclothes. Diving under the covers, she thought she would never be able to sleep, but within minutes she did.

A few hours later, Blaine came in, slipping under the covers. She smiled in her sleep as he gathered her close to him.

Chapter Twenty

The wedding day finally arrived. Jocelyn stared at the tray of food that sat before her. Aggie put her through another torturous sitting of having her hair arranged for the wedding. She was her usual acerbic self, but Jocelyn preferred her company than to be left alone with her frazzled nerves. She did note that Aggie was a wee less critical.

"There, ye look befitting of a laird's wife." She stood back to admire her work. "I believe ye will be pleased to know that the MacDonnell lass left this morn with her husband and clansmen. Seems they wish to get home afore the snow comes. Sir Roderick was kind enough to loan his carriage." Aggie prattled on, "The wee bairn looks just like his da, and I believe that put many wagging tongues to rest."

Having no appetite, Jocelyn walked to the corner window. The sky was full of white puffy clouds. "Dinna look like snow," she said, letting out a long breath that briefly fogged the window.

She had to admit she was relieved that the MacDonnells would not be at the wedding. It gave her some peace—not that she was threatened by Katie. She just didn't care to be fodder for gossip. The whole situation just didn't sit well with her. Why drag a woman across the country when she was so close to her time? It didn't make sense. It wasn't necessary for her to be present only to see if Blaine had married or not. Unless…

Jocelyn jumped when the door opened and in walked Arrabella. Aggie excused herself and left them to talk.

"Oh, ye look beautiful," she exclaimed. Walking around to see the back, she commented on her hair and the intricate arrangement. Most of her hair was crowned in twists and curls. From the center sprung curly tresses cascading down her back. "I see Aggie used the silver beads I gave her. They complement yer gown perfectly." She walked over to inspect her wedding dress, which was a silver-blue satin, the same color as Jocelyn's eyes. It was off the shoulder with a deep V waist, and the sleeves were long and tight around the arms. "Ye will look like a princess," she exclaimed, but then her brows knitted when she saw Jocelyn did not return her smile. Her eyes spotted the full tray of food.

"Come, Jocelyn, let's sit by the fire." She sat down on the

settee, patting the space next to her. "'Tis perfectly normal to be anxious on one's wedding day."

Jocelyn smiled weakly. "Aye, 'tis just nerves."

"Well, ye best eat. It will be hours before the wedding feast, and we canna have ye swooning at the altar." Jocelyn was close to tears. "What 'tis the matter, my dear? It appears 'tis more than just nerves."

She sighed deeply. "I am aware the MacDonnells left this morning. Aggie was kind enough to tell me."

"Aye, I would think this be good news."

"Aye, 'tis better not to have those among ye who do not wish ye well."

Jocelyn pursed her lips. "I canna help but wonder why they came in the first place."

Arrabella thought for a moment then shrugged.

"I mean to say it makes no sense unless…"

"What are ye thinking?"

"Before we left Edinburgh, Lady Charlotte told me how Blaine had offended the MacDonnells by having a tryst with one of their wives. Laird Caelan was forced to make restitution for the offense and insisted that Blaine marry." Arrabella nodded. "Dinna ye see? Magnus doubted the child that Katie carried was his son's. He did not need to come here to see if we had wed. 'Tis been gossip for some time that we are betrothed. I believe Magnus MacDonnell brought his daughter-in-law, expecting Lady Anna would see that her time was near and insist she stay. Had the babe be born with the raven locks, he could press further for some sort of compensation and leave Katie and the bairn here for the MacKinnons to care for."

"But it matters naught, don't ye see? The bairn was Boyd's. Now they have left and hopefully not to return for a while."

Jocelyn shook her head but decided to let the matter drop. Arrabella was about to say something when Miranda and Angela walked into the bedchamber without knocking.

"Sorry to disturb ye, but we thought ye might want some company," Miranda announced. "Mama and Ilyssa will be along any minute." She walked directly over to the tray of food. "No rolls? Pity."

"I see ye have some parcels. Could they be gifts for the bride?" Arrabella pointed out.

Jocelyn perked up a little when she saw the gifts.

"Aye, but mama says we have to wait." Miranda ran back to peer out the door.

"Oh Jocelyn, yer gown is so beautiful," Angela exclaimed,

examining the satin gown.

"Here they come." Miranda bounced back in the room. A moment later, Lady Anna walked in, followed by Lady Ilyssa. "Now, may we give her our gifts?"

"Just a moment, child," Lady Anna said before greeting Jocelyn with a kiss on each cheek. "Why don't ye sit down?"

When they were all settled, Lady Anna motioned to Miranda, who jumped up with excitement. She thrust a small packet at Jocelyn.

"What is this?" Jocelyn asked, untying the string and carefully unfolding the paper. She gasped in delight when she held the beautifully embroidered handkerchief. The edge was a silver blue and in the corners were the initials J.M., embroidered in a deeper blue.

"Do ye like it?" Miranda asked, proudly. "I made it myself."

"'Tis lovely," Jocelyn said honestly. "I shall carry it with me today." She smiled at the younger woman as tears gathered. "It may come in handy."

"I am next," Angela said, handing her package.

Jocelyn was having trouble untying the string when from nowhere Miranda produced a small dirk and sliced through the rope with a quick twist of her wrist. Lady Anna shook her head, giving her daughter a disapproving look. Inside were a pair of dark gray gloves. "I thought these matched your cloak and will keep yer hands warm when ye are up north."

"Thank ye, Lady Angela. They are lovely."

Ilyssa and Arrabella handed their gifts, a large package and then a smaller one. Inside the larger parcel was a silver and black fur blanket and the other held a matching muff. "These will come in handy on the ship."

The ladies beamed at her. Their gifts had touched her heart, and Jocelyn was at a loss for words.

It was Lady Anna's turn, and she placed a small velvet pouch in her hand. "I understand ye plan on wearing the sapphire necklace Blaine gave ye, but since yer gown is silver, this might look nice." Jocelyn looked at her future mother-in-law in disbelief when she withdrew a black pearl and diamond pendant. The delicate silver chain sparkled with small diamonds on every other link. "It was given to my grandmother on her wedding day. Her brother had just returned from the Orient and surprised her with the gift."

"I canna...I mean 'tis most extravagant," Jocelyn sputtered.

"Nonsense," Lady Anna replied in her usual way. "Each of my son's wives received a piece of jewelry from me on their wedding day."

Ilyssa and Arrabella both nodded, one pointing to a brooch and the other a necklace.

Jocelyn was touched by their kindness and found herself again using the handkerchief Miranda had given her. "Well, I must say your gift has certainly come in handy," she said to Miranda, and the ladies laughed.

~ * ~

Jocelyn stared at her reflection in disbelief. Arrabella was right, she looked very much like a princess. Better yet, she felt like one too. Wearing the veil Arrabella wore on her wedding day completed the tradition of wearing something borrowed. The necklace was something old, her gown the new and her handkerchief the blue.

Aggie muttered as she packed Jocelyn's clothes in her trunk. She was clearly displeased by her trousseau. "Ye will surely catch yer death of cold. How can ye expect to wear this gown on a ship?"

Jocelyn was becoming fond of the old servant. "I believe ye are going to miss me when I leave."

"Oh, nonsense. Who leaves so soon after the wedding? Ye should stay 'til spring. Sir Blaine isna' thinking," Aggie complained.

The more she fussed, the calmer Jocelyn became. That was until she heard the knock on her door. Her heart plunged into the pit of her stomach as she squeaked out a weak, "Enter."

Much to her surprise, it was Caelan who greeted her. He looked grand in the MacKinnon red dress kilt. Seeing that Jocelyn wasn't expecting him, he quickly explained, "I asked Braedan if I might have a moment with you before you went downstairs." He offered his arm. "He waits for ye at the top of the stairs."

Aggie had to push her out the door when she did not respond immediately. "Aye, of course," Jocelyn said and put a trembling hand on his arm.

"Ye look beautiful, Lady Jocelyn," Caelan began as they strolled down the long corridor. Then he paused and turned to her. "'Tis important ye are aware of the agreement I made with the MacDonnells. Once ye understand my reason for wanting Blaine to marry, ye will better understand the man ye wed today."

Jocelyn looked up into his blue eyes which revealed kindness in their depth. With a sharp intake of breath, she nodded.

"MacKinnons believe our word is our honor. Therefore, when we swear fealty or take an oath, we stand behind it. Blaine holds one oath above all else—the marriage vows. He would never break them. Do ye understand why I insisted he marry?" She nodded. "He would have to change his way of life, settle down with a wife and produce an heir. I would finally be able to stop worrying about him. Just as ye should not worry."

Jocelyn understood. Marrying her would be for life, and she would never need to worry about infidelity. But was that possible for a man as dynamic as Blaine, whose thirst for life and taste for variety was the very fabric of his being? Could he be pleased with the same woman for the rest of his life? Well, she would have to trust the man.

A man who would honor her with vows he will never break. "Thank ye, my lord, ye have given me the best wedding gift."

Caelan gave her another gift, a smile. And it was not just any smile, it was one of encouragement. "Come, my dear, I believe a groom is anxiously awaiting ye."

They continued down the hall, and as they turned the corner, they saw Braedan nervously looking for them. He smiled in relief and took her arm. Caelan bowed to them and calmly walked down the stairs to the great hall.

Braedan squeezed her hand, his eyes slightly misting. "Ye look beautiful, Joce." Tears prickled behind her eyes. "I just wish father and mother were here."

"Brae, they are with us now."

He smiled and kissed her tenderly on the cheek.

Hearing the music, they went down the stairs to stand at the entrance of the great hall. The hall was packed to full capacity and at the opposite side stood Blaine in the same red dress kilt. Her breath caught in her throat. He looked resplendent. She had never seen a more handsome man in her life. Grateful for Braedan's sturdy arm, they strolled down the long aisle until she stood next to him.

It was if she were walking in a dream. She felt Blaine's hand in hers, the taste of wine and she heard them exchange their vows, but it wasn't until she saw the gold band that he slipped on her finger that she realized that she was wed. She closed her eyes as warm lips covered hers, and a strong arm crushed her against his hard body. The kiss lasted longer than usual, and it wasn't until she heard people applauding that he finally released her.

Pulling away Blaine returned her smile. Leaning close he whispered, "The look of happiness on my wife's face will be the one I will keep forever in my heart.

~ * ~

The wedding feast was more elaborate than the christening. The hall was overflowing with merriment, followed by toast after toast to the happy couple. For hours Blaine greeted well-wishers, danced with them, toasted with them completely relaxed in the merriment.

Jocelyn, on the other hand, was lost in the sea of happy faces and goblets of wine. Her head swimming, she was starting to be giddy. Blaine caught her gaze, and the crowd parted as he made his way to her side. Smiling, he kissed her full on the mouth and claimed that he needed the company of his wife. The word 'wife' sounded foreign coming from him, and she liked it.

She giggled as he led her back to the head table. "I think ye need a bit more sustenance, my love, if ye are to last the evening." He winked as he motioned for a servant to bring over a platter of roasted meats.

The smell made her mouth water as she realized she was famished indeed.

Pouring a glass of water, he handed it to her, not taking his eyes from hers. His intensity made her cheeks heat.

"Yer lips glisten from the juices of the meat, and 'tis taking all my self-control not to throw ye over my shoulder and carry ye back to our room...so I canna lick those salty lips."

Jocelyn couldn't help giggling.

"'Tis your own fault ye are still here and not enjoying yer new bride," Arrabella said overhearing Blaine. "If ye had agreed to spend yer wedding night at the castle, ye would have left by now."

"Aye, Blaine, why is it we are not following tradition?" Jocelyn teased him, popping another piece of meat in her mouth so she could continue to chew seductively.

"Spending the night in that drafty old ruin is not my idea of a wedding night," he growled.

"Och. Ye are mistaken. 'Tis not drafty at all. 'Tis quaint and terribly romantic." Ilyssa was seated next to them. "There be no one fer miles, and ye can scream at the top of yer..." She abruptly stopped when she saw her husband approaching them.

Caelan picked up her hand and kissed the back, looking longingly into her eyes. "Blaine is right. The castle is no place for a wedding night. 'Tis said to be haunted."

She laughed.

"Come, my sweet, I believe we should take advantage and spend the night there ourselves."

Her mouth opened her mouth in surprise. "Are ye saying that we..."

"I am saying we should leave now so we are there afore dark."

She rose from her seat, a knowing smile on her lips. "But what about wee Michael?"

"Arrabella has graciously offered to care for him in our absence, and I have taken measures to make sure provisions are there when we arrive."

Ilyssa positively glowed at the prospect of spending a romantic night with her husband. She threw herself in his arms, kissing him on the lips. "Oh Caelan, what a wonderful surprise." She bid them goodnight and left with him.

"When would ye like to retire, love?" Blaine asked. "'Tis still early, but no one would fault ye if ye want to excuse yerself."

Jocelyn wasn't tired at all, in fact, she was still hungry. "I am ready," she said, reaching for a warm piece of bread and spreading some goat cheese. She closed her eyes as she bit into the tangy cheese.

Blaine laughed, taking a small tart from the platter next to him. "Eat, and when you are satiated, we will go."

Blaine and Jocelyn ended up staying for a few more hours enjoying the music and company. Lady Angela sang a Scottish love ballad. Her voice was high and airy as that of an angel. Just like her name. Jocelyn listened to her, captivated by her performance.

"I will be retiring for the evening, my lady, unless you need my help?" Arrabella leaned over to say.

If she didn't accept Arrabella's offer, she would have to submit to Aggie's administrations. "I will join ye," she whispered. Asking Braedan to inform Blaine, she followed Arrabella out of the hall.

Jocelyn was surprised when they walked past both her and Blaine's bedchamber. She had assumed they would spend their wedding night in one of them. Instead, Arrabella led her back to the laird's bedchamber. The solar was large and spacious and cheery fire burned in the hearth. On a small table sat a tray of fruit and tarts and a bottle of wine.

"I dinna understand?"

Arrabella smiled brightly. "Since Blaine opted not to spend yer wedding night at the castle, Caelan thought perhaps ye would like to use the laird's quarters instead. It would offer ye privacy and plenty of room. Would ye like me to help ye ready yerself?"

Jocelyn nodded shyly.

Thirty minutes later, Arrabella stood back, smiling.

Jocelyn was dressed in a sheer white night rail and robe. Beautifully embroidered around the neckline and sleeves, the gown hugged her slender form. The robe was long with a two-foot train. With her hair down loose, she looked like a wood nymph san the wings.

"Ye are a vision."

Panic filled Jocelyn when Arrabella turned to leave. "Must ye take yer leave?"

"Yer husband will be along any moment, my dear, and I have

no doubt he would appreciate the privacy. Unless ye have any concerns?"

Jocelyn gave her a puzzled look.

"I mean to say, do ye have any questions about yer wedding night?"

She shook her head, giggling when she realized what Arrabella was implying. "Nay, my lady, I am...," she stammered, "um...aware," she said for lack of a better word.

"Good, then I will bid thee goodnight." Lady Arrabella left, closing the door behind her.

Jocelyn looked about the room when she spied the wine on the table. She reached for a glass but had second thoughts. Thinking that she had already consumed a large amount of wine, she opted for water instead. "Well...I am ready."

~ * ~

Placing his empty goblet on the table, Blaine rose to leave. He had to laugh at several of his clansmen's attempts to waylay him.

Fortunately, Douglas John came to his rescue. "Be gone with ye, yer beautiful wife awaits," he said, practically pushing him out the hall.

"Och. 'Tis too early, ye 'aven't had enough drink," one man said, swaying on unsteady legs.

"Aye," another called out. "Ye 'ave plenty o' time. The night 'tis young." A group shouted in agreement.

"Come along now." Douglas John winked at him. "She be waiting in the laird's chamber."

Blaine was somewhat anxious. Realizing that he would soon be joining Jocelyn in more ways than one, he felt like a naïve lad. It had been over a month since they left Heatherwood, and the prospect of making love to her excited him. His body ached for her.

Taking the stairs two at a time, Blaine knocked on the door before letting himself in. He found Jocelyn standing before the fire. Her supple figure was outlined by the firelight. His own desires surging, the sight caused him to grow heavy. Coming from behind, he wrapped his arms around her. Jocelyn leaned back as he started kissing the side of her neck.

"How are ye, Lady MacKinnon?" He smiled.

She turned to face him. "Wonderfully happy."

Slowly he leaned down to capture her soft lips. He kissed her with all the love he possessed. Jocelyn opened her mouth, and he plunged his tongue into her warm and sweet depth. He wanted to consume her, to take in her very essence and then return it in tenfold.

~ * ~

Jocelyn wasn't sure how long they kissed. Blaine's hands explored the curve of her back, waist, and hips. She yearned for his touch, and she wanted to feel his skin against hers. Blindly she sought a way to remove his sporran. She wrapped her arms around his back and unbuckled the clasp. She gasped aloud when she felt his arousal hard against her belly.

"What ye be doing, lass?"

She looked up at him, giving him an alluring smile. "I believe ye are over-dressed my lord."

Blaine raised his brows looking very pleased.

Having successfully removed the sporran, she tugged hard and managed to unbuckle the wide belt that held up his kilt. The yards of wool unraveled and fell to his feet. The end was held up by a large brooch on his shoulder. It was an impressive brooch made of gold, and the pin was stabbed through the folds of the cloth which locked into the ring on the other end. Jocelyn had never seen its kind and examined it closely.

"'Tis a penannular brooch, 'tis ancient, going back to Celtic and Viking times," he said.

"'Tis beautiful," she exclaimed, releasing the pin. Jocelyn smiled devilishly at him, waving the sharp pin under his nose.

Blaine let out a groan. He picked her up in his arms and carried her into the bedchamber. Placing her on her feet, he quickly shed the rest of his clothes until he stood gloriously naked before her. Before pulling her back into his arms, he took the broach she held in her hand and put it on the bedside table. He then pulled her against his arousal. He kissed her hard on the lips, his tongue delving deeply.

"I want to taste ye, lass, I want to taste all of ye." He untied the ribbon that held her robe closed. His hands traced down her arms as the silky material drifted down to cloud around her feet. The night rail left little to the imagination.

Before she realized it, he had somehow untied the ribbon on the top of the gown and pulled the entire garment down over her shoulders and hips in one fell swoop. Exposing her body. "Ye are like silk," he said as he caressed her.

He trailed kisses down her throat until he found her breast. Latching onto the nipple, he laved and suckled sending sensuous currents streaming down her body, stimulating the most intimate area between her legs.

She weaved her fingers through his hair, pulling it free from its queue. She loved how silky it felt between her fingers. The scent of bayberry filled her nose.

Bold, she ran one hand down between their bodies, finding the silken rod, and she grasped it. Running up and down its length, she was pleased by Blaine's reaction.

"God's teeth," he swore as he covered her hand with his own. "Lass, ye have me at a disadvantage, ye ken?"

Jocelyn laughed, then took her other hand to cover the head of his shaft, smearing the glistening drop around the head, causing him to suck air between his teeth.

"Ye are a little minx." He withdrew, breathing hard.

Capturing her hands, he placed them behind her, causing her to arch her back. He went back to loving her breasts and causing sounds to escape her own lips. As he trailed more kisses between the valley of her breasts, he made straight to her belly. He continued to hold her hands down against her sides.

Dipping his tongue in her navel made her titter. His kisses didn't stop until he knelt before her. Biting the curve of her hips, he moved to the center until he reached her most intimate region. Then with gusto, he thrust his tongue between her lips to stroke and suckle her enticingly.

She tried to keep her balance while meeting each thrust of his tongue with a tilt of her hips. Her legs quivered as the sensation started to intensify. He must have sensed that she might not be able to stand, because he swiftly lifted her up and placed her in the middle of the bed.

Before she realized it, he was lying between her legs. "Ah, that 'tis better." His warm breath touching her sensitive flesh.

He resumed his licking and suckling. Twice she neared her release, but each time Blaine would slow down his stroke to enter her wet and velvet passage with his talented tongue. "Please," she begged him.

He refused to cease his delicious torment. "Tilt your hips, it will intensify yer release," he finally said and returned to the task of bringing her to a blinding climax.

She held her breath as she climbed to the precipice, wavering in its height as he gently sucked in and kept her teetering until she was engulfed in warmth radiating throughout her body. With one last stroked, she fell, tumbling through a physical bliss that words cannot describe. Muscles convulsed in surprising strength that defied reason. From somewhere in the distance she heard someone scream. It wasn't until she finally descended to earth that she discovered the sound of ultimate satisfaction was coming from her own lips.

~ * ~

Jocelyn awoke well-rested, albeit a bit sore. Her first glance confirmed her thoughts that she had slumbered most of the morning. She couldn't help but smile softly as she recalled Blaine making love to her for most of the night, but soon stopped when she realized she was alone in the massive canopied bed.

Hearing voices coming from the solar, she sat up.

"That won't be necessary, as my wife is still abed and needs her rest," Blaine said in a clipped voice. Someone responded, but she couldn't make out who it was. "Perhaps in an hour, I will advise you."

She smiled when he referred to her as his *wife*. Lying back down, she closed her eyes and feigned sleep.

Blaine walked into the bedchamber. Taking off his robe, he laid it at the foot of the bed before slipping between the covers. Sensing that Jocelyn was awake, he gathered her in his arm and began kissing her bare shoulder. "What has ye smiling, my love?"

"Mmm..." was all she could manage.

"Then go back to sleep," he yawned, closing his eyes.

Although they were not in any hurry to rise, her stomach had other ideas, and it grumbled loudly. Blaine did not respond. They laughed when both of their stomachs protested in unison. "I will return in a moment," he said and jumped out of bed without bothering to don his robe.

Jocelyn couldn't help admiring his physique. Well-muscled, he could have been chiseled from stone.

As promised, he returned, carrying a tray laden with food. Comfortable in her own lack of clothing, Jocelyn sat up and welcomed the bounty before her. Grabbing a cold piece of chicken, she tore at the tender flesh and closed her eyes with pleasure.

The pillows shifted as Blaine sat back. She opened her eyes to see him studying her. He lifted a silky strand of her long hair as it draped around her shoulders like a cape. "I find I no longer hunger for food."

As she fed him a piece of meat, he brought the tray closer. For a while, they ate in silence until he reached over to smooth the crease between her brows. "What has ye troubled, love?"

"Oh, 'tis nothing," she said. "Braedan is gone, and I didn't have a chance to say goodbye."

"Aye, he and Rod left at first light. Yer brother is most anxious to reclaim yer land," Blaine said. "They sent word to the king, asking for an audience. They hope to have matters resolved quickly." He lifted her chin with the tips of his fingers. "Rod also plans to speak to his parents about Braedan."

"I fear the MacPhersons will not consider my brother's offer, even if he regains the land Graham stole from us. He canna compete with Laird Mackenzie's wealth. I am sure the MacPhersons want only the best for their daughter."

"Well, your brother carries two letters with him, a letter of introduction from Caelan and a second from my mother." Jocelyn sat up. "Rod has agreed to champion yer brother and so has Caelan. My mother has been close friends with Mary MacPherson since they were young. As a matter of fact, Mary is my godmother."

"Do ye think they can influence them?"

"I canna say, but their opinions hold value and they will at least agree to meet hm." Jocelyn smiled, sighing contently. "There is another subject I wish to discuss with ye." He paused as if he sought the right words. "I wish for us to leave on the morrow. I would understand if you prefer to postpone our trip to Stonegate and remain here for a while."

Jocelyn gave him the brightest smile, and threw herself in his arms, almost upsetting the tray. "Nay love, I am ready to start my new life with ye. To meet yer clansmen, to see my new home and most of all, to be yer wife."

Blaine held her for a long time. Lifting her face so he could kiss her lips with a soul-searing kiss. Relishing the warmth of his hands as he ran them up and down her naked body, she felt his arousal grow. Laughing, he flipped her onto her back, ignoring the sound of the tray hitting the floor.

She lost herself in the depth of his emerald green eyes. If this was any indication what married life would be like, Jocelyn would be a very happy wife.

Chapter Twenty-One

Termagant, belligerent, curmudgeon…words that best described Aggie MacKinnon? Nay, efficient. Jocelyn had just returned from breaking her fast to find all of her and Blaine's belongings perfectly packed for their trip.

Aggie gave Jocelyn her usual acerbic glare. "I took liberties in packing all the essentials ye will need for the trip to Stonegate in this smaller trunk. The rest of yer clothes are in the larger two—not much need for a ballgown on a ship." She smirked.

Jocelyn smiled and then did something that caught the old woman off guard. She hugged her. "I will miss ye, Aggie." When she pulled away, she was surprised to see the servant wipe away what looked like a tear.

"Ye best be off as the tide waits for no one," Aggie said brusquely. Seeing two servants waiting in the doorway, she used the excuse to shout out orders. "Take the laird and lady's trunks out straight away."

"Come along, Lady Jocelyn," she heard Aggie's shrill voice.

It was still early, and most of the family were still abed. Blaine and Jocelyn had said their goodbyes the night before, so she was surprised to see Lady Anna standing alongside Caelan, looking fresh and energetic. Jocelyn accepted her warm hug.

"I thought to see ye off, my dear.

The four climbed aboard the waiting cart. Caelan was in his usual stoic mood, while Lady Anna filled in the silence with lively conversation of what they would see along the way. They would sail to Stonegate onboard The Ilyssa. The ship was laden with cargo and ready to leave. Blaine smiled at Jocelyn as he helped her out of the carriage. She was grateful for the warm cloak and gloves as a cold wind blew off the loch.

"My dear, you are already missed." Lady Anna kissed her on both cheeks. "But nay ye worry, daughter, I will be coming for a visit in the spring."

Jocelyn was close to tears as she hugged the woman tightly. Next, Lady Anna embraced Blaine. Jocelyn watched as they exchanged words, a playful smile on his lips as she most likely imparted words of wisdom.

"I have something for ye, Lady Jocelyn." Caelan startled her. He pressed a small pouch in her gloved hand. "'Tis an advancement on yer dividends." He gave her a look when she tried to argue. "Yer brother departed with his share, and his response was to thank me."

She was a little embarrassed when he smiled. His smile was so charming she blushed like a young lass. "Thank ye, Caelan," she managed to say.

"Ye will be a wealthy woman once yer brother regains his land, remember that, so guard it well and invest wisely." She awkwardly curtseyed and then almost stumbled when he leaned over to kiss her cheek. "Safe journey."

Blaine took hold of her elbow and guided her up the plank. The wind was picking up, so they immediately went below to their quarters. It was small but very cozy. The bed was surprisingly comfortable and in the corner was a brazier that was already lit, making the room toasty warm.

Once settled, she decided to remain below while he went up top to meet the captain, the first mate and boatswain. There was excitement amongst the crew. This was *The Ilyssa's* maiden voyage, and they considered the honeymooning couple a good sign.

~ * ~

On the twelfth day of their journey, Blaine came to fetch her. "Come quickly," he said with excitement.

Putting down the book she was reading, he helped her with her cloak. Jocelyn laughed as he pulled her up the walkway and pointed excitedly at the distant shore. At first, she wasn't sure what she was seeing but then remembered that Stonegate was named for the fifty-foot natural stone arch at the point of the harbor. He told her the quartzite structure could be seen from a great distance and was a landmark for many ships seeking a safe harbor, thus making Stonegate a profitable port.

Arm in arm they stood as the shore drew closer. Her eyes grew wider and her mouth open in amazement at the stone structure. "'Tis spectacular," she said in awe.

The harbor was a lot larger than she expected. To the right was a wharf with several buildings and room enough to dock several ships the size of *The Ilyssa*. The other side was a narrow beach with dozens of small fishing boats lined up in rows. Next to the fishing boats was a half-constructed round structure. She assumed this was the ice house he was so set on completing. Seeing the ice house made her grin, and a plan began to formulate in her mind. Lost in thought, it took her a moment to realize there was a crowd gathered at the pier.

When she asked him who they were, he answered her with a laugh. "'Tis nothing, just yer clansmen, so put on a smile and greet them heartily."

"Heartily?" she said, doing her best to appear calm. It took a little time to dock the massive ship, allowing her time to compose herself.

He helped her down the plank. It was exciting to finally be at her new home.

From within the crowd, a man approached them. Similar in likeness to Caelan and Douglas John, his hair was not as dark, yet he had the same cobalt blue eyes. Behind him stood a woman; one could only describe as golden. Her hair was the color of ripe wheat, and her eyes, also gold, had a dark ring around them. Rimmed with long dark lashes, they looked unnatural. The rest of her was sublime, a face that one could only be described as striking.

"Laird, welcome home," the man said and then hugged him fiercely. When he was through abusing Blaine, he turned to face Jocelyn, and he bowed deeply. "Welcome, my lady. All of Stonegate bid ye welcome."

Blaine laughed. "My love, may I present to ye Brode MacKinnon and his wife, Marsali."

The young woman blushed, appearing even more golden. Surrounded by people, Blaine did his best to introduce her to everyone.

Seeing the men from the ship file down the plank, he invited all to join them in the tavern for a drink. They followed the crowd to what looked like an enormous building only to see that it was, in fact, two structures. One was the tavern connecting to a large three-story inn. There was so much commotion that Jocelyn could only smile and nod as dozens of voices welcomed her.

After several tankards of ale and what was an interminable period of meeting people, she was exhausted. Blaine noticed and motioned to Marsali. "Is my room readied? I believe my wife could use some rest."

"Nay, Laird, we have readied the house. Tonight, ye will stay in the laird's quarter." He asked her to explain. "I am saying we have prepared for yer arrival."

Marsali laughed again and pushed him toward the doors leading out of the tavern. "Mistress, if ye will follow me, we had yer belongings sent to the house. The staff is ready and waiting to meet ye."

Seeing that the couple was leaving, Brode announced that

drinks would continue for the revelers, but it was time for the newlyweds to retire. As they walked out of the inn, there was an open carriage waiting to take them.

"Why would we not stay at Stonegate, isn't it yer home?" Joselyn questioned.

"Truth be told, I haven't much use of the house. Considering I ate most of my meals here, I kept a room at the Inn."

"That was afore ye wed, my lord," Marsali said. "Since we heard of yer pending nuptials, we have taken great lengths in preparing yer home to welcome Lady Jocelyn."

Taking a well-used road, Jocelyn saw a proper tower house. It sat upon a small rise with a perfect view of the harbor. She could see a nice size stable in the back, but within the maze of low stonewalls, there grew not a single plant, flower or shrub. Although stark, she thought it had potential. The drive was graveled and clear of weeds. Apparently, someone was tending it.

As the carriage made its way to the front of the house. A small group of servants filed out of the double doors. They stood at attention with the approach of their laird.

Blaine helped her from the carriage, guiding her to stand before a large woman with sparkling blues eyes that crinkled at the corners when she smiled. "Mrs. Anderson, may I present to ye my wife, Lady Jocelyn MacKinnon."

The older woman curtseyed and then smiled, exposing a large gap between her front teeth. "Och, welcome, my lady, we have been most anxiously awaiting yer arrival." Mrs. Anderson then went about introducing each lass and lad who stood in line. The only name Jocelyn recalled was a young gal by the name of Shona, who was to be her personal maid.

Entering the home, Mrs. Anderson led them to a salon well lit by a pair of floor candelabras. Several high back chairs sat around the hearth where a fire cracked and popped. In the center was a large round table with an impressive silver tray. The tray held several goblets and a pitcher of ale.

"Please sit. Let me get ye something to drink," Mrs. Anderson said proudly.

Blaine grinned approvingly. "I must say, 'tis a grand surprise," he said, looking around.

Jocelyn tilted her head, not fully understanding. To her, the house looked charming and most welcoming. "Why wouldna ye want to spend time in your home, tis quite lovely," she whispered.

He said in a low voice, "As I said earlier, I spent most of my time at the inn. I am afraid that if ye had seen the house afore…"

"Ye would have seen bare walls, no furnishings or coverings." Marsali surprised them from behind. She rolled her eyes with great exaggeration. "It was a bachelor's home, but with ye now being wed, we did our best to make Stonegate presentable. I am afraid this was the best we could do on such short notice. The rest of the house needs help." She gazed warmly at Jocelyn. "It just needs a woman's touch."

When they were finished with their refreshments, Mrs. Anderson led them to the laird's quarters. Jocelyn saw that Marsali did not exaggerate. The best description of their bedchamber was sparse. It was basically empty. Besides the large canopy bed, a chair and one small table, there was nothing else, no wardrobe, trunk, screen…nothing.

"How many rooms are there besides this one?" Jocelyn inquired.

"Not counting the servants' quarters, there be a total of eleven bedchambers," Marsali said.

"Well then, I believe I will be very busy for the next few months." They laughed in unison. Jocelyn immediately liked the young woman. She appeared warm and friendly.

Marsali turned to bid them goodnight when a small boy, no older than seven or eight, bound into the room.

"Uncle Blaine, yer home."

Blaine picked him up in his arms, giving him a big hug.

"Ye are late," the lad chastised him.

"Ye little rascal, ye have grown since I've been gone." He laughed. "And nay, I am not late, I am right on time."

There was no doubt who the boy belonged to, he was the spitting image of his mother, with honey skin and golden hair. Except for his eyes—he had the MacKinnon blue, same as his father…*his father?*

"Ian MacKinnon, ye are old enough to properly greet yer laird." Marsali lifted him out of Blaine's arms. "Let us try this again."

Blushing a bright red, he bowed to Blaine and then to Jocelyn. "Welcome home, Laird, welcome, Lady Jocelyn."

"Now, that's a good lad." Marsali took hold of his hand. "Lady Jocelyn, this is my son, Ian."

"Do ye all live here at the house?" Jocelyn hoped they would have the joy of a young person at Stonegate.

"Nay, we have a nice cottage on the property. When Ian is not at school, Mrs. Anderson keeps an eye on the lad while we work."

"Well, it will be a pleasure to have ye here with us," Jocelyn said, secretly wondering when their children would join the household. She hoped very soon.

~ * ~

Jocelyn slept quite fitfully her first night at Stonegate. Rising early, she went to inspect the kitchen. Mrs. Anderson was putting some biscuits in the oven when she walked in. She immediately informed her that Blaine and Brode had already left, both eager to discuss the state of affairs after his long absence.

Jocelyn insisted on helping Mrs. Anderson in the kitchen. It took some convincing, but the kind servant agreed. Sitting at the long table, Jocelyn recounted her days at the bakery and how much she enjoyed rising early to start the long and arduous task of kneading dough. The smell of baking bread made Jocelyn feel at home.

After breakfast, Mrs. Anderson offered to show her the rest of the house. Upon leaving the kitchen, they saw Shona running toward them. "I beg yer forgiveness, my lady. I did not expect ye to rise so early."

Obviously, Shona thought Jocelyn was like most high-born ladies who languished the morning away. "'Tis fine, why don't ye join me whilst I inspect the house?"

Shona agreed and pleasantly chatted away at all they had accomplished.

Every room and bedchamber were cleaned and dusted but void of any furnishings. Thinking about Lady Anna's plans to visit in the spring, Jocelyn decided she should start immediately in putting the house together. "Do ye know where I may find Marsali?"

"Aye, she will be at the tavern," Shona said.

Jocelyn sent her to fetch their cloaks.

~ * ~

The wharf was bustling with people coming and going. The market was set up between the buildings and brought in tradesmen with their carts of wares and supplies. There had to be hundreds of people milling around.

Entering the tavern, Shona led Jocelyn up to the second floor and knocked on a double set of doors. Without waiting for a response, they walked into a spacious and beautifully decorated office. Sitting behind a large oak desk was Marsali.

She stood up and curtseyed. "Good morrow, my lady. How fare ye this day?"

Jocelyn looked around admiring the beautiful room. Books filled shelves that lined three walls. One wall was all windows with a view of the harbor below. "I hope I am not interrupting?"

"Oh please, 'tis a pleasure to see ye," she said. "Is there something I can assist ye with?"

"I was wondering if you could guide me as to where I might purchase some items for the house."

"Of course, what are ye looking for?"

Jocelyn looked down at her list. "Everything."

Marsali laughed, taking the list she held. "I see ye are wantin' to turn Stonegate into a real home." Jocelyn nodded. "Well then, I had best take ye to the warehouse."

"The warehouse?" she asked.

Marsali bobbed her head once. "My lady, ye are going to love this."

The three ladies walked down a long alley behind the tavern that was composed of numerous warehouses. "Here, we have merchants who come to sell or trade goods. There's everything one could possibly need," Marsali explained. "People come from all over on market day, which is practically every day, except Sundays."

They walked past one of the warehouses that held mostly livestock, another was building material and the other farming equipment.

Jocelyn told Marsali she first wanted to properly equip the kitchen. Next, the servants' quarters. She thought to buy floor coverings, warm bedding, and proper window coverings. Mrs. Anderson told her that even during the summer, the rooms could get cold. They had reached the last row of warehouses when Marsali stopped and opened the door. She laughed when Jocelyn gasped aloud.

Stepping in, she saw all one would need to furnish a hundred tower houses. There was everything from furniture to chamber pots. It was an emporium of goods. "I have no idea where to begin."

"Let's start with the servants' quarters first," Marsali suggested. "Ye need just the basics."

Together they disappeared into the vast cavern of dry goods, sundries and dreams.

~ * ~

It had been several hours since Blaine was told that his wife had gone down to the wharf. He had expected her to join him for the midday meal. When she didn't return, he began to worry. Brode was in the midst of explaining an error in the ledger when Blaine looked out the window to see Jocelyn and Shona in the open carriage, followed by several carts filled with goods. He shook his head, marveling at the scene before him.

Brode rose to see what had caught his laird's attention. "I'm afraid the coffer be somewhat low, and I was hoping to send payment to Giamatti's so we could order the rest of the stone to finish the ice house."

Blaine shrugged. "We have waited this long; it will no matter if we wait another few months." He left to greet his wife.

Jocelyn was smiling brightly when she saw Blaine walk out the door. "I see ye have been busy." He laughed as he helped her down from the carriage.

"Oh, I just bought a few things." Counting the five carts pulling up the drive Blaine thought she must have purchased an entire warehouse. Seeing Mrs. Anderson, she instructed her to have the servants help unload the carts. "Shona will show ye where everything should go but do not hesitate to ask me." Walking inside, Blaine helped her off with her cloak.

"Blaine, do ye have a moment?" He nodded and fetched Brode to help with the unloading. He then took her to his study, so they could have some privacy.

"Can I pour ye a drink?" He offered her a glass of sherry which she gratefully accepted.

"I was able to purchase all the furnishings using my own money." She smiled shyly. "I was given an advancement of my share of The White Star's quarterly dividends."

"I would hope ye would use that money to make repairs at Heatherwood."

"Nay, Braedan will take care of Heatherwood. I want to use my money for my home."

"I am perfectly capable of providing anything ye may need."

"Then why does yer ice house stand unfinished? Wouldna it be best to finish the construction now, in winter, so it will be ready for spring?"

"Aye, that was my intention; however, I was somewhat…detained." He gave her his most charming smile, one that was only meant for her. "The inn and tavern are doing well, and we make a substantial profit in fishing. I have spent a good sum so far and was—"

"I want to help," Jocelyn interrupted. "I want ye to order the material to finish the ice house." She opened her reticule and walked over to take his hand. She pressed a gold sovereign in his palm, closed his fingers and then placed a small kiss on his fingers.

"I canna take yer money, love."

"'Tis not my money. 'Tis our future and one I believe in." She wrapped her arms around his neck.

With those words, his mouth came crushing down on hers in a mind-blowing kiss. He ravaged her with his lips and plunged his tongue in her sweetness. After a moment, he whispered, "May I show ye my appreciation for yer generosity?"

He swept her up in his arms and carried her upstairs to their bedchamber where he made love to her in a most appreciative way.

Chapter Twenty-Two

Marsali smiled approvingly at the finished guest bedroom,

"Oh, and I did use the portrait of Lady Anna I found under the stairs," Jocelyn said. "I think she will like it when she arrives next month."

It had been three weeks since Jocelyn came to Stonegate. She had been able to decorate four of the bedrooms using some of the paintings and wall coverings stored below the tower house.

"Have ye finished with yer bedchamber yet?" Marsali inquired.

"Some, but I have much to do." Jocelyn fluffed the embroidered pillow on the chaise lounge.

"I so wanted to do this when I lived here, but alas," Marsali said. "I must commend ye on getting so much done and in so little time."

Jocelyn gave her a side glance. She wondered when Marsali lived at the house as she thought that she and Brode lived in the small cottage next to the property. Well, it didn't matter. Jocelyn took her to see the other completed bedchambers and was thrilled Marsali approved.

"The ice house is finally coming along. How long did Blaine say it will take to complete?"

"We are waiting for the shipment of stone from Italy. Once it arrives, it will be a few months."

Mrs. Anderson came to tell Jocelyn and Marsali that Blaine and Brode would be gone for most of the day. They planned on returning home in time for the evening meal. "Oh good," Marsali said, "then ye have time to join me at the tavern. We be trying one of yer new recipes."

Jocelyn eyes widened.

"'Tis the capon roasted in wine and herbs."

Eager to see her dish prepared, they left at once. When they reached the tavern, they went straight to the kitchen to sample.

"'Tis enough sage and needs a bit more salt," Jocelyn advised, taking another bite of the succulent meat. She went over to a large pot and breathed in the fragrance. "I believe if ye add more celery, it will add to the flavor. All I can smell is the onions."

Marsali took one of the long spoons to taste it and agreed.

After an hour in the kitchen, they decided to have a cup of tea in Marsali's office. Walking out into the tavern, Jocelyn heard a familiar voice call out her name. Her already flushed face burned hotter. She slowly turned to see who it was.

"For heaven sakes, if my eyes do not deceive, it's the baker and the fishmonger's wife...together?" Standing amid a group of men was none other than Lady Charlotte Wickstrom.

Dressed in an emerald green gown with a plunging neckline, she resembled a big fat peacock, especially with the matching green hat that sat atop her head at a jaunty angle. The white feather that sprouted from the top completed the look.

Before either lady could respond, John McDermott stepped around to greet them most gallantly. "Lady Jocelyn, what a pleasant surprise," he said, taking her hand. "May I be the first to offer my congratulations on yer marriage."

Jackson and Terrance Ferguson soon joined him spouting the same good wishes. "Aye, Blaine is a lucky man."

She was pleased to see Lady Charlotte standing behind, clearly miffed at them for interrupting her little show. The men warmly greeted Marsali, who looked ill at ease. Wishing she had worn one of her better dresses, Jocelyn held her head high as she addressed them as mistress of Stonegate.

"I am so pleased to see everyone, as it has been a long time." She smiled. "My husband is away on business, but I do expect him later this evening. I hope ye will join us for dinner." She saw Marsali looking uncomfortable. "I hope ye and Brode will be able to join us," she said to Marsali.

"I best be going, Ian should be finished with his studies," she said, excusing herself.

"I must say, marriage certainly agrees with ye. Ye are more beautiful than ever," John said, ignoring Lady Charlotte's unladylike snort. "We would love to join ye for dinner. We just arrived, and as soon as we make arrangements at the inn, we will be up shortly."

"Nonsense," Jocelyn purred. "We have plenty of room. Ye will stay with us. My husband would insist."

"That won't be necessary, dear," Lady Charlotte piped up. "I have been a guest of Blaine's on numerous occasions, and quite frankly, I am not fond of the drafty old house."

Ignoring her jab, Jocelyn laughed. "Oh, don't be silly, that's when Blaine didn't care who he entertained." She turned to the men. "I believe ye will find Stonegate adequately furnished and staffed. 'Tis quite comfortable, gentlemen."

The men agreed to the invitation which did not sit well with Lady Charlotte. "When we visit Stonegate, we stay at the inn," she said adamantly.

"My dear, I wouldn't dream of troubling ye, by all means, stay." Jocelyn turned her attention back to the gentlemen. "My carriage is just outside if ye would like to follow me. I'll send one of the servants to have your trunks bought up."

She heard Lady Charlotte gasp. "How dare ye turn yer back? I am not some commoner to be treated with such discord—"

"Nor am I." Jocelyn narrowed her eyes at the woman. "I am Blaine's wife, and ye will give me the courtesy as mistress of Stonegate."

Lady Charlotte stared back when she suddenly laughed, throwing her hands in the air. "I do swear, I never understand you Scots, so fiery in nature. 'Tis true what they about your tempers. I have come all this way to deliver a letter from Rod and under no circumstance did I come to do battle."

Jocelyn squashed down her anger. Hopefully, Rod's letter included news of her brother. "If ye will kindly follow me." They walked into the lobby and waited while Lady Charlotte fetched her cloak and reticule.

"Ah, here we are," Lady Charlotte announced pleasantly, handing her a thick letter. "I am sure you want to rip into it, you must be starving for news of your brother." Her words rang true, and it took an enormous effort to calmly put the letter in the pocket of her cloak.

Jocelyn clenched her teeth. "This way please." She led the group out to the waiting carriage.

~ * ~

Blaine walked into their bedchamber to find Shona putting the final touches to his wife's hair. Jocelyn was dressed in a light gray gown edged in navy blue. Around her long neck, she wore the sapphire necklace.

"Oh good, ye are here," she greeted him happily. "Giles will be bringing up yer bath, and I have laid out yer clothes." She blindly motioned to their bed.

"Would ye mind giving us some privacy?" Blaine asked.

Seeing her laird's look of displeasure, Shona left immediately. Jocelyn arched a delicate brow.

"Would ye care to explain what 'tis going on?"

"Nothing is going on, Blaine. We are simply entertaining friends," she said pleasantly.

"Ye consider Lady Charlotte a friend? As I recall, things did not go well the last time ye two spoke."

She rose from her chair to give him a quick kiss on the cheek. "They will be here for a few days."

"A few days?" He looked shocked. "They can all stay at the inn. They always stay at the inn."

"I am proud of our home. We have worked hard these past few weeks," she reasoned. "Besides Lady Charlotte brought news." She motioned to the missives that lay on top of the small table.

"News?" he asked, taking off his boots. "News from Rod?"

"Aye, Rod and Braedan brought their grievances before the king, and Graham was summoned to Edinburg to stand trial. There has been no judgment or penalty for his crimes, yet, but the land will be returned to Braedan immediately. The king wants more information with regards to the shares he stole from our father. Roderick says Graham has asked for time to gather his documents from his solicitor. 'Tis only a ploy to buy him time as he has no case."

"'Tis good news, love. Graham will be punished for his crimes," Blaine said.

"Aye, ye can read the letter yerself after the evening meal, but in the meantime, ye have guests waiting to greet ye." She smiled again and headed toward the door. "Twill be fine, Blaine. Ye need not worry," she said before leaving. "'Tis only a few days."

~ * ~

It was the longest week Jocelyn had ever endured. Lady Charlotte was charming in Blaine's company, but whenever he was gone, or out of earshot, she didn't hesitate to criticize everything or offer unsolicited advice.

Jocelyn had to bite her tongue on several occasions. When Lady Charlotte made references to times she and Blaine spent together, he claimed not to remember. By the second day, Lady Charlotte stopped reminiscing about old times.

Jocelyn also noticed her husband was exceptionally attentive, complimenting her on her attire or the delicious meal she prepared. Much to Lady Charlotte's chagrin, her companions toasted her numerous times, gushing with compliments. She decided to celebrate the small victories and ignore Lady Charlotte's spitefulness.

What Jocelyn had not expected was for her guests to remain so long. They had planned on attending a hunt nearby, but when the weather turned foul, they opted to stay at Stonegate until it was time to leave.

She noticed Marsali's absence too. She did not stop by to visit, nor did Ian come by after his lessons. At first, Jocelyn considered it odd and then remembered the comment calling Marsali "the wife of a fishmonger" so she didn't blame her. She missed Marsali's company and wished their guests would leave.

The day of their departure was finally at hand, the carriages loaded with their trunks sat waiting. Blaine was outside with the men waiting for Lady Charlotte to join them. Jocelyn plastered a smile on her face when she saw her descend the stairs.

She was in the middle of bidding her farewell when Ian ran around the corner and straight into Lady Charlotte. "Oomph," he grunted. "Begging yer forgiveness, my lady, I didn't see ye."

Lady Charlotte had to grab onto him to keep herself from falling, then continued to hold him with a vise-like grip. "Well if it isn't young Blaine. I must say, ye have grown," she said in a sugary voice. "Ye are looking more like yer father."

"His name is Ian, my lady," Jocelyn corrected her.

"Yes, 'tis what some say, but ye must admit the lad could pass as Blaine's son." Ian squirmed, but Lady Charlotte wouldn't let go. She looked at him, strangely scrutinizing him.

"I would appreciate it, Lady Charlotte, if ye would unhand the lad." Three pairs of eyes locked onto Marsali, standing at the doorway to the kitchen. "If ye are injured, then I apologize for my son's carelessness."

"Oh, don't be a ninny, Marsali. I was just having a pleasant conversation with the lad," Lady Charlotte replied, finally releasing him.

He ran directly to his mother's arms.

"Go on, son, Mrs. Anderson is waiting fer ye." Once the lad was out of earshot, she turned to address Lady Charlotte. "So, there be no misunderstanding, Ian is Brode's son, not our laird's. I would appreciate it if ye would refrain from making such comments. Good day." Marsali quickly curtseyed and followed her son into the kitchen.

Lady Charlotte's face was pinched in anger. "She has the nerve to talk to me like that," she spit out. "I am not the only one who sees the resemblance between them." She turned her vicious gaze to Jocelyn. "Don't be a fool, Lady Jocelyn. That woman is a wolf among sheep."

"What drivel." Jocelyn laughed.

"I speak the truth, but if you are too simple-minded to heed my warning, then so be it," Lady Charlotte snarled. "Marsali was Blaine's leman. He threw her out when he saw she was carrying his child. Brode took pity and married her so the boy would have his name. But give her the slightest encouragement and she would see ye gone from Stonegate." Lady Charlotte spun on her heel and stormed out.

Jocelyn stared at the woman's retreating back, her mouth open with shock. She remembered her conversation with Arrabella when she confided that she lived under the same roof with Douglas John's former leman. She knew in her heart Blaine loved her, but could it be possible?

"No," she said.

Marsali made it very clear the boy belonged to Brode, and if there was anyone, she should believe, it was Marsali. Charlotte was nothing but a conniving woman who would stop at nothing to cause trouble.

Jocelyn heard the carriages depart and breathed a sigh a relief. Heading to the kitchen, she was disappointed not to find Marsali or Ian. Well, there was no need to mention Lady Charlotte's blather because that's all it was…malicious blather.

~ * ~

Blaine, too, was relieved to see their guest leave. He had just enough of Lady Charlotte's insipid company. He wasn't surprised when Jocelyn did not join him to see them off. By the look on Charlotte's face, she was in one of her moods. Thinking of a more pleasant way to spend the rest of their day, he went in search of his wife.

He guessed she might be in the kitchen and to his delight, he found her taking inventory of the larder. He walked behind her, and as was his custom, slipped his arms around her slender waist. She leaned back enjoying the heat of his body.

"How do ye fare, my love?" He nuzzled her neck.

"Hmmm," she managed to say.

Relived that life would return to their regular routine, he spun her around so that he could kiss her soundly.

Jocelyn hugged him tightly. "If ye are inclined, may I interest ye in joining me on a trip to town?"

Blaine leaned down and captured her lips in another sensuous kiss. "I was thinking of a more pleasant way to spend the rest our day."

Without waiting for an answer, he threw her over his shoulder and carried her upstairs. The sound of Jocelyn's giggles echoed down the hall.

Chapter Twenty-Three

It had been a fortnight since their guests left, and Jocelyn was disappointed that she had not seen much of Marsali. Each time she sought her out, she would make some excuse that she was busy or late to an appointment. Jocelyn missed her friend and her company. She also wanted to share the news that she was carrying Blaine's child. Well, she suspected she was and wanted the opinion of another woman.

The construction of the ice house was occupying most of Blaine's days, so it was lonely at times. Jocelyn decided she had waited long enough, and today she would finally confront Marsali and find out what was troubling her.

~ * ~

Blaine decided to take his midday meal at the tavern. Taking a sip from his tankard, he spied Marsali crossing the tavern on her way to her office. "Marsali, a word if ye don't mind," he called out.

Marsali pretended not to hear. When he rose from his chair to intercept her, she realized it would be rude to ignore him.

"Care to have a seat?" He motioned toward his table.

"I canna my lord, I am afraid..."

He scowled then took her elbow and guided her back to his table. He motioned to a passing servant to bring another ale. He held up his hand when she tried to refuse. "Ye will oblige me, lass."

Marsali reluctantly took the chair he motioned to.

"I have noticed ye spend little time at the house and, for that matter, no time with my wife. May I ask ye what has brought on this riff between ye?" He regretted his words when he saw her face blush red and her eyes brim with tears.

"I canna speak of it," she answered, looking around. "At least not here."

He escorted her out of the tavern. Together they walked toward the pier. When they were alone, he asked her again, "What has ye so upset, Marsali? Surely Jocelyn has not offended ye?"

"Nay," she said, shaking her head. Looking over the wharf, she took a deep breath and exhaled slowly. "I canna bring myself to say the words."

He was perplexed. What on earth was she trying to say?

"I am too ashamed, my lord."

"See here, I have known ye a long time and 'tis nothing ye canna say to me."

She struggled for a moment and then finally blurted it out, "Lady Jocelyn was told I was once yer leman. She might even suspect Ian to be yer son." Tears that threatened earlier streamed down her cheeks. She wiped them away carelessly.

"How is this possible? Who would say such things?"

"Lady Charlotte," she bit out. "I overheard her telling Lady Jocelyn about us. I feared yer lady wife would loathe me, so I thought it best to stay away."

Blaine's jaw flexed as she told him what transpired that afternoon. His fists clenched at his side.

"I am too ashamed to…".

"Ye have nothing to be ashamed of. I will speak with my wife and explain everything. Jocelyn has a kind and understanding heart, but most importantly, she possesses common sense. I am sure she saw through Lady Charlotte's machinations."

"Forgive me, my lord, I was wrong to doubt Lady Jocelyn." Marsali accepted the handkerchief Blaine handed her. "If ye dinna mind, I will go to her immediately."

She started walking toward the house.

"Do ye need me to accompany ye?" he called out.

She turned around, saying something to the effect that it wasn't necessary, but the wind carried her voice away.

He smiled as she ran up the road. Finally, all would be set right, and he would once again have a happy wife.

~ * ~

The smell coming from the pot was heaven. Jocelyn stirred the mixture of herbs and lemon. She planned to slowly cook the capon in the sauce, its juices mingling with the tangy mix. With her rolls rising and vegetables ready to roast, she just needed to find Mrs. Anderson to see if she could keep an eye on the meal. She planned to run to the tavern and ask Marsali to dine with them. Jocelyn hoped she could finally find out what was bothering her.

Standing next to the long table, she decided to take a quick peek at the dough when she heard someone sneaking up behind her. She waited to feel strong arms encircle her waist when her smile faded. Instinct told her it wasn't Blaine.

She opened her mouth to scream when a grubby hand clamped over her mouth. "Keep it down if ye want to live."

Strong arms lifted her up as her assailant pushed her through the back door. Waiting outside was a carriage, its windows draped closed. She could not see the driver, but when the door swung open, she saw the man within.

She was overwhelmed by a wave of panic when she recognized him as one of the robbers that had accosted them on the road. She struggled in earnest, thrashing wildly about.

For an instant, the man that held her lost his footing, and she fell to the ground. When he reached for her, she started to kick him, almost hitting him in the groin.

The man inside of the carriage jumped out to help, and it took the two of them to lift her up. When they tried to stuff her inside, she used her legs to brace herself.

Jocelyn screamed as loud as she could, hoping someone might hear. When she looked back at the house, she saw Marsali hiding behind the stone wall.

"Please help me," she cried out.

Marsali did nothing. She just stood there watching as the men finally threw Jocelyn inside and closed the door, locking her in total darkness.

"Please help, help," she screamed as the carriage raced away.

They rode for hours till she was sure it must be nightfall. Her thoughts plagued her. She kept seeing Marsali hiding behind the stone wall. Could Lady Charlotte be right?

Shaking her head, she knew it was ridiculous to think Marsali had anything to do with her abduction. She trusted their friendship. She did her best to stay positive, that was until the carriage came to a stop.

Jocelyn heard the voices of at least four men. She suspected they were the men who had robbed her and Braedan. She nearly jumped out of her skin when the carriage door swung open. As expected, it was dark. A man offered his hand, but she swatted it away as she hopped to the ground. Looking around, she hoped she might find a way to escape. They were inside a large barn, and there was no exit in sight.

"Yer still a feisty piece o' baggage. I be wonder'n if ye be so feisty if the master lets me finish what Ned started."

The men laughed crudely at his joke.

"I demand that ye take me back," she demanded, backing away from them. "I swear my husband will see ye all hanged if I am not returned immediately and unharmed."

"And miss the chance for our little reunion, my dear? I wouldn't hear of it."

Jocelyn spun around to see Walrick Graham standing in the

shadows. She didn't need a light to recognize him. His slouch was enough.

"How dare ye?" She walked straight toward him. "Are ye some addle-minded twit? How do ye think ye can abduct me and get away with it? Ye are a witless, spineless fodder for pigs."

He struck her hard across the face.

Her head snapped back. Tasting blood in her mouth, she gave him a murderous glare.

"I will not stand fer yer insolence." He sneered. "If I be want'n some harpy, I would have not gone to all this trouble of bringing ye here. I would have been content to have my way with yer servant."

She looked to where he was pointing. As her eyes grew accustomed to the dim light, she saw a figure lying on the ground next to the carriage.

Pure unadulterated rage coursed through her when she recognized Mrs. Anderson bound and gagged. There was blood on the side of her head, and one of her eyes was swollen shut.

"She's quite a little hellion." He walked over to kick her cruelly with his boot. "In the end, they all succumb to my whim." Leaning down, he leered at her, spittle dripping off his chin as he laughed.

"What do ye want?"

"Why ye of course." Graham smiled in a sinister way. "And if ye are not more agreeable, well then, I would hate to see what happens to yer dear Mrs. Anderson. I am afraid at her tender age she may not endure what my lads will do to her.

"I am married. Ye canna have me."

"My dear, I care not a whit if ye are wed or not. Yer husband took everything from me, so I will take what is his."

"What are ye talking about?" She feared he was mad. "Braedan said ye have given back our lands, that was all."

"Well, let me enlighten ye." He ambled toward her until she was forced to look up. "Because of Blaine MacKinnon, I lost my home, my lands, everything. The king confiscated all except the estate my son resides in."

"'Tis your own fault. Ye took what wasn't yers. Ye stole from my family for years, swindled my father and now ye are caught."

"Shut yer mouth." He raised his hand.

She closed her eyes, waiting for him to strike. Much to her surprise, nothing happened. When she opened her eyes, he was walking away.

Slowly turning, he looked at her with hatred and contempt. "It was not I who swindled yer father. Gordon MacAulay betrayed me."

"Ye are mad," she said under her breath.

Shaking his head, he gave her a most fierce look. "Nay, lass, years ago yer father and I invested in a shipping company. When the company failed, we sold our share of the company but were offered a fraction of the price. At first, I was hesitant to sell, but yer father convinced me. He lied." He yelled the last part. "He did not sell his share. Instead, he bought my share and went into business with Caelan MacKinnon. My solicitor told me that the company was now The White Star and was profiting. At first, I asked yer father if he would sell me back my original share, but he refused. I was duped."

"But ye stole the money," she accused him.

"Nay, at first, I thought to invest in other businesses, but they all failed. They failed while the White Star prospered. I only took what I thought was my fair share. When I had enough, I again offered to invest in The White Star, but yer father went behind my back and made MacKinnon promise not to do business with me. I feared one day I would be discovered, so I offered for yer hand, but Braedan turned me down, even after I offered to give back the land I bought fairly. If ye had wed me, I would have been redeemed. It would matter naught what I took. As yer husband, I would have control of yer share of The White Star."

"So ye lied and made us believe we were still indebted to ye." Jocelyn was sick to her stomach. "Ye sent yer men to rob us, to make us more desperate, more in debt." She was disgusted when he nodded. "Yer man nearly raped me. Did ye not think of the consequences?"

"He was supposed to rape ye, but he failed."

Her breath left her body.

"I knew if he took yer virtue, no man would want ye. Yer brother would be grateful to anyone who offered for ye."

"What if he had gotten me with child? What then?"

"What's another bastard? The world is filled with them." He scoffed when he saw her shaking her head. "When I heard ye had been saved, I thought all was lost. I could not believe my good fortune when I heard ye were betrothed to Blaine MacKinnon. With his reputation, it would be a matter of time that he would tire of ye. Ye would be tarnished beyond repair, and then, ye would be mine. But something happened. My solicitor came to say he would no longer manage my holdings. The next day I was dragged from my home in the middle of the night by the king's men and led to court in shackles. The king would not hear my side of what transpired. Instead, he gave everything to your brother: my home, my lands. He took everything. He even stripped me of my knighthood. My own son disowned me."

She wanted to say he deserved it but thought better. "How is it ye are not in the king's dungeon."

"I begged for mercy. The king agreed to send me to the colonies, and that, my dear, is where ye come in."

She held her breath, dread descending upon her like a suffocating shroud.

"MacKinnon took all that I held dear, my son's love and respect. Therefore, I will take from him. Ye and I are leaving."

"Where are we going?" she asked, fearing the obvious.

"To the ship that awaits us. We leave within the hour for the colonies." He smiled, quite pleased with himself.

"I refuse. I would rather die than leave with you." She leveled her gaze, hoping he would take her seriously.

"I was afraid ye might say that." He walked over to where Mrs. Anderson lay. "Mr. Finch, please take Mrs. Anderson out and dispatch her."

Mr. Finch roughly picked up the poor woman as she cried out in pain.

"If ye kill her, I still will not go with ye," Jocelyn challenged him.

"My men have been told to make sure they see us sail. If they don't, I have instructed them to kill the lad, Ian."

"No!" she screamed at him. "Ye would kill an innocent lad? He has nothing to do with this."

"Aye, and then when they are done with him, they will poison yer beloved Blaine MacKinnon. Whether it takes a day or a year, he will never be safe."

She just stared at him. "I will go with ye. Let us be off." She walked over to Mrs. Anderson and untied the gag from her mouth. "Are ye all right?"

"My lady, dinna go with this monster."

Jocelyn leaned down and whispered, "Blaine will find me. He will never give up." Turning around, she faced Graham. "I am ready," she said.

She was walking toward the carriage when she heard a strange sound. At first, she thought it was some wild animal. The man standing next to Mr. Finch was making horrible noises, his hands around his throat. Blood poured out of his mouth as he pitched forward, falling dead at their feet. Jocelyn almost fainted when she saw the dirk impaled in the back of his neck.

It was as if the hounds of hell had descended on them. The

terrifying sound of a warrior's cry pierced the dark and sent men running, and fists flying. The sound of swords clashing was everywhere. Furiously pulling on Mrs. Anderson's bindings, she managed at least to free her legs.

She heard a woman yelling in her ear. "Follow me." Looking up, she saw Marsali. "Hurry."

Helping the older woman to her feet, the three of them ran toward an open door. Just as they reached it, Jocelyn noticed it was blocked by a wall of flames. Someone had set the barn on fire.

"This way," Marsali said, and they ran to the other side.

The whole building was filling with choking black smoke, and she could hear the horses neighing in fear. Falling to their knees, they crawled toward a small door.

Jocelyn turned around and saw Blaine fighting with Graham, their swords clashing with deadly intent. One of his men came up from behind.

Just as he raised his sword, Jocelyn screamed, "Blaine, behind ye."

Distracted in his fight, he didn't see the other assailant until her warning. Spinning around, he slashed out with so much force he disemboweled his attacker. Turning around again, he took advantage of Graham's shock and pressed the tip of his sword straight at his heart. Defeated, Warrick Graham dropped his sword, holding his hands up in surrender.

"I yield," he screamed. "I yield! What now? Ye just plan to kill me? A fellow knight? Where's yer honor?"

Blaine stared at him with a cynical smile on lips. "I have honor, and I would never take the life of a fellow knight."

Graham relaxed, likely thinking he was safe. Then without warning, Blaine drove his sword straight through his heart, a look of disbelief on Graham's face.

"I warned ye vermin, if ye ever touched my wife again, I would cut out yer black heart." He twisted his sword viciously, and Walrick Graham fell dead at his feet.

Jocelyn had watched the horror before her. Before Blaine could get out, the entire barn was engulfed in flames. Behind her the double doors to the barn flew open, and Brode led out the horses, still harnessed to the carriage.

"Dear lord," Mrs. Anderson exclaimed, pushing Jocelyn with her body out of the barn. They gasped as part of the barn's roof caved in.

"Brode," Marsali called out. "Where's Blaine?"

Brode desperately tried to keep control over the horses. "Here, take the reins," he shouted at Marsali, but there was no way she had the strength to keep the horses from trampling her.

As more of the roof caved in, Jocelyn feared Blaine might still be inside of the inferno. Without thinking, she ran toward the burning building, ignoring Mrs. Anderson's pleading. Just as she reached the small side door, strong arms grabbed her around the waist to pull her back.

"I am here, love." She heard Blaine's voice next to her ear.

They ran from the barn just before it collapsed.

"Graham?" Even though she'd seen him fall, she had to know.

"Dead."

"Are ye sure?" The next thing Jocelyn knew she was being kissed all over, her eyes, her cheeks and her lips.

It was as if he could not get enough.

"Are they all dead?" Jocelyn trembled.

"I need to get you away from all the destruction." He rubbed her arms. "Two are dead. Not sure what happened to the others."

She clutched his arm. "Blaine, if Graham's men don't see me leaving on a ship headed for the colonies, they have orders to kill Ian and you."

"Nay, love, ye need not worry. Ian is well protected, and without Graham, they will flee. There's no one to pay them, and I doubt highly they held any true loyalty to him." He still saw fear in her eyes. "Come, love, 'tis time to go home."

~ * ~

After the ordeal, Jocelyn was plagued with nightmares. She dreamt of trying to find Blaine in the blinding smoke only to awaken in his arms, shaking and crying. He held her like a wee bairn, rocking her against his chest until her sobs subsided. She knew he worried for her health, but soon the nightmares stopped, and she was able to sleep through the night.

She was sitting in the salon next to the fire, a serene smile on her face. She had worried that the ordeal might have harmed her babe. In the morning, when she had properly thrown up her breakfast, she knew she was still pregnant. The sickness wasn't the best sensation, but she welcomed it, relieved that the babe lived.

"Today I will tell him," she said when she heard a knock.

Her smile grew when she saw Marsali. "I hope I am not interrupting."

Jocelyn missed her friend so much that she jumped up from her chair and ran over to give the young woman a hug.

"My lady?"

"Oh, Marsali, I have been wanting to thank ye for saving me. Why have ye stayed away?"

"I was afraid…"

Jocelyn gave her an 'are-ye-jesting?' look.

"I mean, ye saw me hiding behind the wall when the men took ye. I wanted to explain why I didn't come to yer aide."

"Blaine explained everything. Ye could not have stopped those men. In fact, if ye had tried to intervene, they would have taken ye as well, and then no one would have been able to find me."

Marsali released her breath.

"I didn't realize ye were a tracker," Jocelyn said. "I have never met a woman who had the skill."

"Aye, 'tis a talent I always had. My father was a sheep farmer, and whenever there be a wayward sheep, he sent me to track them."

Jocelyn motioned for her to sit.

"When I saw those men take ye, I studied the tracks the carriage wheels left. Also, one of the horses had thrown a shoe, so that made it easy to follow. I left marks along the way for Brode and Blaine to find us. I must admit, I had hardly any petticoat left. The rest was Blaine and Brode."

"But why did ye avoid me? Did ye think I cared that ye once had a relationship with Blaine?" She cast down her eyes. "Marsali, there's hardly a woman in Scotland who hasn't had a relationship with my husband."

Marsali couldn't help but smile. Then they both started laughing. It felt so good. "I am relieved, but I wanted to tell ye…"

"It dinna matter, 'tis not important."

"'Tis important to me," Marsali argued. "Forgive me, but I believe ye will appreciate knowing the truth and not what others think."

Jocelyn nodded and settled back in her chair.

"I was young when I met Blaine. It was no secret that he wasna interested in getting married, so I agreed to become his leman. He can be most persuasive when he wants something. About a month after I came to Stonegate, he left to serve the king. He was gone so long I tired of waiting. I walked the halls waiting. The days became weeks and weeks became months. Brode did not join the king's army. He was left to manage Stonegate and to see to my protection. We spent nights playing chess or reading.

"After a time, we realized we had fallen in love. Brode was overcome with guilt, and he tried to stay away, but we could not be parted. When Blaine returned home, we told him the truth. At first, he acted as if he was upset, but then he started laughing. He was happy for us, and we married immediately. Blaine even gave me away, and that's when I found I was with child. With Brode's child. I have not been able to conceive again, but we are happy nonetheless."

Jocelyn looked at Marsali, tears coursing down her cheeks. "I am so happy ye told me."

She looked at her, quizzingly. "I hope ye are not upset?"

"Nay, I just am so verra happy, and these days, I seem to cry at everything."

Marsali raised her brows. "Am I to assume ye are *enceinte*?"

Jocelyn nodded, and the two women hugged each other. "I plan to tell Blaine tonight."

"May I offer ye my best wishes for a happy and healthy child," she said, and they embraced each other again.

Jocelyn couldn't wait for Blaine's return.

~ * ~

Blaine did not return home that night until late. He could tell Jocelyn had tried to stay awake but couldn't keep her eyes open. The mattress sank as he slipped into their bed. He gathered her in his arms. She opened her mouth as if she was going to tell him something then slipped into a restful slumber.

He awoke the following morning to find his lovely wife retching into the chamber pot. "Love, are ye ill? Is there something I can get ye?"

Jocelyn moaned. "Nay 'tis nothing. I will be fiiigghn." She retched again.

When the illness finally passed, he bathed her pale face with a cool cloth. "I best fetch my stepsister, Simone. She's a gifted healer."

"'Tis not necessary, I am not ill."

"The hell not," he growled. "She lives at Dunn Leigh; I can have her here on the morrow."

"Blaine, I said 'tis not necessary as I am not ill. I am with child," she snapped back.

It took him a moment to realize what she said. "Are ye certain? Well, of course, ye are…I mean, ye are a woman."

She laughed.

"I am going to be a father," he said in disbelief. "I have never thought this day would come." He placed his hand on her still flat belly.

"Aye, 'tis not how I planned on telling ye."

Taking her hand, he kissed the back. "I thank the Saints for the day I met ye. Ye have changed me. What I thought I could buy with a gold coin is insignificant to what ye have given me…your love. I will forever be yer faithful husband, and I am sworn to protect ye and our children till the good Lord calls me home."

Jocelyn eyes brimmed with unshed tears as she held out her arms. "I love ye," she said and immediately found herself lost in his kisses and loving embrace.

Epilogue

Jocelyn wrapped her shawl tightly around her as she stepped out on the balcony of the master bedchamber. It granted her a perfect view of the wharf. Berthed at the harbor was a most impressive ship. She assumed it must have just arrived. Gazing toward the end of the dock, she could not help but smile at the completed ice house. It had proved to be an essential asset to their fishing business, keeping the fish fresher.

She breathed deeply, enjoying the smell of the sea air. She huffed when she heard the squalling of a bairn. Her bairn to be exact.

"Pray forgive me, my lady, but I came to give ye the news when I heard wee Annie. Well, she be fussing so much I thought she might need to be fed."

Jocelyn sighed.

"Oh, dear me, ye be wantin the bairn to sleep, forgive me."

She smiled, taking Annie, whose cries had now grown in volume. "She is most determined not to nap." The women giggled when Annie stopped for a moment only to take in a deep breath and release the most pitiful wails. "Ye were saying ye had news?"

"Perhaps she needs changing?" Marsali suggested.

Annie's crying intensified.

"The news, Marsali?" Jocelyn asked again, hoping she could be heard over the wailing.

"What 'tis going on?" Blaine said, joining them on the balcony. Taking his daughter, he paused to plant a noisy kiss on his wife's lips. "What 'tis all this fussing?" he cooed at his daughter.

"Och. I came to tell ye, Blaine be home," Marsali said laughing, and then both Jocelyn and Marsali stared in amazement as Annie stopped crying.

He continued speaking softly to his daughter until she yawned most ardently then closed her eyes and fell asleep.

"Well, 'tis what they say, yer husband does have a way with the lasses." Marsali excused herself, giving the new parents some privacy.

Walking back inside, he laid his sleeping daughter in the bassinette and covered her with a blanket. Satisfied she was asleep, he pulled Jocelyn into his arms and planted a searing kiss on her lips.

"I have missed ye, wife," he said between kisses. He threw her wrap on the floor and started unbuttoning the back of her gown.

"Nay, Blaine." She placed her hand on his chest. "I want to hear about the wedding."

"Lass, I canna wait. 'Tis been a fortnight, and a man can perish being away from his loving wife."

"Ye can wait a little longer," she smiled at him seductively, "and I want to hear the news."

He sat down on the bed, drawing her onto his lap. "The wedding was grand. Angela was a vision of beauty, and yer brother was the happiest I have ever seen him."

She smiled, but then her smile faded.

"Please, Jocelyn dinna fret. 'Tis true ye hated to miss the wedding, but Annie is too wee to travel."

"They could have waited," she pouted.

"Nay, lass, if they had waited, Angela might have held the bairn in her arms instead of flowers." He chuckled when she rolled her eyes. "It will be hard enough to explain when she delivers this spring."

Blaine was right. Angela feared her parents would not consent to her marrying Braedan, even with Rod's endorsement. Still, there was nothing they could have done to prevent them when it was discovered she was pregnant.

"They will reside at Heatherwood until the bairn is born."

"Do they ever plan to live at Castle Mugdock?" Jocelyn wrinkled her nose at the memory of Walrick Graham's family home."

"Ascar and Heddy are living there since they wed. They plan to renovate the castle until they are satisfied nothing remains of Graham.

It took Jocelyn a moment to realize what he said when she threw her arms up. "Ascar and Heddy are wed? 'Tis another wedding I missed."

He hugged her tightly. "Aye, ye missed their wedding but look at why."

She gazed lovingly at their sleeping daughter. "Well, I hope they change the name. Mugdock, just horrid."

He rose, placing her on her feet. He then handed back her shawl. "Enough talk. Come, I have something to show ye."

After making sure Mrs. Anderson was available to watch over the sleeping baby, he ushered her out the front door to the waiting cart. It took minutes to reach the docks where a small crowd had gathered. Everyone was talking at once, but they hushed at their approach.

Blaine was grinning from ear to ear.

"Blaine, what 'tis going on?" They walked closer to the magnificent ship she spied earlier. Tilting her head to one side, she was puzzled by his behavior. He was saying nothing.

He stopped at the stern and pointed.

Jocelyn's eyes grew wide when she saw *Jocelyn* painted in gold. "Oh, dear heavens…ye didn't?"

"I invested in The White Star," he said proudly. "I hope ye like her."

She threw herself in his arms and kissed him again and again. "I canna believe it. I have no words."

"Shall we go onboard?"

She nodded vigorously.

Taking his hand, she gazed into his green eyes. Once again, they would be taking the first steps to a new future. But this time, a bright and certain future.

Acknowledgement

Writing a book has always been my dream, and none of this would have been possible without the help of Kris Lord, Marilyn Gradov, and my mother in-law, Joy Magoon. These three amazing ladies stood by me during every struggle, and through every doubt and every chapter I threw at them. From reading early drafts to giving me advice, they believed in me and helped me believe in myself.

I am eternally grateful to Norman and Jennifer MacKinnon, who welcomed me into their home during my first trip to magical Scotland. They inspired me to write about Scotland and its rich history, even offering the very books off their shelves as reference and research material. The time spent with them solidified my desire to write about Scotland. It was their deep devotion to family and the depth of their pride in their culture that led me to choose the name MacKinnon for my main characters.

To DeeDee Buserwini, a very special thank you for your editorial support, insight and keen eye for finding every dangling participle and modifier, missing comma, excessive comma, homonym, and punctuation error; you did this with a smile and the patience of a saint. I couldn't have done it without you.

Thanks to Maeve O'Toole, who helped fine-tune my manuscript. Because of her exceptional proofreading skills, I was able to complete the final revisions needed to present for publication. Maeve did this out of the kindness of her heart and for that I will be forever grateful.

And finally, to my husband, Douglas John. You have been my rock throughout our marriage, my partner in raising our two autistic sons, and a giver of strength who encouraged me to pursue my dream. There is no one who compares to you as a father and a husband. It was you who said to me years ago, when I first dared to give voice to my desire to write…You can do this.

About the Author

Barbara lives in Northern California with her husband Douglas John and their two autistic sons, whom they adore.

Barbara loves to connect with her readers on Twitter. Find her at:
https://twitter.com/BarbaraMagoon/status/1236675149983666176

Now turn the page for a peek into *Highland Honor* by Angela Ashton.

RIVAL SCOTTISH CLANS.
AN ANCIENT RELIC.
A BATTLE FOR OWNERSHIP.

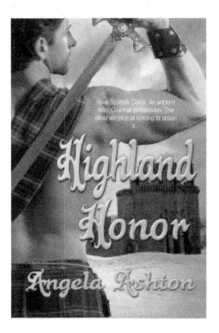

TURN THE PAGE
FOR A PEEK!

Highland Honor

Chapter One

Scotland, 1599

Why had she allowed him to badger her into this? Dread hovered in the frigid air, its gusty fingers threatening to suffocate her.

A shower of guilt trickled down Tegan MacAlpin's spine as she weighed the consequences of backing out of this, her one, mayhap, her only chance to prove her worth to her clan. As if Neil would stand for her disobedience. She'd boast a better chance of surviving an attack of rabid wolves than she would dare she quarter with her obstinate sibling.

Besides, had she not been praying her whole life for such an opportunity; to dispel the rumors and prove once and for all that she deserved to carry the MacAlpin name?

If she failed... Tegan stiffened at the horrid images conjured by the thought.

She couldn't. That's all there was to it.

The beat of her heart boomed like vicious spurts of nerve-shuddering thunder in her ears. Despite her manipulative brother's optimistic coaching, she couldn't help feeling like a helpless lamb being led to the slaughter. An expendable pawn in Neil's deadly game.

The heavy woolen gown she was forced to wear was likening to a ravenous swarm of mosquitoes feasting upon every inch of her hyper-sensitive flesh. The only saving grace was that it was hidden beneath a snow-white cloak fit for a princess. Neil had simply grinned like a menacing toad when she'd asked how he'd managed to acquire the repulsive garments. Not that she'd actually expected an answer.

Neil told her only what he thought she needed to know. But however he'd come by the materials to see his perilous plan to fruition, Tegan was positive it wasn't through any honorable means and might very well see war waged on their struggling clan.

Only when she'd donned the atrocious pattern of colors of her clan's blood rival did the impact of what she was about to do truly sink in. She pressed a hand to her stomach to help calm a violent wave of nausea.

And while she would do anything for the good of her clan, there were many things about this particular adventure that left her unsettled.

A thud pierced Tegan's ear, then another, yanking her back from the fear of what if and plunging her into the fear of what was. Her chest constricted as the drove of ceremonial riders rounded the snowcapped mountain. The earth shuddered with each dreadful blast of the horses' imperial hooves.

Heat flushed her cheeks despite the frigid chill that whipped through the last of the wintry wind. She eyed her eldest brother in need of his unshakable confidence. Neil embodied the daunting guise of a strung-tight predator about to descend for the kill. He was so sure his scheme would work. Yet, he wasn't the one being sent into Lucifer's lair.

Neil reached out and gave her forearm a squeeze. Tegan stifled a startled breath, amazed she hadn't shattered upon impact. A chill trickled down her spine as she met his callous gaze. The dark hood concealed a receding hairline, which made him look much older than his twenty-seven years. Mossy-black eyes squinted beneath calculated auburn brows, peeking at her atop the crook of his nose and reminding her of stories she'd heard as a child about the reaper. And pinching the same bone-riveting fear.

"Doona fash, Tegan. You are doing the right thing. Olga will be there to watch over you." His eyes shrank to thin shards of hatred's fire. "Our kin have waited centuries to take back what is rightfully ours. We'll not get another opportunity like this. Just remember what I told you about the MacDuff and you'll fare well in your quest. Once you're inside, make haste in your search, but," he emphasized with the stern arch of a brow, "do not draw a suspicious eye. The clan is counting on you, lass. Do not let us down."

The menacing threat underlying the shrouded gaze did not escape her: *If she failed, she'd pay dearly for her misfortune.*

Tegan berated herself yet again for agreeing to take part in the risky ruse. It had seemed like some far off dream at the time. To think she held the authority to bring great wealth and long-sought vengeance to her clan. Yet, that wasn't why she'd agreed. Well, not at first. Not entirely.

Neil had never asked, never *needed* her assistance before. In truth, she liked the attention, liked having such power over him. The way the entire clan looked upon her through hope-filled eyes, where before they'd barely noticed her—except to shoo her from the great hall where the haughty men congregated—was an added boon. But when Tegan allowed herself to fully take note of what she had agreed to, as if she'd been left any choice, her blood turned cold enough to freeze an entire loch.

This scene, the entire painstaking plan and her part in it, had been well rehearsed and branded into her mind from the time Neil had learned of the impending nuptials of the Laird MacDuff's eldest son.

His voice dipped into the familiar lethal tenor, penetrating her thoughts and causing her heart to leap into her ears, "Do not get cold feet, woman. 'Tis far too late to turn back now. Are ye not a MacAlpin?"

Tegan flinched. *This* was the Neil she knew. Managing to transform her innermost weakness into an invisible blade and drive it through her soul with a brutal twist at the finish. Determined and cynical, he looked like he wanted to slap her off her horse. He wouldn't of course, for if she arrived at her destination with a bruised face it would ignite a fury of inquiry all the way up to King James himself. And knowing that filled her with a sense of bravery. If she weren't inwardly shaking, she might test his feigned tolerance further.

A MacAlpin, indeed. What if the enemy recognized her as such? Her mind wouldn't allow her to dwell too long on the torturous thoughts, nor would the disquieting gallop of riders suddenly upon them.

"Now!" Neil bellowed and was soon lost in a pack of darkly cloaked kinfolk blocking the snow covered trail, weapons held high. "Auch. His kingship does not think too highly of his bonny niece if the bastard ordered only five of you to accompany the wee lass to her new home."

His voice was strained with hatred's husk. It didn't matter that he riled the king's men. The disguise would make it difficult to pinpoint any one clan to the treasonous crime about to be committed.

It was hard to see the rider's expressions beneath the silver helmets, though the enraged tenor that boomed from atop a beautifully armored Arabian mare dripped impatience and aggravation. "What's the meaning of this? By order of the king, move aside and let us pass."

"Throw down your weapons and get off the beasts." Neil's lethal pitch could strike alarm in the devil himself.

"The devil take you, ye spineless blaggard! We're on a mission for King James. He'll not be pleased when he learns of your treacherous act, you filthy traitor. Now stand down, and I might forget you ever crossed our path."

When Neil laughed the irritated man glanced over his shoulder and threw his head to the right, a muted signal to have his group change course.

Yet Neil had spent every minute of every hour over the past several months plotting his victory over the thieving MacDuff and had anticipated such a random act.

Another dozen of Tegan's clansmen surrounded the small entourage. Trapped like a pack of wild boar, the alarmed riders had two choices: fight or surrender. She prayed they weren't foolish enough to stand against her blood-thirsty kin, especially since the odds were so obviously not in their favor.

The sight of blood left her weak-kneed and dizzy to the point of swooning and from the moment they'd departed Ridgewood, she'd hovered in a semi-nauseous state.

To her relief the reluctant riders seemed to come to the same conclusion and surrendered. Neil had promised no one would get hurt but Tegan knew better than to take him at his word. She'd suffered the results of such empty pledges and had the scars to show for it.

"Take what you will and leave us on our way," a subtle air of warning laced through the escort's tone.

Neil laughed in a way that made her skin crawl and Tegan had to look to be sure the wicked sound came from her sibling and not the dark devil himself. "Get off your horses."

A meek, shaky voice rose above the prickly quiet as the riders appeared to be reconsidering their submission. "Please, sir. Have mercy, you are welcome to my jewels and anything else in my possession, but I beg you, doona harm these good men. If you'll allow us to pass, I'm sure my betrothed will be more than willing to offer a generous reward."

The lass's show of bravery was quite the surprise.

Fear climbed high in Tegan's chest as she admired the King of Scotland's beloved niece by marriage… Alick MacDuff's intended. Skin the delicate shade of alabaster, the woman was truly as beautiful as rumor proclaimed her to be.

Was *she* beautiful? MacDuff had never seen his betrothed, but surely, he'd heard tale of the lass' natural splendor. 'Twas the reason James kept her locked away like a nun at a mission…or a coveted relic. Even if Tegan might be considered bonny, her skin possessed a tawny dust and her voice surely lacked the feminine quality of Lady Kathryn's. In fact, she could almost pass herself off as a lad when she dropped her inherent rasp several octaves.

The courageous woman was trying hard not to show her fear, yet her gloved hands trembled atop the leather reins. Neil stalked over and practically yanked the reclusive woman from her horse. "Most of your clothes and a few jewels shall be sent to Dunnington. Although, I'm afraid your party shall be delayed in your arrival, m'lady."

Lady Kathryn's eyes flailed wide. "Delayed? You mean...ye don't intend to kill us?"

Most of Neil's face was shadowed beneath the hood but Tegan didn't miss the tight-lipped smile escorting the venomous hiss. "Not unless you give me a reason."

The lady blinked, in fear or surprise, Tegan wasn't sure. Both, she surmised. "Then why?"

"Don't ask questions, lass. I shall tell you all you need be concerned with once we get to your temporary quarters. Now, the rest of you follow suit and mayhap my men shall spare your miserable lives."

With a great deal of grumbling, snorts and curses, the king's men, accompanied by Lady Kathryn's trembling nursemaid, were led away by several MacAlpin clansmen.

The royal niece was ushered to Tegan's side. Their gazes locked for one lengthy moment. The terror reflected in the woman's almond-shaped eyes caused a prickle of shame to pinch Tegan's conscience.

"Forgive me, m'lady," she whispered under her breath, resisting the urge to touch her nose and see if it was as dainty and perfect as Kathryn's.

All her life she'd been told her eyes were a deep dung-brown and would surely never be as brilliant as the sea storm that looked to brew eternally in the heart of the pampered woman's pupils. The glimpse of hair beneath the hood of the royal cloak brought somewhat of a relief for it was as black as midnight and matched her own. She couldn't help but wonder if it was straight and flowing like a fine sheet of silk, or bouncy and rebellious like the unruly mane with which she'd been cursed.

A triumphant leer spread scrupulous lips as Neil sized them up. The next instant, he waved the lady be whisked away to join the others. "This shall be easier than I thought," he crooned, watching his kinsman cart her off.

Too bad Tegan didn't share his enthusiasm.

Size was one thing, but the woman's complexion was positively flawless where Tegan had a scar on the corner of her lip thanks to her love of wrestling with Arrow, one of the clan's many dogs. It wasn't her only battle scar, but the only one that need concern her as the vile MacDuff would never come to know any other part of her maiden flesh.

Neil threw back his hood, the sinister gleam lingering in his eye. As did the strangling burden lodged in her throat. His dark gaze descended upon her like an enemy blade. "Come on, Tegan. What are ye stalling for?"

Suddenly, she wasn't so sure she could go through with his scheme. It was hard to separate the line between where her apprehension to proceed stopped and her fear of Neil's wrath if she told him her feelings began. "I'm scared, Neil."

Rage traveled over the cherry-flushed face, and Tegan instantly regretted her choice.

"By the saints, woman. We've been through this. Now get moving or the wretched MacDuff shall be the least of your futile concerns."

"But, she's *beautiful*. MacDuff will take one look at me and know I'm not his intended."

Enraged, calculated eyes rounded on her and Tegan could practically feel the heat of his fury warm her flesh. "Auch, foolish lass. How many times must I tell you? Alick MacDuff has nary laid a treacherous eye on his betrothed. Will you relax? You worry for naught and waste precious seconds with your fashin'. Now, let's be on our way while the daylight travels with us."

Neil turned to Olga, posing as Lady Kathryn's nursemaid, but more importantly, clan informant. "If you don't find the relic beforehand, you shall meet me at the market as planned with an update." Chosen by Neil for her strength and keen wit, the stalwart woman nodded and pulled the cloak further over her peppery head.

Neil settled his duress on Tegan. "No matter what happens in there, if anything should go amiss you are to stick to the plan. Do exactly as I have instructed. Whatever you have to do to get that relic— *do it*. For if you are careless enough to be discovered and start wagging that unruly tongue of yours, pray the MacDuff slices your insensitive throat and doesn't send ye back to Ridgewood. Do you understand what I'm telling you, Tegan?"

The dark undertone in the way Neil had censured her name was the final twist of the knife that had taken up residence in her gullet sometime during childhood. By the saints, if she was forced to carry out the charade in hopes of saving her people, she simply had to stop dwelling on the dangers involved with the hazardous ploy.

Her kinsmen longed for vindication and wealth that should

rightfully belong to them. More than anything, she wanted to gift the MacAlpin what they longed for. All she wanted in return, all she'd ever wanted, was to feel like she was part of the family. To know a true sense of belonging. To be appreciated. Loved. In laying claim to the relic, would she earn her rightful place in the clan? "Aye, Neil. I well understand my duty."

"Very well. Off with you then."

That said, Tegan, Olga and several clansmen took their appointed places atop the royal cluster of horses and made their way toward hell's fortress. Dunnington Castle.

Home of the vile Clan MacDuff.

Tegan ground her teeth against the hefty weight of dread crawling up her back. This was her moment to shine. A chance to prove herself.

The devil himself would not stop her.

~ * ~

The next afternoon, the frigid party of masqueraders gaped at Dunnington Castle from atop the powdery peak of the crescent hill. Not even the blanket of virgin snow encompassing the fortress could hide its malevolence. It looked every bit as dark and sinister as her brothers described. Closing her eyes, Tegan offered up a prayer that no harm should come to her while under the roof of her enemy as every fiber of her being clamored against her taking another step toward the monstrous keep.

Did the God of Abraham care to listen to one whose heart was set on deceit? She cringed and it wasn't from the biting breeze tearing at her cloak en route to reach her goose-fleshed skin like some famished beast.

A mother she scarcely remembered was probably tossing about in her grave. But Neil was right. The MacDuff possessed what rightfully belonged to their clan. The Cross of St. Luke rumored to bestow the holder with God's favor and power beyond the imagination. If her clan was to survive the hardships of late it would require such mystical influence. It was long past time to reclaim the fated relic.

Tegan inhaled, drawing strength from centuries of wronged kinsmen and thrust her chin high. She clipped a courageous nod at her guide and the counterfeit travelers started over the rolling foothills to the black dungeon looming like a menacing thief before them.

Standing tall and proud against the white wrath and snowcapped wilderness covering it like a protective shield; the MacDuff keep was nearly twice the size of Ridgewood Castle and looked nigh on impenetrable. If she were found out, her brothers would never be able to break through the thick walls to free her.

Not that it mattered. Neil had just confirmed he wouldn't come to her rescue. A far cry from what he'd said several months ago when he first broached her with his brilliant and devious scheme.

Then again, if Alick MacDuff discovered her treachery, he would no doubt slay her on spot and send her body parts back to her brother as a merciless warning. What was she worried about? The sheer rattling of her nerves alone would shake her into an untimely grave.

Whatever it took, she had to make the MacDuff believe her ruse. From this point on, she *was* Lady Kathryn. Once she found out where the coveted relic was hidden, she could flee the home of her enemy and mayhap Neil would be so pleased with her, he wouldn't make her marry that atrocious shepherd, Charlie Gordon.

Half an hour later, the hopeful party of regal imposters traversed over a wide ice-glazed moat to arrive at the entrance gate. The lofty stone wall was quite impressive and appeared to encompass the entire fortress. The enemy's garrison was monstrous with its jagged towers scaling various heights into the blurred out heavens. MacDuff clansmen stood as still as pawns dotting a chessboard and lined the outer walls protectively. It would take eons to find the relic in the pile of flashy rock.

Fear seized Tegan's chest, but she squashed it out like a pesky insect before its venom had a chance to penetrate her soul. If she allowed it to take root and fester, she'd never convince anyone she was the king's sheltered niece and would surely be minced meat by nightfall.

They were permitted entrance, then immediately met with another frigid moat. Good Lord, once the relic was in her hands would she be able to escape with it?

A long drawbridge was lowered as if on cue and her apprehensions peaked as the horse's hooves clattered along the wood planks. Each step was like the slash of a whip flailing at her optimism and only damped by the magnified drum of blood bubbling in her ears. In a matter of minutes, she would come face to face with the MacDuff.

All too soon, they stopped moving. They'd reached the main bailey and hovered in the midst of the wide stretch of yardage that disappeared on either side of the menacing castle. The stench reminded her of a stable—horse sweat and manure-saturated.

Tegan looked down to see a strange man wearing offensive MacDuff colors reaching up to her. She accepted the hand and slid down from the gentle mare. It was worse than she'd thought. Her feeling of inadequacy reared its ugly head with a vengeance that would fail the king's grandiloquent army. The man smiled at her in what seemed a genuinely warm salutation.

Paranoia draped its heavy curtain over her heart while the angry whip of the wintry wind tried to bully her to trembling knees. It had seemed like this day would never come. And now that it had...

Tegan took a calming breath and returned the smile. Somehow her mind had pictured it differently. As if Fate might intervene and guide her straight to the relic. There were no magic wands loitering about, no divine beam of blinding light to point her in the right direction. She stifled a sigh. It could take days to locate her treasure. Neil had made it sound so easy.

Olga appeared beside her while men gaited about unpacking her—correction—the Lady Kathryn's things. *Godstoes.* She wasn't even inside yet, and she was as rickety as an old stool. Mayhap there was still hope of divine intervention.

Tegan felt sure her heart would punch a hole through her chest as she stood watching, waiting...

"M'lady Kathryn," a masculine pitch boomed from behind her. Tegan spun on her heels, and gasped. The beaming man rushing toward her was positively stunning. So much so that she almost didn't mind the atrocious rival tartan that hugged his slender, well defined frame.

In the next minute he'd claimed her hand and bent over to place a gentle kiss upon the icy-red knuckle. Eyes as black as a midnight marauder greeted her and his flamboyant smile seemed sincere in its welcome. "I trust your journey went well?"

Tegan offered a proper curtsey and returned the brilliant smile. Perhaps her short stay in the devil's den wouldn't be so bad after all. "Indeed, m'laird. Thank you. A might cold, though 'tis to be expected this time of year, aye?"

"Indeed, albeit we should not have to suffer much more of winter's wrath with spring just over the mound." He nodded amicably toward Olga before his mesmerizing gaze rested on her once again. "I hope your days will be long and happy here and that you shall not be regretting our forthcoming union."

The smile followed the chilling trail of blood and left her face.

Our forthcoming union—*this* was Alick MacDuff?

Well, that certainly changed her view of the egotistical buffoon. Tegan bit back her rage; stomping out all remnants of her sinful infatuation.

Almost a foot taller than she, Alick MacDuff's hair was short and as black as his heart was rumored to be. Long legs peeked from beneath a kilt bearing unsightly MacDuff colors. His body appeared solid and well defined, but as she'd noted before, not overly muscular. Not exactly the picture of the fearsome warrior she'd always dreamed of. Auch. What was she thinking, comparing this peacock of a rival to the man of her dreams!

Oh all right, so he was handsome. But being her blood enemy made his attractiveness all the more repulsive. And by the looks of him, she had to wonder if the puny foe could even wield a sword.

Mayhap her worries were for naught. Breathing easier, Tegan felt sure she would be on her way home within a day or two and couldn't hold back a confident smile.

The MacDuff maggot misread her poised grin and winked as he tucked her hand in the crook of his revolting arm and walked her toward a set of reinforced arched doors that were at least twice her height. She detested having to be under the same roof with the vile MacDuff, much less having to permit the man's bloodthirsty fingers to touch her flesh in any fashion. *And pretend to take pleasure in the despicable offense.*

The treacherous fool was still talking, never minding the fact she wasn't listening.

"I'm glad to see gossip isn't always founded on untruths." Adding to her chagrin, his voice was masculine and soothing.

"I beg your pardon?"

Alick laughed and to her surprise, the sound wasn't entirely unpleasant. *Godsfinger!* In all the endless nights of meticulous planning her brother had failed to prepare her for this dual-faced demon. What had she expected? Lady Kathryn, the king's stunningly beautiful niece, was to be the rat's wife.

"You're a very bonny lass, as whispered throughout the covetous moors of Scotland, to be sure. When a man blindly agrees to an arranged marriage, he can only pray he doesn't wind up strapped to a horse-faced mate for the rest of his life." He snickered. "I have suffered many a nightmare as to what our offspring might look like."

Offspring? Her innards pounded at the waning door of her resistance, begging her to turn back from the mystical prison before it was too late. If only she could. Holy saints preaching in the heavens, she had to move quickly.

The wedding would commence in six weeks. King James and the rest of the royal kinfolk would start arriving the preceding week. Alick might not know what Kathryn looked like, but the lass' family certainly did. Suddenly five weeks didn't seem long enough.

"Tell the truth, lass. Were ye not the least bit curious as to what your future husband might look like?"

Tegan hesitated a moment too long and looked up to greet a frowning foe. She must stop behaving like a half-witted twit. She'd assured her brothers she could pull off the impersonation and find the relic and simply could not—would not—let them down.

She wondered what Lady Kathryn, meek and mindless niece to the Scottish throne, would say.

"Of course I was. To be honest, I am more than a little relieved to see ye doona have horns protruding from your forehead." She lowered her face as if to hide a blush and giggled like a scatty child. *Of course the devil had horns.* Probably kept a file in his chambers and smoothed them down every morning before breaking his fast.

Alick laughed again and she sucked in a breath as they entered the keep. "It pleases me to hear you say as much."

The grand hall was incredibly beautiful in its elegant simplicity, which only served to fuel her hate all the more. Such grandeur should belong to the MacAlpin. Instead, they lived like paupers with rickety tables and wobbly benches to rest weary bones upon after a grueling hunt. No tapestries lined their walls. Indeed, Ridgewood was crumbling in ruins. She hated to think what would become of the MacAlpin, should she fail in her quest.

Aside from the strong smell of pine, richly colored tapestries decorated the gray stone wall opposite the entrance. Winding stairwells vined up either side of the entry. A pair of heavily wooded doors stood directly before her and without asking, she knew they led to the great hall. The heart of every castle. Was the pilfered relic on fashionable display therein?

The ceiling tapered so high it surely touched the foothills of heaven. Two long, deep-set windows decorated the arch, exquisitely perched toward the top of one wall, the pointy tips reminding her of menacing daggers.

Tegan raked her gaze away from the painful splendor to stare at the rush-strewn floor. Neil would undoubtedly view such lavish décor as squandering.

Dunnington was both frightening and welcoming at the same time. The faint smell of sausage broke through the pine, probably loitering from breakfast. Tegan felt a trifle disappointed the fancy dwelling was absent the unmistakable scent of animals that used to greet her whenever she'd enter Ridgewood Castle.

She couldn't fathom how the men did their hunting without hounds to sniff out the kill. That proved the MacDuff were monstrous thieves. There was something wrong with a person that didn't like dogs.

Alick ushered her toward a slightly hunched over, balding gentleman with a prune face standing guard over the right-sided stairwell. Tegan resisted the urge to rip her hand from between knifed fingers when Alick lifted it and touched it softly to his lips.

"Talbors, please show the Lady to her chambers. I'm sure the lass would like to rest a spell before dinner."

Only then did Tegan notice Olga behind them. Alick dipped his head, adding, "I'm afraid I have some pressing business and must depart your company for a short while, m'lady. Talbors will see you settled. Should you require anything at all, just ask. Talbors can show you where the other women like to gather for knitting, gossiping and whatever else 'tis womenfolk do." He winked and flailed a sheepish wrist in the air. "I shall send word to your uncle informing him of your safe arrival straight away." Her ruthless nemesis left her at the mercy of the humble manservant and disappeared into a mystery door beneath the stairs.

Tegan's curiosity lingered on the door as Talbors, who looked more like an overgrown toad than a man, led them up the multitude of exceptionally wide steps to the third floor and all the way to the end of the lengthy and equally wide candlelit hallway. The part of the castle reserved for the lady of the castle, she was informed.

To her delight, the rooms assigned to Lady Kathryn were surprisingly cheery. One could view the coverlet of snow through the man-sized window, yet spring had bloomed inside the spacious compartments. The bed was easily large enough for three men and plushly curtained with silken lilac-laced drapery.

Tegan was mortified by the tide of excitement that poured through her, yet helpless to stop it. Her own bed was small in comparison and her room, while hardly plain, lacked the radiant luster and femininity of this one. A vanity, complete with a small looking glass in the center, rested against the wall opposite the massive window. Wait, was that?

She forced a calm stride to her step as she made her way to the extravagant window that stretched from the floor to several feet above her head. Holy stars. It wasn't a window at all, but an escape onto a balcony overlooking a great portion of Scotland. It was positively breathtaking in all its sugar-coated glory.

"Will m'lady be requiring anything else? Perhaps a little knitting, or mayhap some gossip, to pass the time?" The aging man cracked a smile. Damn his kindred spirit. She didn't want to like the gentle ol' geezer. In fact, she *refused* to like him, or anyone else she might come into contact with during her sentence beneath the enemy's illustrious roof.

But that didn't mean she couldn't enjoy all the comforts of a princess while she was here. *Knitting, indeed.* She'd never picked up a needle and never would, least it be to gouge the sight from her enemy.

"Not at the moment. Thank you, Mr. Talbors."

"Very well, m'lady. I shall return in a few hours to collect ye for the evening meal." He bowed low, closing the heavy doors in his departure.

Tegan spun around, unable to keep the smug grin from her face. Whatever fanciful thoughts she'd entertained were immediately vanquished beneath Olga's stern glare.

"Has Lucifer himself sank his claws into you, lass? Have ye forgotten why 'tis we're here? Your brother will not like the fact that you all but drooled all over the boots of one Alick MacDuff!"

"Drooled?" Tegan refused to meet the bold woman's accusatory stare. "Your sight must be failing you in your old age, Olga. It took every ounce of energy not to whip my dagger from my boot and drive it through MacDuff's treacherous throat. Besides, I'm Lady Kathryn—his betrothed. I have to pretend to like him. Or have *you* forgotten?" She ignored the disgruntled snort and went about inspecting the rooms. "At least there are no bars on the windows."

"Always one to flirt with the devil." Olga made a tsking noise and settled ham-like hands upon padded hips. "You shall be lucky to see a wee bar if the MacDuff uncovers your treachery. Remember what Neil told you, but doona get caught up in the pretending. 'Tis one thing to speak of something, takes a lot more than a mastery of words to carry it out. And a heap of sense to know the difference between the two. We've got work to do. The sooner we start, the sooner we can return home."

Olga was what every nineteen-year-old girl needed…a double dose of conscience. At least the nursemaid's quarters were on the opposite side of the adjacent sitting room so Tegan wouldn't be burdened with the woman's constant nagging around the clock.

She wasn't a fool. No matter how tempting the bait, a trap was still a trap.

She wouldn't get caught.

Out Now!

http://champagnebooks.com/store/vintage-historical/8-highland-honor-ebook-9781771551090.html

What's next on
your reading list?

Champagne Book Group promises to bring to readers fiction at its finest.

Discover your next
fine read!
http://www.champagnebooks.com/

We are delighted to invite you to receive exclusive rewards. Join our Facebook group for VIP savings, bonus content, early access to new ideas we've cooked up, learn about special events for our readers, and sneak peeks at our fabulous titles.

Join now.
https://www.facebook.com/groups/ChampagneBookClub/